If You Needed Me

by Lee Lowry

OPEN BOOK
EDITIONS
A Berrett-Koehler Partner

IF YOU NEEDED ME

iUniverse books may be ordered through booksellers or by contacting:

iUniverse
1663 Liberty Drive
Bloomington, IN 47403
www.iuniverse.com
1-800-Authors (1-800-288-4677)

Because of the dynamic nature of the Internet, any web addresses or links contained in this book may have changed since publication and may no longer be valid. The views expressed in this work are solely those of the author and do not necessarily reflect the views of the publisher, and the publisher hereby disclaims any responsibility for them.

Any people depicted in stock imagery provided by Thinkstock are models, and such images are being used for illustrative purposes only. Certain stock imagery © Thinkstock.

ISBN: 978-1-4917-3171-0 (sc)
ISBN: 978-1-4917-3170-3 (hc)
ISBN: 978-1-4917-3172-7 (e)

Library of Congress Control Number: 2014906694

Printed in the United States of America.

iUniverse rev. date: 01/30/2015

For my husband, with a love that surpasses all things

Prologue

Geneva, Switzerland—September 2000

They talked in the muted light of the hospital room, Olga in a chair and Sandrine propped up in the bed, an IV tube taped to the back of her hand. The cancer that had spread through her bones and her lungs had begun its attack on her brain, but she was still lucid. She knew she was dying.

During her first bout with cancer, nine years earlier, Sandrine had prayed she would survive long enough to see her children grow up. She came very close. Marc had just turned twenty, and Delphine, at eighteen, had graduated from secondary school three months before. She was confident they would make their way in the world.

Her confidence did not extend to her husband of twenty-seven years. Carefully, thoughtfully, Sandrine shared this assessment with Olga. "I do not think David will be able to cope on his own," she concluded.

September, 2000

Grief

On the flat hospital roof
Below the balcony
Where those who do, smoke,
Cigarette filters litter the gravel
Like the ugly beads
Of a million broken rosaries.
When it rains, they float
Bobbing and winking of the worries
They represent - the fears,
Their ashes long ago washed away
By the rain and the tears.
So after her death,
I'm relieved, yet sad, to know the ashes
I've added to the roof,
In the long run they say,
Will also disappear.

Chapter 1

De: David
A: Family & friends
Envoyé: 25 septembre, 2000
Objet: Sandie

Sandrine Caillet Perry died tonight, 25 September 2000, of cancer, at the age of fifty-two. She died peacefully, serenely. "She simply forgot to breathe," the doctor said. She was with a good friend, Olga Gerasimova, at the moment of her death. I was on my way to the hospital and arrived half an hour later. Marc and Delphine came shortly after that and then a steady stream of friends.

Delphine, Marc, and I are terribly hurt, but we had many chances to talk with Sandie about her cancer, our distress, her anxiety, our lives together, and our love for one another before she slipped into a cloud of morphine. She went into the gentle night, scared certainly, as the little girl she had always cherished within herself, and elegantly, as the Parisienne she was. Knowing this, we are in good shape, so don't worry about us. Just keep us in your thoughts for a while. David

Jenny Longworth got the call at midnight, Boston time. It was already morning in Geneva. She reached for the phone, groggy with sleep. "Hello?"

"I sent an e-mail to your office but then realized you may not get it for another seven or eight hours."

"David?"

"Sandie died last night. The cremation is on Thursday, and we're doing a ceremony on Friday. I need to know what time you're arriving." His voice was steady, but he sounded very weary.

"Oh, David. I'm so sorry." What could she say to a man who had just lost his wife of twenty-seven years?

"When does your plane arrive?"

"I'm sorry—I'm still asleep. What?"

"Your plane. When do you arrive?"

Before Sandie's death, David had discouraged far-flung family and friends from going to Geneva for her funeral. "I'd rather you take a trip to somewhere lovely with someone you love. No reason to come over here. Be with your image of Sandie. Light a candle for her."

Jenny had taken him at his word. She had made no plans to attend.

"You really want me to come?"

"Yes."

Jenny agreed without further discussion. Though they lived separate lives on separate continents, David was the love of Jenny's life. If David needed her at his wife's funeral, she would be there.

Jenny was first in line when the airline ticketing agency near her office opened at 9:00 a.m. "I need to leave today so I can attend a funeral in Geneva," she said, trying to calm the quaver in her voice.

The agent hesitated. "We have special bereavement rates in some cases," she offered. "Is this a family member?"

Jenny struggled to reply but dissolved into tears. How could she explain that Sandie was part of the most important family she had—but was no legal relation? The agent immediately pulled out a box of tissues from beneath the counter. "Don't worry," she said. "We'll get you on a plane."

"She was only fifty-two," Jenny blurted out, as if somehow it mattered.

Within minutes, she had a ticket in hand. When she boarded the plane that afternoon, she silently blessed the airline agent for her thoughtfulness. The agent had assigned Jenny a window seat next to the only empty seat in the main cabin, ensuring her some privacy. She tried to nap but couldn't sleep. The events of the past summer whirled through her mind. Moments of hope. Moments of despair. And weaving in and out, moments of confusion—and guilt.

Jenny's friendship with Sandie had taken time to develop. Jenny had still been married to Seth Winthrop when the two women first met, but even so, Jenny made Sandie uneasy. Sandie knew David and Jenny had been lovers during their long-ago college days. David had had several girlfriends before he finally settled down to married life. Given David's warm and caring nature, most of these women had transitioned into lifelong friends, but Sandie spotted an intimacy and a depth to the relationship between David and Jenny that set it apart from the others. She sensed, intuitively and accurately, that despite their lives taking different paths, Jenny's love for David had not diminished. It merely changed expression.

Cautious and skeptical at first, Sandie ultimately accepted Jenny's friendship. Even after divorce returned Jenny to single status, Sandie viewed her as a safe and loyal "sister" to David and allowed her a supportive role in Marc and Delphine's college plans. Jenny had no children of her own. Despite her affection for her nieces and nephews, it was David's children to whom she played Auntie Mame. Jenny's admiration for Marc and Delphine further solidified her relationship with their mother.

Every other year, David and Sandie came to the States with the children, spending part of their time with Jenny. In the off years, Jenny traveled to Europe, joining the Perry family in Geneva, their home base, or on forays into France or Italy.

A newspaper story about renting farmhouses in France inspired the two women to search for a vacation property in Brittany for their August holiday. Always organized and efficient, with the added asset of being Parisian, Sandie checked websites and talked to rental agents. She found an ideal house in Le Croisic, on the Brittany Coast, and reported to Jenny, "This is a part of France I love very much. I am sure you will like it too!" Their exchanges were filled with pleasant anticipation and gave not the slightest hint of the tragedy that lay ahead.

Sandie must have had intimations by April or May, but perhaps denial was at work. Nor was there any clue from David. His e-mails were upbeat, humorous, and profane. A native of Tennessee, David's folksy, wisecracking, and exuberant nature was only slightly modified by his Harvard education and three decades of European living, first in Paris and then in Geneva. Jenny had come to see Sandie as the perfect foil for him—charming, elegant, urbane, and very French.

Then it hit. Their playful vacation planning was transformed by a chilling e-mail.

> *De: David*
> *A: Jenny*
> *Envoyé: 27 juin, 2000*
> *Objet: The Ebb and Flow*
>
> Got problems. Sandie's spinal cancer spot seems to have metastasized. She starts heavy chemotherapy on Friday. The doctor says there is a 75 percent chance we'll be able to meet you in Brittany, but he suggests we take out cancellation insurance on the house rental.
>
> It doesn't mean you have to cancel your trip. If we have to throw in the towel on Brittany, you could come straight to Geneva. Ain't life shit, as the Buddha said.
>
> Love, David.

Sandie had survived two previous bouts with breast cancer. Jenny had survived a serious battle with thyroid cancer, so they often compared notes. For the past two years, Sandie had been coping with a troubling spinal cyst, but she had informed Jenny not six months earlier that her doctor was pleased with her recent lab results. "I am fine," she wrote. "The last yearly testings were good!"

David's sardonic e-mail was a transparent attempt to keep terror at bay—David's terror, not Sandie's. Sandie seemed to take a philosophical view, but she handled being a patient far better than David handled being a helpless bystander.

Flying through the Atlantic night, Jenny shifted restlessly in her airplane seat, her mind relentlessly reviewing the events of the previous months. Throughout the summer, she had worried more about David than about Sandie. Sandie was dying, but David was her primary focus. Although she felt guilty about her upside-down priorities, there was little she could do about them. She appreciated Sandie. She admired and respected her. She was grateful for Sandie's friendship and enjoyed their time together. But it was David whom she loved.

Replying to David's first grim warning, Jenny had suggested that they keep their fingers crossed and go ahead with their August plans.

From: JWLongworth
To: DavidP
Date: June 29, 2000
Subject: Re: The ebb and flow

Unless Sandie needs to be close to her doctor, we can cook, clean, and chauffeur her about, making Le Croisic a totally restful experience. Also, since I'm an old hand on the cancer front, Sandie knows I fully understand what frequent nausea can do to one's disposition.

That being said, I will do whatever you think best. Perhaps, with cancellation insurance, it will be easier for Sandie not to worry about a decision until the last minute. Meanwhile, I'll just think positive thoughts with all my love. J.

De: David
A: Jenny
Envoyé: 30 juin, 2000
Objet: Re: Re: The ebb and flow

Thanks, Ducks. I'll keep you posted. Fatigue and nausea are what it's all about.

Love, David

When Sandie began her chemotherapy, she had a terrible reaction. The cancer was more aggressive and the treatment more devastating than her previous experiences. Jenny's mind kept revisiting the same dark territory. This was Sandie's third time around. No one wanted to say it, but it was going to get her in the end. Still, she had come through before. Maybe she would beat it one more time. David and Sandie had been together for nearly thirty years. "David and Sandie" was a single entity. The thought of David without Sandie was … unthinkable.

Jenny shut her mind to the possibility of Sandie's death. She stilled the disquieting speculation inside herself by focusing on helping Sandie survive. She searched out funny get-well cards and sent letters of encouragement to support Sandie through her first round of chemo. But things did not go well.

> *De: David*
> *A: Jenny*
> *Envoyé: 11 juillet, 2000*
> *Objet: Update*
>   Sandie couldn't do her treatment today because she has a mouth full of sores. Her own damned fault 'cause she refused to "bother" the doctor over the weekend! Oh well, we'll just continue, won't we, Luv?
>   Kisses, David

His message made Jenny uneasy, but she kept her response light.

> *From: JWLongworth*
> *To: Sandie; DavidP*
> *Date: July 12, 2000*
> *Subject: Re: Update*
>   Just to let you know I'm thinking of you, hoping that the yucky treatment is now more than half over and that you're both tolerating it reasonably well. Be patient and be well.
>   Love, J.

Then came David's response, foreshadowing the dark days to come.

> De: David
> A: Jenny
> Envoyé: 17 juillet, 2000
> Objet: Vacation problems
> Love, Brittany ain't gonna work. Sandie's mucous systems have been invaded by sores. She's been receiving intravenous feeding for the last week because it's too painful for her to eat. She's on morphine, and she's very tired. A trip across France is out of the question. I have canceled the rental cottage. I suggest you come to Geneva. I'll try to call this evening to discuss the matter.
> Love, David

He rang that night. He sounded tired. "Sandie's mouth sores are healing," he reported. "The doctors feel her lethargy will greatly diminish after a blood transfusion. So plan on coming to Geneva. We may not be able to go far afield, but we can do short trips, and Sandie can decide on the spot as to whether she feels up for an outing."

"I'll come to Geneva," Jenny agreed, "but I'll also be prepared to leave whenever Sandie wants some solitude."

"So we'll see you on the first of August?"

"Yes, I'll e-mail the flight details."

"Night, Ducks."

David and Sandie's daughter, Delphine, had recently signed up for an extended winter backpacking tour of the Far East. She hoped to attend college in the States and wanted to file her applications before leaving for Asia. David suggested that Delphine accompany Jenny back to Boston after Jenny's Geneva visit, and spend a week looking at campuses in New England. When Delphine contacted Jenny about setting up college interviews, she reported that her mother was better. The blood transfusion appeared to mark a turning point in Sandie's therapy.

The optimism continued for several days, but a week later, David called. Sandie was down again. David couldn't decide whether Jenny's visit would be a positive distraction or a further drain on Sandie's dwindling energy. "A visit would probably be a lot more helpful to me than to Sandie," David allowed.

Sandie joined the conversation using the bedroom telephone extension. Her lethargy was apparent, even over the phone. "I cannot do most of the touring," she said in a flat tone, "but you will still be very welcome to come." Her speech was slow, almost slurred, and she sounded very passive. Jenny cut through the niceties.

"Sandie, you need to concentrate on getting through the treatment and healing. Having a guest in the house, however sympathetic, won't help with your rest and recuperation," she said firmly. They agreed to postpone the visit. It was the last time Jenny ever heard Sandie's voice.

After that phone call, Jenny put together a care package including a blank journal, a hawk's tail feather for luck, and some newspaper clippings about cancer treatments.

> July 27, 2000
>
> Dear Sandie,
>
> I hope you are back home by the time this care package reaches you. I know sometimes it's best to be in the hospital, but personally, I'd rather throw up in my own bathroom.
>
> Since you enjoy making photo albums and creating scrapbooks, I am including a journal designed to help people record their life experiences to share with future generations. I gave one to my parents several years ago, urging them to record their own histories. Now I give one to you, so Dellie's children and Marc's children can read all about the adventures of Grannie Sandie!
>
> I have it on good authority that homemade chicken soup cures just about anything, especially if you add a tablespoon of sherry to it. I will send David my recipe and hope it will help, or at the very least, taste really good.
>
> Love, Jenny

Jenny e-mailed the usual platitudes to David, along with the chicken soup recipe. She felt she had made the right decision. Sandie needed to focus on healing, with no distractions. But Jenny ached to be with David.

> *De: David*
> *A: Jenny*
> *Envoyé: 31 juillet, 2000*
> *Objet: Re: Hi*
>
> Hiya, Good-Lookin'. Thanks for the thoughts. Miss seeing you, too. Miss having someone around who knows what the shit's going on, someone to lean on a bit.
>
> Got a good friend here, Edie Duval, who says that for good chicken soup, you gotta start with a good chicken (according to her Russian grandma) and use tarragon and sugar. We'll try 'em both! Meanwhile, I gotta find things to keep me busy or I'll go bananas. Sandie starts her revised chemo treatment on Wednesday. Find another feather.
>
> Love, David

A few days later, there was a poignant e-mail from Sandie.

> *De: Sandrine*
> *A: Jenny*
> *Envoyé: 5 août, 2000*
> *Objet: Merci*
>
> Dear Jenny, Thank you for all your letters and the package with the feathers. I am still emotional and scared and depressed, but I feel better about the mouth infection. It was lasting three weeks and I could not speak, eat, or even drink water.
>
> Now it is almost cured so we hopefully can go on with *chimio* that we had to put aside for a month. My energy is low, and I become impatient. I am so used to being off and running all the time! The weather is terrible, feels like fall, gray, rain, wind, and this does not help.

I also find it difficult to deal with the input and comments and actually their own fears from the many friends who care and worry about me and probably are not aware of the damage they create in my head. Everybody is so thoughtful, I should not say that.

I am glad (actually is not the right word) that we canceled Le Croisic. It was definitely the right thing to do. Your visit to Geneva was also not the right thing to do at this time. Thank God we are free enough to act this way and not to feel guilty about it. I hope I will survive this experience so we can see each other and have some fun again soon!

Bises, Sandie

In their past conversations about cancer and life and death, Sandie had been pragmatic and serene. She never expressed a fear of death, only an appreciation of the extra time she had been given. Now Jenny was picking up discouragement and depression. Jenny backpedaled quickly.

From: JW Longworth
To: Sandie
cc: DavidP
Date: August 7, 2000
Subject: Input and Comments

Dear Sandie—Don't apologize for finding it difficult to deal with input from well-meaning friends. You have only one responsibility—to concentrate all your energy on getting better. Your friends want to help, but only you can do the real work of healing. It's hard to have positive thoughts when you feel absolutely lousy.

Love, Jenny

To David, Jenny sent practical advice—ideas about how to deal with hair loss, how to reduce nausea—gleaned from friends.

De: David
A: Jenny
Envoyé: 9 août, 2000
Objet: Practical support

Dearest you, thanks for all the suggestions. It doesn't bother me to admit my helplessness and incompetence. All I can do is act as a sounding board for Sandie's hurt and anger, live my own as well, accompany her down this road, and work to fill in the potholes so the trip is as comfortable and sunny as possible. Ain't necessarily of much practical worth since our minds are concentrated on finding or imagining solutions to the cancer, which perhaps don't exist. Thus the anguish and the frustration.

Love, David

It was the first time David had acknowledged the possibility that Sandie might not make it.

De: Sandrine
A: Jenny
Envoyé: 13 août, 2000
Objet: News

Keep those good and lucky feathers coming! We were able to do the treatment on Wednesday. On Thursday and Friday I had blood transfusions so I am hoping the energy will come back and also the spirits should improve. I do not know where to search in myself to find the energy to fight as I did the other times. Fingers crossed. I hope all is well for you.

Bises, Sandie

PS: My problem of the hair is solved. It has fallen so heavily when I was in the hospital and I was so depressed that I have called a hairdresser to come to my room and shave it all. So I am wearing bandanas, and I should have a wig ready next week.

Sandie's focus on details was a good sign. She seemed confident the transfusions were helping. Another hopeful sign came in David and Sandie's decision to follow through with the plan to send

Delphine to Boston in early September. *They wouldn't let Dellie leave Geneva if Sandie were dangerously ill*, Jenny rationalized. *Maybe the treatment is working.*

But toward the end of August, the e-mails from Sandie stopped. David's became terse and infrequent. Was it because school had started, and David had a full teaching schedule? Or was Sandie going downhill again? Jenny hesitated to call. *David has more important things to do than handhold me through all the ups and downs*, she told herself. *I'm supposed to be giving him support, not the other way around.*

> *De: David*
> *A: Jenny*
> *Envoyé: 3 septembre, 2000*
> *Objet: Delphine's itinerary*
> Delphine arrives Boston on Wednesday, 6 September. I'm forwarding her itinerary. Sandie ain't top-of-the-morning.
> Love, David

It was hard to read David's blunt words. Yet when Delphine landed in Boston, she seemed pert and cheerful. In the two years since Jenny had last seen her, Delphine had blossomed into a lovely young woman, combining the best of both parents. She had her mother's dark eyes and chiseled nose, while her face reflected her father's cheekbones and broad forehead. She didn't use makeup; she had healthy tanned skin and didn't need to. She was wearing blue jeans, but the wide leather belt and colorful neck scarf made it instantly clear that her fashion instincts were European.

As Delphine updated Jenny, she echoed Sandie's view that the blood transfusions were helpful. They chatted happily about the schedule of college visits and tourist activities Jenny had planned. Neither of them had any inkling that while Delphine was crossing the Atlantic, David was being handed lab results showing that all hope was lost.

From: J W Longworth
To: DavidP
Date: September 7, 2000
Subject: College tour

Except for the shadow of Sandie's illness, we're having fun. Dellie and I talked a bit about Sandie and the pressures you're facing. She has some pretty adult insights. I think she's stronger than you realize. And she loves you a whole lot. As do I. We're beaming over whatever psychic support may be sent via the trade winds. Wish there were something more concrete we could do.

Love, J.

David responded with a single line, "Wish you were here," then copied Jenny on an e-mail to Marc, who was traveling in Eastern Europe.

De: David
A: Marc
cc: Jenny
Envoyé: 7 septembre, 2000
Objet: Mama

Marc, Mama has taken a turn for the worse. Dr. Blanchard is very pessimistic about her chances of recovery. She is not responding to the chemotherapy. Now the cancer has spread to her lungs and may have attacked her brain. It seems to be very aggressive.

There is nothing any of us can do but hope for a miracle. We simply have to be with her, either by her side or in our thoughts. Being here in Geneva, I have the possibility of doing both. And that helps me even though it may have no effect on Sandie. You must decide how you feel, whether or not you want to cut short your trip. It may have no effect on Sandie, but you may want to live the experience of saying good-bye ... if it comes to that.

Whatever you decide, know that I love you, as does your mother, and that our love will *not* be influenced by your decision. Don't let money be a problem. If you need it, I will send it. *Bon courage.*

Love, Dad

After the third read-through, Jenny put aside her sense of dread and concentrated on the logistics of getting Delphine back to Geneva.

> *From: J W Longworth*
> *To: DavidP*
> *Date: September 8, 2000*
> *Subject: Re: Mama*
> Dellie is over at Boston University right now, having a tour and an interview. I've checked the flight options. I could get her out Tuesday night, if not sooner. I would like a chance to say good-bye to Sandie myself, but it sounds as if that window has already closed. Would an extra pair of hands (and arms in the form of a hug) be of any use if I came back with Dellie? My French is limited, and the last thing I want to do is get in the way, physically or psychologically, but it's a viable option if I could be of value.
> Love, J.

> *De: David*
> *A: Jenny*
> *Envoyé: 8 septembre, 2000*
> *Objet: Re: Re: Mama*
> It's not that urgent, so don't send Delphine back prematurely. The doctor is talking in terms of weeks, not days. If you haven't said anything, don't for the moment.
> Love, David

Jenny had hoped David would respond to her offer to fly back with Delphine. She wanted to be there so she could do something, anything, to help him through this nightmare. It was discouraging that he said nothing—not even no. It occurred to her, however, that she might be confusing her needs with his and that she should trust him to seek help on his own timetable.

De: David
A: Family & friends
Envoyé: 8 septembre, 2000
Objet: Sandie's condition

Many of you may be shocked by this because I haven't written you about Sandie's latest bout with cancer, but I want you to be in the picture. Last March one of her markers went up. In late May she developed a bad cough. Examinations in June revealed widespread metastases— lungs, bones, liver, skull, vertebra. She began massive chemotherapy, but her system couldn't handle it. After four weeks and two blood transfusions, she resumed modified chemotherapy treatments. At the end of last week, she began to get confused, began to forget things she had never before forgotten. On Wednesday the doctor ordered an X-ray of her lungs and did a brain scan.

The scan results indicate irreversible brain lesions. There seem to be three possibilities, all of which are mutually exclusive: either Sandie continues chemotherapy for her lungs and gradually slides deeper and deeper into her confusion; or she undergoes massive radiation treatment for her brain, which may bring her back to a certain level of consciousness with probable, severe secondary effects, but will do nothing for her lungs; or medical science simply makes her as comfortable as possible and lets nature take its course. Hell of a choice.

We seem to be at the end of the process. At the same time, I am grasping at straws, hoping someone somewhere has a solution. Nevertheless, having gone through tears and upheaval for the last couple of days, I seem to have found a way of living with the situation. This is only to say not to worry about me. Be with your image of Sandie. Light a candle for her. David

From: Marc
To: Dad
Date: September 9, 2000
Subject: Re: Mama

dad—well! what can i say, but that i had felt it that way since june ... what a f***** up karma. it is funny how sometime i can deal with it and how sometimes i just feel like shooting people, but i'm here with my friends, i haven't told them anything, except that mom was not feeling very well. i don't know how long i will keep it in … but anyway i want to know what you think about her rest of life on this shitty planet … for real.

well, i will call you … all that i know is that i don't want her to suffer and i know she has suffered already enough … and take care of yourself and i will pray on my side for mom …

love you marc

When he was a child, Marc was a total charmer—polite, outgoing, cute, and lots of fun. When he hit his teens, the chemistry changed, and he morphed into a withdrawn and moody adolescent. While Delphine thrived at school, both academically and socially, Marc was a loner. Jenny sometimes wondered whether the contempt he expressed for his classmates was a preemptive defense. L'Académie Internationale was a private school. High-ranking diplomats sent their children there, as did well-to-do families tied to the multinational corporations headquartered in Geneva. David and Sandie were in no position to pay the school's substantial tuition fees, but one of the perks offered to teachers and administrators was free attendance for their children.

Delphine wasn't troubled by the fact that her family didn't own a yacht or a chalet in Gstaad. Marc, however, had a more vulnerable personality. Faced with classmates who always had the newest and most expensive sneakers, bikes, and electronics, Marc masked his insecurity by disparaging his peers, their materialism, their social class, and their culture. Delphine mixed well with her age group. Marc eschewed contact with fellow Académie Internationale students. During the past several years, he had not been easy to communicate with under any circumstances, but Sandie's illness drove him deep into an emotional cave.

David sent Jenny a blind copy of his reply to Marc. His response to Marc's anger and confusion touched her deeply. Though David sometimes covered his emotions with folksy language and profanity, he had a profoundly gentle and forgiving nature.

De: David
A: Marc
Envoyé: 9 septembre, 2000
Objet: Re: Re: Mama

Yes, as you say, what can we say? We've all feared it since June, and now time has proven us right. Not much comfort in that discovery, is there? I feel the anger in your message, and it reminds me of myself when I was twenty-two. When I was angry so long ago, I discovered that I was angry with myself. The screwed-up karma, the shitty planet, the people I wanted to shoot were just "objects" hiding me. I realized that the people I wanted to shoot (or that the government of the United States wanted me to shoot) also had moms and dads and kids and problems. So I decided there was no reason to shoot them, as they were having the same difficulties I was having. Instead, I decided to be with myself and learn about me, so I moved to Paris. The rest is my story of bliss, and your mother is a big part of it, as are you and Delphine.

On Monday I'm going to do whatever I can to make sure Sandie is comfortable. She is moving toward death, which seems to me must be the beginning of a great adventure. It's kind of Buddhist, but it's the way I see it. So I would like her to go toward that final passage in style, comfort and grace befitting a beautiful Parisian who has given me her love, who has given me Paris.

Thank you for your e-mail. I love you. Take care.

Love, Dad

Jenny sent David a quick update, hoping to provide some reassurance about Dellie's emotional state.

From: JWLongworth
To: DavidP
Date: September 9, 2000
Subject: Your Memo

Dellie may already sense what the situation is. Still, I will not give her your memo about Sandie's condition until you specifically direct me to do so. I underscore my belief that she can handle it. Dellie mentioned that it was difficult to deal with Sandie's depression and withdrawal

17

after the chemo. She felt she was failing Sandie because she couldn't figure out how to cheer her up. I think it would help Dellie to know that you believe everyone did everything possible and that you feel good about the way you and Sandie spent the time you had together.

I am mailing you some letters concerning the education trust I set up a few years back for Marc and Dellie. Sandie is the principal trustee, and it would help if she could sign the letters. If this is too difficult, not to worry. I can deal with this in other ways. Please forgive me if this financial stuff sounds coldhearted and unfeeling. Taking care of these details is one of the few concrete things I can do for Sandie—and the kids—at this point. It was so important to her that they have the possibility of a good education.

Love, J.

De: David
A: Jenny
Envoyé: 10 septembre, 2000
Objet: Re: Your Memo

Show Delphine my letter, Ducks, but only after her admissions interview. We're hanging in there, but every once in a while the tears and grief do get the best of us.

Love, David

From: Marc
To: Dad
Date: September 10, 2000
Subject: Phone number

dad—well! thanks for that answer or that explanation, i guess it makes me realize certain things, such as my feelings about all that!

can you send me the number of the hospital so i can maybe reach mom? what do you think, she may like to hear my voice? i cannot get my mind on how mom's condition is.

love you and take care. marc

De: David
A: Marc
Envoyé: 10 septembre 2000
Objet: Re: Phone number

Marc, Mama doesn't know how to use the hospital telephone anymore. She no longer knows how to sign things. She will soon reach the stage where she no longer recognizes friends, including me. Your mother has changed.

Love, Dad

Jenny tried to concentrate on David's needs, but her own emotional turmoil sometimes took center stage.

From: JWLongworth
To: DavidP
Date: September 14, 2000
Subject: Tears

I have been sitting here working on the education trust letters. Our receptionist, Mary, is the only other person in the office. Everyone else is over at the Park Plaza setting up for a seminar we're running. The phone has been ringing steadily, and Mary has been covering all by herself.

I stuck my head out to say I would come help her, only I suddenly lost control and couldn't get through the sentence. So Mary, bless her heart, threw on the night switch to cover the phone and sat herself down in my office. I handed her your memo about Sandie, which she read while I was blubbering and blowing my nose. She's very levelheaded, and she asked me to share a suggestion based on her personal experience. She felt it was important that you let Sandie know it's all right for her to leave. It's important for the kids, too, to give Sandie permission. Oh, yecch, now I'm crying again and my nose is running so I'm going to stop.

Love you. Bye. J.

De: David
A: Jenny
Envoyé: 14 septembre, 2000
Objet: Re: Tears

    I know there will come a time when I will talk to Sandie about leaving ... we will talk to her ... but I don't think the time is here yet. Squeeze a bit more out of our life before we get down to sharing our grief and her death. I kiss away your tears, each and every one of them.
    Love, David

David's words confused her. He had told Marc that Sandie no longer knew how to use a telephone or sign her own name. How could he believe that it was not yet time to talk with Sandie about "leaving"? Jenny sat at her desk, puzzling about how to respond. Then Delphine called from the house, sobbing. She had just talked with her father. She wanted to read his memo about Sandie before going to the airport that evening. As Jenny was printing a copy to bring home for her, another e-mail came in from Geneva.

De: David
A: Jenny
Envoyé: 14 septembre, 2000
Objet: Delphine knows

    I told Delphine about Sandie over the phone about ten minutes ago. She called to ask why Marc was coming home early, and I didn't know how to avoid it. I told her I had asked you not to say anything until after her last interview. Sorry about this.
    Kisses, David

By the time Jenny reached the house, Delphine had finished packing and was dressed in her traveling clothes. Her eyes were puffy and red, but she managed a brave face.

"Are you okay?" Jenny asked after giving her a hug.

Delphine shrugged and tossed her head. "I sort of guessed before," she replied. "It seems weird, but it's actually better to know. It's easier to deal with one awful truth than with dozens of awful speculations."

> *From: J W Longworth*
> *To: DavidP*
> *Date: September 15, 2000*
> *Subject: Re: Delphine knows*
>
> I trust Dellie is now safely home and has had a chance to see her mother. I think Dellie has known instinctively about Sandie for some time. Part of her was in denial, naturally, but she told me that when you spoke the words out loud, she wasn't surprised. We had a good talk after she read your memo. She had been really disturbed by Sandie's depression and withdrawal under the influence of the chemotherapy. She didn't want that to be a lasting memory of her mother.
>
> She was curious about conversations Sandie and I have had touching on cancer and death. I shared with her everything I could remember, all of which was positive and reassuring. I also told her how much Sandie loved her family and always counted her blessings.
>
> For my part, thanks for your gentle response to my catharsis of yesterday. I spent the early morning sorting out why I was so upset. I'm going to write it all down so I can get myself past this particular pain. Someday I'll share it, but I think you have enough to deal with for now.
>
> Love you, J.

Once the e-mail to David was on its way, Jenny contacted the friends in her own support network. "Many thanks for all the concern and sympathy you have offered throughout the summer," she told them. "The end is near. David is hoping that Sandie will be able to spend her last days at home."

September 16 was supposed to be Sandie's homecoming. Remembering her own relief at getting out of the hospital, Jenny decided to celebrate Sandie's return home. There had been more than enough anguish. It was time to do something uplifting.

In her attic, Jenny had boxes of correspondence and journals going back decades. One by one, she hauled them out, extracted everything connected to Sandie, and arranged the contents on the living room floor. She spent three hours reliving visits and remembering conversations. With her own pain somewhat eased, she wrote to David about her "visit" with Sandie.

> From: JWLongworth
> To: DavidP
> Date: September 17, 2000
> Subject: Update
>
> Hello, Luv. I exorcised some demons by writing about what upset me when I was preparing those trust letters for Sandie, but it's all about me and my issues—nothing that will provide you with aid and comfort. It will keep until some faraway day.
>
> Instead, I pass along the following, which I feel good about: I spent all morning with Sandie yesterday. I read every word she ever wrote me—including notes scribbled on Christmas cards and postcards. I went through all the photos and read my journal entries describing the vacations I spent with you two. All the little details came back. I realized how very lucky I have been to have Sandie as a friend.
>
> With your approval, I would like to excerpt, for Dellie and Marc, some passages that speak to Sandie's philosophy and values. I could put together some form of "Conversations with Sandie" notebook. There was not a single tear prompted by anything I read—only smiles. It might have the same effect on the children.
>
> Hope Sandie's homecoming went well. Dellie said you were planning to use her office for her sick room. I remember Sandie saying that her office was a special sanctuary. I like to imagine that she feels safe and comfortable there, with her photographs on the shelf, her quilt on the bed, and all of you close at hand.
>
> I've been thinking about you day and night. You have all my love and an enormous hug. Be at peace.
>
> Love, J.

De: David
A: Jenny
Envoyé: 18 septembre, 2000
Objet: Re: Update
    Thanks for this, Love. Do it. Sandie didn't make it home.
    Kisses, David

Jenny froze when she read David's words. Sandie didn't make it home? Did that mean she was dead? Or still at the hospital, too ill to move? *Oh—my—god,* she thought. *Should I call? Should I give David some space?* Finally, she crafted an e-mail that was valid whether or not Sandie was still alive.

From: JWLongworth
To: DavidP
Date: September 19, 2000
Subject: Re: Re: Update
    If it would help to have your family come to Geneva, and if the only thing standing in their way is a financial concern, I would remind you that my piggy bank is accessible 24/7. You can use it anytime you wish. No need to respond or acknowledge this. I know you're in pieces right now.
    Love, J.

De: David
A: Jenny
Envoyé: 20 septembre, 2000
Objet: Family Support
    Thanks for your messages. Sandie is drifting. I've already told everyone far away that there's no reason to come over here. Hard to put into words. Better to go somewhere lovely with a loved one. That's as close as I can get.
    Kisses to you, and all my love, David

Jenny assembled the promised packet of extracts from her correspondence with Sandie and put it in the mail to Marc and Delphine.

De: Delphine
A: Jenny
Envoyé: 22 septembre, 2000
Objet: Thank you

Dear Jenny, Thank you very much for the package you sent and for sharing with me memories and thoughts you have shared with my mother. I never really had a chance (or at least I didn't take the chance) to speak with my mother about her illness. Now I really know how she felt about it and it helps me say good-bye to her more easily. This really means a lot to me. I will never to able to thank you enough for everything you've done.

Much love, Dellie

There was nothing left to say, yet the e-mails back and forth increased in number. The Internet was a lifeline for David. The need to keep busy was overwhelming. He started to copy Jenny on his communications with his family, including one particularly poignant exchange with his sister-in-law:

From: Margaret
To: Geneva Perrys
Date: September 22, 2000
Subject: Our thoughts

Dear David, Marc, and Delphine, I just wanted you to know that our thoughts are with you each day. I pulled out a couple of my favorite Sandie pictures and carry them with me so in some way I can feel close. Wish we were there.

Love, Margaret

De: David
A: Margaret
cc: Jenny
Envoyé: 23 septembre, 2000
Objet: Re: Our thoughts

Dearest Meg, No, you don't. Like us, you wish there were something you could do, and like us, you have trouble accepting that there is nothing to do but think about Sandie and us and the cancer. And like us, you don't get much satisfaction from that course of action, and so like us, you fall back on wishing there were something you could do. And the infernal cycle starts all over again.

But you don't wish you were here, because waiting for someone to die—even someone you love—is tedious. You spend a lot of time asking yourself irrelevant, theoretical questions such as, since she looks so peaceful, what would happen if we took her off morphine? Do you think she's managed to eradicate the cancer on her own? Are her brain lesions truly irreversible? It's an exercise I call intellectual cancer because you can't block it, and it eats your spiritual guts away.

Sandie is basically asleep now. She is no longer receiving glucose because the cancer closed her kidneys down. Her energy level is going to start dropping rapidly. That may be good because her heart and pulse are beating away like a teenage girl's. As she gets weaker and the CO_2 accumulates in her lungs, she will go completely to sleep … the doctor hopes. I guess we do too … sometimes.

And that's the way it is, Saturday, 23 September, 2000, the beginning of fall. It's a glorious day outside.

Love, David

De: David
A: Jenny
Envoyé: 23 septembre, 2000
Objet: Sundry and just to talk

Love, I thought I'd sit down with you in cyberspace and chat. I've got lots to say, but I'm not sure I'll remember what as I go along. Not being well organized like you and

Sandie, things tend to slip through the net of memory only to pop up a bit later. At least they pop back up. That way I can deal with them late, which is, after all, better than never. That's how I got the telephone company to restore our service last week. They cut us off because we hadn't paid the June bill. July, yes, August, yes. June, no, so ZAP! True Woody Allen.

Thank you for preparing Delphine. It hurts her every time she goes to see Sandie, but at least she doesn't have any qualms about saying she doesn't like going and is glad she did after it's done. Accepting the contradiction is all part of the experience, and you helped immensely in that. I'm sorry you're not here to continue, but Delphine is open enough with her thoughts and feelings to go to other adult women friends when she feels the need. We also talk, but I understand her movement toward a motherly shoulder to cry on.

Everyone loves the notes you sent of your conversations with and about Sandie, including friends who have come to the hospital to see her. I've left my copy there for visitors. Delphine told me it was wonderful to discover a side to her mother she had never seen. Kisses for your time and compassion. I want to ask you to send me the other thing you wrote, the one you set aside "for some faraway day." The morphine has ended Sandie's pain, so I am no longer suffering for her. I'm suffering for me, myself, and I, and the part of Sandie that is in them—the loss in me. It would comfort me to direct my thoughts elsewhere and read about you.

I spent the night at the hospital, sleeping in Sandie's room. The unit has been very good about that and all the visitors and gay/sad confusion around Sandie. I see no signs that she has found the exit and cracked the door. For whatever reason, she hasn't finished what she's got to accomplish in this life. Tomorrow I'll bring up the subject of bringing her home. I want to make sure, or as sure as possible, that we're not going to violate her comfort by moving her. Any thoughts about the matter?

Now I'm going to go out and beat, cut, and tear back the wisteria, which, like the cancer, is trying to destroy our house. Do me good to use a bit of aggression on the SOB.

Love to you. David

From: J W Longworth
To: DavidP
Date: September 24, 2000
Subject: Conversations in Cyberspace

You do understand that you don't have to be sorry I'm not there to continue my conversations with Dellie. You do understand that I would be on a plane in a wink if you wanted or needed me to come. But I recognize the ambivalence that underlies "wish you were here." Your e-mail to Margaret, gently discouraging a visit, was poignant and very much to the point. I respect the way you are dealing with this. I would walk through fire for you, David, but sometimes walking through fire means sitting tight several thousand miles away from where you ache to go. So sit tight I will.

I'm also going to hold back on that "other thing" I wrote. It's actually a rambling journal entry rather than a letter, and in any event, it's pretty maudlin and self-serving. The flood of emotion at the time I was writing was over the top, but I can at least give you the gist.

In a nutshell, I've often made reference—but always lightly, half-jokingly—to the fact that I envied Sandie. Envied her for her wonderful qualities, and envied her for her relationship with you. Envied, but was not "jealous of," because I liked her and because I saw her as being the ideal companion for you—in a way I could never have achieved had history taken a different path. With jealousy, you want to usurp. With envy, you just wish you could walk in the envied-one's shoes. And so I did, sometimes wish I could walk in Sandie's shoes, wish I could, for however brief a moment, be Sandie.

But you know how children, when something bad happens, often feel that they are somehow to blame? That they wished something that the gods grabbed hold of and twisted into a tragic reality? Well, it hit me, full force, as I was signing Sandie's name to those thank you letters regarding the trust, that in a dark and terrible way my wish was coming true. From my hand and my pen, Sandie's signature was unfolding across the pages. For that brief moment, I was "being" Sandie, and I absolutely fell apart.

27

Now, as I recap the incident, the tears have started again, but I'm not feeling any irrational guilt. When I wrote my journal entry, I was consumed by the conflict that haunts survivors. Why Sandie? Why not me instead? And the guilt and confusion were so strong that it spewed out over two pages. Trust me on this one, David, they are two pages you can do without reading. Someday, maybe, but not now. I'm embarrassed by the self-absorption of it.

About moving Sandie: I don't know a single soul who wants to die in a hospital. If I were Sandie, I would want my quilt and my pictures and the familiarity of my own house. The only reason to keep Sandie in a hospital is if it's easier for you and Marc and Dellie. Before you commit to having her at home, however, you need to be sure that:

a) There is adequate help with her physical needs. I think Sandie would prefer to have her hygiene requirements met by a professional rather than a family member. She was the chief caregiver. I doubt she would take kindly to you or her children dealing with her diapers, no matter how willing you might be.

b) Her dying at home will not cast a pall over the house. She would want you to look at her study and remember her happily at work, sorting mail and filing bills. She wouldn't want images of herself dying to haunt the room or the house. Sandie loved that house. She would be upset if spending her last living moments there undid the sweet memories it holds.

Last thing. You speculate that Sandie hasn't finished what she's got to accomplish in this life. I'm inclined to agree, because I've been waking up in the middle of the night worrying about what I now refer to as "Sandie's Checklist." These are practical issues falling right in line with, "Has anyone paid the June phone bill?" It seems insensitive to be fretting over insurance policies in the midst of a deathwatch. But if your assessment is correct, perhaps Sandie will rest more easily if I forward the checklist now, rather than waiting. I will send it as a separate document.

All my love, Jenny

De: David
A: Jenny
Envoyé: 24 septembre, 2000
Objet: Conversation continued

Dearest Jenny, I don't know what to say about the first part of your letter. I think I might first need one of those sweet sherries we used to guzzle in our youth and a soft fire in the fireplace. You definitely got me with that one. So I'll shift to the second part for my own comfort!

Sandie has so much morphine in her that I don't think she knows where she is, but I could be dreadfully wrong. She hasn't opened her eyes or given us a noticeable sign in two days. She can't even change the position of her head on the pillow or swallow the phlegm accumulating in her throat. She looks calm and peaceful and pain-free, but what's going on inside her hard Parisian mind I no longer know. I'll talk to the doctor about bringing her home ... with help.

Send me the checklist. I began with some matters last week. I also have to start reading the insurance shit.

Love, David

From: J W Longworth
To: DavidP
Date: September 25, 2000
Subject: Jenny's Checklist

Last night, I reread your memo to Margaret and tripped over your remark that "there is nothing to do ..."

There is nothing to do that will stop the cancer, but there's more at issue than the illness or its outcome. Done right, the process of dying can gather up life's loose ends and weave them into something beautiful and transcendent. So, herewith is an attempt to highlight positive actions and viewpoints.

Your shared grief may be a chance for Marc to rebuild some bridges back to you. Marc has clearly found something to do by sleeping at the hospital. What about having Marc take care of some of the action items I sent you? He might appreciate being asked for his help.

The same with Dellie. Could she perhaps sort through Sandie's clothes and designate scarves and costume jewelry to be passed to dear friends who would cherish a final memento?

I understand the pain that prompted you to declare, "There is nothing to do," yet you gave people something to do when you urged us all to be with our image of Sandie. You affirm people are doing something every time you express appreciation for their calls and letters and visits.

Please don't feel there is nothing you can do. Consider what you've already done. Imagine that, after her first bout with cancer, Sandie was told that modern medicine would extend her life for another nine years. Imagine that she made a list of everything she wanted to accomplish and experience in those nine years. Read that list in your mind, David. Read it and tell me what she didn't get to check off.

Granted, she didn't get to have a corner of the garden that was sacrosanct and safe from your horticultural incursions. And yes, you drove her nuts sometimes. But other than that? Nine whole extra years of life together. What a joyous, incredible gift! As I said before, I envy the lady. You gave her the world, David.

Here endeth the checklist. If I think of anything else, you know you're going to hear about it.

Love always, J.

From: J W Longworth
To: David P
Date: September 25, 2000
Subject: Jenny's Checklist II
I know what I forgot. The poems. Write Sandie one of your poems. Write it to make the angels weep … and Sandie smile. J.

De: David
A: Jenny
Envoyé: 25 septembre, 2000
Objet: Re: Jenny's Checklist
Thank you, Love. Once again the wavelength is common.

Love, David

Reflections

I came back alone to Paris long ago
Because of how
Parisian streetlamps glow
Yellow through the dripping
Chestnut trees
And scatter light
On the paving stones
On a rainy night.

But after the rain is over,
Of course,
And we're drinking wine
In a café outdoors,
Is why I stayed.

D.P. - January, 1996

Chapter 2

The flight attendant rolled the trolley with juice and coffee down the aisle. Passengers were stirring, raising the window shades, and rousing themselves to stand in line for the lavatories fore and aft. Jenny had not slept and was physically and emotionally exhausted by the time they touched down in Paris. She had hoped to freshen up before the ongoing flight to Geneva, but what she found was a very dirty restroom—the airport cleaning personnel were on strike—and not even any paper towels to wash with. She looked at herself in the mirror and wished she hadn't. Her hair was flattened against her head. The hair was fine to begin with, and while softly curly in damp weather, it went almost straight in dry settings, which included airplane cabins. She kept it Peter Pan short and normally washed it every morning so it could recover from being slept on. There would be no recovery this morning.

There was a numbing four-hour wait before Jenny's connecting flight made the short hop to Geneva. She whizzed through customs, but there was no familiar face waiting on the other side. She had told David she could take a cab if need be. She suddenly realized she hadn't checked for last-minute messages before she left. Had David sent word saying, yes, please take a taxi?

As she debated what to do, Marc and Delphine appeared. They exchanged hugs, and Marc took Jenny's bag. To Jenny's eye, he bore no physical trace of his father's genes. He had matured into a masculine version of his mother. Sandie had been petite and slender; Marc was short and wiry. He had her bones and her coloring. Marc's brows nearly met in a straight line, separated primarily by deep frown lines acquired at a young age by a nearly constant scowl. Sandie had carefully thinned and shaped her eyebrows, but looking at Marc, it wasn't hard to imagine how full her original brows must have been. Marc also had Sandie's mouth and the potential for a sweet smile, but he rarely displayed it.

They put Jenny's bag in the trunk and drove her to the family home in Morion, a quiet suburb just outside of Geneva. David came down the stairs as she walked in the door. "Hello, friend," she said. They hugged for a long moment. David had never had the best posture, but grief had tugged his shoulders to a new low point. His sandy hair, normally flyaway, was limp, and he looked thin and drawn. Jenny knew that in happier times David was capable of a dazzling smile—a wide grin that crinkled the corners of his eyes, fetched up dimples in his cheeks, and revealed a chipped tooth, which he had acquired at age six. Now he barely managed a wan smile. She could only hope that David's grin and the zest for life behind it would somehow survive the tragedy that enveloped him.

At fifty-six, David looked his age. He had good bones, clearly visible beneath the creased skin, but his face had the deeply weathered look of an outdoorsman. The visage was a gentle one. David's face spoke of character. The trait that dominated was kindness. Not even the sorrow that lay so heavily as a mask could blot it out.

He took Jenny's bag up and settled her in his study at the top of the house, where the couch doubled as a bed. As soon as she finished unpacking, he asked her to join him on a quick shopping trip for wine and refreshments to serve the constant flow of visitors. It helped him to be doing things, and they talked as he drove.

"Sorry I couldn't be there to meet you at the airport," he said. "I was at the mortuary putting some things in Sandie's coffin to be burned with her."

"What did you put in?" she asked gently.

"Well," he began, "there are some flowers we want her to have with her. The kids from school made drawings and wrote prayers and messages. We cut them up into confetti, which I sprinkled into the coffin. Then there's the painted doll Marc brought back from the Czech Republic. And you know she has the Big Bird T-shirt Delphine got in Boston." There was a pause. "That's what she's dressed in," he explained.

The last-minute additions to the coffin required that the funeral staff open it for David. They didn't think to warn him. In life, Sandie had been a beautiful woman, with dark almond-shaped eyes that slanted down at the outside corners. Her mouth featured a dimple-making smile and that inviting pout that is the special province of French women. Her chin was delicate yet firm, giving her face a heart shape, and she had a long, graceful neck reminiscent of Audrey Hepburn's. The feature Jenny envied most was her nose, with slightly flared nostrils and a chiseled upturn at the end to rival a sculptor's masterpiece.

David, who had kissed her still-warm cheeks not two days before, was taken aback by what he saw. "Her face had stretched into a death grimace," he told Jenny. "It was not Sandie," he added, his voice becoming strained. "It was not Sandie," he repeated. "It was not Sandie," he whispered a third time, then fell silent.

The grief weighing on David and the children was grim to witness, but there were positive moments. In a corner of the dining room sat a jumbled pile of posters, pictures, and balloons—the residue from Sandie's hospital room. When Marc first visited the hospital, he angrily announced to everyone within hearing that Sandie's room was ugly and unacceptable. He went home, gathered up a box of things, and returned to redecorate it with bright paintings, photographs, and souvenirs. Marc spent many of his nights sleeping at the hospital, rotating with David. A host of friends came together to ensure Sandie was never alone. Tables and chairs were brought in. Wine and cheese were served. The hospital room was perpetually filled with warmth and love.

Throughout the afternoon and evening, people stopped by the house with words of consolation and gifts of food. David received everyone with appreciation, but whenever there were enough visitors to sustain a conversation without his presence, he drifted over to the CD collection and listened to different tracks from Bach's cello suites. The viewing room at the mortuary would be available for exactly fifteen minutes prior to the cremation. There was no service planned. David's intention was to play one of the cello suites and let people be with their own thoughts. He hadn't yet made a final choice.

Jenny was exhausted from travel and the barrage of French. She climbed up to David's attic atelier not long after sunset and went to bed. When she awoke the next morning, she could see through the skylight that nature had served up a glorious fall morning. The crematorium *veillée* was scheduled for two o'clock. The morning passed slowly. The phone rang with inquiries about the time and location of the service. Between calls, David read incoming e-mails filled with sadness and sympathy.

At lunch, as the family and houseguests addressed the logistics of transportation, David and Marc were tense, and Delphine was fragile. Marc announced to Delphine that they would need to meet soon with the bank officials to sort out the mortgage and other financial issues. Delphine didn't want to hear it. "Well, you gotta face it," Marc insisted. "Mom's dead and everything's gonna be a mess if we don't take care of it."

Delphine burst into tears and retreated sobbing to her room, slamming the door behind her. David turned on Marc with a fury Jenny had never witnessed in him before. "Goddamn it, Marc! I can't handle this right now! Don't do this," he shouted, "or I'll kill you! I love you, but so help me god, I'll kill you! Make it up with your sister *now!*"

Marc's pain erupted as defiance, and he stormed out of the house. David was beyond comfort. Rather than reacting in her usual practical manner, Jenny felt out of her league and useless. The only thing she could think of was to give David space and try to calm the children. When Delphine emerged from her room, still angry with Marc, Jenny gently urged her forgiveness by putting Marc's behavior into context. "This is how he cries, Dellie. This is how he cries."

Once Delphine was calmer, Jenny changed into a black dress for the service. She was halfway down the stairs when she saw David standing by the front door. In total defiance of convention, he was dressed in blue jeans and a work shirt, as if he were off to the garden store—or about to dig a grave. Their eyes met. He could see she was startled by his choice of attire, but she said nothing. Neither did he.

David took Sandie's blue Volkswagen and drove alone to the crematorium. Delphine went with the neighbors. Jenny waited at the house for Marc, who was still AWOL. She hadn't thought about what she would do if he didn't return, but at the last minute, he showed up, still sullen and angry. Jenny explained that the others had left already and asked if she could ride with him. *David may have invited me for other reasons*, she thought to herself, *but this is why I needed to be here.*

Though David had originally intended to limit the cremation ceremony to family, scores of friends appeared. The somber Bach piece David chose was played, and the room echoed with low cello tones and soft weeping. Jenny sat next to David, alternately holding his hand and passing him handkerchiefs. His body shook with quiet sobs through the entire service.

They headed home. Friends gathered to share wine and stories. People sat out on the terrace or stood chatting in small groups on the lawn. Jenny discovered that inhibitions about speaking an unfamiliar language tended to disappear when everyone was crying together, yet it wasn't all sad. There were even moments of laughter. When David told Edie Duval, an American colleague, that Jenny had sent Sandie a chicken soup recipe, Edie offered her own variation. "Still," Edie opined in conclusion, "so long as you start with a good chicken, it's hard to go wrong. That's how I knew my marriage would work." This was said in English, but Jenny still had trouble understanding.

"Your marriage?" she puzzled.

"My husband Jeremy is French," she replied, "but we met in New York. Our whole courtship was in New York. After he proposed, suddenly I had to go to France and meet his mother. There I was, a good Bronx Jew, going to meet this cultured Catholic lady, on top of which she didn't speak English and my French was, well, pardon my French, but my French wasn't worth *bupkis*. So what was I going to say to her? What were we going to talk about? I didn't know then that what the French always talk about is food. So there I am, meeting my future mother-in-law, and of course we're in her kitchen, because it's afternoon and already she's starting to fix dinner. What is she making? She's making chicken soup.

"'Ah!' I say, in French so bad I won't repeat it, 'I love chicken soup! My grandmother made chicken soup. But you must teach me your recipe so I can make it for Jeremy.' Obviously I said the right thing, because Jeremy's mother smiled a big smile and pulled me over to the counter so I could watch closely. 'Here,' she said, 'it's not so difficult. But you must always start with a good chicken.'

"That's what my grandmother used to say! 'Always you have to start with a good chicken!' And that's how I knew our marriage would work," she finished triumphantly.

People came and went throughout the afternoon but took their leave as the light began to fade. When the last one departed, David retreated downstairs to his computer, to relieve the pressure of the day by writing about it.

> *De: David*
> *A: Family & friends*
> *Envoyé: 28 septembre, 2000*
> *Objet: Sandie's cremation*
>
> The sun is glorious—a fall day that you dream of. Not a cloud. Picnic weather. There we are, standing in the parking lot of the crematorium, waiting for our 2:00 p.m. entry time to start our fifteen-minute ceremony. Cars arrive, friends join us, men take their coats off, and people introduce themselves, joke quietly, and talk about Sandie. Groups form and dissolve as newcomers arrive, people venture into the manicured park, conversations stop and recommence.
>
> At 1:55 p.m., I hail the group and proceed toward the crematorium, a building decorated in beige stucco organ

pipes with an entrance designed for bank management seminars. Inside I meet with one of the guardians who explains procedures and is upset to hear that someone wants to observe the actual cremation. It should have been requested when the details were worked out with the funeral home. However, he checks with someone and reports that it won't take place for another two hours—enough to discourage even the most curious or most suspicious. He ushers us into the chapel flooded with autumn sunlight and two altar candles.

People file in and take their seats. I tell everyone that because we're in precise Switzerland, we have a very precise amount of time to meditate on Sandie—fifteen minutes exactly—and then we'll meet outside. There will be music, but if anyone wishes to speak, they may do so. I thank them for coming. I sit down and the first Bach cello suite begins. The music overwhelms me, and I cry. I have no idea what the others are doing. Wave after wave of sadness washes over me. Jenny is sitting beside me, and she takes my hand. Is she crying? She passes me a handkerchief. The piece ends, and Marc says, *"Vive Maman!"*

The second cello suite starts. Silence grips us once again. I have things to say, but the music is too strong, too beautiful. I look at the coffin. The bouquet sent by the former principal of the school rests on it. The bouquet will burn with Sandie, as will all the students' drawings and texts, Delphine's bracelet and Marc's bunny rabbit. Prayers for the gods. How much time do we have left? Only Marc has spoken. What are the others doing?

I look around and see that the guardian is trying to get my attention. The music pauses. I get up. Everyone gets up. We begin to file out of the chapel. I turn back to help those who brought bouquets place them on the coffin. I invite everyone to the house for a glass of wine. We spend the rest of the afternoon together, laughing and crying, talking about Sandie, toasting her journey until, as every day, the evening chill begins to settle and the sun sets.

Peace be with you—David

On Friday morning, Delphine had a scratchy throat. She announced this in the kitchen. Jenny responded instantly with sympathy, and—remembering how they dealt with the threat of flu that hit during her US college tour—Jenny made a comment about smothering Delphine in Vicks VapoRub and tucking her in bed to watch cartoons. It was a light and welcome moment. Jenny found it reassuring that Delphine planned to stay in Geneva until the end of the year. She was still going to backpack through Asia, but she and her fellow travelers had pushed off the departure date until after the Christmas holidays. Marc also planned to remain in Geneva for a while. This lessened Jenny's worry about David being left alone.

Two of Sandie's childhood friends, one from Rome and one from Paris, arrived to attend the evening tribute and stay the night. Around four o'clock, they drove in various combinations to the Morion Community Center for Sandie's memorial service, which David kept referring to as a celebration ceremony.

"I can usually describe important events I have witnessed in detail," Jenny noted later in her journal, "but this remains a blur of sensation." She soaked her own handkerchief very quickly and had to borrow tissues from the woman sitting next to her.

There were scores of tributes, many of which Jenny couldn't follow because of the incredible range of languages. David was a teacher and Sandie had served as an administrator at l'Académie Internationale, which drew the bulk of its students from Geneva's diverse diplomatic community. David once mentioned that the student body encompassed over a hundred different nationalities. It felt as if they were all represented at the celebration.

David read poems in English and French, some of which were his own. One poem described the time thirty years before when David's youthful love affair with Jenny ended and he met Sandie. "I came back alone to Paris long ago," he began, not needing his notes,

"Because of how Parisian streetlamps glow yellow
Through the dripping chestnut trees and scatter light

On the paving stones on a rainy night.
But after the rain is over, of course,
And we're drinking wine in a café outdoors,
Is why I stayed."

With every word he spoke, Jenny could feel his ache for Sandie and his despair at losing her.

Toward the end of the ceremony, Delphine offered, in French, a list of sweet memories—songs she and her mother sang together, the lighthearted chatter of their morning rides to school, the adventures of their shopping trips, the shared secrets, the clothes they borrowed from each other, the cooking lessons Sandie gave her. Tears glistened on her cheeks, and her voice broke. "Now I must learn to do all these things alone. I'm afraid of not being strong enough. I miss you, Maman."

After three hours, the event ended. Jenny rode home with Marc. David stayed to supervise the final cleanup. Marc was angry with himself because he hadn't said anything publicly. He thought it was all going to be personal statements. He didn't realize how many people would sing songs, read poems, or quote from literature. "You've already said all the important things directly to Sandie," Jenny said, seeking to reassure him. "It was enough that you were present to hear the love and praise everyone had for your mother." Marc grunted in response. Jenny wasn't convinced that her words got through.

Once back at the house, Jenny visited briefly with her fellow houseguests, but she faded early on and, pleading lingering jet lag, went up to bed. Despite her exhaustion, she couldn't sleep. David's attic study was a loft partially open to some of the rooms below. She could hear him typing two floors beneath her, laboring over an account of the ceremony to send to family and friends in the States. The house was packed. Even the master bedroom had been given over to guests. When David finally abandoned his computer in the wee hours of the morning, he crawled into a sleeping bag laid out in the TV room on the couch for which Sandie had made new slipcovers just months before.

De: David
A: Family & friends
Envoyé: 30 septembre, 2000
Objet: Sandie's Memorial Ceremony

I have arranged everything I can think of: the orchestra, the room, the food and drink (compliments of the school), the parking, and god knows what else—oh yes, those who will speak or sing or play, and my tie, a garland of flowers for my love's rebirth. Not the program, however, for I can't imagine how to organize the program.

I wander around the garden surrounding the auditorium—actually a gymnasium with giant bay windows overlooking the Alps—trying to figure out what to say to invite people to speak when they want to. I'm sure it's going to come to me, and it's going to work. I feel unbelievably calm. Cigarettes help. We've put out three hundred chairs. How many people are going to show up? I really don't give a damn because the ceremony is for me and my friends—Sandie's friends—and I know my friends will be there.

4:15: some of my students, dressed to the nines, are outside with or without parents. The cafeteria crew rolls up, and we help unload the cases of wine, water, and fruit juice. Colleagues arrive. Friends arrive. Parents arrive. I greet them in the soft, autumn sunshine as they gather in small groups to talk and feel comfortable in this unusual situation. We hug and chat, and I move from group to group.

4:50: the leader of the orchestra comes up and suggests that the band begin playing to draw folks inside and get the ceremony going. I'm grateful for the suggestion. Don't have to yell or bang on a pot.

A last cigarette. The band strikes up the music—a hot number I don't recognize. People move to fill up the seats. The band continues to play, improvising while the room fills up. No more chairs. Newcomers are heading toward the benches. I put on my flower necklace of red roses, white gypsophilia and yellow woodland sunflowers. I feel light. I feel sad. I feel gay. The mood is rich, infectious. The band is working into a final swing.

The music stops, and I feel my own and everyone's curiosity: what next?

I look out over the seated assembly. There must be four hundred people of all ages. I want to set the rules. This is meant to be a celebration of all of life, including death. For each of us there will be moments of sadness, moments of laughter, moments of contemplation, moments of confusion. I invite them to live those moments as they wish. To do what they have to do within themselves to be at peace.

I have asked certain people to say or sing or play something, but I invite everyone to express themselves whenever the Spirit moves them. There is no protocol or hierarchy. I will try to manage the flow so that the Dixieland band can perform as well. Sandie loved jazz. She loved a party, a celebration. Dixieland is street music, bar music—all a part of life—but in New Orleans it is used at funerals—the sad side of our celebration.

I call for music and sit down in the front row next to Marc. The band plays "St. James Infirmary," my only formal request. It's wonderful. I do not cry. I'm with my memories of our trips to New Orleans. I feel the mixture is working.

The music stops. Applause. I get up and read a poem by Robert Frost. People applaud. Why not? I sit down. Michel goes to the mike and reads Charles Peguy's letter to his wife, written in the trenches in 1915, shortly before his death. Applause. He returns to his place. More poetry readings follow. One teacher reads a story in Chinese—no translation. I laugh and watch the amazed faces of the band. More applause. I stand up and read another poem. The band plays something hot. People start to clap with the beat. People are tapping their feet, beginning to talk to one another. Kids have moved out of the hall and into the grassy plot in front of the bay windows. They're running around, playing outside. I feel lighter and lighter.

The music ends. Applause. More poems, then a prayer from the Koran. Kaddish is said, both in English and in Hebrew. Verses from the New Testament are read in Greek. I break in again, and the band swings into another tune. Some people are forming a line in front of me to offer their condolences. We kiss and chat quietly. The music rolls on. Applause.

I read "Le Pont Mirabeau" by Appollinaire. My voice cracks. I want to read it well, not forget to sound the final "e" on certain words. This is for Paris, Love. Applause. One of Sandie's choir mates sings "A la claire fontaine." I choke and cry. Applause.

6:00: The bandleader comes over and says they're going to have to leave soon. They close with the traditional Dixieland funeral march. Confusion reigns. I remind the assembly that the celebration has not ended. The bandleader comes up, and I suddenly realize he expects me to pay him. Being in Switzerland, I hadn't even thought about anything other than receiving a bill. I apologize and give him my address, borrowing a pencil from one parent and a piece of paper from another. Reality trip. He and the band members thank me for the ceremony. Never seen anything like it (me neither). Really enjoyed it, learned a lot, wished they could stay. *Bonne soirée.*

I return to the hall where a former student and his friend have plugged in their instruments and are now performing a soft rock number. People are returning to their seats. Delphine walks to the front and speaks of precious moments with her mother. She chokes and cries her way through it. I cry as well. A group of eighth-grade girls and boys come up and recite "Fire and Ice." One girl blows her line, and the others immediately jump on her. I give the line. They finish and go off hectoring the one who blew the "performance." Applause and gentle laughter.

The director of the school's theatre department sings "Ave Maria." She finishes in tears. I cry too. It's so beautiful. It's so Sandie.

7:00: I decide to end it by telling the Taoist story of The Lost Horse: "Once upon a time, along the northern border of China, there lived a man skilled in foretelling the future, and his son. One day their mare ran off over the border. The son went to his father, bewailing the family disaster. His father suggested that it was perhaps a blessing. A week later the mare returned, bringing with it a magnificent black stallion. The son rushed to his father with the news of their good fortune. The father suggested that it was perhaps a catastrophe. The son soon learned to ride the powerful stallion. One day the horse threw him, and he broke his hip. He dragged himself to his father, bemoaning his fate. His father looked at him compassionately and asked how he could be sure it wasn't a blessing.

"Several months later, barbarians north of China attacked the border towns. Imperial officers were sent into all the villages to conscript the able-bodied men. The son, who was lame, was not taken into the army. In the war that followed, nine out of every ten Chinese soldiers were killed. And so disasters turn into blessings and blessings into disasters. The wheel of life is always in motion."

While I tell the story, I watch Delphine and her friends, who are laughing and talking. They know the tale well. I'm sure Delphine has been expecting it. I end the assembly by saying that Sandie has concluded her affairs in this life and is off on a new adventure. Her absence hurts, however, we still have our affairs here. So while celebrating her and wishing her *Bon voyage*, we shall get on with our lives. I thank everyone for coming. Applause. People are smiling, talking, crying, getting more wine, eating canapés, shaking hands, kissing one another. People tell me Sandie would have loved it. Perhaps she did. Who knows? We put the hall back into order, stack the chairs, clean off the tables and leave. Socially it's finished. David

The house slowly emptied until Jenny was the only remaining houseguest. She took advantage of the relative calm to sit down with Delphine. It wasn't a long conversation. She wanted to erase any anxiety engendered by Marc's recent remarks regarding the impact of Sandie's death on the family finances. Jenny reassured Delphine that the education trust she and Sandie had organized was securely in place and all of Delphine's anticipated college expenses would be covered. Jenny also promised to assist the family with the unfamiliar territory of financial management.

A call came in from Graham Wells, David's college roommate and one of their oldest mutual friends. Their junior and senior years, David, Graham, and Jenny had shared trials and triumphs in an off-campus apartment building on Ware Street in Cambridge, just blocks from Harvard Square, along with a small band of fellow students.

Though they now lived on different continents, Graham and David were as close as brothers. Each had served as best man at the other's wedding, and each was godfather to the other's firstborn. Their trust in one another was absolute. Oddly, one of the poems David had chosen to read at Sandie's celebration made reference to Graham. The oddity was that the poem portrayed David and Sandie engaged in a disagreement. It began, "'Your poetry is trivial,' she said, 'Like you and Graham talking.'"

David and Graham sometimes spoke in their own private code, using puns and points of reference unfamiliar to outsiders. To the uninitiated, their conversation might sound silly, meaningless. Instead of playing tennis with one another, they sparred with wit and words. David's Southern charm and European graciousness often obscured his complex character and razor-sharp intellect. What Sandie missed was that the point of the exercise was the game, not the dialogue.

Graham had been at a Gestalt conference in Moscow and had missed the memorial service, but he arranged a detour through Geneva en route home. David and Jenny met his plane. He normally cut a handsome figure, lean and dark with an angular face, high cheekbones and straight hair, cut so it fell across his forehead and could be swept aside when a dramatic gesture was called for. The day was absent dramatic gestures, however. Graham was tired and sad, and looked it.

The conversation in the car was brave but sparse. Graham carried a double burden of grief—pain for the loss of Sandie, whom he had loved as a dear friend, and pain for David, whose life had been upended by her death. When they reached the house, all was quiet. The children were out and not likely to be back until the wee hours of the morning. Jenny installed Graham in Sandie's office, having managed a quick turnover of linens, and David opened a bottle of wine.

Michel and Josette DuPont, David's closest friends in Geneva, came by shortly afterward. They hadn't realized Graham would be there, weren't sure of Jenny's departure schedule, and didn't want David to be alone. Michel stood about two inches taller than David, but sorrow over Sandie's death had somehow diminished his height. He was bowed and bent, sagging under the weight of the loss. Josette was similarly affected. Normally bouncy, bright, and full of enthusiasm, her face was drawn, devoid of energy. The color had disappeared from her skin. Her voice, usually pitched to reverberate throughout a classroom, was reduced to a near whisper.

It was because of the DuPonts that David and Sandie had left Paris and come to Geneva. Michel and Josette were fellow teachers. They invited David and Sandie to work with them at Geneva's Académie Internationale after meeting them at a teachers' seminar. The two couples had become the staunchest of friends. In addition to their common experience at school, they spent time together skiing, playing golf, traveling, and sharing domestic hospitality.

There wasn't much conversation. Everyone was emotionally drained. Jenny helped David bring out some of the photo albums Sandie had compiled over the years. Looking at the albums helped cover the frequent silences. After an hour, Michel and Josette departed. David busied himself with heating up one of the many gift meals delivered by friends. Graham and Jenny set the table, and they shared a quiet dinner.

Jenny left the two of them to talk while she went up to bed. From the atelier she could hear their voices, but she fell asleep as soon as her head hit the pillow. Graham was a good listener as well as a trained psychologist, so she trusted they would stay up until David said everything he wanted and needed to say.

Sunday morning, they took Graham to the airport to complete his homeward journey. Once back at the house, Jenny organized the bills and bank statements while David steadied himself by working on his e-mails. Jenny was due to leave the next morning, and she wanted to put the family finances in some semblance of order for him.

Olga Gerasimova, the friend who had been with Sandie when she died, invited the Perry family and any remaining houseguests to a luncheon at her home, a forty-minute drive away. Delphine declined, preferring to spend the day with her friends. Marc was tired and depressed and didn't want to get out of bed, much less go to a luncheon.

It was just David and Jenny who went. Jenny wasn't much of a talker in a car, but she made an effort to offer casual observations about the countryside and the villages they passed through. David remained silent as he drove, so she tried a different tack. She wanted to interject an idea that might give David something to look forward to.

"You know," she commented, "you mentioned the possibility of taking the kids to the States to spend Christmas with your family. If you can route your travels through Boston, I'd love to host you for a few days. Or if I end up joining my siblings in Florida, you could soak up a few days of sunshine before heading up to Chattanooga."

David gave a noncommittal grunt, then tossed off a remark that chilled her to the bone. "I don't know what we're going to do," he said. "Hell, I don't even know if I'll still be around then." Jenny knew from his tone that it wasn't the time to argue. She changed the subject, but his comment stayed with her, cold and hard, with spiked edges.

The farmhouse where Olga and her husband lived was charming, almost storybook, set high on a hill, overlooking a valley with pasture, barns, and cows. Olga greeted them softly, giving David a hug as well as the usual double kiss. She tilted her head sideways as she looked at Jenny and put a hand on her forearm. "I am so very glad that you have come," she said in English.

Olga had steely gray eyes that could see into your soul, yet her face at first glance was almost expressionless. Everything was in pleasant proportion, set into a rounded oval, but her features were held in neutral, like a mask in a Greek chorus. Her flat bone structure immediately revealed her Slavic origins. She was in slacks and a gray sweater. She wore neither makeup nor jewelry, and her hair was pulled back into a slightly frizzy bun at the back of her neck. Jenny was introduced to Olga's husband, Jacques, who spoke no English. Their exchange was limited to *"Enchanté."*

Everyone sat out on the terrace in the soft autumn air, eating white grapes from Jacques' vineyard and cherry tomatoes from Olga's garden, and drinking wine. Had it not been for the heavy sorrow that lay over the guests, the entire scene would have been idyllic. They moved into the house for lunch. The dining room was rustic, opening onto the terrace. At that time of day, it was filled with streaming sunlight. Olga had created an incredibly festive table. The linen cloth was strewn with seeds and nuts amidst plates, glasses and cutlery. There were symbols of harvest everywhere.

Even without Marc and Delphine, it was a large group. Olga invited friends from the teaching staff at school, and there were two teenagers—Olga's daughter and a friend—who hung around the edges and joined them at the table briefly. At Olga's urging, the girls nibbled a bit of casserole, but they were fidgety and departed well before dessert, bidding farewell and dancing off. In doing so, one of the girls left an empty chair next to David.

The symbolism was awful. Jenny held her breath and hoped that in his fog, David might not notice it. Her hope was in vain. In less than a minute, he saw it. She could see his eyes fill and his face set behind a mask. He went outside twice during the meal, ostensibly to have a cigarette. The first time, Jenny walked out after him and gave him a hug. The second time, she just watched. The chatter around the table stilled as the guests realized she was staring anxiously out the window. To her relief, one of the men went out to stand with him, smoking in companionable silence, looking out across the valley.

After dessert but before coffee, David rose abruptly. "I need to leave. I promised to take care of something for Delphine," he said. Jenny started to stand up, but he looked at her sternly and said, very firmly, "Jenny, you're staying. Someone will give you a ride home." She was startled—and immediately uneasy. David knew that she had little

French and was shy in a large group. Why was he abandoning her? She felt fear slowly rising in her chest, her skin prickling, adrenaline pumping. But before she could muster an argument, he was out the door and gone.

As soon as he left, all eyes turned to Jenny. Everyone leaned several degrees in her direction. "How is he doing? How is he, really?" they asked, assuming Jenny had the answers—that she was somehow better at reading him than they were. It felt to her as if they knew the secrets of her heart, though she didn't see how that was possible.

"How is he? Not good. At the moment, I think he's mostly numb from the shock," Jenny offered, counting on the Anglophones to translate for those who didn't understand English. "I suspect the most difficult time will come after the first wave of grieving has passed, because friends will gradually resume their normal lives. His will still be in shambles." Then she swallowed hard. "But I have to tell you, right this minute it makes me really nervous that he left early—and without me."

She didn't add that Sandie's medicine cabinet contained enough morphine to kill a horse. There was sufficient alarm in her voice that she was immediately offered a ride back to Morion. She accepted with alacrity. When she was walked in the door, David was sitting in the kitchen with Delphine. Jenny was relieved but could feel the adrenaline still coursing. She couldn't let go of David's morbid comment in the car: "I don't know if I'll still be around …"

"Are you free to take a walk?" she asked him, her voice quavering slightly. "Or at least to go stand at the edge of the field so I can yell at you without disturbing anyone?"

David offered no resistance. He shrugged and said, "Why not?" telling Delphine they would be back "whenever."

They crossed the street and walked down the lane that led to a sylvan retirement complex. At the entrance to a path that skirted the woods, Jenny stopped.

"Okay," she said, "here it is." Deep breath. "I like to think that you can say anything to me. That we're the kind of friends who can just come right out with whatever we feel and think, and not be afraid to speak up." He nodded.

"But don't you ever, ever again, as long as I live, say anything about offing yourself." Her eyes flooded. "Not even in jest. Not even as a joke."

He drew her to him as the tears streamed down her face. "Do you not understand what you mean to me?" she sputtered. "That I love you as much as you loved Sandie? That I could not bear to live in a world without you in it? That if you died, I would suffer the same kind of pain you're suffering now?"

She choked. She coughed. Her nose was running copiously and slowly turning red. "If you harm yourself, David, I will never forgive you. And if I don't mean enough to you to keep you alive, for god's sake think of your children! Sandie's children! Think of Sandie! She would be furious!"

At this point Jenny was shaking violently, and they were both crying and clinging to each other. "Promise me," she said. "Promise me."

"All right, Kid, all right," he answered. "I didn't really mean anything by it. It's just that I try to see the future, and there's nothing there. It's empty. It's just a hole. It's all I can do to get to the end of each day."

And so they walked. And cried some more. And laughed some, as well. For over an hour they meandered, their arms about each other the whole time, David stopping here and there to light a cigarette. Finally they returned to the house.

Jenny had no appetite for supper. By eight o'clock she was emotionally and physically wiped out. "I really need to crash," she said. David replied that he would probably turn in early too. Marc had disappeared. Delphine took off to visit friends. Jenny went upstairs, did most of her packing, and got into bed. She thought about the day, about the week, and considered, her mind in a jumble, whether there was anything more she could do before leaving for Boston.

As she lay in the dark, she slowly realized that her thoughts were not the only things churning. Her intestines were suddenly active, and the first sensations of stomach cramps swept through her. For a moment she wondered if it was something she ate. Then it dawned on her that the day's prolonged overdose of adrenaline was probably the culprit. She used the bathroom twice. Then the queasiness began. And grew. She took some antacid tablets. Her stomach turned. She tried to bring up the contents and got only a small amount of liquid. Finally she gave up and went downstairs. David was sitting outside on the terrace, smoking. She knocked softly on the frame of the open French doors and described her predicament.

"Do you have anything for nausea?" she asked.

"Of course I have anything for nausea," he replied. "That's what Sandie's last months here were all about."

He looked at her and shook his head at the irony of it. "I was just sitting out here," he said, "envying you your ability to go to bed early and sleep."

He started Jenny on Alka-Seltzer. She walked around sipping the fizzy water, first standing outdoors to feel the cool air, then coming back inside because she was shivering. After an hour of this, with no improvement, Jenny went upstairs and again forced herself to vomit. She was standing at the sink in Sandie's bathroom, thinking she would only cough up bile. She brought up her entire lunch and completely clogged the drain in the process, spattering her robe as well. She was utterly chagrinned, but David, climbing the stairs to her rescue, was sweet and supportive and gentle. He took her robe and put it in the washing machine. He offered her one of Sandie's. She hesitated. He gave her one of his instead. When Jenny apologized for the mess, he looked at her with misty eyes. "You don't understand, Love. You remind me of Sandie."

For about ten minutes afterward, Jenny felt fine, filled with relief that the awful sensation was gone. She sat down with David to have a cup of tea. Then the queasiness reappeared. "One of our neighbors is a doctor," David pointed out. "I could call him and have him come over."

"No," Jenny replied firmly. "It's best just to let nature take its course. This is what adrenaline does to me. It will pass," she insisted.

More tea. More Alka-Seltzer. More antacid tablets. More nausea. Jenny settled next to the upstairs bathroom, on the bottom step of the stairs that led to the loft. It got to be eleven o'clock. Despite Jenny's protests, David called his neighbor and walked over to get some antiemetic medication. When he returned, she took the pills but remained where she was.

"Woman, why don't you get into bed?" David scolded. Jenny's bed was only half a flight of stairs away—a mere six steps—but she wasn't sure she would have enough warning to make it down to the bathroom in case of need. She had already done enough damage stopping up the sink.

"I want to be near the bathroom," she pleaded.

"Then why don't you get into my bed?" David's room was immediately adjoining the bathroom. "There isn't enough room to lie down in the hallway. At least you can lie snug in bed until you either go to sleep or need to get up again."

"I'm likely to be up and down all night, and I don't want to keep you awake."

"I'm not sleepy," he countered.

Jenny stood up to test her body's reaction, then resumed her perch.

"Jewel, you're being ridiculous. If you sit there in the hallway, you'll catch double pneumonia. You won't be able to fly home tomorrow, your office will run amok without you, and the Charles River will dry up and disappear."

A smile found its way out despite the nausea. David was teasing. It was a good sign. And besides, it always made her smile when he called her Jewel. It was a part of the easy intimacy that Sandie had spotted long ago and digested carefully as they took each other's measure. Jewel was an ancient nickname, a play on Jenny's initials, J. W. L. It had come into being during their college years. Jenny yielded, but conditionally. "I'll lie down until midnight," she told him. "If I'm neither asleep nor improved by then, I'm going back out in the hall with a blanket, or upstairs, so you can sleep."

With the bedside light on and the door wide open, they both lay down on top of the quilt. Jenny concentrated on breathing deeply because that quelled the flutters and seemed to help. Somewhere around midnight, Delphine came home and stuck her head in the open door to say goodnight. Jenny could see that Delphine was somewhat startled to her presence.

"Jenny's been sick all evening," David explained. "She was going to sit on the stairs and freeze her ass off, but I ordered her to lie on the bed instead."

"How are you feeling now?" Delphine asked.

"A little better," Jenny replied. "My stomach is slowly settling down."

Delphine said good night, went to her room, and closed her door. David immediately got up and shut his door, then turned out the light. "Enough of this shit, woman! Get under the covers," he commanded.

Jenny didn't protest. She wanted the balm of sleep. She moved next to David for warmth. He put his arms around her and drew her close. She nestled her head against his shoulder, and they lay still, hoping for sleep.

Then, suddenly, he stirred. "*Merde!*" he whispered. "I wasn't expecting this." He drew a deep breath, held it, then let it out. His hands started slowly down her back then slid over her hips. She said nothing. She nearly forgot to breathe. She followed him. She led him. Finally he threw the covers back and peeled away her nightgown.

Jenny was governed totally by instinct. As David reached for her, she took him to her with the fierceness of a mother who snatches up her child from harm's way. From her perspective, David was in mortal peril, and she held on to him for dear life.

There was a long-buried familiarity in his scent and the feel of his skin as their bodies merged, but their joining was different from the rambunctious sex of their youth when they were lustful and limber. This time their touch was sweet and lingering, encompassing the emotional intimacy that had spanned more than three decades.

Afterward, arms wrapped about each other, they talked. Jenny spilled things out in a jumble. All those early memories of him—of them. Revisiting their decision to pursue different lives. Sorting out her relationship with Sandie. Confronting the power David had over her. Fighting the ongoing desire she had felt for him. "I couldn't help but envy Sandie," she said, "but whenever I did, I felt guilty and confused."

Like a broken record, she kept repeating how much she respected Sandie and appreciated her and wished to honor her memory. Finally David shook his head.

"Jewel, grieving for Sandie—honoring her, missing her, loving her—is in no way incompatible with my loving you, and you loving me."

Jenny couldn't remember later what she babbled in response, but David leaned over her whispering, "Shut up, shut up, shut up," then covered her mouth with his own.

Once David dropped into sleep, with the deep snoring that Sandie had often teased him about, Jenny lay there wide-awake. She was well past the worst of her stomach problems, but her body was still alert to its internal stress. She stretched out, curled up, lay on her tummy, switched to her back, and went from side to side. Finally, concerned that her restlessness would disturb David, she got up, went down to the kitchen, and made a cup of tea. She walked around with it but felt cold, so finally she came back up and climbed into David's bed again. She still couldn't sleep. A little before five, she went down and made more tea, with a bathroom stop in between. The liquid was going straight through, which she took as a good sign. The nausea was gone, but sleep was still not on the agenda.

Shortly afterward, David woke up and saw her sitting beside him with a cup in her hands. "*C'est pas vrai. C'est pas vrai!* Woman, you are out of your goddamn mind! I can't believe you haven't slept a single wink!" Jenny set the tea aside, shushed him softly, and moved over to snuggle up against him. He held her while she worked her hands softly up and down his spine to send him back to sleep. After a few minutes, it became clear the backrub was having the opposite effect. They made love gently and then dozed again.

The alarm went off at 6:00 a.m. David got up, fed the cats, showered, shaved, and dressed. He brought Jenny's robe up from the laundry room, clean and dry. She padded down the stairs barefoot to join him for breakfast. Given the love she felt, her heart should have been spinning like a top, yet she felt totally calm. It wasn't the exhaustion slowing her down. It was the familiarity, the normality—as if this were their daily routine, as if she had been waking up with him for years. Which in a sense was true.

It was the sweetest of good-byes. David thanked her for coming, for being there. "It really helped," he said. "It was a great comfort." And then he was gone. Off to school. Back to work. They hadn't spoken a single word about the future. No attempt was made to analyze what had transpired. No attempt was made to project what might follow. She had gotten him through the night. It was enough. She didn't cry. She didn't even get misty. *Be practical, Jenny,* she said to herself. *Finish your breakfast, then go upstairs and take a shower.*

She got dressed and finished packing. She stripped the attic bed and tidied the room, gathering her things and taking them downstairs. She made another cup of tea. *How can I be so much at peace?* she wondered. *Every other time I've left him—or he, me—there have been tears and trauma, however carefully hidden. I have longed for this man's love since our paths first crossed. We live on opposite sides of the world,* she reminded herself, *but I have never felt closer to him. Now, beyond the shadow of a doubt, he knows how much I love him. How much I always have and always will.*

Jenny well understood that most people would be aghast at the events of the previous night—shocked by David's behavior and horrified by hers. But there was really only one person whose opinion was critical. "Sandie," she whispered to the photograph hanging on the wall, "I hope you understand."

Marc appeared. While he had breakfast, Jenny went up and knocked gently on Delphine's door. She was awake, but just barely.

"I want to say good-bye," Jenny told her, "but first I want to talk about what happened yesterday. Is that okay?"

Delphine yawned and raised herself against her pillow. "Okay," she said. Jenny sat on the edge of the bed, then laid out the whole of Sunday for her—Olga's luncheon; David's remark in the car; the empty chair. "When David suddenly stood up during the lunch and announced he was leaving, then told me to stay and get a ride with someone later, I was stunned. All I could think was that he was going to take the car and sail off the mountainside, or go to the house and swallow all the pills left in your mother's medicine cabinet. That's why I was so upset when I got back. That's why I dragged him over to the park across the street so I could yell at him." Jenny described for Delphine the conversation and the tears from their long walk. She talked about how she and David held each other as they followed the woodland paths.

Given that Delphine had walked in as they lay together on David's bed, Jenny told her candidly that they had made love during the night—a love born of caring and concern—and that inherent in the gift was an affirmation of life and an abiding respect for Sandie.

"Based on your own experience, I'm sure you already understand the instinctive need for comfort which accompanies sadness and grief. What's especially important to me," she told Delphine, "is that you understand how much I appreciate and honor your mother."

Delphine shrugged and looked at Jenny. "I understand," she said. Her face was blank. It was hard to gauge her thoughts.

Is there anything else I should say? Jenny wondered. *Does Dellie really understand?* She searched her mind but could find nothing helpful to add. She could only hope her words had hit home.

"Thank you, Dellie," Jenny finished quietly. "I believe Sandie would understand too," she added as she gave her a big hug.

As Delphine ducked back under the covers, Jenny gently closed the door behind her, then went downstairs, where Marc was waiting to take her to the airport.

Missing Her

I haven't moved the lotions in her bathroom on the shelf,
Nor touched the perfumes on her chest of drawers.
I haven't bagged her shoes, nor switched the closet broom,
Nor changed address books, nor modified the phone,
Nor cleaned the sheets, nor rearranged the living room.
Why do I still consider here *her* home?

Her teas are where they were, her closet's closed,
Her robes hang where she hung them last,
Her upstairs bathroom towels are folded, neatly posed
In cupboards as she liked it, as she did it in the past.
Her fountain pen is tightly sealed and cased,
Her arcane household binders shut, no note erased.

As evening falls, I sip my wine, awaiting her
Return, listening for her car, expecting her
To enter, hands full of shopping bags, to hear her
Say the trunk is full, could someone help her
Bring the groceries in, pour a glass of wine for her.
Only my breath jumps up. I just sit. My eyes water.
How I miss her! Oh, God, how I miss her!

Chapter 3

Jenny tried to read on the plane, but it was impossible. She kept reliving the last twenty-four hours, examining each moment, each word. Was their shared night a one-time response to an extraordinary circumstance, or would they go forward as lovers? Their coupling hadn't been about desire or simple lust. It was about life and death—about comfort, solace, and survival. Whatever was in David's thoughts, his body had gone straight for the most life-affirming act in its repertoire.

She considered his words. "Grieving for Sandie is in no way incompatible with my loving you," he had said. Jenny knew the love David expressed was real, but she couldn't assign it a clear category. Their emotional intimacy had endured for decades. She felt it time and again, in his phone calls and letters, his visits, his poetry, his teasing, and his steadfast trust. Jenny had total confidence in that aspect of his love. It had survived their split thirty years before when David decided to make his life in Paris. It had endured through David's marriage to Sandie and Jenny's marriage to Seth Winthrop.

It wasn't until after her divorce that Jenny realized the desire she felt for David had also survived. She thought her ancient passion for him was safely buried, but no, wham, out it had sprung full force on her first post-divorce visit to Geneva. She was embarrassed and ashamed. Wanting David was covetous and unacceptable, because David and Sandie obviously loved each other. Jenny struggled mightily at the time to close the Pandora's box that had sprung open in her heart. She cried more on the plane home from that visit than on the long-ago flight when she left David in Paris to go build a separate life in Boston.

Now, here she was in the present, with David suddenly a widower. The challenge was to keep her feet firmly on the ground, and keep David's survival and well-being as her primary focus. She knew that for her own sake, as well as David's, she had to get her spinning heart back under control. Her wanting him and his needing her were not the same thing.

David was devoted to his teaching job at l'Académie Internationale. Jenny couldn't imagine him leaving Europe and returning to the States to live. She was equally grounded in Boston, as a senior partner and mainstay of a small accounting firm serving the Bay State's nonprofit community. She couldn't stop her mind from toying with a fairy tale ending, but her practical side counseled caution. *Be sensible, Jenny*, she told herself. *Just help David go forward one step at a time.*

Jenny cleared customs and spotted Ross Barrett's tall, slender form at the edge of the crowd hovering at the arrivals gate. Though he was nearing sixty, he was still extremely handsome. His close-cropped hair had gone totally white, but his chocolate skin was wrinkle-free—something she considered very unfair. Ross was quietly gay, conservative in demeanor and dress. He liked good clothes and wore them well. When he entered a room in his three-piece lawyer's suit, he drew admiring glances from both genders.

Jenny felt lucky to have him in her life. When Ross was wearing his attorney hat, he could appear stern, but underneath he was a sweetheart, generous and considerate. In their youth, unknown to one another and in very different ways, they had loved the same man—Ramon Delgado. Ramon was part of the close-knit student group living in the Ware Street apartment building in Cambridge. Since Ramon had no sexual interest in Jenny, he served as her trusted confidant and a shoulder to cry on during the multiple occasions when David pursued other women. Ramon was a soul mate. She loved him like a brother. When she learned he had died of AIDS, she was devastated.

Ramon had moved to New York after their graduation. Over the years, their communications gradually tapered off as marriage and career took up more of Jenny's time. After a while, they lost touch. When Jenny and her husband, Seth, finally called it quits after fifteen years of marriage, she spent months trying to track Ramon down. Ross was the one to give her the sad news, answering a forwarded letter she had mailed to an old address. When Ross telephoned and told her Ramon was dead, she fell apart. There wasn't much exchange through the sobs, but before they hung up, Ross quietly asked if she was the woman Ramon called Jewel.

"Yes," she managed.

"I've heard a lot about you," Ross went on. "I'd like to talk when you feel up to it."

And so the friendship began. Jenny took a train to New York to meet Ross and see the apartment where he and Ramon had lived for ten years and where Ross had nursed him through the final stages of the virus. Ross in turn came to Boston and was sufficiently drawn to the city that he ultimately gave up the Big Apple for an old brownstone in Boston's rapidly gentrifying South End. He had his own social set, but he and Jenny often spent time together.

Jenny was perfectly content to have Ross be the man in her life. Over the years, Seth had conducted multiple affairs with increasingly younger women and had finally sailed off into the sunset with a perky graduate student half his age. Jenny was in her mid-forties when the divorce was finalized, sufficiently crushed by Seth's betrayal that she quashed any thoughts of seeking another husband.

In the decade since the divorce, Jenny had found both purpose and solace in her work, routinely logging fifty- and sixty-hour weeks. She had good friends and interesting neighbors. She had, in Ross, a charming escort and a mixed-gender relationship where sex wasn't on the agenda. And she had David. Though he was an ocean away, his existence filled an emotional need even though physical intimacy had been off-limits—until the events of the last twenty-four hours.

Ross drove Jenny home to Shawmut, and she filled him in on her trip—Olga's luncheon, her fears for David, her declaration of love and concern, and their subsequent tearful walk. But after that, she stopped. She trusted Ross with her life, but the night in David's arms was not something Jenny could share with him yet. She wanted time to digest it on her own before she sought more objective input.

She felt no guilt. *Had I been Sandie,* she reassured herself, *I would have wanted my husband to realize my death didn't doom him to living out the rest of his days in a sad and solitary state.* Still, Jenny understood that her actions were in serious violation of social convention.

When she returned to her office the next day, Jenny's coworkers offered condolences. They assumed, reasonably, that Sandie's death filled her thoughts. Jenny answered questions and talked about the memorial service but said nothing about the radical change her relationship with David had undergone.

Jenny was a confirmed workaholic, and the firm was a large part of her life. Jenny enjoyed the people she worked with. The staff all socialized casually, but Jenny was private by nature and reserved by upbringing. No one in the office had any idea of the depth of her attachment to David, and for the moment, she chose to keep it that way.

There was a week's backlog on her desk, but before she touched it, she reread the e-mails David sent to everyone about the cremation and the celebration. She had seen them in Geneva, but their power did not diminish on second reading. David had let fall all his defenses. He made no effort to hide his helplessness or his grief.

From: JWLongworth
To: DavidP
Date: October 3, 2000
Subject: There are not words
The descriptions of the cremation service and the memorial celebration are so beautiful, David. Sandie has blessed your life. And she has blessed mine. May she bless our future as well, however it unfolds.

> Just so you know, I spoke with Dellie before I left, and we talked about the events of Sunday night. She seemed very understanding. She is her mother's daughter. J.

Jenny already missed hearing his voice. She called to make sure he was all right. Reassured on that score, she asked, "How is Dellie doing? Have you spoken to her to make sure she's okay with what we talked about?"

Delphine was apparently home and within range. In typical fashion, David called out to her, "Delphine? Jenny's on the phone. She wants me to be sure you're okay with what you and she talked about."

"Yeah," Delphine called back, "I'm okay with it."

They didn't stay on the line long. Jenny promised to be in touch every day but also warned David that her office e-mail went through a shared computer and was not secure.

"I love you, David. As I told you long ago, it is a love that surpasses all things. But many people will have trouble understanding and accepting what has passed between us, and I'm not ready to share my thoughts with friends because they're still in a jumble. Just don't you worry that my affection is waning simply because I don't spill it all over my e-mails."

"I won't," he said.

> *From: JWLongworth*
> *To: DavidP*
> *Date: October 4, 2000*
> *Subject: Settling Down*
> It didn't hit me until this morning that yesterday was Ash Tuesday for you. I can only think it was excruciating to bring Sandie home that way. I have no words to soften that process, only loving thoughts.
> Hope the meetings with the insurance and bank folks have gone okay. Let me know if there are ways I can help.
> Love to everyone, J.

De: David
A: Jenny
Envoyé: 4 octobre, 2000
Objet: Re: Settling Down

Life's a goddamn hoot. The engraver misspelled Sandie's name on the urn, and I only noticed it once I was home. Tomorrow I'll go back and complain. How do you complain about a misspelling for a bunch of ashes? JEEEEzus F. Christ!

Kisses, David

David's sardonic tone didn't fool Jenny. She knew his tricks for coping with pain, and this was one of them. She responded with a direct probe.

From: JWLongworth
To: DavidP
Date: October 5, 2000
Subject: The week in review

Dearheart—I'm heading down to Provincetown with Ross tomorrow. I won't be near a computer until Saturday, but I'll send you mental e-mails nonstop. Whenever you need distraction, write and tell me how your day has gone. What was the worst thing that happened? What was the best? Has it been harder than you expected? Or easier? Are you getting enough hugs every day? I have an unlimited supply and will send several if you're running short.

Love, me

De: David
A: Jenny
Envoyé: 6 octobre, 2000
Objet: Re: The week in review

It's the edge of nausea that's permanent. Never really sick but just want to be. Somehow it gets to the mind. I go over and over things or just mope about. Teaching helps. I forget while I'm in class, but I haven't found a self-generated activity that has the same effect.

Tried cooking the other night—didn't work. I'll try golf tomorrow with Michel and Josette. It's definitely the most difficult thing I've ever had to do or live through. Went to the notary this morning to have the Will explained. See the bankers on Wednesday. In the process of getting Sandie's car shifted to me. Really interesting stuff. I did cut the wisteria this afternoon. That gave me a moment's respite. Hope you put flowers in the Provincetown cemetery to honor our visit years ago.

Love, David.

From: J W Longworth
To: DavidP
Date: October 7, 2000
Subject: Safety bowl

Being at the edge of nausea is second only to being in the middle of it, and it's at the top of my list of unbearable natural sensations. I have half a mind to get back on a plane. Sadly, you can't just take on someone else's nausea, and there are a certain number of tears that must be shed. If all distraction does is postpone them, it just prolongs the agony. Still, I wish my own tears could count in your tally and hasten the day when you greet the dawn with a smile.

We spent our time in Provincetown hanging out with some artist friends, so I didn't have a chance to visit the cemetery, but the memory is a very clear one. What you and I got up to in our student days was pretty naughty. Sleeping bags on the marble. Romance à la Edgar Alan Poe! Love amidst the ruins ...

Do let me know about any financial worries. I realize this is officially none of my business, but I am a CPA, and I intend to butt in anyway, so you might as well tell me about anything of importance.

Hugs, J.

On Sunday, Jenny called him. He dodged her questions. She knew his feelings were deep and raw, so she didn't push. He preferred to talk about the evolving plans for a trip to scatter Sandie's ashes.

"The school's mid-October break is coming up. I'll use that time to go to Paris with Marc and Delphine, and then on to Brittany. Sandie wants her ashes cast into the Atlantic." Jenny noted the use of the present tense but said nothing.

"Delphine is thinking about college in Paris rather than Boston," he continued.

This was good news. It meant Delphine would be within a short train ride of Geneva. She could get home quickly in a crisis.

"As far as the taxes go, I don't know jack shit," he announced. "But you're welcome to butt in all you want. Never known you not to butt in … albeit discreetly. Little Miss Busybody. Must be part of your charm."

"Take good care of yourself, David."

How she wished she could give him a hug.

"You too, Jewel. Loved talkin' to ya."

> From: JWLongworth
> To: DavidP
> Date: October 9, 2000
> Subject: Week II
> Americans are busy celebrating Christopher Columbus's navigational skills today, so I have free parking, which is why I am at the office.
> I have neither new insights nor helpful homilies to arm you as you begin another week. It gets darker and darker each morning, making a cheerful start increasingly challenging. Whatever the weather, you are surrounded by love on all sides, even if it feels as if you are isolated and alone.
> Hugs, J.

David announced that he planned to host a luncheon in appreciation of the friends who served as Sandie's caregivers. "November 18. There'll be about thirty people. Can you come?" he closed.

From: JWLongworth
To: DavidP
Date: October 10, 2000
Subject: Re: Sandie's celebration lunch

November 18 is feasible. If you want to celebrate Thanksgiving and need an apple pie baker, I could stay through the holiday. Can you get cranberries in Geneva?

Love, J.

De: David
A: Jenny
Envoyé: 11 octobre, 2000
Objet: Re: Re: Sandie's celebration lunch

Listen, Kid. You come as early as you want and stay as long as you want, and no, there are no cranberries in Geneva, and yes, I need an apple pie baker. Any other silly goddamn questions you have to ask?

Love, David

From: JWLongworth
To: DavidP
Date: October 13, 2000
Subject: Cranberries

It's settled, then. I will bring fresh cranberries, canned pumpkin, cranberry sauce, brown sugar, etc. It's fun to think of festive meals and good company, but I am mindful that your pain is doubtlessly still searing. I still cry when I have to explain it to people.

I delivered a huge Swiss chocolate bar to the ticket agent who was so helpful getting me to Geneva in time for the funeral. She was quite moved, and I had to reach for my handkerchief again. I'll be there in a few weeks to give you hugs in person; meanwhile, know that I am sending them through the atmosphere nonstop.

Love, J.

De: David
A: Jenny
Envoyé: 14 octobre, 2000
Objet: A week without e-mails
    We're off to Paris tomorrow, Love, and I doubt that I will figure out how to capture my cyberspace at a distance. That means I ain't gonna be answering before the twenty-second. All is well (?), I guess.
    Love, David

Jenny hated the thought of being out of touch, especially knowing what lay ahead. This was the week they would take Sandie's ashes to France, make her one with Paris, and share her with the rocky coast of Brittany, as per her request. The profanity and banter about Thanksgiving plans showed bits and pieces of the old sense of humor, but Jenny knew David was in acute pain. She had told him about her family's experience in scattering her father's ashes and how positive and healing a process it had been. She hoped David and the children would find some release in their expedition, yet it was obvious the process would be wrenching. She wished David a journey filled with warm and healing memories. There was little else she could do.

De: David
A: Jenny
Envoyé: 22 octobre, 2000
Objet: We're home
    Just got back, Love. I'm in a funk, even though the trip went as well as one could have hoped. Tell you 'bout it tomorrow.
    Bises, me.

De: David
A: Family & friends
Envoyé: 23 octobre, 2000
Objet: Sandie's ashes
    We drove to Paris on Sunday and listened to news reports of deadly mudslides in the Alps. It fit the

mood. Not much conversation. No one really wanted to make the trip, but there was no getting around it. Sandie wanted it this way. And in a strange sort of way, so did we. Got to Paris in the rain, crossed it glinting, shimmering wet, people huddling in cafés, laughing, jumping back from splashed puddles, coming out of shops, dodging traffic, crossing against the lights, strolling, roller blading, helping children across streets, deep in conversation, hailing taxis, window shopping, buying crêpes. Doing all those things any normal, sane human being does in Paris on a fall afternoon. We were transporting ashes. In all probability, so were others.

We worked our way across town to visit Mme Lamont, Sandie's surrogate mother following her own mother's death from cancer when Sandie was Delphine's age. Everything dovetails. Around and around in circles trying to find a parking space. What's the building code? Someone was going in and let us follow him. Mme Lamont opened her door. Hugs and kisses and tears. Put the umbrella in the corner. Into the dining room, the television on. It will stay on. Mme Lamont says she needs the noise. We talk of Sandie and her death and our disbelief and would you like something to drink and no, we can't stay but wanted to come by and see you first. And the tears and the laughter. Then switching to problems with her apartment, so I could tell that the healing process had already begun, and then with a glance at Sandie's photograph, more tears and memories.

The cycle of sorrow and healing repeated itself at each visit. Only the memories that triggered it would differ. Monday it was still raining. The day was for Camille and Isaac Bloch, my oldest friends in Paris. It was Isaac who took the picture of Sandie we used for her memorial announcement. We had lunch together. Then Isaac's mother called and asked to speak to me and choked up talking about Sandie. I cried as well, trying to console her and myself. Crying into a goddamn phone! And yet the hope was and still is that somehow the answer is there and the process will be reversed. I spent the afternoon buying a pair of shoes and a belt and racing through the Picasso Museum. Life goes on.

Tuesday was glorious. Heavenly blue sky, bright sunshine, fat white clouds. We opened Sandie's urn.

Copper-colored metal, about the size of a small flower vase, a cover screwed on, her name engraved on the cover and the seal of the State and Republic of Geneva. Upon opening it, we found a plain, white bag, closed with a strip of gold wire twisted around its neck. Must have weighed two kilos. We opened the bag and transferred several handfuls of tiny but rather rough ashes (bones don't burn completely even in an hour and a half, not to mention fillings) into plastic baggies. I resealed the official white bag and put it back in the urn. It would await Brittany.

Transferring the ashes was like slicing vegetables and not wanting to cut your finger. You had to mind your Ps and Qs or you risked spilling them on the table. So there were no tears or emotions. We talked and joked with Sandie while we were doing it. We then put several of the small packets of ashes into a paper bag and went out into the generous Parisian sunshine to scatter them. First to the Parc Monceau, where Sandie played as a little girl and where we had wedding pictures taken in 1973. The park was closed for repairs, so we had to cast her ashes through the elegant fence. Then by bus to the Place de la Concorde. The place was a madhouse of traffic, Parisians, and tourists.

We cast some ashes into the reflecting pool where she used to sail model boats, some around a classical statue of Grief, others at the base of Diana's statue (the goddess, not the princess). We ate lunch in the upstairs room at the Rubis—*tête de veau,* which Sandie loved, brie and chiroubles. We walked over to the Pont des Arts across the Seine and cast more ashes into the river. Emptying the packets, watching the wind separate the finer powder from the particles, seeing them bounce off the parapets of the bridge or settle among the blades of grass around the statues, all the time talking to her and among ourselves. There were moments of tears and hurt, but there were also moments of silliness and laughter.

A long river barge approached the bridge. We didn't want Sandie's ashes mixed with the load, so we waited until it had passed, only to discover it was hauling sacks of flour. And what if we dusted one of the *Bateaux mouches*?

That evening we had dinner with an old friend, then walked back up the Boulevard St. Michel to see a photographic exhibit displayed along the fence of the Luxembourg Palace. The night was deliciously mild, and we chatted of the time when I lived just up the boulevard and had first met Sandie.

Wednesday was miserable. Pouring rain. A perfect day to visit the cemetery and put ashes on Sandie's mother's grave. Row upon row of wet graves and tombstones. Dripping, fading flowers by the thousands, mountains of brown, wet leaves. Thank god we went with Sandie's cousin Giselle, who knew exactly where the grave was. Otherwise I would have wandered around lost with a dissolving paper map. No planter at the base of the tomb, so we sprinkled ashes in the gray marble vase, which someone had filled with chrysanthemums. Who was left in the family to do that? Mystery.

Thursday was superb. Not a cloud in sight. A royal blue sky. Low autumn sunlight transforming the Parisian limestone into butter. People strolling, coats over their shoulders, reading newspapers on park benches, bustling here and there. I had nothing to do but errands and good-byes—Mme Lamont over a glass of wine and a cigarette, then the *pharmacienne* who was so helpful over the years with our Paris apartment.

We made a side trip to the suburbs to visit with Mme Lamont's son and daughter-in-law. Memories of the memorial ceremony that they had traveled to Geneva to attend. The moments that touched them. Come whenever you want, stay as long as you want. I know, I know. Got to go. Kisses and hugs. Off to the highway, heading north. We spent Thursday night in Les Maisonnettes, a hamlet not far from Rouen where Giselle and her husband, Jean-Luc, have a Norman country house.

We were ready to go the next morning at seven. It rained solidly for the seven-hour drive to Audierne, the last large village in Brittany before the Atlantic. It rained so hard you had to use your fog lights. It rained through dinner. It rained as we got ready for bed. It rained while we slept, but it had stopped by the time we woke up. Off the port was a thin line of cloudless sky over the horizon, dark in the early-morning light.

We met for breakfast. When we finished, the cloudless line had grown to a band and turned electric blue. We packed and paid the hotel. The band of clear sky off the coast had expanded. During the drive to the ocean, the sun began to break through the dark clouds directly overhead, dropping ladders of light and casting giant golden pools on the bay below the cliffs and far out to sea. The island of Sein suddenly burst into glimmering white. The purple cloud cover began to break into enormous flagstones. Blue appeared in the cracks. A wind out of the northeast picked up, steadily pushing the clouds farther and farther away. I wondered if Sandie had arranged the change.

We parked and slowly hiked the last two kilometers along the cliff path through the gorse. Despite the late date, wildflowers were still in bloom. The cold wind drove them down with gusts. We zipped up our jackets and walked along, talking about the change in the weather. Jean-Luc's dog marked bushes. Delphine carried Sandie's ashes. I checked to make sure I had the texts I wanted to read.

At the base of the navy lighthouse, where a nineteenth-century monument commemorates those who have died at sea, the path takes a sharp curve toward the craggy point at the land's end. The point features great chunks of rock rising out of the ground like the scaly back of a dragon. The dorsal crests form gigantic humps and saddles on their way to the ocean some five hundred meters away. I head over the rocks toward the open sea. Everyone but Giselle, who suffers vertigo, follows.

I take the bag of ashes and open it. I offer it to Marc, Jean-Luc, and Delphine. Each takes a handful. The wind whipping around me, I open my envelope and delicately extract the poems I have brought, then clutch them to keep them from blowing away. I feel tears beginning to flood my eyes. I take a handful of ashes and try to hold the sheets flat with one hand. Marc helps me hold the pages against the wind.

My voice cracks completely as I start. Marc moves to my side and helps me read. I fight my way to the end, crying, step to the edge of the cliff and release Sandie's ashes into the wind above the sea. I recite Frost's "Nothing

Gold Can Stay" and continue scattering Sandie's ashes, watching them bounce and scamper down the cliff, making their way toward the pounding water's edge. Delphine, weeping, steps forward to my side and does the same. Marc climbs to a ledge well above us and, tears streaming down his face, hurls his mother's ashes into the sky. The wind picks up the powder and lifts it, letting the particles scatter and bounce among the granite crags of the precipice on the way to the thundering surf. Each of us takes another handful and, choosing another spot, scatters Sandie's ashes among the elements. I recite another Frost poem, "Once by the Pacific." Despite the sun, it captures my inner darkness. I climb further down the cliff, trying to find a spot that will allow me to scatter her among the crashing waves. I launch a handful into the fierce wind, which whirls it into the sky and dashes it against the rocks.

We regroup and rejoin Giselle at the top of the slope by an old gun emplacement. We repeat the ceremony, looking out over the glistening sea, now dotted with sailboats and ferries. Finally we turn and head back toward the cars. Before returning to Paris, we make a last stop in Breton, where a long, sandy beach allows us to scatter the remaining ashes directly into the waves, to take her away. She would have wanted us to be certain.

David

Jenny felt she would have to read David's report several times over before she could reply. "Once by the Pacific," she was familiar with, but she had to look up "Nothing Gold Can Stay." "I'm so sorry," she whispered as she read. "I'm so sorry."

De: David
A: Jenny
Envoyé: 23 octobre, 2000
Objet: Your ETA
Feeling better this evening, Ducks. When you've figured out your final arrangements, send me the info. All is better.
Bises, David

Because David felt better, so did Jenny. She took her cue from his tone and responded in kind rather than dwelling on the report about Brittany.

From: JWLongworth
To: DavidP
Date: October 24, 2000
Subject: Catch-up
    I will arrive November 16. My return flight is November 27.
    I will happily take primary responsibility for Thanksgiving dinner. I usually make turkey soup, and for that I need barley—is it readily available? I've never been a fan of sweet potatoes, but I could bring some if you wish. Do make a list.
    Now, about Xmas. I would be pleased to accompany you wherever my companionship would be welcome. I assume during Christmas you will be in Chattanooga with your siblings, and that should provide a reasonable support system. I worry, however, about New Year's Eve. It's a difficult holiday—depressing in all sorts of ways. I really want to be with you then.
    Love, me

De: David
A: Jenny
Envoyé: 24 octobre, 2000
Objet: Xmas
    Dear You, Barley and sweet potatoes are available although no one eats the latter except me and then only in sweet potato pudding, which you, as a Yankee, wouldn't know deep doodoo about. You can stay as long as you like, take care of Thanksgiving, and make soup. I don't think we're going to do Florida after all. We're trying to work out a flight to Chattanooga, then to San Francisco. You're welcome and invited to accompany us on both legs of the trip.
    I normally go to bed at 8:30 on New Year's Eve. Never have liked it. Sandie used to sit up and watch TV

with a bottle of champagne while I snored my head off upstairs. Can't agree on everything.

Love, David

From: JWLongworth
To: DavidP
Date: October 25, 2000
Subject: Re: Xmas

Joining you in San Francisco works best for me. Are you planning to stay with Jack? I have a friend in Sausalito whom I could stay with if need be. Keep me posted as the dates and places solidify.

Love, Jenny

Jenny admitted to herself that she really wanted to sleep with David again, but she hesitated to presume or put him on the spot. She was trying to be both neutral and subtle. It got her nowhere. Not a hint, not a clue was forthcoming in his response.

De: David
A: Jenny
Envoyé: 25 octobre, 2000
Objet: Re: Re: Xmas

Jack has enough beds to put up a national political convention, but you can work that one out when we cross that bridge.

Love, David

PS—I invited my next-door neighbors, Mehrak and Manuela Pashoutan, for Thanksgiving dinner. I think you met them at Sandie's ceremony.

From: JWLongworth
To: DavidP
Date: October 28, 2000
Subject: T-Day

I'm delighted you've invited the Pashoutans to join us. Yes, I did meet them. They kept bringing over wonderful Iranian soups and casseroles the week of Sandie's funeral.

Now, logistics. Does one have to order a turkey in advance? Do pumpkins exist over there? Mehrak is Muslim, yes? Does he have any dietary restrictions I should know about?

Love, *moi*

De: David
A: Jenny
Envoyé: 29 octobre, 2000
Objet: Re: T-Day

Pumpkins exist in all sizes. Turkeys also exist in all sizes. No dietary restrictions that I know of, though I suspect that Mehrak would rather not sit down to a roast suckling pig.

I plan to invite Josette and Michel. Marc will presumably bring his girlfriend Valerie. Delphine will likely want her best friend Marie-Claire, and in that case, I'd like to include M-C's mother, Cybèle. That gives us something between ten and twelve people.

Kisses, David

From: JWLongworth
To: DavidP
Date: October 30, 2000
Subject: Monday

With that many diners, I think I'll make pumpkin pudding *and* pumpkin chiffon pie.

Had our first snow yesterday. Nothing is sticking, but it's raw and gray. When I retire I'd love to spend winters in some wonderfully warm and sunny spot. Presumably there should also be a good golf course nearby in case you decide to visit.

Saw a great poster: "If you're going through hell, keep going."

Hugs to Marc and Dellie.

Love to you, Jenny

Jenny came home the next afternoon to find a message from David on her answering machine: "Called to say hello, and not even the cat answered. Wanted to tell you that your retirement spot definitely needs a golf course."

From: JWLongworth
To: DavidP
Date: October 31, 2000
Subject: No one at home at 9 a.m.

Sorry I missed your call. How are you doing? The thought of you facing breakfast alone each morning is depressing.

Ending on a more cheerful note, I have found a recipe for genuine Durgin Park Indian Pudding. It needs cornmeal and molasses. Can I get them in Geneva?

Love, me

De: David
A: Jenny
Envoyé: 31 octobre, 2000
Objet: Re: No one home at 9 a.m.

Yep, it's depressing, but twelve out of twenty-four hours each day, that's definitely the dark side I prefer.

If you're planning Indian pudding, you'd better pack the cornmeal and molasses.

Can't wait.

Love, David

From: JWLongworth
To: DavidP
Date: November 1, 2000
Subject: Are you okay?

Suddenly got a weird sense that you're having a rough day. I'm still digesting your reference about being depressed twelve hours out of every twenty-four. It hurts that you feel down so much of the time, but I imagine that having people tell you to cheer up is at best useless and at worst really annoying.

Love, me

PS—Regarding Christmas, is your family prepared to handle an extra guest if I come to Chattanooga?

De: David
A: Jenny
Envoyé: 2 novembre, 2000
Objet: Re: Are you okay?
    I don't mind people telling me to cheer up because I know it's not currently possible. Everyone has a role to play.
    Chattanooga is not a problem.
    Kisses, David

Jenny noted David's swings between candor and what she considered cover—moments when he confronted his grief and moments when he sidestepped, joked, and changed the subject. She called Rachel Aronson, a former colleague who had given helpful advice during the last months of Sandie's illness. Rachel had lost her husband, Josh, to pancreatic cancer just three months before Sandie died. Petite and trim, with smooth skin and frosted hair, Rachel's energy and positive focus belied the pain she was living through. She knew firsthand how devastating the death of a spouse could be.

"You've got to take things one day at a time," Rachel counseled when they met for dinner. "Even now, five months later, I can't focus on anything more than a few weeks ahead. Certain tasks still feel overwhelming, and frankly, I approach them with dread. Josh always took care of starting up the furnace in the fall, for example, and draining the outdoor water spigots. My son has shown me how, but I keep forgetting, mostly because I hate the reason why I now must learn to do these things."

"That sounds like David and bill paying," Jenny commented. "He hates having to file the invoices and balance the checkbook. Sandie was the one who took care of everything financial."

"Most people don't understand the psychological toll it takes," Rachel said, nodding. "They think it's supportive when they tell me, 'Of course you can do that—it's easy.' I know they mean well, but they have no idea how distressing it is. Don't be surprised if David gets irritated over what seems like nothing. He needs your patience and your tolerance, no matter how irrational his behavior seems."

"Are there triggers I should look out for?" Jenny asked.

"There are too many to count," Rachel replied, shaking her head, "and the worst moments sometimes hit you out of the blue. I have an elderly neighbor who thought it would be helpful to describe her own experience of widowhood. 'My husband died thirty years ago,' she began. I didn't even hear the rest of the story. I felt dizzy with horror at the idea of contemplating thirty years without Josh. I know intellectually that what I feel today is not what I'll feel in five, ten, or twenty years, but I got shivers just thinking about it. It was awful! Really awful!"

"What's the most positive experience you've had—assuming there is such a thing?"

"The most positive?" Rachel tilted her head back, took a deep breath, and closed her eyes. Jenny was briefly afraid she had pushed Rachel to the brink of tears, but Rachel quickly brought her focus back to the table. "It's quite a recent one," she said.

"Josh and I always enjoyed the symphony, but the year before he died, I let our season tickets lapse. About six weeks ago, some friends who often accompanied us to past concerts called and asked if I'd like to go in with them on season tickets. At first I hesitated, but then decided, why not? For the initial concert, I invited them to come to my house beforehand for a light supper. I prepared one of my favorite recipes, put flowers around, and set a festive table. When the bell rang, and I saw my guests at the door, I felt a little surge of happiness. I was completely astonished by it. It didn't last all that long, and the clouds rolled back in later, but now I know empirically that I can feel happy again. It really helps me to keep going."

When the dinner was over, Jenny gave Rachel a big hug and thanked her profusely for sharing her thoughts. "The education you're giving me will really help me with David," she said as they parted.

When she got home, she sent David a lengthy missive describing the evening's conversation. At the end she added, "When you say

Chattanooga is not a problem, may I infer that you have already cleared this with your family?"

> *De: David*
> *A: Jenny*
> *Envoyé: 9 novembre, 2000*
> *Objet: Re: Dinner with Rachel Aronson*
>> The name sounds familiar. Isn't Rachel the woman you invited to join us in Le Croisic before Sandie's decline forced us to abort? Glad to hear she's surviving with a modicum of hope. Gives me a future. Meanwhile, don't worry about me; I don't want to miss the Indian pudding.
>> Now back to the Christmas trip: you're invited (and you damned well *know* you are) for *all* of the trip— Chattanooga as well as San Francisco. If you're worried about sleeping arrangements, know only that neither you nor I will be sleeping in the bathtub, as Sandie used to say, because after the last time I have no intention of depriving either you or myself. And I say that with all the respect and love I have for you—and Sandie.
>> But you, Jewel, Ms. Proper Bostonian, have got to decide on your own what you can and cannot do because you are *you*.
>> Kisses, David

It was reassuring to know that David wanted her—that their night of lovemaking in Geneva had not been a purely circumstantial event, never to be repeated. She understood that there was no guarantee their new status would be permanent. David was operating in a state of emotional chaos. She was his life raft, but someday he would make it through this stormy sea back onto dry land. When that happened, he might well look to rebuild his life with a woman who better reflected Sandie's qualities. Try as she might, Jenny could never be French. *Still, he is in my care and keeping for the moment*, she concluded. *And for the moment, that's sufficient.*

From: JWLongworth
To: DavidP
Date: November 11, 2000
Subject: Sunday

I am relieved to know we will not be sleeping in any bathtubs. I will therefore join you for both Chattanooga and San Francisco.

Love, J.

De: David
A: Jenny
Envoyé: 12 novembre, 2000
Objet: Re: Sunday

Gotcha, Good-Lookin'. Will inform Nate and Margaret officially. Maybe they'll organize a rebel ball. Need something to get me out of my ice cave. David

From: JWLongworth
To: DavidP
Date: November 13, 2000
Subject: Re: Re: Sunday

Don't get too attached to that ice cave. I intend to radiate some heat when I get to Geneva. Can't wait.

Love, J.

November, 2000

Like Trees in November

Like trees in November, the mailbox is bare now.

The cold winds of late September spared
Neither her nor me. October blew in piles
Of cards and letters, filling the box,
Some formal and styled, others simple and sad,
All of which I was somehow glad
To gather in, eager to open and read, hoping
Their decomposition would lead me to answers
Flowering in rows planted not in May
but now, today, among Toussaint Chrysanthemums.

My mind's fields have yet to yield
A single hint, the plot inside me lies sourly
Fallow, my thoughts wander hourly
Up and down the furrows they've already walked,
Furrows from which the autumn wind
Has blasted even the yellowing leaves of sorrow.
Now face to face with Winter, sitting here alone,
I strain to hear her voice, her music, her call
Over the storm wind, my mind's roar,
The quiet of night fall.

Chapter 4

David was waiting for Jenny on the other side of Swiss customs. He was pale, but he smiled and gave her a big hug. Grief had etched new lines in his face in the six weeks since she had seen him last. David had beautiful eyes, chestnut-brown and cocker-spaniel soft, wide set beneath bushy eyebrows, but now they were clouded and dull with sorrow. The sparkle was gone.

When David was young, his skin was smooth and warm, and his cheeks featured deep dimples. Now there were tiny warts and spots scattered like freckles across his cheekbones. Some of what Jenny noted was just age. His nose, once boyish with its slightly snubbed tip, had thickened and become veined and mottled by a steady diet of French wine. But the grief was clearly having an impact.

When they stepped out into the clear Swiss daylight, Jenny noticed that his frown lines had deepened. She could still see in him the young man she had fallen in love with so many years before. It didn't bother her that his face now reflected the outer end of middle age. So did hers. What was hard was looking at a visage that manifested so strongly the loss he had suffered and the pain he was enduring.

When they arrived at the house, Delphine was there to welcome her. Marc was out and likely to remain so for the evening. David carried Jenny's suitcase upstairs, set it on his bed, and came back down. Delphine went up to her room a few minutes later to retrieve something. She spotted the suitcase through David's open bedroom door but gave no outward sign of reaction. They all ate a light supper together, and then Delphine took off to go to the movies with friends.

Jenny went up to unpack and faced a momentary dilemma. Sandie's chest of drawers and her closets were still full. There were no free hangers and no free space. She didn't feel comfortable removing anything, so she doubled up her slacks and blouses with Sandie's on the hangers and mounded her blazers on top of the clothes Sandie had left hanging on hooks. She placed her suitcase in a corner and used it to house her underwear and sweaters.

She noted uneasily that the wig Sandie used to conceal her hair loss was still on its stand on the dresser. Sandie's medicines were still on the bedside table. Jenny didn't think Sandie would want David surrounded by reminders of her illness, but if her visit hadn't motivated the removal of these things, she had to assume he wasn't ready to deal with it. When everything was put away, Jenny went down to help David finish the kitchen cleanup. A quick hug turned into a clinging embrace, and she felt her knees go weak.

"You want to do this here in the kitchen?" he asked, half joking.

"Wouldn't be the first time," she smiled, remembering a summer morning many years ago. "I'm just not sure I can wait," she teased. "I've been counting the hours."

"Me too," he concurred. They went upstairs and tumbled into bed like puppies.

The next morning, David was up early and had a glass of freshly squeezed orange juice waiting for her. Jenny loved fresh juice and reached for the glass with delight but was not prepared for the tartness of European oranges. David laughed as her eyes opened wide in surprise and her lips puckered. "I always made fresh juice for Sandie in the mornings," he told her, "but she was never one for sweet tastes."

"Well, I appreciate the thought," Jenny responded, "but maybe I'll just stick to tea."

David had to teach but came back to the house for lunch since he had two open periods mid-day. He arrived with Delphine, who had gone out mid-morning. She was puffy-eyed and obviously agitated.

"We need to talk," he said tersely as Jenny came down the stairs to greet them. She had no idea what was wrong. The three of them went into the kitchen, which had always served as the heart of the house. Then David explained. Delphine had intercepted him at school. During the ride home, she had broken down in tears, distressed by Jenny's presence in her parents' bedroom. "I'm afraid to lose my mother's scent," she sobbed.

Jenny felt awful. It hadn't occurred to either her or David to discuss how they would conduct themselves in Geneva. Their only communication on the subject involved Christmas accommodations. Delphine knew about Jenny being with David the night after Olga's luncheon, but she presumably saw that as a special instance because David had been so dangerously down—an entirely reasonable construct on her part. David had said nothing to her since. She had been distressed by the sight of Jenny's suitcase on the bed and the prospect of Jenny's clothes in Sandie's closet. She wasn't hostile, but her pain was manifest from the anguish in her eyes and the tautness in her face.

David was candid, open, and gentle. "I've asked myself—and Sandie—all the moral questions you're struggling with," he told Delphine, "and it's very clear to me that this is the right path to follow. The emotional relationship I have with Jenny is one I've always had. Sandie was aware of it, she was comfortable with it, and she respected it. She knew that it didn't take anything away from her."

Jenny echoed his sentiments. "I've had to process all these issues too," she told Delphine, "and I truly believe Sandie would want me to comfort David and give him such peace as I can. But I understand your confusion and your pain. Intellectually, I'm fine with what we're doing, because I see it helping David, yet even I still wish I had some sign from Sandie saying, 'Yes, you have my blessing. Take care of him for me.'"

With remarkable maturity, Delphine told Jenny she would be her first choice for a stepmother, but the fear of losing the last vestiges of her mother was overwhelming. David spoke words Jenny had never heard him say—things she hadn't known until that moment. He told Delphine about how close he and Jenny were when they were younger. "For a long time," he mused, "I could never really articulate why I chose to marry Sandie when I continued to feel such affection for Jenny. And it was you," he said, turning to Jenny, "who finally gave me the explanation—you who introduced me to the writings of Joseph Campbell. 'Follow your bliss.' Campbell counseled. Paris was my bliss. And for me, Sandie was Paris."

"Sandie was Paris," Jenny agreed, "but she was everything else you wanted as well. I could see that from the time I first met her. That's why it was possible for me to be grateful for all she gave you, rather than being jealous."

Jenny told Delphine of her recent dinner with Rachel Aronson, explaining that Rachel's husband had died just three months ahead of Sandie. She shared Rachel's description of the startling bubble of happiness she felt when her guests arrived—an experience that gave her such hope for healing. "That's what I'm doing here, Dellie. I don't want to take Sandie's place. I can't. I just want to give David bubbles of hope to keep him afloat for as long as it takes so he doesn't drown in sadness."

Delphine listened, then issued a quiet sigh. "Well, I guess I can understand, but I don't know if Marc will," she warned. Marc was still unaware of the first instance.

"Dellie," Jenny said quietly, "I will in no way be offended if you prefer that I put my clothes up in the atelier. I know you understand the situation logically, but it can take a while for your heart to catch up to your head. You must never be afraid to express yourself about it."

She shrugged. "Nah. It's okay."

After Delphine left, Jenny went to David and gave him a hug. "Your daughter was pretty amazing," she said.

David shook his head. "My daughter was pretty upset," he countered.

Jenny stepped back, startled by his grim tone. "But she said she understood the situation."

"What she said was, 'How could you?' She came to school, waited for my class to finish, walked in, and said, 'How could you?' She was furious."

Jenny absorbed this in silence. David stood motionless, head down, lips pursed.

"Do you think she's okay now?" Jenny asked after a minute.

"I think she is, but I'm not sure I am," he replied.

"How did you handle it when she said that?"

"When she said, 'How could you?' I told her the truth. I told her I'm really lonely."

"I'm so sorry," Jenny said quietly.

"Nothing to be sorry about," he replied. "We just have to accept that this isn't going to be easy—for anybody."

They agreed that David should speak to Marc as soon as possible. The logistics became tricky, however, when Marc called to say he wouldn't be home till late. Jack Pogue, an old friend of David's, was flying in from San Francisco to attend the luncheon for Sandie's special friends. He had been unable to come to the funeral and wanted to pay his respects. David had to meet his late-evening plane. Jenny decided to stay at the house in case Marc came home while David was collecting Jack.

Marc walked in not long after David left for the airport. "Marc, have you got maybe fifteen minutes? There's a really delicate issue I need to discuss." He took off his jacket, and Jenny gave him the whole story, starting with Olga's luncheon and ending with their afternoon discussion with Delphine. She repeatedly underscored her deep respect and regard for Sandie and her concern for David. Marc digested it all without comment, then said it was okay with him. Jenny didn't know whether to believe him or not. She was shaken by the degree to which she had misjudged Delphine's pain.

Marc was still up when David and Jack arrived, so David, too, had a chance to speak with him. "How did the conversation go?" Jenny asked later as they climbed into bed. David offered no details but said the conversation had been a good one. Marc wasn't strong on feedback. Jenny could only hope David's assessment was correct.

Despite his long flight and the nine-hour time difference, Jack was up and clear-headed the next morning. He and Jenny renewed their acquaintance over breakfast. Jack had known David since college and Sandie since before she and David were married. They were frequent companions during the year David and Sandie spent in San Francisco in the mid-'70s and had maintained a close friendship ever since.

It took just under two hours to drive to the small French village that was home to *L'Ancienne Auberge*, a renowned restaurant run by Georges Blanc. There were two dozen guests in all, everyone knowing everyone else with the exception of Jack and Jenny. David had divided the seating into smoking and nonsmoking. It was a practical decision, but it put David and Jenny at opposite sides of the room.

At the end of a two-hour repast, David stood up and addressed the gathering.

"When we first came here," he began, then described a long-ago visit to what at the time was a rustic country inn with delicious local fare. "The next time we came here," he continued, and described a similarly splendid gastronomic experience. "The only thing I haven't mentioned," he said, "is that the 'we' is not the same in the two stories. The first 'we' was Jenny and me. The second 'we' was Sandie and me."

Jenny felt her cheeks go red. Everyone in the room was casting surreptitious glances at her. David's tale included the fact that, on the first visit, "we" had taken a room upstairs in the inn and stayed overnight.

"Through the years," he told his guests, "my life, Jenny's life, and Sandie's life have been interwoven. We felt blessed by one another's friendship—as I now feel blessed by my friendship with each of you in this room. Through time, you have all been drawn into the connection, and here we are together, celebrating Sandie and friendship and each other."

It was a lovely presentation, tying together past and present, with hope for the future. They drove home, completely sated, and spent a quiet evening chatting. After a very light supper, Jenny retired so Jack would have a chance to talk with David one on one.

In the gray light of morning, she and David made love again. She wanted to spill out her heart to him, but David had an aversion to the language of romance when spoken. He could express love in writing. The poems he wrote for Sandie as he struggled to cope with her death were filled with loving phrases and beautiful imagery, but he was uncomfortable with verbal expression face-to-face. It was a lesson Jenny had learned long ago, so she contented herself with snuggling against him and breathing in the scent of his skin. Ultimately they arose and had a leisurely breakfast before driving Jack to the airport for his return flight. Jenny found it incredible that Jack had braved a forty-eight-hour round-trip from San Francisco. It was a remarkable tribute to Sandie. It was an even greater tribute to David.

They came back from the airport through a village that held an open market on Sundays. From the scores of stalls lining the streets, they bought vegetables, fruit, cheese, and sausages. Stopping at his favorite butcher's, David ordered the turkey for their Thanksgiving meal. They also stopped at a garden store for a bale of flax, to serve as winter mulch for the rose beds. While there, they bought several trays of pansies, which tolerated the mild Geneva winters, and some packets of spring bulbs.

It was not warm, but the sun was out when they got back to the house, and David wanted to spread the mulch. Jenny had not come equipped with work clothes. David gave her Sandie's blue overalls and quilted garden jacket to wear, plus Sandie's work gloves and her rainbow-colored kneeling pad. Sandie had shared her clothes with Jenny on past occasions, so Jenny felt no discomfort, especially since the application was so practical. As David spread the flax, Delphine poked her head out the French doors to ask if he could take a break and help her practice for her driver's test.

"We'll be back in an hour," David promised Jenny as he escorted Delphine to the car.

Jenny planted some of the pansies and bulbs, then tackled the weeds in the shrubbery bed that divided David's yard from that of his neighbor. The neighbor spotted her from an upstairs window. Jenny was kneeling on the ground, bent over, so all he could see were Sandie's coverall, Sandie's jacket, Sandie's rainbow-colored kneeling pad, and the back of Jenny's head. Her hair was short and dark brown, as Sandie's was when she chose to leave it natural. The neighbor came out and peered through the hedge. When Jenny realized there was someone on the far side of the shrubbery, not five feet away, she abruptly sat up. The man was partially obscured, but he was clearly looking right at her. "*Bonjour,*" she said, a little startled.

"*Bonjour!*" he replied, equally startled, and beat a hasty retreat with a slightly ashen face. When Jenny told David about the incident, he actually laughed.

On Monday, with David at school, Jenny decided to test out some Thanksgiving recipes. Despite David's giving her a thorough kitchen tour, she had a day filled with one culinary setback after the other. She had conversion charts for cups and teaspoons, but she had no instructions for converting a "square" of baking chocolate, a "packet" of gelatin, or a "cake" of yeast. She couldn't find any cookie sheets. She couldn't find a chopper for the cranberries. By the time David got home, she was bordering on hysteria. He had never seen Jenny defeated by a kitchen, and he found it amusing. He calmed her down, handed her a glass of wine, and made her sit on the dining room side of the open counter while he resumed control of his kitchen.

Michel and Josette invited the family over for dinner the next evening. Delphine begged off and went to meet some schoolmates. Marc came home not long afterward, and when he learned Delphine was out with her friends, he became enraged. David and Jenny were completely taken aback. Marc was seething with anger, charging

IF YOU NEEDED ME

that Delphine was "getting away with things" and "not carrying her weight." It was difficult to make any sense of his accusations. As far as Jenny could see, Delphine was being pleasant and helpful, despite the difficult circumstances.

Was Marc angered because Delphine was enjoying an evening with friends? Did he think her mourning should preclude the comfort of companionship and distraction? They couldn't escape the obvious implication that his father should not have had, and should not now have, the comfort of Jenny's presence.

"Is this about me?" Jenny asked. "If you're angry at me, it's okay to say so."

"No!" Marc shouted, then said he didn't want to talk about it because he knew Jenny would worry that it was her fault. With that, he started in on his sister again.

David challenged Marc, keeping his voice even, trying to address the substance of Marc's comments. Since the comments were neither logical nor reasonable—nor, in all likelihood, accurate reflections of what was truly bothering him—Marc got angrier and angrier. He actually tore the hand railing from the wall in stairwell—literally ripped it out. Those walls were made of cement, not wood. Jenny had never witnessed this kind of violence up close. She had absolutely no idea how to deal with it.

Concerned that she was indeed part of the problem, she withdrew upstairs, thinking Marc might better articulate his feelings if she were not present. Her withdrawal was brief, because suddenly she heard David shouting, "Okay, so come on, kill me!"

Jenny raced back down to find David with a large kitchen knife, the handle offered in Marc's direction. "What in the name of god are you doing!" she demanded. She was shaking inside, but her voice was outwardly firm. "What would Sandie think if she could see the two of you!" That brought them both up short. She then tried a halfhearted attempt at humor. "If I were in charge here, I would send you both to your rooms for a time-out!" After a pause, she added, "In lieu of that, I'd be grateful for a few minutes alone with Marc."

Perhaps because it offered a face-saving way out, they disengaged. Marc and Jenny went down to Sandie's study. In her most neutral, practical voice, Jenny suggested that David and Marc had trouble talking to each other because David was arguing about the symptoms of Marc's anger, not its cause, whereas Marc could not express the cause, since he himself wasn't sure where his anger was coming from. "What's important to realize," she said "is that your dad is trying to help, even if he goes about it in an unhelpful way. I feel frustrated, Marc, that I can't be of much help either—but if I can facilitate your communication with David, or Dellie, I would be glad to do so."

Things calmed down, but it was a deeply troubling episode. "Marc as much as told me he wishes I had died instead of Sandie," David confided.

They went to the DuPonts' house, as planned. Marc did not join them. Michel greeted them at the door looking very professorial in his wire-rimmed glasses, beige turtleneck, and brown slacks. Josette was in a simple skirt with a honey-colored sweater topped by a moss-green vest and a matching scarf. She was short and full-figured, but she always managed to look chic. *I can do proper,* Jenny thought as she shrugged out of her plain quilted jacket, *but I have yet to master chic.*

Much of the dinner conversation centered on Marc's behavior and what, if anything, could be done to get him back on a positive course. Everyone was at a loss. Josette moved to shift the focus by presenting David with a framed collage she had created from photos of Sandie taken over the past twenty years. They were wonderful pictures, capturing different aspects of Sandie's personality. David had to work on his composure for a few seconds, but he held on to it and thanked Josette profusely for the gift.

After they got home, David and Jenny talked long into the night about the family dynamic. Suddenly the ground shifted. "What is it you see happening between us?" David asked. "What is it you want?"

Jenny was unprepared for the question, and she fumbled. *What I want is to be with him always and forever,* she thought. *What I would settle for is being with him as long as it's helpful.* She didn't know which answer to give him. Some component of her brain was sending out warning signals cautioning against total candor. Sharp curve! Hidden turn! At that moment, David was a man in danger of drowning, and she was a sturdy plank to hold on to. The order of the day was keeping his head above water. But someday—in a year? or two? or three?—the floodwaters would recede. He would reach a safe shore and take up his life again. It was a life committed to a European domicile, defined by French culture, and anchored by Francophone friends. More to the point, it was a life that had centered around a lovely, sophisticated, outgoing Parisienne.

"Paris was my bliss," David had told Delphine. "And for me, Sandie was Paris."

Whatever he was feeling now, it seemed to Jenny that eventually David would want a life partner who was, in every way possible, like Sandie. *I love him down to his toes*, she thought, *but I'm a shy, no-nonsense New Englander. I buy my clothes from mail-order catalogs and cut my own hair. Elegance is an iffy proposition even if I work hard at it—and I have no fairy godmother to turn me into a French femme-du-monde.*

"I love being with you," she said out loud, "but I can't see the future clearly because there are so many factors. Maybe the future means visiting back and forth as often as our schedules allow. Maybe it's sharing part of each year, vacationing together during the summer. I would like to spend as much time with you as possible, but the possible lacks definition. That depends on you, really." And then she heard herself saying wistfully, "It would be a pleasure to grow old with you."

She tried turning the tables. "What is it that you see happening? What is it that you want?"

He ducked the questions by saying words got in the way, words were inadequate, words carried the wrong message. David was a man with keen awareness and deep feelings, but Jenny knew from experience that he was also unexpressive in some key dimensions. Yet her own insecurities were hard to keep down. The only situation she could imagine in which words "carried the wrong message" was one in which David needed her presence to see him through this crisis but didn't want a lifetime commitment and didn't want to hurt her feelings. Her mind was suddenly tripping over old baggage. In a flash, she was back in her early twenties.

Their youthful romance had seesawed back and forth half a dozen times. As a young man, David had places to go and people to see, with no interest in restricting his social life. He wasn't callous. He wasn't deceptive or insensitive or indifferent, but whenever things got serious between them, he would back off and start dating someone else. Yet he was so engaging and so much fun to be with—and Jenny was so determined to stay within his orbit—that their relationship survived countless downshifts. His unrestrained, ebullient, and inclusive nature was part of what attracted her. Whenever they readjusted to being "just friends," he would renew the courtship, curious as to whether he could upset the apple cart one more time. With his Southern charm, that gleam in his eye, and his infectious grin, he drew her like a magnet. Jenny never could resist his exuberance—his "world is my oyster" enthusiasm—so the cycle would repeat.

She followed David to Europe after graduation, getting a job in England when he went to France and commuting back and forth across the channel in the hope that eventually he would tire of life in Paris. After a year in London, waiting for the proposal that never came, she finally concluded that she had to go back to Boston and build a life of her own. What she wanted and what David wanted were too different. With candor and caring and mutual respect, they released one another from future expectations. Yet true to form, no sooner had Jenny returned to the States than David sent a two-page letter that made her long to book the next flight back to Europe:

> Dear Jenny, I wrote you another letter Sunday night, but the damn thing oozed self-pity so I tore it up. Two days have given me time to adjust to the fact that you are no longer around; perhaps this letter will be more reasonable or at least, less self-centered. Since you left, I have found myself musing about what we would do this

weekend in London, only to realize that we wouldn't do anything. Then I start wondering what you will do this weekend or where you will be and with whom.

Thanks for spending a year with me in Europe. I'm sorry things refuse to advance between us. Perhaps they really are, only very slowly—so slowly that I'll miss my chance because of waiting. I love you very much, and I have come to depend on you and your way of handling me. I think that is why I didn't want you to leave and am sorry that you did. I realize that I am unwilling to accept your conditions but expect you to suffer mine. Bad situation, that.

So we'll start writing each other again, but I have a strange inkling that this will be the last time around. As you said, it is your year. Be gay, be Jenny, get married, be happy. This episode is ending between us, but we will always be lovers.

Take care, and love—David

That was thirty years ago. Jenny forced her mind back to the present and mentally kicked herself. *I can't believe I'm setting myself up for this again,* she scolded.

Jenny spent the next morning with Delphine, helping her work on her driving and parallel parking. When David returned from school, he consulted with Delphine about where to hang the DuPonts' photo collage of Sandie. They decided to put it in the hallway just outside their respective bedrooms, at the top of the stairs. "That way," David said, "we can say good morning to her every day."

After the collage took its place on the wall, David and Jenny sat in the kitchen, searching through cookbooks for suggestions about butternut squash. She found a notebook filled with handwritten recipes. Mixed in with them was a long-ago postcard from David to Sandie, featuring a restaurant where he had eaten. *"Bon Appetit,"* he had written. *"Je t'adore, David."*

Would there ever come a day when he would say *"je t'adore"* to Jenny? She couldn't see him ever adoring her in the way he had adored Sandie. *Don't go there,* she told herself. *You're making your own problems, Longworth! We're in our fifties, not our twenties. The man loves you and trusts you and needs you. Adoration is not required.*

David normally set his alarm for 6:00 a.m., but on Thanksgiving Day, he set it for an hour earlier. Jenny put her arms around him to say good morning and soon realized in sleepy delight that he wanted her. By the time they finished making love, he looked at the clock, grinned, and said, "Well, so much for getting up early to correct papers!" He left for school, and she started cooking.

Jenny asked Delphine if she would be willing to set the table the way her mother would have done. "I want to be sure," Jenny told her, "that everything is up to Sandie's standards."

Delphine got out a special tablecloth she had given her mother as a present and some century-old monogrammed linen napkins—a legacy from David's maternal grandmother. Jenny felt really pleased that Delphine was being such a willing helper. Crystal glasses, guest china, and Sandie's wedding cutlery were laid out, and they brought down extra chairs from David's study. Jenny filled some bowls with nuts, placed them in the living room, then came back to the dining room. She was in house slippers. Delphine didn't hear her return. She was standing with her back to Jenny, looking at the table. "*Tu es partout, Maman, et ta place est si vide,*" she said quietly. Jenny translated in her mind. "You are everywhere, Maman, and your place is so empty."

Jenny tiptoed back a few steps, then walked forward again as noisily as she could. "That table looks fabulous, Dellie. Really great! Your mother would be so pleased."

Delphine didn't turn around right away. "Thanks," she replied, as she centered some of the plates and straightened a few forks.

David got home late afternoon, drained by some problems at school and annoyed that they had delayed him. Jenny decided on the spot to postpone her own tale of woe. At noon she had unwrapped the turkey and discovered, to her horror, that there were no giblets or neck for gravy. The wing tips were gone, and the flap skin had been removed, front and back, leaving no way to secure the stuffing inside the bird. Fortunately, she had all afternoon to adjust to these setbacks. By the time David walked in, the turkey was in the oven, and the kitchen and dining room were under control.

David poured them some wine, and they settled on the sofa in the living room. Jenny asked him about school. She sounded like a character out of *Father Knows Best*—"How was your day, Dear?"— but it was exactly what David needed.

After unloading his frustrations, he gradually calmed down and talked about Sandie's former role as a school administrator. "Frankly, the school's current problems would never have arisen if Sandie were still alive. She was as good at managing the principal and the teachers as she was at handling schedules and notices." Jenny couldn't judge how accurate his assessment was, but it didn't matter. She was glad she could serve as a sympathetic listener.

Then, from out of nowhere, David said that what had saved him from jumping off a cliff when Sandie died was reading Joseph Campbell's commentaries on myth and spiritualism, which Jenny had given him after their classmate Ramon died. They had a warm hug, and Jenny sensed that David was actually glad he was still alive. Or at least glad that he hadn't jumped off that cliff.

The doorbell signaled the arrival of their guests. Their neighbors, the Pashoutans, were first on the scene, and David poured everyone a glass of champagne. Mehrak was slender and short, but his ramrod straight posture added to his stature. He had dark hair, black eyes, and a timid smile. He was slightly shy, which endeared him to Jenny immediately. Manuela was yin to his yang—round and maternal, bubbling with chatter. She was dressed in an exotic Pakistani outfit, and her hair was dyed a shiny copper color. They were part of the diplomatic community and had fluent English, which made opening chitchat dramatically easier for Jenny.

Michel and Josette DuPont followed within minutes. The conversation shifted into French, but the DuPonts knew Jenny's limitations and were careful to speak slowly and distinctly. Then Delphine's friend Marie-Claire Baeschler arrived, with her mother,

Cybèle. They were introduced, and despite being strangers, Cybèle and Jenny "kissed," placing cheek on cheek, kissing the air, and making a slight clucking sound. Cybèle then stepped back with a careful smile and let out a stream of French so rapid that Jenny didn't understand a single word. Jenny offered an apologetic, *"Pardon, je ne parle pas bien français"*—"I'm sorry, I don't speak French well." Instead of repeating herself at a slower speed, Cybèle pursed her lips, frowned, and turned to Josette.

"Oh, god," she said in French in a low voice. "Does this mean we have to speak English all evening?" Unfortunately, Jenny understood that phrase, and her self-confidence plummeted.

Josette immediately came to her rescue, telling Cybèle that Jenny was eager to improve her French, so of course they didn't have to speak English. Jenny summoned up a simple but grammatically correct sentence to confirm this. Still, she was quietly grateful that the seating put her next to David and the Pashoutans, while Cybèle and her daughter were at the other end of the table.

They started dinner at 8:30 p.m. and didn't end until after midnight. The feast was presented in the French manner, in gentle waves, with a different wine for each course. Three kinds of paté were offered as an appetizer. A clear mushroom soup was served, then different vegetables. David carved the turkey and sent platters around the table heaped with dark meat, light meat, and classic bread stuffing.

The cranberry jelly was a novelty. None of the guests had ever seen cranberries. Some had never heard of them. The desserts overwhelmed, because there were four—cranberry walnut loaf, pumpkin chiffon pie, pumpkin pudding, and apple pie. The Europeans found the pudding's strong molasses flavor to be very strange, but the meal was clearly a success. Everyone had a good time, including David.

That night, he fell asleep the minute he lay down, but Jenny stayed awake for a long time, thinking about the day and studying his head against the pillow. She found him inordinately handsome, but it would not have been odd for others to consider him homely. She tried to imagine how she would react if she were gazing upon him for the first time, but she had trouble separating what her eyes saw and what her memory retained from their early years as lovers and the interim decades as friends.

In the waking world, David's large, dark eyes were obscured by a pair of thick glasses, as they had been since his childhood. In sleep, the eyes were naked. Sandie once said that if David walked in with contact lenses instead of glasses, she doubted she would recognize him. The glasses were an integral part of his face.

In the soft light of her reading lamp, Jenny could see the gray in David's otherwise sandy hair. When he was young, he wore it in an unruly silken mane. It was much shorter now, but the unruliness was still there despite a small bald spot at the back of his head and a gradually receding hairline. Lying asleep, his mouth seemed thin, but when he was awake and the mood suited, he could still produce that ear-to-ear grin that so dazzled her when she first met him. She smiled at the memories and turned out her bedside light.

That weekend, David took Jenny to Provence. Jenny had never been to the south of France. She was struck by the looming rows of evergreens and massive stands of bamboo that served as windbreaks against the Mistral—the fierce north wind that swept down the Rhone Valley in the winter. They visited a renowned Cistercian monastery, lunched at a rustic restaurant, and then drove through the hills to a charming inn. They dined in a room where a huge leg of lamb was roasting on a spit in the great open fireplace. They lingered over snifters of brandy until it was time for bed.

On Sunday morning, they drove to the former hilltop fortress of Les Baux. The view down into the Rhone Valley was extraordinary, and the rich color of the fields and the ochre soil generated a surprising aura of warmth. As they walked the town's narrow streets, they passed a quaint-looking hotel called Le Prince Noir. "Sandie and I stayed there the last time we visited Les Baux," David commented.

Jenny recalled Rachel's counsel. "Sandie will be with David wherever he goes, just as Josh is always with me," she had advised. "If you want to engage all of David, you have to recognize that Sandie is part of him, part of his whole."

Jenny appreciated the awareness Rachel had given her. "Do you want to go inside?" she asked David.

"No," he answered without elaboration. Instead, they walked through the town's ancient graveyard. She worried that the graveyard might depress him, but David viewed it in strictly historical terms. Sandie's remains had been cast to the winds and mixed with the sea rather than buried beneath a stone. The setting offered no parallel.

They stopped for a quick lunch, then headed back to Geneva. Marc was on his way out the door as they arrived home. The kitchen had clutter on the counters and dirty dishes in the sink. David registered annoyance as he surveyed the room. His mood swiftly went downhill. He perused the mail and produced a profane comment in reaction to a letter from the bank. Jenny asked what the problem was and got an unexpected warning.

"Not a good time to be a busybody, Jewel."

She immediately pulled back and gave him space, making turkey soup while he checked his e-mail. There were some jokes in his inbox that brought a momentary smile, but he was uncommunicative during dinner and afterward was withdrawn and tense, sitting in front of his computer with a large glass of brandy. Was it Marc? Was it the gray skies and rainy winds? Was it the prospect of her departure for Boston the next day? Was it the awful pain of Sandie's absence?

Finally Jenny confronted him. "You've been down all evening. Would it help to talk?"

"No."

"Would you like company, even if we don't talk?"

"No."

"All right, Angel. I'm going to get into bed with my book. But there are some issues we need to discuss before I leave. I'd be grateful if you could allow some time for that when you come up."

He finally started up the stairs, climbing slowly, wearily. He undressed, used the bathroom, and got into bed. "Ready?" she asked.

Silence.

She plowed ahead. "Given Dellie's initial reaction to my suitcase on your bed, I think it's imperative to discuss our new relationship with Nate, Margaret, and the rest of your family before we arrive in Chattanooga. If it poses a problem, we need to respond in a way that protects the children from any fallout. They're still very vulnerable, and they're going to be watching the reactions of the adults around them."

Silence.

"We also need to ask the kids if our being together in full view of the family is a problem for them. It is possible to be totally discreet. We can stay at a hotel. No one needs to know whether we have one room or two."

Silence.

"David, I know you are generally impervious to other people's opinions. What's at issue here is not the impact of other people's feelings on you, but on the children." She was tempted to add that Sandie would surely agree, but she bit back her tongue.

He grunted. "All right," he said. "I'll talk to them." He was clearly pained that they should have to concern themselves with social convention, but he agreed.

The next morning, he was up at 5:30. Jenny arose shortly afterward, showered, and then padded downstairs. The sky was black. The kitchen was dark. No lights had been turned on. David was sitting at the dining room table, smoking and drinking coffee.

Jenny hesitated. "Which would you prefer—that I go back up and read—or sit in the dark with you while you drink your coffee?" Turning on the dining room light was not an option, and she knew it.

"You're welcome to sit."

She made a pot of tea, relying on the light from the stove hood to find what she needed. As soon as she settled with her steaming cup,

David proposed that he withdraw from the afternoon airport run. "I think Marc should take you to the airport, so you and he can talk about Chattanooga."

That meant they would have to say good-bye right after breakfast. Jenny was taken aback by the idea of cutting short their time together. "No," she said, rallying, "I'll speak with Marc sometime during the morning. That way I can fill you in when you come pick me up."

After David left for school, Jenny and Delphine drove to a nearby sports field with a large parking lot, where Delphine practiced her parallel parking, using Sandie's brightly colored, oversized knitting needles stuck into water bottles as markers. On the way back to the house, with Delphine at the wheel, Jenny recapped her discussion with David about Chattanooga and the impact of other people's reactions. With poise well beyond her years, Delphine replied that Christmas in Chattanooga would go smoothly if everyone could see that she and Marc were comfortable with Jenny's new role. She also said—which made Jenny weak with gratitude—that she knew they were doing the right thing because David was so much happier with Jenny there. "He was really down and was drinking a whole lot before you came," Delphine said candidly. "I've been really worried about him."

Once back at the house, Jenny woke Marc. They spoke only briefly, but his response was the same, albeit rather more profane. "If they don't approve, screw 'em." He sounded like his father. With both children, Jenny underscored that if they thought David was becoming dangerously depressed, they should contact her immediately.

David returned early afternoon to drive Jenny to the airport. He was quiet and preoccupied. She filled him in on her conversations with Marc and Delphine. He had little comment. "I'll e-mail Nate and Margaret," he promised. Their farewell was brief. He was not in good shape. "I have to get back to class," he said.

"I love you, David Perry," she told him. "More than words can say."

"You take care," he replied. Then they turned and went their separate ways.

She wasn't in turmoil, but somewhere over the mid-Atlantic, Jenny ached for him so much that she couldn't sit still. She reviewed the visit in her mind. She had arrived in Geneva anticipating a good visit—a helpful visit—one in which any unrealistic fantasies about the future would be reined in by the simple wear and tear of real life— David's smoking, his snoring, the cultural differences, her introverted nature, his mood swings, her language limitations, his grief, and even just the relentlessly gray Geneva weather.

Although reality was front and center throughout the visit, her feelings for David had not only been sustained; they had strengthened. Decades before, she had made the painful decision to leave David in Paris and return to Boston. Giving up hope that he might tire of life in France, she faced the hard truth that her interests and passions were best pursued in her own country, with her own language and her own culture. David traveled to London on a cold January day to see her off and went back alone to Paris. During her flight westward, Jenny wrote in her journal, "Who knows where we are, or where we're going. Doesn't matter if I go back to Boston. Doesn't matter if I go to China! I will always love this man. It simply surpasses all things."

Now, decades later, there she sat on another airplane, once again winging her way back to Boston, once again leaving David behind. And once again, she didn't know where they were in the relationship or where they were going. She knew only that all those years ago, she had been right. It was a love that surpassed all things. "I'm in real trouble here," she confessed quietly to the seat-back in front of her.

Ross stepped forward from the milling crowd at arrivals, handsome and well turned out as ever. Jenny, in contrast, was rumpled and decidedly unchic. In an odd turn of mind, it occurred to her that it wouldn't be a bad idea to ask Ross for some fashion advice. They exchanged a quick hug, and he took charge of her suitcase. It was cold out, but after eight hours in a plane, the crisp, salty air felt good. As they walked to the car, he asked how David was doing.

"He's ... well, you know better than most. The grief is overwhelming. The wound is still extremely raw, but it was a good visit."

He put her bag in the trunk, and they got into the car. He started the engine, but before pulling out, he searched Jenny's face. She could feel a blush creeping up her cheeks. "Aha!" he said, breaking into a slow smile. "Our Jewel seems to be sparkling!"

Ross once told her that a good lawyer never asks a question to which he doesn't already know the answer. "And are we in love?" he queried.

"We singular or we plural?" she countered.

"Does the answer differ?"

There was no point in fencing with Ross. He could read her like a book. "For me, it's a simple yes. For David, I think the answer is really complicated."

Ross pulled into the airport loop and headed for the tunnel. "I put some groceries in your fridge. You have the makings of an omelet. Invite me to dinner. I'll cook while you talk. I want a full deposition."

When they got to the house, Jenny recapped the visit while Ross chopped and sautéed an onion. This time she openly admitted that the love affair had been rekindled. "The weirdest thing, Ross, is my sense of déjà vu. I can't tell you how many times I sat with Ramon and covered this same territory. My early romance with David was continually on-again, off-again. Intellectually, I knew what I was dealing with. David was a free spirit—unrestrained, uninhibited, curious about everything, and full of fun. He was always honest about wanting his freedom, but he was, by nature, so caring and affirming that each time we resumed our affair, part of me fantasized that he might be ready to make a commitment."

"Do you regret leaving him in Paris and coming home at the end of your year in Europe? Do you think that he would have chosen you over Sandie if you had stayed?"

The questions were posed gently, but they reminded Jenny that Ross was skilled at cross-examination.

"No," she replied. "I knew that if I hung around in Europe, my neediness would become a drain on the relationship. Better to return to Boston, let David enjoy his freedom, and hope that when the time came, I would be the one he chose to settle down with. Pretty pathetic, right?"

"How is that pathetic?" Ross asked. "You have an exceptional capacity for patience and long-range planning, Jewel. Thirty years ago you stepped back to allow David to get his emotional bearings. You were secure enough in your own being to allow him to define the relationship in a way that worked for him. Perhaps that was the happiest ending possible. It certainly was a successful one. Within that definition, you have sustained your love for each other for decades. Your strategy was correct, even if you don't recognize it as such."

Jenny considered Ross's words. She hadn't thought of herself as implementing a strategy, but Ross had a way of seeing into the heart of things. "You're right that David defined our relationship in a way that let him keep my love even though he married Sandie. I guess I'm just afraid that history will repeat itself. We loved each other back then, and we love each other now, but I'm not French. Maybe that's no longer a deal-breaker, but I'm not so sure. In truth, I'm not sure of anything except that I'd like to share the rest of my life with him. Question is, what's next? And how do I handle it so I'm not trampling on Sandie's grave, so to speak? At least there is one big difference this time around. This time he really needs me. He's loved me before, wanted me before, but he's never needed me before. It's the need that has me ready to risk everything for him."

Blizzard

I do not like the bright blue sky and glowing

Sun which stop the snow from falling,

Nor Christmas Day

Which ends the piles of presents growing

Brightly wrapped beneath the tree.

I would the snow could blur the air

And hush the clamor in my soul.

Yet can I say what depth of white

By blizzard's end,

Would succor me?

Chapter 5

De: David
A: Jenny
Envoyé: 27 novembre, 2000
Objet: Welcome Home

Welcome home, Ducks. I'm forwarding you my e-mail to Margaret. David

Message original de: David
A: Margaret
Envoyé: 27.11.2000
Objet: Chattanooga Visit

Howdy, Meg. Been meaning to write to tell whoever is hosting Jenny and me that we only need one room, not two. You think about it, and if it poses a problem for anyone, we'll go stay in a motel. If that ain't good enough, we'll go stay in Nashville. We don't want to screw up Santa Claus in Chattanooga.

The tone is light, but the message is serious. Marc and Delphine are aware and okay with it.

Love to everyone, David

From: Margaret
To: David
cc: Jenny
Date: November 28, 2000
Subject: Re: Chattanooga Visit

The single room is no problem—one less room to come up with! So just don't get uppity on me, Monsieur Perry. Remember you're still a Southern boy, and we do have brains down here in dogpatch. I am looking forward to meeting Jenny. Margaret

From: *JWLongworth*
To: *DavidP*
Date: *November 28, 2000*
Subject: *Home*

Got your note to Margaret, composed in your usual thoughtful and subtle style. Also got her response. I can tell I'm going to like this woman. I will e-mail her directly and trust her as point-person for logistical details.

I had an uneventful journey back to Boston. Cramped seats and people in front with their seatbacks in the full reclining position. Mostly I just read my book and tried not to think about the fact that the plane was carrying me away from you at five or six hundred miles per hour.

All was in order at home. Nemesis was asleep in the loft with no interest whatsoever in my arrival. She finally deigned to come down and take over her usual corner of the bed. She twitched her tail once, started snoring, and for the first time in my life, I had no desire to quiet her down. I just let her wheeze away. Didn't even put a pillow over my head. I miss you.

Love, J.

Jenny had met David's middle brother, Nate, during their college days but knew nothing of the rest of the family. Despite Margaret's suggestion that Jenny's accompanying David would present "no problem," Jenny wanted to reassure Margaret that she had David's best interest at heart.

From: *JWLongworth*
To: *Margaret*
cc: *DavidP*
Date: *November 28, 2000*
Subject: *Xmas Trip*

Dear Margaret—David cc'd me on your exchange re the upcoming visit to Chattanooga. I am grateful for your welcome and your openness. I intend to do everything within my power to help David and the children get through these dark months, but my efforts are made far easier by your acceptance and understanding. Loving David and looking out for him is a gift I offer in Sandie's honor, with

108

respect, admiration, and affection for the woman who made David happy for so many years. David knows this, as do Marc and Dellie. It is my sincerest hope that you and all the rest of the family will come to know it too.

Uh-oh. I have to stop writing about this because I'm getting all teary, and when that happens my eyes puff up and my nose gets red. Everyone in the office will wonder why I'm wearing dark glasses indoors on a gray, cloudy day. But we'll talk when I come.

May I mail a package to your address? Many thanks.
Love, Jenny

From: Margaret
To: Jenny
Date: November 29, 2000
Subject: Re: Xmas Trip

Dear Jenny, Thank you for your letter. I know how much you have helped David and the children. It was difficult being so far away during Sandie's illness, so we're all real happy about the Christmas reunion.

A good friend is spending the holidays in New York and has offered her house for y'all. It's got a darling little guest cottage, and it's real close by. It would be a getaway if y'all want a little time alone, but we hope that y'all will spend most of your time here and just sleep there.

Please feel free to send a box here anytime. Margaret

From: JWLongworth
To: Margaret
Date: November 30, 2000
Subject: Re: Re: Xmas Trip

Dear Margaret—Your neighbor's offer sounds lovely. The option of an occasional retreat from the holiday hubbub is very appealing. I will let David speak for himself (as if I could stop him!) but for my part, I would be entirely content to share this "guest house" with Marc and Dellie, unless you (or they) would prefer they stay elsewhere. I trust you will plug me in as a willing worker for any and all holiday chores.

Love, Jenny

In her daily e-mails to David, Jenny reported on Christmas plans and her communications with Margaret. David kept Jenny abreast of happenings in Geneva but eschewed references to his true emotional state.

De: David
A: Jenny
Envoyé: 2 décembre, 2000
Objet: Re: Friday

Fighting a personnel firestorm (someone fired) at school. Really needed that additional problem. Might even manage to get my own ass fired if I'm not careful. But what's life without adventure?

Correcting papers, doing reports, bullshit items. Miss you.

Kisses, David

From: J W Longworth
To: DavidP
Date: December 2, 2000
Subject: Re: Re: Friday

If they fire you, and you find yourself penniless, you can always follow the example of Walter Matthau in *A New Leaf* and start wooing some trusting woman who will swoon with your attentions and turn over half her assets to you.

Love, me

De: David
A: Jenny
Envoyé: 3 décembre, 2000
Objet: Re: Re: Re: Friday

Half her assets leaves me the choice between her ass or her ets. I'll take the first, thank you; never was one for ets. Do you know any trusting women who might swoon? Send me their addresses.

Kisses, David

From: JWLongworth
To: DavidP
Date: December 3, 2000
Subject: Sunday

Your address book is quite full enough without my adding names to it. Consider yourself lucky that you can practice your swoon-producing techniques on me.

Meanwhile, are you doing okay? It doesn't do much good at this distance, but I worry about you anyway— when I'm not swooning.

Love, me.

PS—Have you discussed San Francisco housing with Jack Pogue? How does he feel about swooning on the premises?

Jenny hoped her expression of worry might elicit some feedback about how David was feeling. To her surprise, the conversation veered in an unexpected direction.

De: David
A: Jenny
Envoyé: 4 décembre, 2000
Objet: Re: Sunday

You're worse than Carrie Nation and Rev. Falwell combined. I can't imagine anybody giving a tinker's dam where we sleep or how, but maybe I've been on this side of the Great Waters too long. So I will inform Jack officially and place an announcement in the San Francisco Chronicle.

I'm already practicing on you. What more can we do? What are you getting at, Good-Lookin'? Don't tell me you want to get married. I have yet to figure out the advantages. Disadvantages, yes, but they all occur when one of the partners dies (bureaucracy, notaries, bills to pay you've never paid before, etc.). It seems easier just to wander on down the road a bit together. Maybe I don't understand the drift of things, so why don't you set me straight? I'm kinda slow. I'm also in something of a funk. And looking at all the shit I have to do before we leave for the States ain't helping matters.

Kisses, David

From: JWLongworth
To: DavidP
Date: December 5, 2000
Subject: Ooops

Sorry, Angel. Didn't mean to spook you. I wasn't "getting at" anything, at least not consciously. I'll try to set you straight, but if I know anything about you, it's that you can't be set any way you don't want to be set, period.

First, however, a note on guest etiquette. Even in the wild lands outside of Boston, it's proper to give prospective hosts a bit of warning as a basic courtesy. And in this case, it's a lot more. I would be blown away if something happened to my sister-in-law, and my brother suddenly walked in within weeks of her death with a woman I'd never met—no warning or explanation—and shepherded her into his bedroom. I would feel really confused about how I should relate to this woman. I have no qualms re what we're doing, but it's human nature for others to be uneasy. Jack and your family are important in your life. They deserve to be at ease with my presence.

Okay, back to issue number one. "Do I want to get married?" What I want is what I told you in Geneva. I love being with you. I want to grow old with you. But more than anything, I want to be there when you need me.

Your suggestion of just "wandering on down the road a bit together" is perfectly fine. Where we're headed, I don't know. The only thing that really matters is that someday you wake up and discover you're glad you're still alive. So go as slowly as you want. You have my love no matter what you do. You always have. J.

De: David
A: Jenny
Envoyé: 6 décembre, 2000
Objet: Re: Ooops

Ducks, you can't spook me. I ain't no horse. I'm a jackass and by definition unspookable. I was reading my issues into what you were saying. I'm still not sure I understand. Howsomever, we'll chew the fat together when we rendezvous in Choo-choo Land.

Love, David

To Jenny's relief, the following day brought confirmation that David had forewarned their hosts regarding their new relationship.

De: David
A: Jack Pogue
cc: Jenny
Envoyé: 7 décembre, 2000
Objet: 1 bedroom, 1 set of sheets, but 2 towels

Dear Jack. Would you and Janet mind if Jenny and I had the above equipment for our stay with you in San Francisco? Following Sandie's death—human existence being what it is—we have rekindled a very old and very dear relationship. It's important to me. It's important to Jenny. I think Sandie would agree.

Hugs to Janet.

Best to you, David

From: JWLongworth
To: DavidP
Date: December 8, 2000
Subject: Follow-up

Dearheart, thank you. Your note to Jack is perfect.

Now off with my Emily Post apron. I was so taken aback by the marriage question that I didn't address your list of marital disadvantages: "Bureaucracy, notaries, bills to pay, etc." You're not having to cope with these things because of marriage. You're having to cope with them because you've lost the person who used to take care of them—and you. Anger is a natural part of grief, yet you can't consciously vent it toward Sandie. She left you alone with this mess, but you can't blame her, because it's not her fault. So you vent it on pieces of paper. And notaries. And marriage. Which is weird, because by all accounts you had one of the best I've ever seen.

Don't worry about my romantic fantasies. I'm a big girl, and you've never promised me a rose garden. I'm fully aware that wandering down the road with you is a very iffy prospect, especially since you only like to walk when you're chasing a golf ball.

Love, J.

De: David
A: Jenny
Envoyé: 8 décembre, 2000
Objet: Re: Follow-up

Hell of a psy, Love, but I vent my anger on Sandie every day. The bitch done run off and left me saddled with the gas bill. Regardless, I truly don't understand the advantages of marriage even though I agree that Sandie and I had one of the neatest and most successful ones around town. I just see no need for notarized papers "officializing" the situation. Always willing to listen, however.

Kisses, David

Jenny decided to let the issue rest until they could "chew the fat" in person, as David had suggested. She turned her attention to their visit to Chattanooga.

From: JWLongworth
To: DavidP
Date: December 11, 2000
Subject: Countdown

I remember Nate from his long-ago visits to Cambridge, but at some point, I would love a "who's who" of the rest of the Perry family—spouses' names, children's names, and who belongs to whom. Bundles of love to you and the children. J.

De: David
A: Jenny
Envoyé: 11 décembre, 2000
Objet: Re: Countdown

In order of appearance on the planet: My parents, may they rest in peace, begat three boys, starting with me, then Nathan Forrest Perry, then Isham Harris Perry, the latter two named for illustrious Tennessee Confederates who, as best I know, are no kin whatsoever. I'm the only one with a middle name that is real family: Irwin. But I don't use it because D. I. P. spells dip. R. I. P. would have been better.

Nate and Margaret (Meg) begat Gilbert (Gil) and
Lillian (LeeLee)—now college and high school age.
Isham and Sue Ellen begat Hubert (Bert) who is in junior
high.
　　Love, David

Jenny's plane was jammed with holiday travelers, but the flight
went smoothly. She collected her bags and transferred over to the
international arrivals terminal to wait for David and the children.
After they cleared customs, there were hugs all around, but the
conversation was subdued. Jenny was thrilled to see them, but the
Perrys had been in transit for over twelve hours and were dealing with
a six-hour time difference. They picked up the rental car, headed up
I-75, and were in Chattanooga two hours later.

En route Jenny asked David to give her any background
information he thought might be helpful—family history,
personalities, subjects to avoid (religion and politics!). He teased her
about being anxious. He was right. They arrived to find a dozen people
gathered for an informal gumbo supper. Throughout the holiday,
Nate and Margaret's house would serve as the gathering point for
the Perry clan and half the neighborhood. Jenny was introduced to
all the family members and was grateful for the homework she had
done memorizing the names. After dinner, she and David said good
night and headed over to the guest cottage that would serve as their
residence for the duration. Delphine and Marc were going to stay put,
bunking with LeeLee and Gil respectively.

In response to Jenny's suggestion, Margaret had placed roses—
Sandie's favorite flower—throughout the house to honor Sandie's
memory. As David and Jenny were leaving, she handed Jenny a single
perfect rose in a small vase to take over to the guesthouse. Once they
had settled in, Jenny placed it on David's bedside table.

The mattress was overly soft. Jenny feared they would both have
bad backs in the morning, but the lovemaking was intense and good.
The stiff foam pillows were useless for wrapping around her head
and blocking the sound of David's snores, but she was so happy to be

with him that she didn't mind. She also forgave him for stealing the blankets. She had discovered over Thanksgiving that David was an inveterate blanket thief, but she had not yet perfected her recovery tactics. It took a while to discover that brute force was the most effective ploy.

Waking up in the quiet of their little bungalow, they made love gently in the morning. "You know," she ventured afterward, "if there is anything that especially pleases you, I hope you won't be shy about saying so."

"You're doing fine," was his reply. With that, he considered the discussion over.

Jenny knew from her own youthful experience and from Sandie's confidences that David didn't talk easily about sexual intimacy. He delighted in earthy humor and could more than hold his own swapping ribald jokes, but he shied away from serious conversation. Still, with the subject broached, she pushed to keep it on the table.

"Sandie had nearly thirty years with you," she said. "She had the luxury of learning about you through trial and error. I don't have that kind of time."

"You might," was his response.

Was he suggesting they might be together for the remainder of their lives? Or was he just alluding to actuarial possibilities? He did retract a bit when he projected the figures. In thirty years, they would both be past the four score mark—assuming they lived that long, which Jenny doubted, given her cancer history and his smoking. But David didn't further clarify his remark, and Jenny didn't ask him to. She preferred to hear what she wanted to hear.

They rejoined the family for breakfast, then took Delphine out shopping for her Christmas present. Later, with Marc, they did a similar search. The run with Delphine was easy. She chose a trim and fashionable ski parka and seemed very pleased with it. The trip with Marc degenerated into a clash between father and son.

Marc was searching for some used camera equipment. David and Jenny expressed a wish to buy at least one of the items on his list as

Marc's Christmas present. At the first store they visited, the last of a particular lens Marc wanted had just been sold. The saleswoman made an innocent joke about missing the boat, but Marc decided she was deliberately teasing him. He was defensive, sharp, and borderline rude in response

They went to a second photo store. Within minutes, Marc found something of interest. David and Jenny were standing nearby when a salesman called out to see if they needed help. At the time, Jenny was reaching into her pocketbook. "No," David replied, pointing to Marc. "We're with him."

The sales rep then said, in a jovial tone, "I see! He's got the camera but you've got the credit card!"

Marc turned his back, whipped out some cash, and bought the part, giving his father no chance to participate in the purchase. "I didn't appreciate the remark about the credit card," he fumed as they left. "I'm not like those kids with rich parents who spoil them and buy them expensive equipment they're too stupid to know how to use correctly."

Wham! Jenny was startled, and David was furious. As soon as they got in the car, he and Marc began to argue. "Why would you resent the idea of a gift?" David demanded.

"I can make my own way!" Marc insisted, bristling with truculence.

Perhaps it was Marc's emotional outburst that prompted David, or perhaps he had planned to do it all along, but that evening, after a family supper, David requested that everyone gather in Nate's living room.

"I appreciate everyone's effort to make this Christmas seem normal," he began once they were assembled, "but it isn't. Sandie's death and absence are clearly on everyone's mind. It's important to talk about it together. It would help me, and it might help you."

Sue Ellen spoke up first, saying that, because of the tragedy, she felt closer to the family than she had before. Margaret told of how she felt when she lost her father and how strongly she could identify with the children's pain. There were words of encouragement, attempts to reassure Marc and Delphine that their mother was still with them in spirit. Delphine began to cry softly. Marc stated bluntly that he didn't feel Sandie was with him at all. He just felt her loss. It was emotionally wringing, but David managed to draw people out, and eventually everyone in the family said their piece. As the gathering broke up, Isham passed by Jenny's chair, put a hand on her shoulder, and quietly said, "This must be awkward for you." It was a thoughtful gesture.

"It's kind of you to be concerned, but no," Jenny said. "I truly feel I'm doing what Sandie would want. The only thing that would be awkward for me," she added, "is if people didn't understand that and thought we were somehow slighting her."

The next day, the women of the family scattered for last-minute shopping, then regrouped for a ladies' lunch. Margaret commented on what fun it was to have a table taken up with two generations of Perry women.

"All except one," Jenny corrected.

"Oh, well," said Delphine, "You're almost a Perry."

Jenny smiled. What a little diplomat Delphine was!

That afternoon, David took Jenny on a driving tour of his old neighborhood, conjuring up memories of ballgames, bike rides, and boyhood. Most evenings were taken up with parties. Everyone wanted to help make David's visit home a happy experience. People were concerned for him—and curious about Jenny. Coming from Boston, she represented a different social culture and in most instances a different political culture from that which prevailed in Chattanooga. "Nate and Margaret must have laid some careful groundwork," she later told David. "Everyone has been so gracious and welcoming."

Christmas morning, they were up early. The guesthouse shower was designed for two people, and they took full advantage of it, soaping each other from head to toe and playing in the water. They arrived at Nate's to find the household still asleep. Jenny seized the opportunity to compose a note to Marc. Given the events at the camera store, she was worried that her planned gift of cash might be offensive. After two false starts, she wrote:

Dear Marc—I'm unsure I have made the right choice,
since you are uneasy about certain gifts. But I offer this
with respect, as well as my very best wishes, and hope
it will be useful in San Francisco. If you prefer, think of
it not as my gift to you but as my gift to Sandie, whom I
promised I would look after you—or as my gift to David,
who wants you to find your own way but also wants
you to get there in one piece—or as my gift to myself,
because it gives me pleasure to share my good fortune
with people I care about.
    Love, Jenny

Jenny ran her draft by David, who simply said, "Go with it."

Isham and Sue Ellen were celebrating at their own home, but
with everyone else at Nate and Margaret's, the house was more than
full. The Perry tradition was for everyone to open a present at the
same time. It made it hard to appreciate the individual gifts, but it
certainly made things move faster. They had few classical CDs, so their
holiday listening was primarily country music and twangy renditions
of "Rudolph the Red-Nosed Reindeer." In the midst of all this, their
fox terrier raced about, barking and chasing after crumpled pieces of
wrapping paper that Nate and the children tossed in his direction.

Despite the merriment, David was tense and distracted. Jenny
gave him a homemade gift certificate for a golf weekend "anywhere,
anytime." She had no idea that Sandie had given him a nearly identical
gift the year before. He gave no outward sign that anything was
amiss. Months would pass before she learned of her error. Delphine
was presented with the ski outfit she had picked out previously. She
feigned surprise, but her delight was real. When Marc opened the
envelope with the money and Jenny's note, he read it, gave a rueful
grin, and came over to plant a kiss on her cheek.

Delphine handed Jenny a present from "The Geneva Perrys."
She removed the wrapping and saw the logo *Hermes* on a flat box.
The box was worn and had been opened and closed many times. She
lifted the lid and found herself looking at one of Sandie's favorite
scarves. It still smelled of her perfume. Given the trauma initially

engendered by Jenny's clothes in Sandie's closet, the gift carried enormous symbolism. She accepted it gratefully, struggling to keep tears at bay.

Following an afternoon Christmas dinner that included the Isham Perrys, David asked everyone to come into the living room for a special presentation. Once they were seated, he pulled out two small packages, about the size and shape of film cartridges, wrapped in gold foil and red ribbon. Jenny drew in a sharp breath. She realized what they were before David started talking,

"Sandie never liked Chattanooga," David said, "but she loved this house and the people in it. It's fitting that part of her should rest here." He handed a vial of Sandie's ashes to Margaret. Margaret was speechless. "You might want to scatter them in the garden and the woods behind the house," he suggested softly. Jenny thought the second vial would go to Isham and Sue Ellen, but no. David crossed the room, and handed it to her. "This one is for Boston."

"Thank you," she whispered as she clasped the vial to her heart.

The day after Christmas dawned cold and windy. Marc and Gil went off together. David wanted some father-daughter time with Delphine, so he took her to a film matinee while Jenny stayed behind with a book. That night, David filled Jenny in on his afternoon and summarily dismissed the movie he and Delphine had seen as "classic American Cinderella fare—the kind of movie that Sandie loved." He viewed the genre as uniquely American. European films, he observed, were far less likely to have happy endings, and even if they did, they were reality-based, not "happily ever after" fantasies.

The following day, David took Jenny, Marc, and Delphine to a famous rib joint for lunch. Afterward they went to a record store, where Marc loaded up on hard rock albums. David invested in some country music for Geneva, plus some classical records to expand Nate's meager collection. Among the classics he bought for Nate was a complete set of the Bach cello suites—Sandie's funeral music. Jenny observed the purchase but made no comment. What could she say?

When they returned to the house, Jenny helped slice ham for the impromptu cocktail party Margaret had organized for the evening. As they worked in the kitchen, the somber tones of the cello suites suddenly filled the house, emanating from the stereo system in the living room. Jenny thought maybe Nate had selected the recording from the stack of new CDs, not understanding its significance—but no, it was David. He had settled on the living room couch with his head back and his eyes closed, a half-empty glass of bourbon on the table. Jenny tiptoed out of the room as softly as she had come in. Once back in the kitchen, she quietly explained to Margaret what they were listening to.

Once the evening guests arrived, David seemed fine, moving effortlessly among the visitors, but he was clearly tired by the time they retreated to the guesthouse. The bedroom was cold, and so was Jenny. She hopped into bed and snuggled close, but told David she didn't dare touch him because her hands were icy. He felt them and let out an expletive. "Your hands are as goddamn cold as Sandie's were!" he exclaimed. "I've never known anyone other than the two of you whose hands could freeze hell in winter!"

It was a restless night. David wasn't feeling well. Jenny suspected a combination of grief, exhaustion, and alcohol. Margaret alerted them in the morning that Delphine had a rough spell that night also, missing her mother and breaking down in tears.

After breakfast, David packed the car with the suitcases and dropped Jenny at Nate's while he drove over to say good-bye to Isham and Sue Ellen. Jenny helped the children gather their things and offered her appreciation to Nate and Margaret for their extended hospitality. She handed Sandie's memorial rose and its vase back to Margaret with special thanks.

"Looks like Sandie approves of the way things are going," Margaret commented, examining the rose, which was as fresh and lovely as it had been the first day. Then she looked at Jenny and asked point blank, "What about you? I'll bet you wish David would move back to Boston."

"I don't think David will ever move back to the States," Jenny said cautiously, "though obviously I'd love it if we could be closer to each other. It's way too soon for David to plan his future. I want to give him whatever he needs, without expectations on my part. I'll worry about myself once he's back on solid ground."

Jenny meant what she said, but she also knew it was absolute balderdash. David disparaged the American penchant for Cinderella stories. Yet during unguarded moments, a happily-ever-after ending, however vaguely structured, was precisely what Jenny longed for.

David returned, there were good-bye hugs all around, and the four of them headed for Atlanta and the flight to San Francisco. Once they landed, they made their way easily to Jack and Janet Pogue's house. Jenny was glad she had gotten to know Jack a little when he flew to Geneva to attend the luncheon David gave in Sandie's memory. Jack was two years older than David and according to David, had been responsible for David's decision to apply to Harvard. Had Jack not been so persuasive, Jenny and David might never have met.

The Pogues lived in an oversized Victorian with lots of spare bedrooms, but Marc chose not to stay with them. After Marc's graduation from l'Académie Internationale, he briefly attended an art school in San Francisco. Once there, he had opted out of the program, hung out in the city for a while, then set out on an open-ended hitchhiking trip through the southwest. Marc announced to his father during the plane ride from Atlanta that he had people in the San Francisco he wanted to see. It would be easier to stay with his friends, he argued, than to commute back and forth to Jack's house. He stashed a suitcase at Jack's and struck out for the nearest bus stop with a backpack.

David, Delphine, and Jenny breakfasted with their hosts, then headed south to Santa Cruz. When David and Sandie lived in San Francisco, Sandie worked for a time in a French bakery and café. There she became friends with a gnomish Swiss-German pastry chef named Gretel Munger. They corresponded occasionally after the Perrys' return to Europe and stayed in touch after Gretel retired to Santa Cruz. Gretel had only recently learned of Sandie's death. David sent a memorial card that she opened thinking it was an early holiday greeting.

Gretel's house suited her name—a funny little cottage, like something out of Hansel and Gretel, tucked away on a side street, with an eclectic décor, inside and out. Gretel was thrilled to see David and Delphine, hugging them effusively when they arrived. "But there is one missing," she noted sadly, tears starting in her eyes.

Gretel was pleasant to Jenny but not at all curious. She served homemade cookies and tea, and with raised mugs, the group toasted Sandie. David admitted it was a tough time for the family but added that there were "moments of respite." Jenny didn't know if that was a bouquet for her or just a general reassurance. Whichever, she was pleased to hear him say it.

As they drove back north, David revisited the conversation he and Delphine shared after her tearful bout in Chattanooga. "I've been thinking of what you said," he told her, "about missing all the little things that Sandie used to do. I have no way to get past that because I miss them too. The only thing I can suggest, to make something good of it, is to see the little things that those still living do for us, and appreciate them now, rather than waiting till they're gone. Like Jack's hospitality, or Gretel's cookies," he added. A few minutes later, they pulled off the road and into a State Beach parking lot, where they watched the sun slip behind the watery horizon of the Pacific. It had been a good day.

New Year's Eve came and went with little notice, for which Jenny was grateful. Jack and Janet treated them to an evening of caviar, oysters, and champagne in honor of the occasion, but they didn't come even close to staying up till midnight. Since it was Delphine's first visit to San Francisco, New Year's Day was spent introducing her to the city, with a trolley tour, a visit to Chinatown, and a stroll through Ghirardelli Square.

On their last evening, it was Jenny's turn to set the agenda. Decades back, after she returned to Boston from her year in London,

Jenny became involved with a group dedicated to cleaning up the Charles River. She was earning her CPA credentials at the time, but she had holes in her calendar that she filled by volunteering on river clean-up and water-sampling projects. She met Bibi Birnbaum while hauling trash up the riverbanks and dipping collection vials into the sometimes-toxic water.

Jenny had been raised in a Boston tradition of Victorian manners, faultless etiquette, and modest dress. Bibi was a gregarious flower child in rainbow apparel who, in her youth, wore her thick, wiry hair in a reddish Afro. Now, in middle age, she bore a more-than-passing resemblance to Bette Midler, and her hair color was subject to frequent change. She and Jenny were polar opposites and became instant friends.

Bibi didn't know David. She had barely even heard of him until Jenny started sharing the pain of Sandie's cancer and inexorable decline. Jenny had been back in the States for two years and had started dating Seth Winthrop by the time she and Bibi first crossed paths. When Jenny and Seth married, Bibi came to their wedding. For the next fifteen years, Bibi knew Jenny as a contented partner in a happy marriage. When the marriage fell apart, she proved herself a steadfast friend through the divorce. Not long afterward, Bibi moved to California to be near her two children. She fell in love with Sausalito and had been living on a houseboat ever since.

Jenny and Bibi saw each other rarely but kept in frequent touch. Jenny was eager to have her meet David. Delphine joined their expedition to Sausalito, intrigued by the idea of seeing a hippie houseboat community. They parked near the dock, and Bibi gave them a tour before they backtracked into downtown Sausalito for dinner. David did his best to be social, but he was tired and down after a fight with Marc. David had alerted Marc that he needed to sleep at Jack's that night. The respective return flights to Boston and Geneva had very early departure times. David didn't trust Marc to get to the airport on schedule and insisted that he collect him on the way back from Sausalito. Marc was not happy about the early pickup.

There was some backfill, but much of the dinner conversation was about parenting. Bibi had had her share of raising difficult adolescents, so she was sympathetic to David's frustrations about Marc. At the end of the meal, she turned to Jenny. "When do you get back to Boston?" she asked casually. Jenny gave Bibi her projected arrival time. They parted with hugs, went to pick up Marc and headed home to Jack's.

They said their farewells that night and went upstairs to ready everything for their predawn departure. The Perrys' flight left at 6:30 a.m., and David needed to return the rental car. He planned to be on the road by 4:30.

"It's been a good trip," Jenny observed as they got undressed. "I'm exhausted, but we got to do everything on your list."

"We did everything but one thing," David said quietly. "We didn't talk about us." Jenny sifted through his tone for signs of playfulness. There were none.

What was there to talk about, she wondered. *He had made it clear he just wanted to "wander on down the road a bit together."* Had she inadvertently done something to make him concerned that she might want a stronger commitment than he was prepared to give? Had there been conversations with others that made him feel he needed to clarify things between them?

It was late. They were both tired. In less than four hours, the alarm clock would rouse them in the chill dark and start them on their respective journeys home. It seemed an unwise moment to explore the complexity of the relationship. When the time came to talk about "us," Jenny wanted everything working in her favor. She wanted the sun shining, flowers blooming, and gentle breezes blowing. She wanted David sitting with a gourmet meal on his plate and a vintage wine in his glass. Or maybe it would be the moon that was shining and David lying in her arms. Whichever, she wanted him rested, relaxed, and happy. At the moment, he was none of those things. So she ducked.

"No," she concurred, "we didn't talk about us. But I'm not sure we need to. You said at the outset that you want to take this one day at a time, and I think you're absolutely right." Case closed.

When the alarm rang, David and Jenny showered and dressed, then woke the children and started packing the car. Marc drifted off to sleep again and needed a second wakeup call, which annoyed his father. They managed to get off at 4:30 a.m., as planned, but there was a moment en route when David thought he had missed the airport turnoff. He blamed Marc for the tight timing, and for a moment, the car was full of fireworks. David usually reserved his temper for inanimate objects. His stress level was almost palpable.

At the airport, Marc, Delphine, and Jenny shuttled the suitcases into the terminal while David returned the rental car. The Dallas flight that was David's connection to Geneva posted an on-time departure on the monitor. Jenny's nonstop to Boston was due to leave from the same gate an hour later. They waited together, sitting on a row of anchored seats, surrounded by bright lights and sleepy people. When their boarding call came, Jenny hugged Marc and Delphine, wishing them a safe journey as they got in line.

David held back. They embraced for a minute. He kept touching Jenny's hair and her cheek. He started to turn toward the gate, then swung back, his eyes locking on hers. "Come at Easter," he said. "I have two weeks, one before and one after. I don't know the date, but come at Easter."

"I'll do my best," she replied. And then he was gone.

"Do my best—nonsense!" she breathed. "I'll see him at Easter come hell or high water!"

Waiting in the Evening   January, 2001

Wet she waited, standing, just inside the swinging doors
   In the evening, with her luggage,
   A friend from Paris having asked permission,
   Then left.

Embarrassed, she waited on the crowded café terrace—
   Streetlamps glowing,
   Cars flashing past,
   Passers-by splashing in the streets.

From where I sat among the chat and noise,
   She watched anxiously
   For someone who never came
   While I was there smoking, looking at the rain

Several times I thought of asking her to have a seat,
   Knowing that she felt so ill at ease,
   Knowing how it feels to wait,
   How it feels to long,

For I have waited since September,
   Knowing ever since the fall,
   Knowing all along,
   She'll never come again,

But I didn't ... after all.

Chapter 6

Jenny hadn't been home half an hour when the telephone rang. She didn't have caller ID, but she knew who it was. Blunt as always, Bibi's first words, when Jenny picked up the phone, were not, "Hi, how are you?" but, "What the hell is going on?"

"Well, for one thing," Jenny stalled, "it's snowing. We may get five or six inches."

"He's the one in the photograph, isn't he? I kept thinking, why does this man look so familiar, and then it clicked. That poster-sized print you always had in your office. You and young Romeo, forehead to forehead in Paris, dewy-eyed and on your way to a kiss."

"Yes, he's the one," Jenny conceded.

"So?"

Jenny paused to consider how much to reveal. David didn't care about appearances, but Sandie would have. Subsumed under genuine grief was genuine propriety. Jenny started to describe how devastated David was by Sandie's death and how concerned she was for his safety and survival, but Bibi's radar was not to be gainsaid.

"You're sleeping with him." It was not a question.

"Bibi, what I'm doing is taking care of him in every way I can think of."

"Right. That's Proper Bostonian for, 'Yes, I'm sleeping with him.' Lemme get a cigarette," she interjected. "I want to hear every detail from start to finish."

"I thought you quit smoking."

"I did," she replied, "but I keep a pack in the freezer for special crises."

"This is a special crisis?" Jenny rejoined.

"I won't know that until I've heard the whole story, but the odds are pretty strong."

Bibi was back in less than a minute. "So why didn't you tell me about this before? Who else knows?" she demanded.

Jenny could hear her drawing on her illicit cigarette at the other end of the phone.

"Ross knows, and the people we stayed with over the Christmas holidays know. And now you. But that's it."

"What about your sister and brother? What about what's-her-name, the widow, the one who's been your grief counselor?"

"Her name is Rachel Aronson," Jenny interjected, "but what she knows is what everyone knows—that since Sandie's death, I've been lending a hand and spending time with David and the children. That's all they need to know."

"Why haven't you told anyone you've become lovers again?"

"Because it doesn't really matter. Everything I'm doing for David, I would do regardless of our sleeping arrangements."

"'It doesn't really matter,'" Bibi mimicked. "So why has your nose suddenly grown a foot long like Pinocchio?"

"Bibi, you're three thousand miles away, and we're on the phone. You can't possibly see what my nose is doing."

"I don't have to. I can hear your mind spinning rationalizations like crazy. Why don't you want your family and friends to know?"

"The fact is, I'd rather that nobody knew. The sexual element isn't what's important. It's a distraction. Talking about it feels like being in the tabloids, distorting the picture and creating sensationalism where none exists."

"Are you embarrassed?"

"Bibi, no."

"Feeling vulnerable, maybe?"

Bibi made her living as an editor for a small feminist publishing house. She was good at it, but she had missed her calling. She should have been a psychiatrist or a lawyer or maybe a rabbi. There was no defense against her barrage of questions. Wherever the truth lay hidden, she would ultimately ferret it out.

"The only point on which I feel vulnerable," Jenny told Bibi after a pause, "is public opinion. If you did a poll and asked people what their reaction was to a woman who seduced a grieving widower before his wife's ashes were cold, I don't think you'd find a lot of sympathy for the interloper."

"And is that how you see yourself?" Bibi questioned. "A seductress? An interloper?"

"Of course not. I would do anything to keep David going. And so far, what I've done has worked. It's been absolutely the right thing."

"So, truth be known, you're actually Mother Theresa. Altruism personified. If you could find some other woman—someone in Geneva—who could do the job better, you'd hand David over to her without hesitation."

"Bibi, I didn't say there was no side benefit for me. I only said that isn't my motivation."

"And are we quite, quite sure about that, Miss Mayflower? If things are as you say, why operate behind this veil of silence? I agree with you about public opinion, but your siblings aren't John Q. Public. Neither is your friend Rachel. If I hadn't sniffed this out," Bibi went on, "you would never have said a word to me, would you?"

"Bibi, I know it seems strange to you, but I just don't feel ready to go public on this, even among trusted friends. I can't explain exactly why. It's kind of a gut thing. The pieces aren't all in place yet. "

"You wanna know what I think?"

"Do I have a choice?"

"Hold on a sec. I need to get a new matchbook."

"Bibi, wait. I just got in. I haven't unpacked yet. And I'm kind of wiped out. Let's both digest this for a while. I promise to keep you updated, but right now I really need to get some groceries and change the cat box."

From: JWLongworth
To: DavidP
Date: January 4, 2001
Subject: Easter Vacation

Glad to hear you made it back in one piece. Hope it feels good to be home.

Easter will work. My office team is being totally understanding. Do you want me to come for the whole two weeks? It might be fun to get a small group of friends together. We could rent a place in Provence, or maybe near Paris, as a base of operations for day trips. What do you think?

Love, J.

De: David
A: Jenny
Envoyé: 4 janvier, 2001
Objet: Re: Easter Vacation

Yes to two weeks. The Paris area offers the most options. I'll come up with something that permits us to do both the city and the outlying areas. Liked the trip and loved being with you.

Kisses, David

Jenny took "loved being with you" to mean that their "wandering down the road a bit together" was going well. Maybe a happy-ending scenario wasn't so far-fetched.

She wrote her holiday hosts, thanking them for their thoughtfulness and the support they gave to David. To Delphine, she sent thanks for the Hermès scarf. "It's special not only because it was Sandie's but also because you chose it as my gift," she told her. Jenny interpreted the scarf as a sign that Delphine had made her peace with the love Jenny felt for David. Within weeks, Delphine would depart for Asia. Hopefully she now felt easier about leaving, knowing her father had someone who would move heaven and earth to keep him afloat.

Marc was trickier. For him Jenny saw a lengthy struggle ahead. The only comfort she could offer was to assure him, "Sandie believed you would come through all this okay, and I believe it too."

Several days went by without an e-mail from David, so Jenny finally called. His voice was flat and devoid of energy. The neighbors were attentive, he reported, but to little avail. "People are wonderfully kind and want to take care of us by having us over, but it doesn't really help," he said with a sigh.

Jenny tried to be upbeat and cheerful, but nothing drew David out. For an instant she had an awful image of all the morphine in Sandie's cabinet. *Why didn't I get rid of it at Thanksgiving?* she moaned inwardly. She tried to shift her thoughts in a more positive direction, but when they finally hung up, she felt defeated and uneasy.

From: JWLongworth
To: DavidP
Date: January 7, 2001
Subject: Open me NOW; This is a hug
　　You sounded really depressed when I called, so I'm sending you a warm and snuggly hug with no cold hands or cold feet, hoping you will sleep well tonight.
　　Love, J.

It felt as if they had returned to the dark days when Sandie lay dying. Jenny committed to communicating daily. She wrote about the weather. She wrote about what she had for dinner. She quoted newspaper articles. She speculated about politics. She chatted about her cat. She kept David apprised of her weekly calendar. It didn't much matter what she said. It was her "presence" that counted.

From: JWLongworth
To: DavidP
Date: January 8, 2001
Subject: Gray days
　　As if you didn't have enough weighing on you, the *Boston Globe* advises that this is Lump Week—the week

after all the holidays are over, but we haven't caught up on our sleep yet or dealt with whatever piled up during our vacations. So if you're feeling lumpy, you're not alone.

Big hug and a little nibble on your left ear. Mmmmm. That was tasty. A little nibble on your right ear as well.

Love, me

De: David
A: Jenny
Envoyé: 8 janvier, 2001
Objet: Re: Gray Days

Thanks for the nibble. Kisses from gray Geneva, the home of Protestantism. David

From: J W Longworth
To: DavidP
Date: January 9, 2001
Subject: Tuesday

Nothing to report, except an uneasy feeling that you're having a rough time. I know Sandie's birthday is coming up soon. Perhaps you could think of something pleasant in her honor. Fill the house with roses. Light a fire, write her a note, and send it up the chimney in smoke. Give her the gift of your smile. It's a real dazzler. I've known it to make women swoon. Hang in there, Luv. The crocuses aren't far away.

Love, me

De: David
A: Jenny
Envoyé: 10 janvier, 2001
Objet: Today was better

Back up today after four days down. Must figure out a way to reverse the statistics. Delphine is visiting friends. Marc and I cross like ships in the night. I hope he'll be home for dinner for we must talk, and I'd rather start while Delphine is out of town. Question of yelling and screaming without bothering the rest of the progeny.

Kisses, David

Jenny was distressed by David's report but felt it was better to have him admit to his sadness and depression rather than avoid all reference to it.

From: JWLongworth
To: DavidP
Date: January 10, 2001
Subject: Re: Today was better

I am relieved that you are "back up." I, too, wish I could figure out a way to reverse your statistics, but it's only month four. Just be careful, Love. Keep my number pasted on the phone. If you start sinking, call me. I don't care how incoherent you are or what time it is. I'll stay on the line with you all night if need be, until you're back on safe ground.

Re you and Marc, I understand that he may yell and scream at you. What I don't understand is why you yell and scream at him, knowing it doesn't work. Who is the grown-up, and who is the child? Or is it more complex—with two adult males, the aging lion king and the young challenger? I don't have the answer. I just pose the question.

Love you, J.

De: David
A: Jenny
Envoyé: 11 janvier, 2001
Objet: Lion kings and such

Ducks, temper has nothing to do with whether it works or not; it has to do with not knowing what to do and getting pissed off. Sandie used to duck and wait for the blast to pass. I just live with it. And I can tell you that when Marc said he doesn't know where his driver's license is, I wasn't a happy camper.

Kisses, David

Marc was clearly not a reliable support system for his father, and Delphine's departure was imminent. They had only been apart for two weeks, but Jenny wondered whether she should fly to Geneva for a long weekend. She picked up the phone and called Bibi, unloading her worries and seeking advice. After much back and forth, Jenny decided she should organize things so she could take off at the drop of a hat if need be but hold off unless David seemed in immediate danger.

"Have you told anyone else about your affair yet?" Bibi asked.

"It's just not relevant, Bibi," Jenny answered wearily.

"See, I don't believe that," Bibi replied. "You're making too big a deal of saying it's not a big deal. You've never been one to shy away from controversy, and you're not afraid of criticism. If you're skittish about people learning that you're sleeping with David, it's not because you're worried about their reaction. So maybe what you're worried about is an inside problem. Maybe it's survivor's guilt. I mean, why did Sandie, with a husband and two children, have to die, when you, with no one dependent on you, sailed through a scary diagnosis and came out on the other side with a clean bill of health? And now, because Sandie's dead and the road is clear, you've got her husband where you've always secretly wanted him—in your arms. You didn't exactly waste a lot of time getting him there, either."

Bibi was blunt, but she wasn't being mean. Her tone was speculative, analytical, and free of judgment. She was Sherlock Holmes, applying logic and observation to the unraveling of a mystery.

"I didn't waste a lot of time because I didn't have a lot of time," Jenny commented dryly. "I was afraid he'd kill himself. As for survivor's guilt, I felt some when Sandie died, but I'm well past that now. When you're as much of a nature lover as I am, you see death as a normal part of life, not something separate and evil. It wasn't anyone's fault. So let's just give the issue a rest."

There was a brief silence on the other end of the phone.

"Change of subject," Jenny announced. "The trip to Paris in April is definitely on, and David thinks it would be fun to have friends join us. Any interest?"

De: David
A: Jenny
Envoyé: 14 janvier, 2001
Objet: Grayness on a Sunday

Today is so sad, cold, and ugly it could convert the Pope himself to Calvinism. Thank heavens for Handel and Vivaldi to splash a bit of spiritual sunshine around the house. Delphine and I will spend this week doing last-minute things for her Asian adventure.

I went onto the Internet to look for places in or around Paris. We'll need to decide how many people we're talking about. I think it will be more interesting to be in Paris and then travel outside whenever we want. After all, you haven't been to the Center of the Universe for a long time.

Kisses, David

From: JW Longworth
To: DavidP
Date: January 14, 2001
Subject: Calvinist Hug

Dearest David—Since it's such a Calvinist kind of day over there, I am sending you a Calvinist kind of hug. It's simple, clean, and pure (well, maybe not totally pure), but comes with cold hands and feet.

Love you, J.

Jenny sent David a care package with recipes and a funny card, and considered what else she might do short of getting on an airplane. David was facing a grim and lonely couple of months. She contacted his immediate family and branched out to his friends, encouraging frequent calls and letters. In her note to Graham Wells, she included some sensitive details that she had screened out of her other e-mails. Since Graham was a psychologist, she trusted both his wisdom and his discretion.

From: J W Longworth
To: Graham
Date: January 15, 2001
Subject: Friend in Need

Graham, I'm worried for David. There is serious tension with Marc. There is political strife at school. Dellie is off to Asia. David is beset with the legal details of settling Sandie's estate, plus the bill paying and financial juggling that he hates. He goes out when people invite him over, but his preference is to sit home drinking while listening to sad music. His Geneva friends are trying to keep a close watch, but the more of us puffing air into the life raft, the better. A million thanks.

Love, Jenny

From: Graham
To: Jenny
Date: January 16, 2001
Subject: Re: Friend in Need

It's not surprising he's having such a bad time. The drinking worries me. It takes a couple of years to begin feeling anything like oneself after a loss like this, but drinking is going to make everything worse.

I also think it will be almost impossible for David to handle the paperwork without someone sitting down with him and walking through it. You could be a big help there. What do you know about the kind of financial shape he's been left in—mortgage payments on one income and so forth?

Barbara and I have invited him to join us for a weekend in Italy in March. He's said yes, so that will be both a chance to distract him and to assess how he's doing.

Don't feel helpless. You have already done so much. Knowing and loving Sandie over the years, I know it meant everything to her that you were standing behind her kids and were going to help them with their education.

Much love, old friend—Graham

From: JWLongworth
To: Graham
Date: January 17, 2001
Subject: Re: Re: Friend in Need

It's a relief to talk to someone who knows the history and the cast of characters!

I don't know how to deal with the alcohol. David is obviously anesthetizing himself most evenings. I can tell the difference between e-mails he sends in the morning and e-mails he sends at night. My big fear is that he'll suddenly decide to go out for cigarettes and end up wrapping his car around a telephone pole.

It's great that you've asked him to come to Italy in March. The DuPonts are going golfing with him in February. I will meet him in Paris mid-April. So he has something to look forward to each month that will get him out of that house and out of Geneva.

I agree with you about the paperwork. I was there at Thanksgiving and went through everything in Sandie's desk. The problem isn't that the financial management is difficult or confusing. The problem is that Sandie isn't there anymore to take care of it. Coping with the bills is acknowledging her death with every check he writes.

About his solvency, I'm looking into it. I don't have a totally clear picture yet.

Love, Jenny

Serious e-mails were mixed with lighthearted ones. Jenny tried everything she could think of to dispel the dark shadows around David, even if only for a moment or two.

From: JWLongworth
To: DavidP
Date: January 17, 2001
Subject: Mush

I don't know where you are when I write my e-mails, but I do know where you are when you read them! I can picture you sitting there at your desk, squinting at the screen. I can imagine I am tiptoeing up behind you, startling you with a gentle but nonetheless telltale love bite on the right side of your neck, a little to the back, just where the shoulder muscle comes in. This will scandalize everyone at school unless you wear a turtleneck for the next few days.

Well, that's enough excitement for one day.

Love, *moi*

De: David
A: Jenny
Envoyé: 18 janvier, 2001
Objet: Re: Mush

Do believe that one drew a wee spot of blood! I plan to go topless.

Love, David

From: JWLongworth
To: DavidP
Date: January 18, 2001
Subject: Paris rentals

I checked out some of the websites you suggested re Paris rentals. I don't know the local geography well enough to know what I'm looking at. As long as there is good food and drink, decent plumbing, space for guests, and enough hot water for morning showers, I'll be a happy camper.

I just want to be sure hanging out in Paris isn't going to be more painful for you than hanging out somewhere else. Sandie and Paris are inextricably bound together for you—as you and Paris are inextricably bound together for me. I never went back because I was afraid it would make me sad.

I love the idea of spending two weeks in Paris with you. It will undo a dark spell of long standing. But I don't want to break the spell at your expense. You're going to grieve for Sandie no matter where you are, but I don't want to deepen your loss by choosing a site whose memories will heighten your pain.

I leave the decision in your hands.

Je t'adore, J.

De: David
A: Jenny
Envoyé: 19 janvier, 2001
Objet: Re: Paris rentals

This is difficult to explain because I don't really understand it myself. I felt freer of Sandie's absence while we were spreading her ashes in Paris than anywhere else I've been since her death.

I came to Europe to follow my bliss, something you helped me to understand years later. My bliss was Paris—its layout, its style, its atmosphere, its urbanity, its Frenchness, its magic, its light, and its fabulously elegant women. Sandie gave me a person to live with who embodied something of all that. She was my pocket Paris, with whom I went everywhere, so my bliss was always with me in Sandie. However, when I returned there in October, I realized that Paris was either greater than Sandie and me together or of a different nature (this is the part that I don't understand) because I felt appeased being in Paris. Sandie was with me more as thoughts or presence than the aching absence I carry with me elsewhere.

So, Jewel, being with you in Paris would be blissful. Even showing you Sandie's Paris would be blissful, regardless of whether we stay in Paris or travel to and from.

Kisses, David

From: JWLongworth
To: DavidP
Date: January 20, 2001
Subject: Re: Re: Re: Paris rentals

You have extraordinary insight for someone who doesn't understand things, exceptional linguistic ability for someone who finds explanations difficult, and you turn prose into poetry without even thinking.

Love you, J.

Jenny called Rachel Aronson, and they met in town after work. Over dinner, Jenny brought Rachel up to date on David's progress and expressed her hope that spring would bring some respite. "Spring certainly improves the psychic environment," Rachel cautioned, "but we're not dealing with a gently graded road that climbs steadily out of the swamp onto higher ground. It's a roller coaster. Just when you think you've reached a safe plateau, you're pitched over the edge straight to the bottom of the chasm again."

Rachel said that while some things were better for her after six months, some things were worse. "I've started going places, attending events, and taking on new clients. But when I come home, precisely because I am doing these things, I want to tell Josh about my day and ask his opinion of this or that. And he's not there. The crutch of denial is gone. The recognition of his absence is absolute.

"People think," she continued, "that when you're widowed, the most difficult part is getting yourself to the point where you will go out and about again. But that's not it. Going out is easy. It's coming home that's hard."

"David says he has conversations with Sandie. Do you talk to Josh?" Jenny asked.

"Well, I talk to myself," she replied. "I ask myself, 'What would Josh think?' or 'What would Josh do?' And there is one really bizarre thing I find myself doing. When I have committee meetings at the hospital, I deliberately use the elevators and travel the corridors that Josh used during his treatments. I half expect him to come around the corner or stick his head out the door. Odd as it seems, I find this comforting, as though this is a place I can be near him."

Jenny told Rachel of David's decision to hang a collage of Sandie's photographs outside his bedroom so he could say good morning to her every day. Rachel nodded in recognition. "I placed pictures of Josh everywhere I would normally have seen him, like the view from my breakfast chair, or over his dresser where there used to be a mirror.

"I banished relics of Josh's illness. His bathrobe is now gone. I haven't yet dealt with his general clothing, but I made a good discovery you might pass along to David. Josh always stored his off-season clothes in a hall closet. For a long time, I couldn't face removing them. I would open the closet door and close it again, not wanting to further diminish his presence in the house. Then I visited a friend who, like me, has young grandchildren. She had recently cleaned out a former clothes closet and converted it for toy storage. The shelves and cubbyholes were filled with blocks, puzzles, and stuffed animals. I felt like those cartoon characters with the lightbulb suddenly flashing over their heads. I realized that, if I had a positive, grandchild-oriented reason to clear out the closet, it would be okay. I knew Josh would love the idea and emptying the closet became almost a team effort in my mind. The specifics may not translate to David's situation, but the concept might prove helpful."

Rachel asked how David had handled Christmas. Jenny described their time in Chattanooga, including the family discussions and the distribution of Sandie's ashes. "It sounds as if he did a good job," Rachel commented. "Holidays and traditions have become more important than ever, yet I've had to make changes. The prospect of dealing with Josh's empty place at the head of the table at Rosh Hashanah filled me with dread. We solved the problem by installing my youngest grandson, who sat there in his highchair and symbolized all that is good about one generation yielding to the next. He was past and future bound together. It was another bubble of happiness for me," she concluded.

Jenny found it invaluable to listen to Rachel. She could ask sensitive questions and get straight answers. Rachel enhanced her awareness of what David was facing and pulled no punches about the harsh and painful realities that surviving spouses struggle through on a daily basis. She also gave Jenny much-needed reassurance. "I think it makes it much easier for David that you knew Sandie so well and appreciated her. He doesn't have to explain anything."

When Jenny got home, she recapped as much of the conversation as she could remember and sent it off to David via e-mail. When she didn't hear back from him, she worried that he was withdrawing again.

From: JWLongworth
To: DavidP
Date: January 21, 2001
Subject: Quiet time

You're not talking much, which makes me suspect you feel down. And the fact that I can't do anything about it makes *me* feel down. In addition to hugs, I think I'll try sending bubbles of hope and happiness. Every circle, every sphere you see, from now until bedtime, is one of my bubbles. I love you, Angel, and I know you can do this. J.

De: David
A: Jenny
Envoyé: 21 janvier, 2001
Objet: Re: Quiet time

You're right, I feel like shit. Apart from the fact that Delphine is leaving, Christophe St. Jean, an old French friend I've known since the '70s, is dying of cancer. I'm debating about a visit, but I don't know what good it would do.

Kisses, David

One look at that e-mail and Jenny called. Christophe and his wife, Germaine, lived in Nîmes, in the south of France. David finally decided he would take a train down the following weekend. Jenny hated the thought of his doing the journey alone and wondered if she should arrange to go with him. She needed on-site intelligence. She wrote to Josette DuPont, asking for an assessment of David's mental state. She was somewhat mollified by the swift response, which, dictionary in hand, she was able to translate fairly easily.

De: Josette
A: Jenny
Envoyé: 22 janvier, 2001
Objet: Re: Jenny is worried

Chère Jenny, I understand well that you are worried because to be far away is horrible. But to be near is also difficult. Difficult to know the critical moments. Difficult to be present at the right time. I avow that we do not always know what one should do. The return was very hard. I see David each day at school, and I find that he is not too bad. He knows always to be present with others, to have humorous conversations, to be in tune with his students, but I find also certain days that he is sad, unhappy, and depressed. To tell him that we are with him in his sadness seems to us the best thing to do. We also are dispirited, also uneasy—and the right thing to do, does it exist? I know that he is happy when you call. He tells me your messages. But I do not know that you are able to do more.

We will try to be more present after Delphine's departure. But I know also, for he has said it to Michel, that David does only that which is essential. He has no desire to do the things he did before. In a couple, one often does things for the other at the same time one does things for oneself. And without the other, the motivation disappears, and this energy, this desire—it doesn't exist for the moment.

Keep me informed of your worries, for perhaps we do not notice the same things. We will try our very best to help him. Thank you for your confidences. I send you an affectionate hug. Josette

Michel and Josette were aware of the situation with Christophe, and it was reassuring to know they were keeping an eye on David. Then, out of the blue, David telephoned, confused by some tax questions. Jenny was unfamiliar with the Swiss tax code, but she could at least explain the meaning of certain technical terms. When David started making wisecracks in response to her efforts to educate him, she knew he was okay—at least for the moment.

From: JW Longworth
To: DavidP
Date: January 23, 2001
Subject: Chat
Dearheart—It was lovely talking to you yesterday. You sound much better. You have no idea how close I was to booking a flight and coming over. Sometimes I underestimate how much inner strength you have.

Please forgive me if I hit the panic button more often than need be. I just want you to get through this in one piece.

Word has it that you've got golf plans with the DuPonts, and you're cooking up a weekend in Florence with Graham and Barbara. Here I was, worrying that you were going to pine away in grim Geneva. Now I discover you'll be golfing in February and frolicking in Italy in March. I shall henceforth keep my inclination to worry in check. Maybe.

Much love, J.

De: David
A: Jenny
Envoyé: 23 janvier, 2001
Objet: Ruminations on chat

Don't know why you want me in one piece. If I blew myself to bits, there could be multiple memorial celebrations.

Yup, I'll be in Provence in February with Michel and Josette. I don't have confirmation from Graham, but the plan is to meet them in Florence about the fifteenth of March. Wanna come?

Love, David

From: JWLongworth
To: DavidP
Date: January 23, 2001
Subject: Re: Ruminations on chat

I can think of several reasons for wanting you in one piece.

I'd love to join you in Florence, but if I'm going to do two weeks in Paris in April, I need to put in some serious office time first.

Re the Paris trip, I'm thinking of inviting Ross to join us, along with Bibi (whom you met in Sausalito) and also Rachel Aronson (whom you will really like). Bibi and Rachel could share a room if space is tight.

One more week, and we've made it through January!
Love, J.

Sandie's birthday was the twenty-fourth of January. She would have been fifty-three. David suggested that family and friends "do something lovely today in Sandie's honor."

From: JWLongworth
To: DavidP
Date: January 24, 2001
Subject: Wednesday

Hi, Angel. Re honoring Sandie's birthday, the loveliest thing I can think of is giving you an enormous hug and not letting go for the longest time. I expect Sandie often entertained similar sentiments, so perhaps that is the best gift to honor you both. Consider this a rain check; I'll give you the real thing in April. May today go gently for you.

Much love, Jenny

De: David
A: Jenny
Envoyé: 24 janvier, 2001
Objet: Re: Wednesday

Ducks, I accept the rain check on the hugs. It fits with the weather; it is *pissing* with rain and has been since last night.

I'm definitely going down to Nîmes this Friday unless Christophe dies beforehand. I'll be back Sunday late afternoon. Disjointed message, but that's the way I feel.

Kisses, David

From: JWLongworth
To: DavidP
Date: January 24, 2001
Subject: Re: Re: Wednesday

Wish I could be with you to brave the trip. I'm sure it will help Germaine to have you come. You of all people understand how she feels. I stand in awe of how honest you've been about the pain, and how hard you've worked to find things that are positive—even joyful—in your life.

Christophe will surely be grateful for anything you can do to comfort the family.
Love, J.

Sandie's birthday was a time of special remembrance for the children as well as for David, as evidenced by a poignant note from Delphine.

From: Delphine
To: Dad
Fwd: Jenny
Date: January 25, 2001
Subject: Re: Sandie's Birthday

Dear Dad, I bought some incense, a votive candle, and a lotus flower that I set at the foot of a Jade Buddha at the Grand Palace in Bangkok to honor Mom for her b-day. I think that la parisienne will be pleased. At least it helped me during that difficult day. I hope you were okay. I thought a lot about you and Marc. Take care!
Kisses, Delphine

From: JWLongworth
To: DavidP
Date: January 25, 2001
Subject: Thursday

That was a sweet note from Dellie.

All's quiet here. My condo association's annual meeting went smoothly. No contest re the board. I'm on for another year. Have a good trip to Nîmes. I know you're not looking forward to it, but I'm glad you're going.
Love, J.

De: David
A: Jenny
Envoyé: 28 janvier, 2001
Objet: Sunday

I'm back and kinda wiped out. Christophe is still all there in terms of his mind and cerebral connections. However, he's terribly thin and in growing pain.

He's shifting to a palliative care center next week, but he considers it a rehab facility from which he will go home after a couple of weeks. As he says, he does not consider the hypothesis that he is going to die. I asked him to do so on the off chance he might, and to check out things with Sandie if they ran into each other in the beyond. Germaine said it scared him, but I wanted to get that in, for him and his family—try to get the ball rolling as I wish we had done earlier with Sandie. However, Christophe is very much the French intellectual, so not much else exists.

I spent quite a while with both Germaine and their son. They were most receptive to a little straight talk. Christophe seems to me to be about where Sandie was in August before the final decline, but I could be very wrong.

Kisses, David

"I'm clear for April in Paris," Bibi announced, "and now that that's settled, I'm going to ask you a tough question. You don't have to answer it, but if you do, you have to be absolutely honest. You might as well, because I'll see through it anyway if you aren't. Were you and David having an affair before Sandie died? All this visiting back and forth … sharing vacations … you being divorced. Was there something going on between the two of you while Sandie was still alive?"

"No, there was nothing going on between us while Sandie was alive," Jenny stated emphatically. In a softer tone, she added, "Certainly not once they got married."

Bibi caught the hesitation. "Not once they got married?" she repeated, turning it into a question.

"David and Sandie dated for three years before they got married," Jenny said matter-of-factly. "During that time, David saw other women besides Sandie."

"And you were one of them?"

"It only happened once. By then I'd been back in the States for a while and had started dating Seth. David had to go to New York for an educational seminar and came up to Boston for a weekend before flying back to Paris. He stayed with me."

"And?" Bibi asked.

"And," Jenny answered. "But that was the last time."

"How long after that did he marry Sandie?"

"I think it was about a year."

"And how long before you married Seth?"

"Maybe another six months. Something like that."

"Would you have married Seth if David had still been single at the time?"

"Why not? At that stage of our lives, David and I had totally different goals. I wanted to save the world. He just wanted to enjoy it. Look, I know I rationalize. I know it wasn't as tidy as I make it sound. But once I started dating Seth, I began to think of David as an adolescent fantasy. David was my perfect partner in a dream, but not in the real world. He was the prince in the fairy tale, Peter Pan to my Wendy.

"I was never in love with Seth the way I was with David, but we made a good team. Our backgrounds were similar, our ambitions were similar, and our values were similar—or so I believed. I admired Seth's ambition. He was disciplined, focused, and hardworking. And he wanted to use his engineering training to help protect the environment. He was like me, a cause person—serious and practical. In marrying Seth, I was signing up for genuine adulthood. I committed to a grown-up relationship with a grown-up partner. David's marital status wasn't relevant one way or the other."

"So, during all those years when you were being a responsible married grown-up, you never once thought about having a fling with David?"

"Bibi, I never said I was a saint. I admit David showed up in erotic dreams. And maybe there were a few waking moments when he came to mind that way as well, but not as much as you might think. Until Seth starting getting careless about his infidelities, I thought we had a good marriage. I was busy. I was happy. I never had the emotional intimacy with Seth that I had with David, but it wasn't until after the divorce that the passion I felt for David climbed back up to a conscious level. Even then, it's not as if I was unhappy with my life. I had my work, my causes, my garden, my friends—and a wonderful companion in Ross.

"I admit to getting excited whenever a visit was planned. I loved every minute I spent with David. But after each visit, we returned to our separate lives, and I was usually back to normal within a few weeks, content with my daily world."

"No jealousy that his separate life was with Sandie?"

"I felt bereft when the visits were over, and I certainly envied Sandie her role and her access, but envy is not the same as jealousy."

"Not the same but close enough. And you actually liked this woman? Even though she took the man you loved away from you?"

"What choice did I have, Bibi? And besides, she didn't take him away from me. Paris took him away from me. He wanted a Francophile life— French friends in a French city with a French wife. I couldn't give that to him. She could. She made him happy, Bibi. I'm as capable of jealousy as the next person, but if I'd treated Sandie like the competition, I would have lost my access to David. I could hardly blame her for falling in love with David. We both wanted the best for him, so I chose to view her as an ally. I respected her and admired her. She was a nice person. She really was. And once she decided that I posed no threat, she accepted me as part of their extended family. She knew I was important to David. She not only allowed our friendship. She actually encouraged it."

There was a brief silence on the other end.

"So," Bibi resumed slowly. "On the one hand, you're sad that Sandie died. And other the other hand, you're glad that David is back in your life, front and center, with no one in the way."

"That's a harsh way to put it," Jenny answered.

"It's not Boston tidy, but reality rarely is. I'm not blaming you. You've been performing a pretty amazing balancing act all these years. It's natural to feel torn. And maybe that's why you also feel vulnerable. It's hard to have feet of clay and keep your halo polished at the same time."

"Bibi, if you don't let go of this, I'm going to rescind your invitation to Paris."

When their call was finished, Jenny checked her inbox and found sad news.

> *De: David*
> *A: Jenny*
> *Envoyé: 31 janvier, 2001*
> *Objet: Christophe's death*
>
> Ducks, it's kind of shitty. Christophe died last night. He went into a coma on Monday, so it was very quick. The funeral is next week, but I'm not going to make it. I don't have time for another ten-hour train trip. Marc and I are going to Paris over the weekend to see friends. We both need some respite.
> Kisses, David

> *From: JWLongworth*
> *To: DavidP*
> *Date: January 31, 2001*
> *Subject: Re: Christophe's death*
>
> Dearest David—I'm so glad you saw Christophe and his family last weekend. I expect your presence was far more important then than it would be at the funeral. I have to believe that you brought them a strength and perspective that they needed and appreciated.
> What I know for sure is that your visit to Nîmes marked a turning point for me. You took the pain and suffering you have endured, got a hold on it, and forged it into a powerful tool to help other people. For the past four months, the grief has managed you. Now, you're beginning to manage the grief. You're starting to channel it in positive ways. When I saw that happen, I stopped being afraid for you. Don't you dare think, however, that you can start again with the suicide jokes!
> Have a lovely few days in Paris, and be at peace.
> Love, Jenny

From Paris, David mailed Jenny a simple postcard featuring a young couple kissing beneath the Arch de Triomphe:

> Dear Jewel—Sitting in a café across from the Gare de Lyon, sipping a glass of wine, biding my time before taking the train back to Geneva, and thinking about you. Love, David.

Spring's Promise

For Jennifer,

       to remind you that Spring is on its way.

We have crocuses and primroses
Though the cold is sharp,
And the wind blows hard
From the Arctic pole across the snow -
Ice fields and frozen desolation.
I'm still loathe to let them go.
Their hold I nonetheless know now
Will fail as the pale sun's warp
Grows warm and forces
Winter's grisly straps to tear,
Releasing shoots through rips
To slip me back to where
New life on earth eagerly grips
A tendered stand, sending vines
Spinning ever so slowly, winding as wisteria,
Waltzing unseen at times round wires.

The grass will once again be green and
Though I putter midst weeds for hours
I'll notice only flowers
That we planted or I've planted since.
Their beauty will be ours.

D.P. - March, 2001

Chapter 7

From: JWLongworth
To: DavidP
Date: February 2, 2001
Subject: Groundhog Day
Happy Groundhog Day! Bibi says yes to joining us in Paris. Rachel can't make it, but Ross is definitely interested. I've been candid with Bibi and Ross about our relationship, and they seem pleased by the notion of me and thee sharing a bed. Hope your weekend in Paris was rewarding.

Much love, Jenny

De: David
A: Jenny
Att: Spring's Promise
Envoyé: 4 février, 2001
Objet: Paris
Just walked in. Paris was wonderful—definitely where I feel best, freest, and most at home, with and without Sandie.

Kisses to everyone. A special one for you. Talk to you soon.

Love, David

The e-mail came with a poem attached, titled "Spring's Promise." "For Jennifer," David wrote at the top, "to remind you that spring is on its way." Jenny read it twice. It was filled with hope. "One day the grass will once again be green, and ... I'll notice only flowers," he said.

"Thank god!" Jenny breathed. "He can see the light at the end of the tunnel. He's going to make it!" Since Delphine was far from home, Jenny was moved to reassure her that her father was making progress, but she focused on David's trip to Nîmes rather than mentioning the poem.

> *From: JWLongworth*
> *To: Delphine*
> *Date: February 5, 2001*
> *Subject: Note to Delphine*
>
> Hi, Dellie! Just a quick note to say that your dad seems measurably better than he was just a few short weeks ago. I'm sure you were aware of how depressed he was after the return from the States. Mixed in with that were some fears about your trip to Asia. But since your e-mails started coming, and he knows you're safe and having fun, he is much happier—and very proud of you.
>
> Last weekend, David went down to Nîmes to see his old friend, Christophe St. Jean, who was dying of cancer. Amazingly, it turned out to be a positive experience. He was glad he made the trip and felt his presence was genuinely helpful to the family. My sense is that he was able to take his own pain and do something really good with it. I think he no longer feels weak and helpless.
>
> He had a good time in Paris this past weekend. He and the DuPonts will play some golf in Provence this month. David also plans a weekend in Florence in March with Graham Wells and his wife. In April, he and I will have two weeks in Paris. So there are many good things for him to look forward to while you're away. Hope your own travels continue to be wonderfully fun.
>
> Much love, Jenny

Delphine's response came indirectly, via an e-mail that David forwarded to Jenny.

From: Delphine
To: Dad
Date: February 14, 2001
Subject: We're back

Hi there! Burma was *fantastic!* Exhausting but beautiful. I'll tell you all about it in Geneva.

I have dreamed of Maman every night since I arrived here. The dreams aren't very realistic, but she is always present. I miss her a lot. It's even harder because you are also far away, but in general my morale is fine. It's not messing up my trip. So don't worry.

Sorry about your friend Christophe. I hope it wasn't too hard. Next time you talk to Jenny, tell her thanks for her note. Lots and lots of love to you and Marc! D.

From: JWLongworth
To: Delphine
cc: DavidP
Date: February 17, 2001
Subject: Re: We're back

Dear Dellie—A very strong memory came to mind yesterday, perhaps inspired by what you said about dreaming so often of your mother. The memory was from the summer you, Marc, and your parents stayed with me in Maine for a week. The image was of Sandie, David, and me, sitting by the edge of the lake in the evening, enjoying our wine and looking out over the water.

That was when I first raised the idea of creating an education trust for you and Marc. You had both expressed an interest in coming to the States for college, but US tuition was beyond your parents' means. I had the means and no children of my own to educate. The discussion was primarily between Sandie and me. We agreed that education didn't just mean going to school. It could include travel and other valuable life experiences. Once the discussion ended, we returned to sipping our wine and watching the reflection of the moon on the lake. There was a dreamlike quality to the setting and the moment.

I wonder if Sandie had a vision that night encompassing the very trip you are taking now. I don't mean a mystical vision. I mean the natural kind of vision parents have when they look at their children and think about the possibilities ahead. Sandie might very well have imagined your trip as clearly as she would see it today if she were still alive. Your trip would then be one of her wishes for you, coming true. The memory pleased me, and I hope it will bring you a smile.

Much love, Jenny

Unfortunately, smiles were in short supply. Jenny got a report from Josette that David was very low. Rachel had warned her that grief was a roller coaster ride, but she was still taken aback. Just weeks before, David had written Jenny a poem filled with such optimism. Now he was down and depressed again. In stilted French, Jenny replied:

From: JWLongworth
To: Josette
Date: February 23, 2001
Subject: Re: Bon courage!

Chère Josette—It is hard to hear that David continues to be so sad, but in my heart I already knew this, so it is not a surprise. I am reassured that you feel he is making progress—managing to live his life! It is hard for me to judge when I am so far away. I am glad he is becoming active and getting away from the house. Even Dellie was surprised to learn that he has made so many visits to friends, and planned little vacations such as your drive to Provence.

I appreciate your keeping me apprised of David's emotions. I cannot think how it would be if you and Michel were not there to support and encourage him.

I bless you both.

Love, Jenny

De: David
A: Jenny
Envoyé: 2 mars, 2001
Objet: Our return to Geneva

We're back early. There was snow in Aix-en-Provence. The daffodils were covered with hail, drowning in the rain, shivering from the cold. To hell with it. We saw some friends—inner sunshine—had some excellent meals and drank some good wine. The golf courses were closed because of bad weather. Decided to surrender. Had to drive through a bloody blizzard to get home.

Days like these, I could do without. Gray inside and out. Gloomy enough that the crocuses in the garden are not enough. I need more splotches of color. Sigh!

Miss you, David

From: JWLongworth
To: DavidP
Date: March 3, 2001
Subject: Countdown

What you need is a hug. So stand up for a minute. Come on. Up, up, up. Long snuggly squeeze. Hold it. (It's okay to breathe.) Little rocking motion. One more squeeze. All right—enough. We'll get into trouble if we keep going.

I'm starting my official countdown today. In one month, Bibi and I will board the plane for Paris. It's almost worth doing an advent calendar!

Love, J.

De: David
A: Jenny
Envoyé: 4 mars, 2001
Objet: St. Germain

Got the hug, Ducks. A pleasure. I booked an apartment on the Boulevard St. Germain yesterday. It's exactly where I want to be to show you my Paris.

Kisses, David

Jennifer read David's e-mails with an eye out for warning signs that he was in trouble, but he seemed to have found a semblance of balance.

> De: *David*
> A: *Jenny*
> Envoyé: *9 mars, 2001*
> Objet: *This week ...*
>
> Just tried to call, wanted to chat, but you're obviously out somewhere.
>
> Our former landscaper stopped by the other night and announced that I was at risk of losing the azaleas out front. There are hundreds of little shell-like bugs sucking the life out of 'em. Shit. I'm hoping they'll survive, but survival isn't much in vogue around here these days.
>
> Sandie must be laughing her heart out. When we first moved in, the strip in front of our new house was completely bare, so I had the landscaper put in a bunch of azaleas. I wasn't thinking about cost. I was only thinking about flowers. Sandie had our move budgeted down to the last centime, and when she got a bill for five thousand francs for landscaping, it was a toss-up as to whether she would sue for divorce or just kill me.
>
> Big kiss.
> Love, David

> From: *J W Longworth*
> To: *David P*
> Date: *March 9, 2001*
> Subject: *Re: This week ...*
>
> Sorry your azaleas are in trouble. Still, I don't think Sandie would laugh about them. She must have moved mountains to make the finances work once you blew the bank balance. She would surely want them to survive, if for no other reason than to remind you of your wanton ways and her wise management. If the azaleas go, I hereby promise Sandie that the circumstances of their arrival *chez* Perry will not be forgotten.
>
> Love you, J.

De: David
A: Jenny
Envoyé: 12 mars, 2001
Objet: Azaleas

Don't worry about my forgetting the azalea story. 'Tis burned into my mind.

I leave Friday for Florence. We're staying at a *pensione* Graham has reserved. I fly back Sunday night. Meanwhile, it's raining cats and dogs and has been for days. Sigh.

Love, David

From: JWLongworth
To: DavidP
Date: March 15, 2001
Subject: Firenze

Dearest Love—Have a gorgeous time in Florence. Think baroque. Feel rococo. If the sun shines, have a gellato (sp?) for me. Big Italian hugs for Graham and Barbara, and a naughty little French kiss for you.

Ciao, J.

De: David
A: Jenny
Envoyé: 15 mars, 2001
Objet: Re: Firenze

Gelato, Ducks. And not Baroque, that's Rome. Florence is Early Renaissance, which is why I like it. I'm gonna have to take you in hand! You're good at naughty French, but European culture? Think Paris.

Love, Cellini

Graham sent Jenny a brief note saying David was "up and down" during the visit to Florence, but David's report carefully avoided revelations about his emotional state.

De: David
A: Jenny
Envoyé: 20 mars, 2001
Objet: Back Home

Florence was pissing with rain, I mean pissing! So I was glad to get home to Geneva ... where it's raining. Sigh. However, Florence is so beautiful and so appealing that I was happy to be there despite the weather. We spent a lot of time doing what I love to do in cities— walking around, drinking and eating in cafés, watching the crowds, window-shopping. I also got to see most of the museums and sights I wanted to see, and they remain as inspiring as ever. We'll definitely have to go to Florence.

Love, David

Jenny understood that David generally put up a brave front, but on the six-month anniversary of Sandie's death, she chose to confront the date rather than avoid acknowledging it.

From: JWLongworth
To: DavidP
Date: March 25, 2001
Subject: Six Months

I'm hoping today is not too difficult for you. I'm proud of how far you've come in the six months since Sandie died. You often accuse me of thinking "just like Sandie," so I take that as evidence that she, too, would feel good about where your head is. Enclosed is a big warm hug. J.

De: David
A: Jenny
Envoyé: 25 mars, 2001
Objet: Re: Six Months

Today wasn't difficult until I got your e-mail, and Josette brought over a bouquet of roses, but what the hell, that's the way it is, and it's good to cry. Got to go out and mail my Swiss tax forms ... late. The garden is wonderful. Tulips blooming. End of the daffodils. Definitely spring. Kisses, and see you in a week. David

The flight to Paris arrived an hour late. Neither Bibi nor Jenny had slept, despite inflatable pillows and earplugs. At Charles deGaulle, they spent a frustrating hour waiting for their luggage, with no information as to what the problem was, nowhere to sit, and people chain-smoking all around them. They later learned there was a transport workers' strike. When they finally got through customs, David greeted them each with a hug, helped them with their bags, and they all piled into a cab.

The apartment was a fifth-floor unit at the corner of Boulevard St. Germain and Boulevard St. Michel, with a view of Paris chimneys, rooftop gardens, and the steeple of St. Chapelle. It had gabled windows with one tiny balcony, a fully-equipped kitchen, a washing machine, a TV, and a CD player. David came prepared with some favorite Handel and Vivaldi pieces, plus a collection of renaissance music he picked up in Florence.

There were fresh croissants waiting for them. Bibi caught up on her sleep while David and Jenny went to La Rhumerie for lunch. There they ate spicy fish dumplings and drank hot rum punch as an antidote to the cold, wet weather. Bibi was up and re-energized when they returned. It was Jenny's turn to feel the jet lag, so she napped while David took Bibi out to explore the neighborhood. That evening they had dinner at a restaurant within walking distance. The food was good, but Jenny encountered what was to be a perpetual problem— smoke. The radiation treatment she underwent for her thyroid cancer had damaged her saliva glands, leaving her with chronic dryness in her mouth and respiratory system. David always went outside to smoke, but other diners lit up at their tables. The ventilation systems were rarely adequate to refresh the air.

They headed immediately to bed when they got back to the apartment. Jet lagged as she was, Jenny was still eager to take David in her arms. He inserted himself between the sheets, gave her a peck on the cheek, said good night, and rolled over. She took about twenty seconds to digest this. Was he exhausted from the logistics of getting the apartment ready and meeting them? Was he being considerate because of her own fatigue? Was all the wine at dinner having a dulling impact? If that was the case, why didn't he say so? Or—gut-wrenching thought—was this all a mistake? Was being in Paris—Sandie's Paris—making it impossible for him to respond to another woman? Was she going to just lie there, silent, tense, and confused? No.

She snuggled close. "Do you know how lovely it is to have you here where I can touch you, instead of at the other end of a computer several thousand miles away?" He acknowledged this opener with a grunt. Undeterred, Jenny moved her hands slowly and gently over his back and his arms. She felt him relax a bit, and finally he turned to face her, so her hands could more easily access the rest of him. She almost laughed with relief when it became clear that he was responding. *Here's to April in Paris*, she thought, but the rational part of her brain registered tension beneath the seemingly smooth surface.

On their first full day, there was rain and more rain. They abandoned any notion of strolling the glorious boulevards of Paris. They abandoned plans to drive out into the countryside. The Loire Valley was soaking wet, the Seine was overflowing its banks, and Normandy was underwater. Given David's enthusiasm for all things Parisian, however, they never ran short of activities. They wandered through galleries, explored museums, and browsed through bookstores. Whenever the rain threatened to drown their spirits, David hustled them into the nearest café for espresso and hot chocolate.

"He's fun!" Bibi exclaimed a few days into the visit. "When you brought him over to Sausalito at New Year's, he seemed like a nice guy but nothing special. Here, I'm beginning to see why you're in love with him. He has such a positive outlook on life! I know from you how much he's grieving inside, but he keeps it pretty much under wraps. He's got all this energy, and he's so passionate about Paris. On top of that, he's such an old-fashioned gentleman! I'm not used to having someone hold the door for me or pour my wine. He lit my cigarette too!" she added with a grin.

"Your cigarette? You brought cigarettes with you? Bibi, shame on you!"

"I didn't bring cigarettes. I just wanted to try one of his French ones, and he very graciously lit if for me. He really has beautiful manners."

"You smoked a Gauloise? They're absolutely gross," said Jenny, wrinkling her nose.

"Yeah, but I felt so very French!" Bibi chuckled.

Ross joined them at the end of their first week, making it a foursome. Bibi and Ross knew of each other but had never met. The personalities were quite different, but the mix worked well. Sometimes they did things as a group. Sometimes they struck off in different directions and in different combinations.

They rode practically every bus in the city, with David pointing out sites of interest at every turn. They lunched at sidewalk cafés and watched as Parisians and tourists alike scurried by, avoiding the puddles and the ubiquitous dog droppings. After a day of sightseeing, David often "relaxed" by whipping up a three- or four-course dinner at the apartment.

The kitchen gave David a place to withdraw when he was down, without being obvious about it. Cooking almost always lifted his spirits. His homemade meals were delicious and appreciated. The informality created a pleasant environment for his Parisian friends and helped Jenny relax as well. In addition to her innate shyness and minimal French, she was nervous about how David's friends would regard her. They were, after all, Sandie's friends too, and her love for David was so obvious she might as well be flashing a neon sign. Meeting people at the apartment allowed her to busy herself slicing bread or clearing the table when she needed to retreat.

Among the first of David's dinner guests were Sandie's cousin Giselle and her husband, Jean-Luc, who had accompanied David and the children when they cast Sandie's ashes into the Atlantic. Jenny sensed that Giselle's opinion of her might be very important to David. She drank a glass of wine before they were due in an attempt to calm her nervousness. When they arrived, Giselle was wearing a gorgeous scarf, vibrant with fantastic birds and flowers in tropical colors. David had told Jenny that Giselle was a fashion designer, so after the initial introductions, Jenny asked if the scarf was one of Giselle's creations. The answer was *"Oui,"* which allowed Jenny to employ the French phrases she had practiced all afternoon, saying how honored she felt to meet the designer in person.

David played translator to keep everyone in the loop. When the last morsel of dessert was gone, David disappeared for a moment and returned with a small package that he handed to Giselle. She opened it to find one of Sandie's Hermes scarves and was suddenly stricken. Jenny's French failed her, so she just gave Giselle a hug, then stood by helplessly as Giselle cried.

They cleaned up the kitchen after Giselle and Jean-Luc departed. Bibi and Ross said good night and retired to their respective rooms. David refilled his brandy snifter and sat down on the couch, lamp low, head back, staring at the ceiling. "Would you like some quiet time?" Jenny asked, "Or may I join you?" He wordlessly patted the seat next to him. Jenny sat and chattered on for a minute. "Giselle is so nice— the evening went well—the wine was a good choice."

David's responses were monosyllabic. Finally she put her head on his shoulder and wrapped her arms around him.

"I'm so sorry," she whispered. "If I could make it right for you, I would."

"I know," he said gently, "but you can't."

The next morning David made Jenny tea and ran her bath. When she emerged, the table was set for breakfast, with thick jam, sweet butter, and fresh bread. No one else was up, so she and David had a pleasantly intimate start to the day. Through the windows, looking out over scores of tiled rooftops, they could see fat pigeons perched on top of the myriad chimneys, oblivious to the rain, enjoying the warm air wafting up beneath them.

David went out on his own to have lunch with an elderly French friend. When the rain turned to mist, Ross, Bibi, and Jenny decided to attempt a walk. They headed up the Boulevard St. Michel. Jenny pointed out David's first apartment where she had spent many a weekend during the year she worked in London. The temperature began to drop so they didn't linger, hurrying back through the Jardin de Luxembourg. When they reached the apartment, they fixed mugs of hot cocoa and settled into the living room.

"What's your assessment thus far?" Bibi asked.

"He had a tough time last night," Jenny told them.

"I could see that," Ross interjected. "What about you?"

"I sort of go up and down when David does," she answered. "There are memories of Sandie everywhere. These reunions with old friends have emotional moments. Still, it seems to me that he is steadier than he was during the Christmas vacation. There has definitely been improvement since December. It manifests itself in little ways: his interest in an exhibition—his enthusiasm for a trip to a bookstore—his appetite for a good meal—his delight in a vintage wine."

But then there was the withdrawal. Jenny wasn't sure what it meant. During their Christmas and New Year's travels, David constantly sought the reassurance of her touch. Now, in April, in the City of Lovers, he needed—wanted—less physical affection, and he gave less. When she took his arm as they walked the rain-slicked sidewalks, there was no gentle squeeze in response. Their interaction at times seemed more like siblings than lovers. Did being in Paris make him wish he were with someone who was more like Sandie— someone more urbane, more cosmopolitan, more French?

Bibi was looking at Jenny expectantly. Ross was watching her as well. Jenny realized her mind had wandered. She tried to remember what she had been saying. "It's confusing," she admitted. "I'm not sure when to worry and when to relax. Over Christmas, we did everything together. He wanted me at his side every minute. Here in Paris, he goes off on his own. If he's regaining his independence, if he's less needy, that's healthy. If he's withdrawing because he's depressed, it's a problem."

"It could be all of the above," Ross suggested. "Grief isn't a rational process, Jenny. It's not a problem you can solve. You've known David all your adult life as a warm, funny, engaging guy full of energy and mischief and enthusiasm. But he's had a body blow the likes of which you've never experienced. I had years to prepare for Ramon's death, but when I actually lost him, I felt as if my insides had been kicked out. Nothing made sense. I had no purpose—no direction. The future was a cold, dark, gaping hole.

"Considering that Sandie died—what, six months ago?—David is being an amazing host. The man wears one hell of an effective camouflage suit. But he has to be hurting, no matter how well he hides it. And it's not something you can change by waving a magic wand, Jenny, no matter how much you want to. Grief is a very lonely ordeal, even when you're surrounded by loving friends. I was grateful for the support and encouragement I got, but often as not, what I wanted most was to go off and lick my wounds in solitude. Just stick close, Jenny, and be there when he needs you. It'll all work out."

Jenny gave Ross a hug. So did Bibi. They were all smiling when David returned.

The weather report for the weekend offered the possibility of a few patches of sun. David suggested a drive to Giverny, the home of Claude Monet. Ross wanted to wander about Paris on his own for a while, but Bibi and Jenny signed on with enthusiasm. Once there, a guide led them through Monet's house. David loved the bright blue kitchen and the shiny yellow dining room. Jenny's decorating choices tended toward naturals and earth tones, but David thrived on strong colors. Fortunately, their different tastes were usually a point of discussion, not dissention.

They walked through the gardens—dense and formally planted, crisscrossed with graveled pathways—then wandered around the edge of Monet's lily pond, enjoying the ancient willow trees and the feeder stream, which was swollen with the rain.

That afternoon, despite cascades of water washing across low-lying roads, they drove to Beauvais to see some of the area's cathedrals. En route, they chanced upon a flea market masquerading as an antique show. David mentioned that he was looking for a sunburst mirror for Sandie's mirror collection, so Jenny was surprised to see him halt by a table laid out solely with china and glassware. He asked the vendor a question, then took out his wallet.

Jenny walked over to see what he was buying. He held up a small ceramic creamer, mustard-colored and plain, and showed her the underside with the name of the town where it was made. "That's the town," David explained, "next to where we scattered Sandie's ashes into the sea." Sandie had maintained a collection of small creamers on the windowsill in the kitchen in Morion. "This will close her collection," David announced.

They made it back to Paris with minimal traffic. Over supper, they filled Ross in on their adventures. It had been a good outing, but David was restless that night. He got up before dawn, and as light filled the sky, Jenny heard him go out on an early-morning run to get fresh bread and croissants for breakfast.

Walking back from the baker's, David discovered that his car, parked overnight on a side street, had been broken into. Sandie's creamer, wrapped in newspaper and tucked into the glove compartment, was gone. There had been nothing else to steal. David spent most of the morning filing a theft report with the police so his insurance would cover the damage to the car door. But it wasn't the door that upset him. It was the loss of the pitcher.

Madame Lamont, a close friend of Sandie's grandmother and a longtime honorary family member, was invited to lunch, along with her son and daughter-in-law, whom Jenny had met briefly when they came to Geneva for Sandie's memorial service. In David's eyes, Madame Lamont was Sandie's family matriarch. Jenny felt as if she were being presented to "Mother" for her approval.

Madame Lamont arrived at the apartment on her son's arm. She was in her eighties but looked ten years younger. Her hair was iron gray, her eyes blue and piercing, and her skin nearly wrinkle-free.

After a splendid meal, which David had spent all morning preparing, Madame Lamont asked to take a short nap while the rest of the company talked. "You can sleep in my room," David told her. Jenny's clothes and toiletries were put away. She thought there would be no indication of double occupancy, but that night she realized she had left a pair of earrings on the bedside table. Jenny had no way of knowing whether Madame Lamont noticed them, but before leaving, Madame Lamont had peered straight into her eyes. "I have heard so often of Jenny," she commented.

The next day, while Bibi and Ross went shopping at the *Marché de Puces*, David and Jenny took a bus to the apartment David and Sandie had shared on the Rue Capron, just off Place Clichy. The apartment now belonged to a timeshare consortium of American friends, including Jack Pogue. David had promised Jack he would stop by briefly to make sure everything was in order. When they walked in, Jenny asked David how it felt to be there. "It doesn't make me sad, if that's what you're asking," he replied. Then, out of the blue, he added, "Sandie actually hated that apartment. Her childhood memories were not happy ones. She was relieved when we sold it."

On their way home, David and Jenny visited the antique shops at the *Louvre des Antiquaires* at Palais Royal. Jenny's grandmother had given her a cameo tea ring set in a heavy gold band for her twenty-first birthday. Jenny lost it years back and hoped she might find something similar to replace it. They wandered in and out of different shops, looking through trays of antique jewelry. David was more than patient. He seemed almost enthusiastic. His interest, however, was not in cameo tea rings.

"Well," Jenny said finally, "I didn't find what I was looking for, but it was fun."

"I didn't find what I was looking for either, but I agree. It was fun," David echoed.

For a minute, she hesitated. Perhaps he was looking for something for her? But he had told her once that he didn't give jewelry as a present because jewelry didn't mean anything to him. "What were you looking for?" she asked.

"I was looking for a sapphire ring," he said simply. Jenny silently considered this. Then, unbidden, David came out with the story. He designed the diamond and sapphire wedding ring he gave to Sandie. Sandie loved the ring, but because of its style, she regarded it as more of an engagement ring. She lobbied for a second ring. In response, David promised that someday he would get her a ring that was all sapphires. Someday never came. Would he now buy a sapphire ring if he found the "right" one? What would he do with it? Jenny asked him about the first ring, the one he designed.

"Did you give it to Dellie? Or are you saving it for Marc's future bride?"

"The ring was burned with Sandie," he replied quietly.

Neither of them spoke the rest of the way back to the apartment. Everything Ross had said about David's level of grief seemed to be right on target, Jenny thought. *He looks for a sunburst mirror. He looks for a creamer. He looks for a sapphire ring. Sometimes I think he's moving forward, then other times, it's as if Sandie died yesterday. He thinks about her all the time. It's not that I want him to think about her less, but I want—what? I want him to be more present with me, even though that may not be possible right now. Is that disloyal? To Sandie? To him? Bibi was right. It's difficult to keep your halo polished when you have feet of clay.*

Toward the end of their Paris stay, the four of them went to the Modern Art Museum to see a pop culture exhibit, then had dinner atop the museum at a restaurant offering a magnificent view of the city. After the main course, David went out on the balcony to have a cigarette. As he returned, Bibi spotted a celebrity—or celebrity lookalike—at the next table. David, still standing, peered in the direction in which Bibi nodded. Jenny gently tugged at his sleeve, suggesting that he be more discreet in his curiosity.

"David," she cautioned in a low voice, "you really shouldn't stare like that. You'll make the man uncomfortable."

"Goddamn it to hell!" he bellowed. People at adjacent tables turned to look at them. "I can't believe how much you and Sandie sound alike! You say the exact same things! All the time! It feels like the two of you are ganging up on me!"

Sandie and Jenny alike, ganging up on him, like a team? Jenny smiled at the thought. "Maybe it's a sign," she teased. "At the very least, it means you should sit down and lower your voice." To be likened to Sandie was always the supreme compliment.

Her delight was short lived, however. When they got back to the apartment, they went immediately to bed. David said good night and rolled over, turning away from her. Her spirits sank. Almost every exchange of physical affection since she arrived had come at her initiation, not his. She reminded herself that David's grief wasn't something she could fix. And there was also the possibility that she was making a mountain out of a molehill. They were no longer teenagers filled with rampaging hormones. David had been playing cook, interpreter, history teacher, and tour guide for nearly two weeks. Maybe the man was simply exhausted.

She let him be, but in the middle of the night, he was still unsettled, tossing and turning. Jenny reminded herself that this time was supposed to be focused on David's needs, not hers. "You're wide-awake," she whispered. "Let me see if I can relax you." She gave him a long, slow back massage. He accepted it, but after twenty minutes he was still alert. She finally changed strategy and shifted from hands to lips, starting at the back of his neck and moving ever-so-softly down his body. She had just reached the small of his back when he turned over, silently inviting her, and at last they made love.

As the second week wound down, David asked about going to Geneva versus remaining in Paris for the final weekend. Jenny had mentioned the Geneva possibility to both Ross and Bibi, but they wanted to stay in Paris straight through to their Monday departure date. Jenny knew David had things to prepare for the spring school term. "I could always hang out here with Ross and Bibi," she offered, "and free up your weekend."

"No way, Good Lookin'," he replied. "You're coming to Geneva."

She suddenly felt foolish about her anxiety. *The day will come when he doesn't need me*, she observed, *but it hasn't arrived yet.*

On Saturday morning, Jenny packed while David fetched the car from the parking garage. Jenny made plans to reconnect with Ross and Bibi on Monday. After a light breakfast, she and David bade them farewell and drove through gently rolling farmland and vineyards before ascending the French Alps and reaching Geneva. There was little conversation en route, except as David pointed out various sites of interest.

The cats met them at the door. Carotte, the family's rotund orange cat, was still uncertain of Jenny, despite her past visit. She took one look, then quickly disappeared. Minuit, sleek, black, and several years Carotte's junior, came over after greeting David and wove about Jenny's legs in search of a gentle scratch behind the ears. Jenny suspected he wasn't particular about who provided it.

The first item of business was inspecting the garden. Despite the drizzle, it was bright and cheery. There were tulips everywhere, and the pansies David and Jenny bought at Thanksgiving created clusters of contrasting color throughout the beds. Sandie's favorite roses had started to unfurl their leaves. Spring had not come to the inside of the house, however. All of Sandie's things were still in place, including the wig on the dresser.

David tackled his backlog of newspapers, bills, and mail. Jenny watered the houseplants. It was very domestic—very tranquil. Marc came home late afternoon with his girlfriend Valerie in tow. He was pleasant and seemed relaxed. It was nice to see him smile after all the dark moods in Chattanooga and San Francisco.

The weather turned sunny on Sunday morning. They did an early market run to replenish the fridge and stock the larder for the week ahead. David stopped at all his favorite stalls, asking Jenny again and again, "Do you like this? Or would you prefer that? And should we get some of these?" He was ready to buy out the market. Jenny had to keep reminding him that she was leaving the next morning.

David had paperwork to deal with in the afternoon, so Jenny sat in the kitchen and wrote postcards. It was a lovely day, but she felt unsettled. She had no idea when she would see David again or where the relationship would be when the next visit took place. *Why am I having such trouble keeping all this straight?* she wondered. *The goal here is to help make him whole again. I'll worry about the future when it comes,* she resolved. She finished the postcards and picked up her book.

At the end of the afternoon, David put away his schoolwork and walked into the kitchen. "Some wine? Let's sit out on the terrace," he suggested. The sun was still out, but it was cool, so Jenny got a wool throw and wrapped it around herself. They sat and drank their wine as the sun lowered. The conversation was idle and interspersed with companionable silences. "We should go in," David suggested when the sun disappeared. "Bring your glass."

"Living room or kitchen?" she asked.

"Kitchen."

They resettled themselves, he near the industrial-strength stovetop ventilator so he could smoke indoors. He lit up a Gauloise and tilted back in his chair. "So," he asked casually, "when are you coming back?"

"That depends on your schedule," she replied. "When do you want me?"

"My schedule doesn't matter," he countered. "Come when you want."

"That doesn't work," she insisted. "You're the host, and I'm the guest. I can't just pop into your life whenever I feel like it. I need an invitation."

"Then I invite you to come whenever you want to." He grinned. This was a man who took a certain pleasure in being difficult.

"No, come on. Be helpful. When do you want me to come back? Give me some dates that work for you."

"Well," he said, "let's see. Tomorrow's Monday," he observed. "You're leaving in the morning. How about Tuesday, day after tomorrow?"

Had she heard him correctly? "What are you saying?" she asked.

"I'm saying come back on Tuesday—and stay as long as you want."

Surely he was teasing. "David, you're not understanding the situation. If I came when I wanted to, and stayed as long as I wanted, I might be here all the time."

"So," he shrugged, "be here all the time."

Jenny felt a shiver go through her. "Are you inviting me to come live with you?"

"Yes."

"Do you really mean that?"

"What do you think?"

Did she look as dumbfounded as she felt? The words spilled out of her heart. "I've loved you forever, David Perry."

"Will you come?"

There was no point playing games. There was no point pretending that this was an idea that had never occurred to her.

"Yes," she told him. "Yes, yes, yes."

Neither of them moved. Jenny's heart was racing. Was this real?

"When should I come?" she asked.

"As soon as you feel comfortable. There's a plane every day."

Her mind was suddenly flooded with practical details. She started blurting out issues that would have to be addressed. David just smiled and repeated. "Come when you're ready. There's a plane every day."

The next morning, David drove Jenny to the train station. He walked her to the checkpoint and told her how to auto-punch her ticket, how to identify the right train car, and where to stow her luggage so she wouldn't have to lift her heavy bag into the overhead rack. He was sweet and protective, giving her a long good-bye hug.

"I love you," she said.

"There's a plane every day," he replied.

"I love you," she repeated.

"Thank you," he whispered.

It was an easy train ride, with comfortable seats and pleasant scenery, but Jenny wasn't paying attention to the countryside. She was totally preoccupied sorting out the implications of David's proposal that she come live with him. "Yes! Yes! Yes!" she had said, but her brain was engaging the issue at a far more cautious pace than her heart. Unsettling questions started to pop up. David needed her presence, but would there be a backlash? How would Marc and Delphine react? Would Sandie really have approved? Getting David through the worst of his grief was one thing. Moving in with him was another. And what would the neighbors think? At this last worry, Jenny had to chuckle. *Good Lord*, she thought. *I sound like my mother!*

She replayed their good-bye at the station several times. David had always used humor or understatement to mask deep feelings. Knowing this about him, Jenny forgave his inability to say, "I love you," out loud as she boarded the train. It was as if he spoke in code, and Jenny was one of the privileged few who could interpret the cipher.

Much of the trip was spent confronting the enormous upheaval that a move to Geneva would engender. It was clearly going to take months, not weeks, to settle everything out. When Jenny arrived at the Gare de Lyon, Bibi and Ross met her on the platform. They walked upstairs to Le Train Bleu to see if the restaurant could take them for lunch without a reservation.

"So," Bibi asked as the hostess consulted her seating chart, "how was Geneva?"

"Chilly, but at least we had some sunshine," Jenny answered.

"You think I'm asking for a weather report?" said Bibi, cocking her head and scrutinizing Jenny's face.

"Let's wait until we're seated," Jenny replied.

The hostess led them to a table and handed them menus. Bibi looked at Jenny expectantly. "We should decide on our orders first," Jenny suggested.

Bibi had confidence in whatever restaurants offered as their *plat du jour*. Her decision was swift. Ross enjoyed reading menus from cover to cover but allowed that he could read and listen at the same time. Jenny knew she couldn't leave Paris without having a plate of snails drenched in garlic butter. She had no excuse to delay her report.

"Okay. Geneva." She tuned her voice to its calmest level. "David finds it really helpful to have me around. He asked me to consider coming to Geneva for an extended stay."

Ross looked at Jenny over his reading glasses, raising his eyebrows in the process.

"How extended?" Bibi demanded.

"Well, his exact words were, 'Stay as long as you want.'"

"Like, a month? A year?" she pressed.

"It was pretty open-ended," Jenny replied. "Actually," she corrected, "he in essence asked me to move in with him."

"Move in with him?" Bibi exclaimed. "Permanently? As in marriage?"

"We didn't talk about marriage. He's not enthusiastic about the institution. He just suggested that I stay in Geneva all the time."

"And give up Boston?" Ross queried, his tone cautious and lawyerly.

Jenny hesitated. "I'm going to have to juggle on that one."

"What did you tell him?" Ross continued.

"I said yes," Jenny replied.

"I'm hearing a 'but,'" Ross countered.

"No, no buts. More like a reality check. I'm a planner. I'm a detail person. I don't overdrive my headlights. I like to see what's coming. With David, there's no way to bring the long-range picture into focus. His situation is too volatile. The immediate is clear: he needs me. He loves me, too, but not with the same passion and commitment I feel for him. Will he get there? Maybe, but it won't be anytime soon. Sandie is still front and center.

"One of the qualities I admire in David is his loyalty. He holds on to the people he cares about. Most of his old friends are still in his life and still important. He's not going to let go of Sandie just because she's dead. Did I tell you that all her things are still in place? Toothbrush, bedside reading, wig—the works. This is going to be a *ménage-à-trois* for the foreseeable future."

"And you're okay with that?" Bibi asked, frowning.

"It's not my first choice, but isn't there some rule about the course of true love never running smooth?"

The waiter appeared with their orders. Their subsequent conversation ranged from commentary about the cuisine to a philosophical discussion of the complex and sometimes baffling nature of love.

From the restaurant, they took a cab to Charles deGaulle and boarded the plane for Boston. Ross had booked his flight separately and was assigned a seat four rows away, but their fellow passenger kindly exchanged places with him, allowing the trio to sit together.

They talked about the implications of an "extended stay" in Geneva. Any past fantasies Jenny had entertained about sharing her life with David were just that—fantasies, devoid of details such as what to do with her house or her car, her clients or her cat, her healthcare or her retirement plan. Most of Bibi and Ross's questions zeroed in on precisely those details, and Jenny had no easy answers.

"You've also got to think about what you'll do once you're there," Bibi interjected. "You didn't much like living in London way back when, but at least the Brits speak English. Now you're looking at life in a French-speaking city. Obviously, David is fluent, but how are you going to manage? Plus, he'll be teaching all day. You don't like exploring cities by yourself. What are you going to do while he's at work? You're not the type to be happy sitting home and crocheting doilies."

Bibi was clearly concerned that Jenny's decision was precipitous. "I'm not saying it's bad or wrong, but for an otherwise practical person, you're putting a lot of faith in romance."

"I don't think it's a question of faith in romance," Jenny replied. "You're right that I wasn't enamored of my year in Europe. Much

IF YOU NEEDED ME

as I loved David, I was sufficiently homesick that I couldn't hang on indefinitely, waiting for him to make a commitment. And now, looking at Geneva, well, yes, I have some serious doubts about how independent I can be. But if I don't try, I'll never know. And I can't fail this man just because the leap is a scary one. He needs me. He really needs me. As long as that's the case, I'll figure out a way to take care of him. It's not romance, Bibi. It's love."

They arrived in Boston to a sunny afternoon. Ross took the subway home. Bibi and Jenny cabbed down to Shawmut. It was only 5:45 p.m. when they arrived at her condo, but that was close to midnight Paris time. They went to bed almost immediately, and Jenny ran Bibi up to the airport in the morning for her flight to California.

Jenny was back on familiar ground. Her daffodils were blooming. On the surface, nothing had changed. But her world had been turned upside down.

From: JWLongworth
To: DavidP
Date: April 24, 2001
Subject: Safe Landings

Hullo, Luv. We arrived safe and sound yesterday. I just took Bibi up to Logan. I slept straight through the night, so I am rested physically, but my mind is whirring away. Bibi, Ross, and I talked about my move on the plane. They share my sense that Marc and Dellie's feelings could be critical to the success of this endeavor. The children seem comfortable with our current relationship, but merging our lives will lead to a different dynamic.

My arrival will hasten the day when decisions must be made about Sandie's clothes and her personal items. My presence will have an impact on household routines. I'm hoping you can give Marc and Dellie a preview of likely areas of stress so we can talk before any real conflict arises.

On the legal front, I did some quick research. At first glance, there isn't much wiggle room. I know you're not enamored by the concept of marriage, but Swiss immigration isn't likely to issue me a residency permit on the strength of my being your once and future girlfriend, and I don't relish honoring the three-months-here, three-months-there limitations of a tourist visa.

I don't see making the official move before late September, but I could schedule a short visit midsummer. This would give us an opportunity to talk together with the children and also find out what's involved in a Swiss marriage license.

Love, J.

De: David
A: Jenny
Envoyé: 24 avril, 2001
Objet: Re: Safe Landings

Goddamn, that's a shopping list! I too want to sit down with the kids, but that means waiting until Delphine's return in mid-June. I disappear at the end of June for a two-week seminar in Deutschland. That gives me a window of thirteen days—similar to the Cuban missile crisis. Decisions, decisions. Sigh. Back to the drawing board while I try to answer your four hundred questions.

Kisses, David

Jenny was fully conscious of the importance of laying groundwork. Her move to Geneva could only work if she and David gradually created an environment that honored Sandie and respected the past, but that also evolved to reflect what she and David needed to function, comfortably and equitably, in the new life they built together.

From: JWLongworth
To: DavidP
Date: April 26, 2001
Subject: 400 Questions

Dearheart—Did I really ask four hundred questions? Lord knows there are at least that many swirling around in my head. When I'm in Geneva with you, nothing else exists. Back here, suddenly there are all these *issues* to deal with. I'm looking at bridges to be burned and feeling a little nervous about it.

I know that I am absolutely perfect for you, and you're incredibly lucky that I'm willing to come file your bills and put up with your bad habits. But once I'm installed, you will have to start dealing with *my* bad habits. You may begin to regret the invitation.

Love, me

De: David
A: Jenny
Envoyé: 26 avril, 2001
Objet: Your queries

Jewel, no matter how hard we try to anticipate the problems, all sorts of shit is going to hit the fan. At times we'll be aware enough to wipe it off gently, and other times we'll cry or yell or god only knows what. That's the way I've always lived, and I don't know how to do it otherwise.

Make sure you're on the right side of the bridge before you set it on fire. Don't do it with the cat in your arms. You're absolutely right about filing my bills, but I'm shocked to learn that your mother permitted you to have bad habits.

I have to decide whether to speak to Marc now or wait for Delphine's return and talk to them both at once. If you want to get married because it's important to you, I accept willingly. If it's for other people's perceptions, I really don't give a fart in a high wind what they think.

Loving you with the part of my heart that doesn't hurt and wishing with all my heart that you were here to share a glass of wine, David

From: JWLongworth
To: DavidP
Date: April 26, 2001
Subject: Re: Your queries

Thanks, Luv. Your note was reassuring. I feel I'm standing on solid ground. I also feel schizophrenic. I spent the morning picking out fixtures for the bathroom renovations I'm doing this summer. I considered

canceling the work, then decided to keep going. The bathrooms need redoing whether I sell, rent, or keep the condo for our visits to the States. But it's sort of a weird situation to be in.
    Love, J.

Jenny made a list of everything that needed doing before she moved to Geneva. Organizing was one of her fortes, but as she rearranged the list in a chronological sequence, a little voice inside kept cautioning her to slow the process down. The practical obstacles loomed larger and larger. She needed objective input from someone she could count on for balanced yet candid feedback. That meant Ross. She asked him to come down to Shawmut after work on Friday. He picked up a deep-dish pizza en route, and Jenny opened a bottle of wine.

"I've got to look at some practical issues, Ross, starting with money. My accounting credentials have no validity in Switzerland, and my French is *de minimus*, which makes it unlikely I'll be able to get a job over there. I've got to generate some income, if only to make up for the loss of Sandie's salary. If I stop reinvesting the dividends from my retirement fund and use them as operating capital, that will get me part of the way, but I may need to rent out my condo as well. Question is, can I word the lease so I could regain occupancy on short notice if necessary?

"And then there's the firm. Do I go for a severance package, which would give me a cushion, or should I try for an open unpaid sabbatical so I could have my job back if circumstances required it?"

Ross held up his hand. "Stop," he commanded. "You should listen to yourself, Jewel. You say you want to be with David, but it almost sounds as if you're calculating escape routes. Moving to Geneva is a huge step. It's going to require an absolute and unwavering commitment to make it work. What's happening? Are you changing your mind now that you're back home?"

"No, I'm not changing my mind. As long as he needs me, I'm his. But I can't completely ignore the past. The day may come when it's time for me to come home to Boston. It happened thirty years ago even though we genuinely loved each other. It could happen again."

"Do you think that's likely?" Ross asked.

"Likely or not, would you ever allow one of your clients to enter into a contract that had no dissolution clause?"

"No, but we lawyers earn our living by anticipating worst-case scenarios. I repeat my question. Do you think it's likely?"

"There's a lot of history, Ross. If Ramon were here, he could tell you stories. David and I were on-again, off-again several times when we were young. David was adventurous and didn't want to be tied down. He never toyed with me or led me on. He's not that kind of person. And he's not toying with me now. I expect that he can't imagine letting go of me. But someday, down the road, he'll find his feet again. He'll come close to being his old self. And his old self wanted a woman who was French. I couldn't become younger for Seth. I can't become French for David. I love him, but I won't hold him prisoner."

"Don't sell yourself short, Jewel. You've got a lot going for you. I wonder if you're not still processing some of the hurt from Seth's betrayal and instinctively setting up a line of defense. And don't sell David short, either. He seems like a really good person. You talk as if he blew hot and cold about you all those years ago, but I remember Ramon commenting that despite the different women David dated, he always came back to you. It's all boils down to how you look at it."

Jenny had to smile. Ross had a way of making everything seem possible. Small wonder Ramon had loved him so.

De: David
A: Jenny
Envoyé: 6 mai, 2001
Objet: Sunday
Stopped raining long enough for me to do a bit of summary weeding. Used the lawn mower and cut 'em off at ground level so I don't have to look at them. Marc has

gone to see a friend whose dad just died of cancer after a long struggle, and so the series continues.

How's the travel schedule shaping up? The garden needs you.

Big kiss, David

David's reference to another cancer death was off-hand, but Jenny understood it as a sign that he could use some cheering up.

From: JWLongworth
To: DavidP
Date: May 8, 2001
Subject: Tuesday

I'm thinking of a quick trip at the end of July. I could stay for ten days—maybe two weeks. The permanent shift should wait until late September. I don't want to move in until we've passed the anniversary of Sandie's death. You may think that a year is an arbitrary marker, but I expect Sandie would appreciate it.

In any event, it's going to take a while to extricate myself from work. Given my history of chronic overtime, we'll need two people to replace me. We've got to run ads and do interviews. I've also decided I should hold on to my condo. Your garden in Geneva may prove too small for the both of us.

Love, Jenny

Jenny saw no point in saying that holding on to her condo also gave her a safety net—a place to come home to if Geneva didn't work out.

De: David
A: Jenny
Envoyé: 9 mai, 2001
Objet: Re: Tuesday

Honeybuttons, you come when you goddamn well decide to come. You're welcome to have the garden all to yourself as long as you keep flowers blooming from February to December. It's not gardening I like so

much as looking at the flowers. I wish they just grew automatically. It's warm and sunny today—nice to sit outside and daydream (my way of gardening).
Kisses, David

Jenny called Rachel Aronson and arranged to meet her for dinner after work. Rachel's grief was nearly as fresh as David's, and Jenny valued her tutelage enormously. "I hope this isn't going to shock you," she told Rachel they settled at their table, "but David has asked me to come live with him in Geneva."

Rachel looked at her wide-eyed. "And your answer?" she managed.

"I said yes," Jenny replied.

"Maybe we should order a whole bottle of wine instead of just two glasses," Rachel said. She confirmed Jenny's preference for red, requested a bottle of William Hill Merlot, then spread her hands. "From the beginning," she requested.

Jenny condensed the story but gave her the highlights. At the end, Rachel nodded. "Grief hits people in different ways. Most people don't speak of it, but the question of survival is a key element. You have to decide whether or not you're going to go on. I've seen people who just gave up—withered away in loneliness or anger or depression. But choosing to survive is no picnic. You have to find a reason to keep going forward through the pain. It looks as if you are David's reason," Rachel concluded.

"I certainly hope I'm part of the reason, but the children are surely a major factor. And then there's David himself. He's always had such a zest for life, such a deep appreciation of art, music, and literature, and such a love of travel and exploration! If there is anything positive or motivational to be found in loss and grief, he'll find it. He's pretty amazing."

Rachel studied Jenny's face. "Are you at all concerned that it might be too soon to take this on? For both of you? And for the children?"

"The children, I don't know about. There's been some ambivalence, but that's to be expected. We've all been comfortable in the past. I've was kind of an Auntie Mame to the kids when they were younger. They're aware that David and I are intimate, and he's told them he's convinced that Sandie would approve of our revived relationship."

"Do you think that's the case?" she probed gently.

"It may be a matter of wishful thinking, but we wouldn't be where we are if David thought Sandie would disapprove. I never had a chance to talk with Sandie about her wishes for him, but had it been me—had I died and left behind a husband I loved—I'd want him to find happiness again."

"This soon?" The question was posed quietly.

"Touché. I realize a lot of people will have trouble with the timing. But I want David back on solid ground as quickly as possible. One of the ways he's coping with the pain is alcohol. I can't sit here and worry about propriety when I could be over there making a real difference."

"Will it be enough for you? Even if the most wonderful man in the world walked into my life tomorrow, it would be a very long time before I could give him the emotional commitment I gave to Josh—if ever. With David, you're the one who's likely to be doing most of the giving."

"The relationship isn't in perfect balance by any means, but still, it works. Granted, he's needy, but he's also hugely grateful. And he gives me more than is obvious on the surface. I feel safe with David. He has an instinctive awareness of my latent agoraphobia. He's chivalrous and protective, but it's never overbearing. He fills so many blank spaces. Where I'm shy, he's outgoing and engaging. Where I get bogged down in details, he's a big-picture person. Our personalities are radically different, so our strengths and weaknesses really complement one another. We have a special bond that comes from sharing formative experiences in college, from coming-of-age rites to the assassination of our youthful heroes. We can talk about anything, and we enjoy being silent together."

Rachel smiled. "You really do love him, don't you?" she observed.

"I really do," Jenny answered.

"My hat's off to you," Rachel said, shaking her head. "It's a real high dive!"

From: JWLongworth
To: DavidP
Date: May 17, 2001
Subject: Dinner with Rachel Aronson

I had a good dinner with Rachel Aronson. She seems to be doing well. The pleasant moments are more frequent, she reported, although Josh's "yahrzeit" is coming up. She deals with the pain differently now, but when it hurts, it hurts as much as it did in the beginning.

"It goes so slowly," she said, "this process. On the surface, I'm much calmer, but the truth is, I'm still never very far from tears, and it doesn't take much to bring them forward." She values our periodic dinners, she told me, because she feels totally free to talk about Josh— something she hesitates to do with various other friends. "It really helps," she said. "I love to talk about him; it makes him feel close."

She wanted to know how things were going with you. She sends you best wishes and looks forward to meeting you someday soon.

Much love, J.

De: David
A: Jenny
Envoyé: 18 mai, 2001
Objet: Re: Dinner with Rachel Aronson

My kisses to Rachel. What she tells you about the process *is* the process, although I have no qualms about talking to anyone about Sandie. Often makes me cry, always makes me feel close to her, frequently reminds me of what a wussy I am. Broke down the other day in seventh-grade English. The grounds manager brought me the first rose from Sandie's memorial garden at school—silken, lemon-yellow chiffon. I asked the kids to write a poem. Tears stream just mentioning it. That's where I am, one day at a time.

Love, David

Based on Rachel's input, Jenny decided it was better to emphasize her awareness of Sandie rather than minimize it.

> *From: J W Longworth*
> *To: DavidP*
> *Date: May 24, 2001*
> *Subject: Signs*
>
> David, there is some truly mystical chemistry between me, thee, and thy first wife. I took advantage of a suddenly clearing sky this morning to hit the local nurseries. At the last nursery I visited, I noticed a large ceramic planter with a rose that was so perfect it didn't seem real. *Wow,* I thought, *That is one spectacular rose! Too bad this isn't Switzerland, or I would get it for David in memory of Sandie.*
>
> It was a luscious, soft, blushing peach. They don't normally have roses there. I wondered if it was even for sale. It might have been just to market the planter. I carefully lifted up the pot in search of a price. The price sticker was on the flip side of the planting/care directions. So was the name of the rose: Abbaye de Cluny, Romantica. It was developed in Provence.
>
> I thought of how much we enjoyed the Cluny Museum in Paris, of our trip to Provence in November, of Sandie's beloved roses, and of the romance that binds our three lives together. The rose is now sitting on my patio, waiting to be planted. It is nothing short of fabulous.
>
> Love, Jewel

For the next two weeks, David said nothing to either of his children about inviting Jenny to move to Geneva. He was waiting for Delphine's return from Asia so he could announce the news to both of them, in person, at the same time.

De: David
A: Jenny
Envoyé: 12 juin, 2001
Objet: The return, the weekend, the conversation

Delphine is back, safe and sound. I'm thankful and happy. We sat around listening to her stories until one in the morning. She had a marvelous trip.

Things here are a bit more discombobulated than normal. Marc has moved in with Valerie. Delphine has been slapping order into her home life and dealing with jetlag. I've been doing end-of-school-year things, so nobody's been around at the same time or in the right state to have "The Conversation."

Kisses, David

PS—I need a lesson in how this education trust thing works. Delphine wants to sign up for a business school in Paris for the fall.

From: JW Longworth
To: DavidP
Date: June 12, 2001
Subject: Education Trust

Re the trust, I'll fill you in when I come. It's not difficult.

Meanwhile, it sounds as if your household is in a state of pleasant chaos. I'm sure "The Conversation" will happen in its own good time.

Love, J.

De: David
A: Jenny
cc: Marc, Delphine
Envoyé: 17 juin, 2001
Objet: Conversation

Conversation done. They are happy for us, but they were surprised and somewhat befuddled. They expressed the same concerns we have. Delphine is worried about my not being on this side of the Atlantic since Europe is where she now wants to go to college. I told her I had no intention of moving. I told them we would get married, probably near the end of September, in order to associate Sandie as intimately as possible with the ceremony. I told them I could easily imagine Sandie watching over the scene, laughing at our social anxiety while she blesses the whole undertaking.

I feel calm, happy the news is out. One more Rubicon crossed. To you.

Love, David

The die was cast. Jenny called Bibi. "David told his children that he wants to marry me," she announced, without preamble.

"When was this?"

"Today. Or maybe it was yesterday. The time difference is always confusing."

"You already knew, presumably."

"That he was going to tell them?"

"No, that he wanted to marry you."

"I don't think 'want' is the right verb. He doesn't consider the institution of marriage to be meaningful. I agree with him that love doesn't need a title to make it work, but the kids and I will have to deal with people whose perceptions and opinions are influenced by such definitions. 'Dad's live-in girlfriend' doesn't bespeak permanence. For people who aren't sure how we relate—and are therefore unsure how to relate to us—giving them a generally understood definition really helps. Psychology aside, I can't hang out in Switzerland without some legal standing. Girlfriend doesn't cut it with the immigration authorities, so David accepts that we have to get married." Jenny paused. "I'm making this sound like a shotgun wedding, aren't I?"

"Why are you not more excited? Is there some kind of Boston etiquette that says you can't shriek and holler when the love of your life proposes marriage?"

Jenny had to laugh. "Those Puritan genes can put a damper on anything, but I think it's more a fear of jinxing things if I start sounding too confident. Don't count your chickens, and all that."

"Too confident about what?" she queried.

"It's hard to explain. I had dinner with my friend Rachel recently, and she expressed concern that we might be moving too fast. I understand her perspective. I myself worry about the timing, but I want David so much that altruism is out the window. If I wait until he's no longer grieving, someone else could snap him up. I know I blow hot and cold on this, but my selfishness could be setting us up for a rough ride."

"Maybe you should stop with the hot and cold and trust the signs."

"The signs? What signs?"

"The ones you've been talking about for the past six months. The memorial rose that stayed fresh the whole time you were in Chattanooga. That time in the restaurant in Paris when David swore a blue streak because you sounded just like Sandie. The little creamer David bought at the antiques fair when we went to see Monet's house. The rosebush you found in Boston—the Cluny Romantica or whatever it was—that connected a bunch of unconnected pieces."

"Bibi, I don't believe in signs. Talking about signs always makes a good story, but I don't really believe in them. Looking for a sign is shorthand for saying I'm looking for resolution of an emotional dilemma. My happiness with David is predicated on Sandie's death. David believes Sandie would bless our union. I like to think she would, but I'll never know for sure. When I stand in front of Sandie's portrait and ask her for a sign, the truth is I'm just searching for peace inside myself."

"Does David know you're still feeling uneasy about this?"

"He senses it, but he thinks I'm nervous about having to learn French. Anyway, it doesn't matter. I keep saying I would die for this man. If I really mean that, I have to be willing to live for him as well, even though there might be some pain involved."

Bibi gave a little snort. "So how can you lose? Isn't pain supposed to be good for Puritans?"

"We'll see," Jenny said, laughing.

When her conversation with Bibi was finished, Jenny called her siblings and filled them in. Then she composed an e-mail to Marc and Delphine.

> *From: JWLongworth*
> *To: Marc, Delphine*
> *cc: DavidP*
> *Date: June 17, 2001*
> *Subject: The future*
>
> Dear Marc and Dellie—I don't think I have to reassure you about how deeply I love your father. And I hope I don't have to reassure you about how much I respect and honor Sandie's memory. She will always be a strong and welcome presence in the life I build with David.
>
> I've always felt close to you both, but motherhood (step- or otherwise) is not something I have any experience with. I want to be there for you, but I don't know how to act as a mother—only as an older friend. I'm planning to stick with what I know, be just that, and hope it's okay with you. Since you're already young adults and had a terrific mother to get you this far, I'm confident it will work out.
>
> There are going to be some practical issues to deal with. I'll do my best to tread softly, but I'm bound to disrupt some things, mix up the laundry, move some furniture, and gradually alter the rhythms of daily life. If I do something that concerns or upsets you, I trust you to tell me.
>
> I wish I could be there right now to give you both a big hug.
>
> Much love, Jenny

There was no response from either Marc or Delphine, but Jenny didn't expect one. If there were questions, they could be addressed when she arrived in Geneva.

The weeks flew by. Although the weight of grief remained, David's communications showed no signs of distress. When he returned from his July seminar in Berlin, he was eager for Jenny's arrival.

De: David
A: Jenny
Envoyé: 17 juillet, 2001
Objet: Berlin

Hiya, kid. Just got back.

Our travel plans are shaping up. Once you're here, we'll drive up to the Valais (Switzerland's central valley) to spend a couple of days in the high Alps with Michel, Josette, and some colleagues who have a chalet in the mountains. Then we'll go to Sion to spend the Swiss national holiday with some other colleagues. Watch the traditional bonfire and drink white wine. Then back to Geneva for a day or two before going to central France to play golf, once again with Michel and Josette. Give you your first lesson.

Afterward, we can come straight back to Geneva, or we can go spend a day or two with friends in Provence. Tell me what you'd rather do. After all, the garden here does need care.

Love, David

From: J W Longworth
To: DavidP
Date: July 17, 2001
Subject: Tuesday

I trust you completely as tour guide, but gardening in Geneva would also be pleasant. I leave it to your inclination and your take on the weather. Whither thou goest ...

I have my ticket. I'm arriving the twenty-eighth, at 9:30 a.m. I will be tired and stiff, but if Snow White and Sleeping Beauty had it right, I can be revived with a kiss.

Much love, J.

You're with me still

You're with me still in Paris
    on the wicker seats
    in the rain on St. Germain,
    at the bus stop for the 95,
    window-shopping, crossing the courtyard,
    coming out in the Place des Vosges,
    sipping wine at 5 and watching people
    walking on their way somewhere.

You're with me still at the light
    waiting to cross or cutting between cars
    stalled to a crawl, at the bakery
    choosing which bread to buy,
    weighing madeleines for 3,
    watching the women's hair bob and blow
    in the west wind off the ocean
    while we stroll across the Pont des Arts.

You are here, there, behind,
    in front, next to,
    beside, just outside
    and forever inside me.
    Your presence warms me,
    inspires me in Paris.

Chapter 8

David met Jenny as she came out of customs. In the past, greeting each other after long absences had always been a joyous occasion. This encounter, however, was different. They embraced, yet it felt stilted—almost formal. This visit might decide their future, and they were both aware of that. They drove in near silence across the bridge, through the left bank of the city, and out to Morion.

David took Jenny's suitcases into the house while she poked her head around back to see how the garden was doing. Marc was elsewhere. Delphine was just getting up. Jenny asked her directly for permission to clear some space in Sandie's closets for her clothes. Delphine was sweet about it.

"No problem," she said. "You've got to make room for them somewhere," she added practically.

They had a light lunch, which doubled as Delphine's breakfast. When they finished, David turned to Jenny and said, "Let's take a walk." Delphine's mouth dropped open in amazement. David didn't like to take walks, unless you counted golf. He led Jenny across the street, onto the path that wound through the nearby woods and fields. There he hugged her with the intensity that was missing at the airport. They walked with arms about each other, retracing the steps of the journey they made after Olga's luncheon on that fateful October day some ten months earlier.

"Glad you came, Ducks. Wasn't sure you would."

Jenny looked at him in surprise. "What, you thought I'd stand you up?"

"I'm not much of a prize at this point. Gotta lotta shit in the minus column."

David was in folksy mode. It was the easiest way for him to talk about feelings when face-to-face with someone. As they followed the trail that meandered alongside the stream, Jenny realized that David harbored worries similar to hers. He knew that grief had rendered him surly, withdrawn, and depressed. He feared Jenny's desire to be with him would fade in the harsh light of the compromises she had to make and the things she had to give up.

"I'm hardly an angel myself," she said lightly. "I have lots of positives, but there's usually a negative to balance each one out."

"Uh-oh. You're telling me you have faults? You'd better come clean now, Ducks, before it's too late."

"Well, I appreciate a clean, well-ordered house, but I don't like housework, and I've never learned how to iron."

"I'm not very good at ironing either," David admitted. He had old-fashioned manners but was completely flexible with gender roles, which Jenny very much appreciated.

"I love your cooking," she continued, "but I can't handle spicy foods, and I dislike anything that hints of coffee or licorice—like fennel! I love the country, but I'm not much of a city person. Touring churches and museums holds a very limited appeal. I love traveling with you, but I don't know how to drive a stick shift, I have a small bladder, and I prefer to avoid gas station restrooms."

"Just like Sandie," he commented. "She always wanted to get back to her own bathroom."

"All women prefer their own bathroom to public facilities," Jenny commented. "I'm pleased to think that Sandie and I share certain traits, but you need to be prepared for the reality that the differences outweigh the similarities. Comparing Parisians and Bostonians is like comparing apples and oranges."

"I accept that you're a proper Bostonian. But is that a plus or a minus?" he teased.

They gently reassured one another of their commitment throughout their walk. When they got back to the house, Jenny began the painful process of going through Sandie's drawers and closets, packing clothes in boxes and bags to be stored until Delphine felt ready to look through them.

"I'll be downstairs if you have any questions," David offered.

"I would feel easier about this if you or Dellie or even Marc were willing to participate," Jenny had told him.

"The kids can't deal with it yet. They accept that things need to be moved, but they can't do it themselves. They'll go through everything at some point, but I don't know when that will be. Meanwhile, we'll just store everything until they're ready."

"Are you sure you don't want to at least oversee the process?"

"I can't, Love." His voice broke, and he turned away. "I just can't."

Sandie's things were exactly as Jenny remembered them from her visit in April. The bedside table still housed Sandie's medicines, the book she had been reading, and the last of the get-well cards she had received. Her dresser top was covered with perfume bottles, costume jewelry, and her wig stand. In the bathroom, her robe and nightgown still hung on a hook behind the door. All the surfaces were taken up with her cosmetics and toiletries. Her toothbrush still sat in a glass by the sink.

Jenny had done a lot of moving in her day. She could be ruthlessly efficient in cleaning things out and packing things up. It took her several minutes, however, before she could start. She was alone, but she felt Sandie's presence so strongly that Sandie might as well have been perched on the bed, watching with interest to see how Jenny would proceed. And in that felt presence lay Jenny's answer. She deferred to Sandie in death as she had in life. She would perform the removal according to Sandie's standards.

Sandie was one of the tidiest and most organized women Jenny had ever known, and with that in mind, she began. She handled her clothes with careful respect, honoring the order in which Sandie kept things—summer blouses together, winter slacks together, dressy sweaters in one bag, everyday sweaters in another. Some outfits Jenny could remember her wearing.

After five or six bags, Jenny's composure began to slip. She felt tears welling up. Part of it was the image of Sandie in this jacket—that skirt—smiling and pretty and alive. Part of it was her continuing concern about Delphine and her feelings. Delphine had seemed genuinely okay with Jenny tackling the closets, yet it was clear that neither Delphine nor David could bear to move anything from where Sandie had left it. Jenny felt some of their reluctance as she looked at the bare hangers and empty shelves left in her wake. When David came up to check on her, he found her sitting on the floor wiping her eyes.

"This is a lot harder than I thought it was going to be," she confessed. "I'm going to remove that wig and stand," she said, "but after that, I need to stop for the day."

"You can leave it there for now," David suggested, "and when school starts again, I'll see if the drama department would like it."

"Giving it to the student theatre is a good idea," Jenny replied, "but I'd like to store it somewhere else in the meantime. If Sandie had recovered, she would have gotten rid of that wig immediately. She hated losing her hair. There is nothing positive associated with the wig—no happy memories attached. It's a symbol of illness." She hesitated. "And to be honest, it makes me really uncomfortable," she finally admitted.

David scooped up the stand and its hairpiece. "I'll take care of it," he said, marching it upstairs to the atelier.

Not long afterward, David and Jenny relaxed barefoot on the front porch with glasses of iced tea. One look at David's feet told Jenny he hadn't clipped his toenails in months. She scolded him forthwith and asked where the nail clippers were. He laughed and scoffed and seemed delighted that he had shocked her Bostonian sensibilities. "I like my toenails just the way they are, thank you very much, and I have no intention of cutting them," he announced with a grin.

Jenny decided to fight that battle another day, so she searched out the photographs she had brought and gave them to him. They included two shots of the Abbaye de Cluny rose, planted near the patio in Shawmut, but most of the pictures were views of the new garden along the woods' edge. David had forgotten that Jenny had dedicated the garden to Sandie. He was caught up short by the final print, which featured a flat rock engraved "Sandie's Garden." She could see him struggle for control, covering his emotion by going back through the photos again, very slowly.

That night, as Jenny climbed under the covers, Carotte jumped up on the bed. She twitched her tail, gave Jenny a wary look, then circled her chosen territory twice and curled into a ball. After months of considering Jenny an alien, Carotte finally deemed it acceptable for her to share David's bed. *That's one down*, Jenny thought.

On Sunday morning, her internal clock was still on Boston time, but Jenny got up with David at seven so she could join him for the weekly trip to the farmers' market. When they got home, she returned to the task of emptying Sandie's closets and dresser. She couldn't help but note how different she and Sandie were in their dressing habits. Jenny possessed, at most, five belts. Sandie had two boxes full—thin belts, thick belts, all colors and styles. Jenny had three pocketbooks—white for summer, black for winter, and beige for spring and fall. Sandie had well over a dozen, plus several evening bags. Jenny knew how frugal Sandie was. This impressive inventory was clearly the result of some serious bargain shopping.

Jenny did all right until she got to the T-shirts. Sandie loved T-shirts with souvenir logos and cartoon figures. On top of the stack, there was an oversized one with a Tweety Bird logo, which Sandie had used as a nightgown. It was almost identical to the Big Bird T-shirt Delphine bought in Boston and gave Sandie just before she died—the T-shirt that ultimately became Sandie's shroud. Jenny was suddenly transported back to the cremation service, sitting helplessly by David's side as he wept. She picked up the Tweety Bird shirt and hugged it, tears running down her face. Delphine walked in in the middle of this, and seeing Jenny's distress, asked if she was okay. Jenny pointed to the shirt, took a deep breath, and said, "It reminds me of your Big Bird shirt."

Delphine understood exactly where Jenny's mind had gone. "Yeah," she said, with quiet calm. "Mom always liked T-shirts like that."

Once again Jenny had to stop. She took the bags she had filled down to Sandie's study. Over a leftovers lunch of cold spinach quiche, she mentioned to David how much it had meant for her to receive one of Sandie's scarves. "And I'm not the only one who was touched," she added. "Remember how deeply moved Giselle was when you gave her one in Paris?"

David agreed that it might lessen the trauma of removing Sandie's clothing if Sandie's friends were invited to choose a personal item as a remembrance.

"I'll talk with Delphine and Marc about it," he promised. Delphine, he knew, was already favorably disposed to the idea. Marc, however, was an unknown quantity. He hadn't been much in evidence since Jenny's arrival. He came by to welcome her and had been pleasant, but he was again at odds with his father. He seemed directionless, and there was a disturbing degree of cynicism and anger that had resurfaced in his behavior. David was worried by it but didn't know what to do.

David shifted the conversation to taxes. He had lived in Europe for thirty years, paying taxes first in France, when he worked in Paris, then in Switzerland, after he and Sandie moved to Geneva. His teacher's salary was always well below the allowed foreign exemption, so he owed no US taxes and had never filed anything with the IRS. When Jenny initially advised him that citizens were supposed to file even when they owed nothing, he had strongly resisted the idea of dredging up a decade of Swiss tax forms for a back accounting. "Wait a minute, Lady!" he objected. "I don't want to get you in trouble with the US government, but I ain't got no intention of giving the IRS as much as a Bronx cheer!"

Now, as they finished their lunch, David announced quietly that he accepted the necessity of filing. No contest. Jenny was astonished. "I understand that marrying you places certain obligations on me, and I want the marriage to go forward," he said simply.

It was not a minor concession. His yielding represented retreat from a longstanding principle. He had disassociated himself from the officialdom of the US government since the Vietnam War. In his mind, that included the Internal Revenue Service. Jenny had assumed they would battle over the filing question until the eleventh hour. Instead, David handed her his consent without a word of protest. This was an extraordinary gift on his part, and she recognized it as such.

"I keep finding new things to love about you," she said, smiling.

"Hmpff!" was his reply.

That evening, she and David talked about the timing and nature of their wedding.

"My preference," Jenny started, "is to take care of the legal work quietly—a notary-public kind of affair—then do a small home-based celebration or invite a few friends to a really good restaurant. I have an aversion to large gatherings and public events. I'd really like to avoid having a crowd. We're very different on that score."

"Differences aren't a bad thing," David mused. "Before Sandie and I got married, a fortuneteller warned us that we were completely incompatible!"

"You mentioned the end of September," Jenny continued. "For sentimental reasons, I was thinking October 1 or 2. The first is the anniversary of Olga's luncheon and the afternoon you and I cried our way along the meadow paths across from the house. The second is … well, it was after midnight when you ordered me to stop futzing around and get the hell under the covers. So either one works for me."

David wanted to frame his marriage to Jenny as an extension of his marriage to Sandie. "I want to do something symbolic to show the connection between the three of us. Frankly," he said, "I'd like to hold our wedding on September 25, the anniversary of Sandie's death."

Jenny was dumbstruck. David started to offer his reasoning, but she found her voice and spoke strongly against the idea. She knew how important it was for David to feel he had Sandie's imprimatur, but this was not the way to go about it.

"That's Sandie's day," she said. "It's a day when your friends and family will want to be with Sandie in their thoughts. September 25 commemorates the loss of her presence. It's not a good wedding date, David. If you need to tie our marriage to Sandie, it would be better to choose your wedding anniversary in November, although personally, I still prefer the anniversary of Olga's luncheon." He heard her, but he wasn't ready to abandon the idea.

They set the question aside and considered the ceremony. They agreed that the civil ceremony required by Swiss law would be sufficient. David wanted Marc and Delphine as witnesses and at most, a few friends in attendance. They did not expect their respective siblings to cross the ocean for what was to be a very low-key event. They would celebrate with them the next time they were in the United States.

"Do you want a ring?" Jenny asked.

"Nope," David answered firmly. "Don't like 'em. Sandie tried to make me wear a wedding ring. Insisted on giving me one. I managed to lose it the year we were in San Francisco. After that she gave up. And if you want one," he added, "you'd best pick it out yourself. I ain't much on jewelry."

Jenny had an antique gold band from her mother's family, which she wore on her right hand. She suggested that they convert it into her wedding ring. David agreed, then began to reminisce about Sandie's wedding ring, the one he had designed, despite his claim that he wasn't "much on jewelry." He had mentioned it when they were in Paris, but he didn't remember telling Jenny about it, so he repeated his description—a narrow band with diamonds and sapphires interspersed.

Jenny realized, with a start, that she had come across just such a ring in one of the boxes in the bedroom. David told her in Paris that

Sandie's wedding ring was gone—that Sandie had been wearing it when she was cremated. "There's a ring like that in Sandie's dresser," Jenny told him. His jaw literally dropped.

She went upstairs, got the box, and brought it down. There were several pieces of jewelry, mostly costume, but among them was a ring studded with tiny diamonds and sapphires. "*Tiens!*" he said in wonderment. "That's it! Sandie must have taken it off before she went into the hospital."

Jenny watched him carefully. He showed no distress that Sandie and her wedding ring had been parted. Sandie had obviously removed it to safeguard it. She didn't want it lost. "I'll save it for Delphine," he said. "Maybe give it to her at Christmas or on her twenty-first birthday."

There were other surprises in store. Before Jenny's arrival, David had arranged for an excursion with Michel and Josette DuPont to visit friends and tour the Swiss countryside. "I'm going to take advantage of the trip to tell Michel and Josette of our wedding plans," he announced on the morning of the trip. Jenny was suddenly nervous. She thought the DuPonts already knew. David considered their blessing as important as Marc and Delphine's, but he wanted Jenny at his side when he made the announcement.

"I'll tell them once we're on the road," he said, as much to himself as to Jenny.

The two couples set out after breakfast, each taking a separate car. In Chamonix, at the base of the towering Mont Blanc, the foursome found a little café and sat outside, surrounded by green forest and snow-capped peaks. As they waited for their coffee and tea, David said calmly that he had invited Jenny to move to Geneva, that she had accepted, and that they would be married sometime in the near future.

Michel was instantly and obviously pleased, coming around from his side of the table to hug David and then Jenny. Josette struggled with the news—Sandie had been her best friend—but she gamely joined her husband in welcoming Jenny with an embrace. She was genuinely glad that David would not have to suffer another year alone. Jenny couldn't muster more than a sentence in response, but she repeated *"Merci"* several times and smiled happily.

David reiterated his sense of the connection between his relationship with Jenny and with Sandie, and he floated the idea of getting married on September 25. Michel and Josette were openly horrified. To Jenny's relief, David quickly backed down and told them that Jenny, too, was strongly opposed to the idea. He asked them not to mention the wedding plans to anyone else yet, as there were people he felt he should tell directly.

They got back on the road to continue the journey, glad they had taken two cars. Clearly Michel and Josette would spend much of the drive ahead discussing the news between themselves.

Their destination was a rugged chalet used as a summer retreat by a couple who taught art and French literature at l'Académie Internationale. Jenny found herself feeling anxious as they approached. She was nervous about how David's friends would react to their relationship. When they arrived, their hostess greeted Jenny in English, and her tension began to dissipate. Everyone settled with a glass of wine on the chalet's high, narrow balcony. The farm buildings immediately below were roofed with massive slabs of stone, hand hewn and covered with moss. The play of light on the mountains was spectacular.

Later, seated at a sturdy country table surrounded by benches, they enjoyed a traditional *raclette*—a half wheel of cheese set against an open fire, with the melted portion continuously scraped off and eaten with small boiled potatoes. After dinner, a bottle of schnapps was brought out, but the host offered it only to the men. Swiss women, Jenny was advised, do not drink schnapps.

Their hostess had obviously been forewarned, because she put David and Jenny together in the living room, where the couch converted into a bed. As they snuggled beneath a layer of quilts, Jenny discovered, despite David's recent protestations, that he had finally clipped his toenails on her behalf. Her heart melted. "If that's not love, what is?" she said, laughing.

They breakfasted on coarse country bread and homemade preserves. The women packed the makings of lunch, and then everyone set out through spectacular scenery to a gently graded hiking trail that led to a mountain plateau. The Francophones were careful with their diction, and everyone understood English even if they didn't speak it. The group went back and forth in two languages, and it worked.

The men built a small cooking fire in a storybook meadow filled with alpine flowers and bordered by a little brook. They opened bottles of cider and wine. Later, as the picnickers sat, sleepy with the food and the warm sunshine, a doe crossed the meadow just above them, skirting the edge of the forest while keeping a wary eye on the small herd of humans below her.

David, Jenny, and the DuPonts took their leave the next morning, choosing alpine routes with one breathtaking view after another. Their destination was the Valais, where another set of school colleagues had retired to a modest villa overlooking the broad valley below.

"You may remember Hans and Maria-Luisa from Sandie's ceremony," David advised.

When they arrived in the late afternoon, Jenny was introduced to their hosts but had no memory of either of them. As they brought in the bags, Maria-Luisa indicated that Jenny should share a room with Josette. "David can share with Michel," she announced.

Did this mean no one had forewarned her? Or did it mean she disapproved? Jenny feared the latter and was suddenly unnerved by the thought that she and David might be separated. Josette pointed out that David and Jenny were sharing a suitcase. "It will be easier if they stay together," she suggested diplomatically. Maria-Luisa shrugged and said they could do as they wanted, but Jenny detected no warmth in her tone.

After a tour of Hans's terraced garden and orchard, the party arranged itself around a long picnic table next to a small brook that tumbled down the hillside. The gurgling noise of the water, the overlapping conversations, and the rapid French made it difficult for Jenny to understand what was being said.

As soon as the wine was served, everyone but Jenny lit up a cigarette. She was surrounded. The smoke hit her no matter how the wind shifted. Her eyes began to sting, and her mouth and throat dried up. Worse than the physical discomfort, however, was a growing anxiety that Maria-Luisa did not welcome her presence.

Jenny couldn't contribute, but she kept her eyes directed to each speaker, showing her effort to follow the conversation. Yet throughout the entire evening, Maria-Luisa never once looked at her, always skipping over Jenny as her glance moved around the table. Jenny's head ached from the smoke, and her nose began to run. She could feel the warning signs of a looming panic attack. Her throat was tight, and she had trouble breathing.

David sensed that Jenny was uncomfortable, but he mistook it for fatigue. When they broke after dinner, he suggested that Jenny go to bed, but she didn't want to be parted from him. She insisted on climbing to the top of the hill with him to watch Hans light the Independence Day bonfire. There were similar bonfires on mountaintops all across the Valais. Although she had to move a few times because of the shifting smoke, she sat on the hillside for over an hour as beacon after beacon was set afire in a stirring reenactment of the ancient ritual.

When she finally gave up, David walked Jenny down to the house and tucked her into bed like a little girl before returning to the others. She didn't hear him when he came in later and didn't hear him when he got up in the morning. By the time she woke up and went downstairs, everyone else had finished breakfast.

After a quick cup of tea, Jenny joined the others as they watched the Swiss Air Force jets that zoomed back and forth through the valley in celebration of the national holiday. "It takes only two minutes for the jets to cross the entire country," Hans observed, "so they have to spend most of their flight time turning around."

As the visitors prepared to depart, Maria-Luisa cut a large chunk of Spanish cheese for David to take back to Geneva. With a friendly and pleasant demeanor, she handed it to Jenny. Perhaps David had found an opportunity to talk with her—or perhaps the DuPonts had said something. Perhaps Jenny's sense that Maria-Luisa disapproved of her was a figment of her imagination or a product of her exhaustion. Whatever the truth of it, Jenny's distress of the night quickly dissipated.

Driving back to Geneva through ski country and glaciers, David apologized that the visit had been so boring for her. "That wasn't boredom," Jenny explained. "That was a panic attack, complete with tears, hyperventilation, and an adrenaline hit." She had told David about her handicap, but he had never witnessed it. Perhaps the evening's suffering was a blessing in disguise, she thought, because it offered a real-life example of the kind of situation that started her down that path.

"Why didn't you just say you were tired and excuse yourself?" David puzzled. "I asked you if you wanted to take a nap, and you said no."

"It was too late," she answered. "There's a certain stage in my panic attacks when I'm so fragile I can't even speak without bursting into tears. I just want to be invisible. I avoid anything that might focus attention on me, even if it's standing up and excusing myself from the company." Jenny offered the comparison of a deer in someone's headlights that freezes in the hope no one will notice it. "It's not a rational response," she said. "It's just misdirected instinct."

David shook his head. "I don't remember you ever being scared of anything," he remarked. "Is this a new thing?"

"No," she answered. "I've always been extremely shy. When I was younger, it embarrassed me terribly. I never talked about it, and I went to great lengths to hide it. I finally realized that it's not a personal failing. It's just my chemistry. Where possible, I avoid situations that might lead to a panic attack, but I'm no longer ashamed of it."

Delphine was home when they walked in, and she alerted Jenny that the surface-mail package she sent from Boston had arrived. Jenny took it up to the bedroom and put away the contents—extra underwear, sneakers, and blue jeans. When she came back down, Delphine was standing in the living room with David, tears streaming down her face.

"What's wrong?" Jenny asked. "What's happened?"

Delphine looked at Jenny. She looked at David. Her face was a portrait of anguish and confusion. The arrival of Jenny's package had brought with it the realization that, once they married, things would come for Jenny addressed to "Madame Perry." "But there is only one Madame Perry," Delphine choked. She was not ready. A wedding in October, which David and Jenny had tentatively settled on, was too soon for her.

On the spot, Jenny put her arms around Delphine. "Delphine Perry, don't you understand that you are far more important to me than any piece of paper?" Jenny looked her straight in the eye, shaking her head. "David and I don't have to get married in October," she told her.

Jenny blurted this out without consulting David, but he agreed wholeheartedly. "It seems to me that Delphine needs someone other than us to talk to about her feelings," he counseled as soon as they were alone.

"How about the DuPonts?" Jenny suggested. "Wasn't Josette Sandie's best friend?"

"Yes, but it may be easier for Delphine to talk with Marie-Claire's mother, Cybèle—the woman who joined us last Thanksgiving. Marie-Claire is Delphine's closest friend in Geneva. Marie-Claire went with Delphine on the trip to Asia, and Cybèle was Delphine's German teacher at l'Académie Internationale, so there's a well-established relationship. I'd like to clue Cybèle in on our plans and ask if she and Marie-Claire could help Delphine deal with this."

David called Cybèle and asked her over for an early drink on an evening when Delphine would not be home until dinnertime. After a few moments of banter, David told Cybèle about their plans. She nearly spilled her glass of wine. Jenny could see she was struggling with her composure. Cybèle pursed her lips and looked at David. She shrugged and said something Jenny didn't understand. She then rose, kissed cheeks with David, nodded her head in Jenny's direction, and walked out the door.

"What happened?" Jenny asked in dismay. "What did she say?"

"She isn't sure it's wise for me to be making such a significant decision so soon after Sandie's death," David said ruefully. "She said it would be difficult for her to help Delphine accept an action that is so precipitous."

David continued with a painful but honest observation. "It will be hard for some people to accept your presence," he said, "because they will no longer be able to imagine that Sandie is just away for a time. Intellectually, people know this isn't your fault, but emotionally, it may be difficult for them to feel comfortable with you at first."

Jenny understood the dilemma well. How could she justify being happy with David when Sandie had to die in order for it to be possible? The quandary found its way into her journal on a regular basis.

At David's request, Marc came home to join the three of them for dinner. As they were eating, David told Marc what had happened with Delphine and the package from Boston. He then raised the issue of the proposed wedding date and asked Marc to share his feelings.

"Whatever I think won't make a difference," Marc said, "so there's no point in discussing it." His tone was truculent. He would not be drawn out. Delphine kept numbly repeating that she didn't want to upset their plans.

"Dellie, you're not upsetting our plans," Jenny interjected. "I would rather postpone the wedding than see you uncomfortable with it."

It was a difficult situation all around. David and Jenny thought the marriage had the children's blessing. They had failed to read between the lines. They were now confronted with the painful gap between Marc and Delphine's intellectual position, which was supportive of

LEE LOWRY

Jenny's commitment to their father, and their emotional position, which was opposed to anything that diminished the symbols and remnants of their mother's presence. They were fine with Jenny being Jenny, as she had always been, but the title of Madame Perry belonged to their mother.

"It takes time," David offered gently. "Last week, when I drove out to the airport to meet your plane, all I thought about was seeing you. I drove the whole route without thinking of Sandie's dying. For the first time in over a year, it was just a road, and I was aware of the change. It takes time." Jenny had not registered, until that moment, that the road to the airport was also the road to the hospital.

They debated canceling their planned golf trip, but David decided it would be best if the children had time to themselves to sort out these latest events. Delphine walked in while Jenny was doing some last-minute packing for the trip. As Jenny stuffed pens and a writing pad into a small bag, she dislodged a greeting card that had been tucked into the pad. It fell on the floor, and Delphine picked it up. The front of the card read, I LOVE YOU MORE TODAY THAN YESTERDAY.

"Is it a love letter?" Delphine asked as she handed it to back.

Jenny laughed. "Yes, in a way it is, but it hasn't been sent yet. I'm saving it for the right moment." Jenny showed her the inside of the card, still unsigned: YESTERDAY YOU REALLY GOT ON MY NERVES! "Whenever I have to wait for prescriptions at the drugstore, I browse through the greeting cards and buy the ones I really like, so I'll always have cards on hand when I need them. The day will come when this card is perfect for David."

"I remember the cards you sent on my birthdays," Delphine told her. "They were always the best and funniest cards I received," she said brightly. It was a thoughtful peace offering.

David and Jenny took off shortly afterward and collected Michel and Josette so they could do another tandem drive. After checking into their hotel, they went to the golf course for Jenny's first lesson and eighteen holes of play. Jenny was given Sandie's golf bag and

210

clubs. David started her out with a seven iron. He wanted her to work on the rhythm of her swing and not worry about power or direction. Unfortunately, even moderate swings required a swivel of the hips with a fair amount of pressure. By the third hole, Jenny's left hip was issuing sharp and serious protests. Her golf career ended before it began. Luckily, it was only the pivoting that was painful. Walking normally at a steady pace was not a problem. Jenny studied the wildflowers. She listened to the birds. There were deer grazing on the roughs and frogs plopping into the water hazards. She was entirely content to walk without the distraction of hitting a ball.

Jenny had never seen David involved in a sport. He clearly loved the game and was drawn by the beauty of the pure physics involved— the relationship between the club, the ball, the lay of the land, and the force brought to bear by the player. Watching him, Jenny was reminded that there was still a lot about this man she didn't know.

After three more days of golfing, they headed back to Geneva. The DuPonts took the shortest way home. David and Jenny drove through the brooding vistas of extinct volcanoes in the Massif Central and took long, winding roads through the mountains. Jenny held the map and was officially the navigator, but David rarely needed her input. "We won't have time to do it this trip," he said, "but next time we're in this neck of the woods, I'll take you to Avignon. There's a restaurant there that Sandie loved." Was there any part of France, she wondered, where he and Sandie hadn't been?

By early evening, they were back at the house. David set about doing little things the children had neglected—putting the trash out, emptying the dishwasher.

"What can I do to help?" Jenny asked.

After a moment's thought, David handed her a planter containing a bonsai ficus that Olga had given to Sandie for her hospital room. "It's gotten straggly," he said, "and I don't know how to prune it. Do you?"

Jenny wasn't an expert pruner, but she was a fearless one. She got a small pair of shears from the garage and went to work. Stuck in the dirt at one end of the planter were two mangy seagull feathers. She pulled them out and held them up disapprovingly. "Do you think we could deep-six these?" she asked.

"No," was the reply. His voice was even, but David turned his face away from her and found something in the sink to occupy him. "They came from the beach in Brittany where we cast Sandie's ashes," he said.

"Ah," Jenny responded, trying to match her tone to his. "In that case, I'll just clean them up and put them back."

They invited Marc and Delphine to join them for lake perch at a nearby restaurant. Delphine played chauffeur, practicing her new driving skills. During dinner there was a discussion about Marikit, the housekeeper who helped with the cleaning and ironing. The children were unhappy that the house seemed less than sparkling. Jenny had observed Marikit at work and thought she did a very conscientious job, but she came only four hours a week. Four hours were insufficient to cover everything that needed doing. Clearly Sandie had taken care of many things herself. Delphine was teary-eyed when she complained, "The house is not the way Maman kept it."

No, of course it wasn't, but the problem wasn't that the house was dirty. The problem was that the house was empty of Sandie's presence. The life had literally gone out of it. When David suggested increasing Marikit's hours, Marc became critical and questioned the quality of her work. Jenny didn't discover until months later that Marc was angry with Marikit because she had broken a piece of china from one of Sandie's many collections. Marc then switched tactics and argued against increasing Marikit's hours,

"Because," he told his father, "this winter you'll be alone."

Jenny was startled by his words. She and David had agreed to postpone the wedding in deference to the children's sensibilities, but did Marc think this meant Jenny would wait out their engagement sitting in Boston? That she wouldn't come back to be with David through the winter? Jenny was on the verge of posing a question when David's eyes met hers in silent signal, and he changed the subject. She had never been a parent, but she could see at close range that it was a job fraught with peril.

As the meal progressed, Marc announced his decision to go to San Francisco, where he intended to take classes in photojournalism. He planned to leave in September, which was when Delphine was due to start her first semester at a business school in Paris. Was that what Marc meant by David being alone?

Lying in bed that night, David and Jenny rehashed the dinner conversation. David didn't think the "you'll be alone" reference was aimed at her or at their relationship. "Marc reacts to things with emotion rather than logic," he observed.

The next day began with errands and homey little projects. David teased her about it, but Jenny was enjoying her venture into domesticity, darning holes in his sweaters and figuring out how to iron his rumpled shirts without leaving scorch marks. David passed the early afternoon making soup and spaghetti sauce while Delphine packed for a trip to Zurich with Marie-Claire and her family. He was in a good mood, displaying a moment of gallows humor when the mail brought a marketing letter addressed to Mme Sandrine Perry, offering guaranteed life insurance with no health exam required. "Goddamn!" he exclaimed. "Maybe we should sign her up!"

David asked if Jenny wanted to join him in taking Delphine to the train. She thought it would be better for Delphine to have David to herself for a bit, and told him so. After they left, she went upstairs and started tidying the twin night tables on either side of their bed, removing outdated magazines. Mixed in with an old newspaper, she came across a handwritten poem, undated and untitled. "You're with me still in Paris on the wicker seats, in the rain on St. Germain, at the bus stop," it began.

It went on for three stanzas. It was beautiful and devastating. When did he write it? Was it during the trip to Paris with Marc back in February? The last line made her think so, because David had told her the February trip was healing. But it might have been written earlier when he went to Paris to scatter Sandie's ashes. Or—and this one cut her to the quick—it might have been written during the April vacation they had spent there only four months ago. It would explain the remoteness she sensed while they were there. He was with Sandie.

After Paris, when Jenny came back to Geneva with David—when he invited her to come and live with him—they had talked long into the night. One of the things she told him, although it seemed almost foolish at that point, was that, in Paris, she sensed he was withdrawing from her. "Well," he had explained, "we weren't alone, and I didn't want Ross and Bibi to feel as if they were intruding on a couple. I didn't want to exclude anyone, so I pretty much treated everyone the same." What he said made sense, but now, in light of the poem, she felt there was more to it.

Delphine had started an album for the sympathy letters they received, plus the tributes offered during Sandie's memorial service. It was labeled simply "Maman." Jenny took it out, tucked the poem inside, and then restored the album to its shelf.

She felt akin to a trespasser. David didn't hide his grief. He would have no objection to her reading the poem, but it hit a nerve. Jenny had long since accepted David's love for Sandie. She would always accept it—and respect it. She had told everyone, including herself, that the difference in intensity between David's love for her and hers for him was not a problem. "It doesn't diminish the validity or power or beauty of what we have," she argued. Yet the poem unsettled her.

When David returned from the train station, Jenny couldn't hide her distress. She had dabbed makeup on her red nose, but her puffy eyes were a dead giveaway.

"What's wrong?" David asked.

Jenny couldn't bring herself to mention the poem, but spoke instead about other areas of mounting stress. "Marc's on-again, off-again hostility has me on pins and needles, and the whole situation is really upsetting. Marc is talking about going to San Francisco in September. Dellie will be starting school in Paris at the same time. They won't be in Geneva except for holidays. Why does it matter to them whether or not we're married, once they've left home?"

The tears returned. "I came to help people heal," she said, face buried in David's shoulder, "but it feels as if all I'm doing is opening wounds. The wedding date shouldn't matter to me, but somehow it does."

David was gentle and reassuring. "I think this will all take care of itself once we get past the anniversary of Sandie's death," he counseled. "I think everything will begin to fall into place at that point."

The tears paved the way for an exchange of confidences and reassured Jenny that their ongoing emotional intimacy would be sustained by the deep trust they had in one another. "I feel so lacking in the social skills at which Sandie excelled," Jenny said, sighing. "My limited French, my discomfort with cities and crowds, my anxiety in social situations with strangers—all these things make me acutely dependent on you, and I'm afraid my dependency will become a source of irritation. I need to feel confident that you can accept and be tolerant of my social limitations, as I accept and am tolerant—at least up to a point—of your temper and your addiction to cigarettes."

It was a sweet night, prompting Jenny to raise another issue. David showed his affection through his thoughtfulness, but he didn't hug easily or cuddle up on the couch.

"Sandie used to reproach me for the same thing," he said, "but I've never succeeded in altering my behavior. It's just not something I think about."

Jenny didn't ask for change, since it seemed a matter of David's basic nature, but she did want to clarify his feelings about being on the receiving end. "I love to touch you as I pass your chair, or when you hand me my tea, but I don't want to do so if you feel an aversion to it," she explained.

"I'm quite happy to be touched," he replied. "I'm not very good at reciprocating, but I assure you, I enjoy it, and I appreciate it." They fell asleep with their arms about each other.

The morning brought another day of domesticity. David introduced Jenny to Sandie's accounting systems. He showed her the Swiss method of paying bills—very different from the United

States—and he showed her Sandie's filing set-up, with rows of carefully labeled binders lining shelf after shelf in Sandie's office. He declared that lesson sufficient for a starter and prepared to tackle a pile of bills on his own. Jenny offered to sit with him as he paid them, but he declined. Once they were paid, they had to be filed, and David often had tough moments with the storage binders, seeing Sandie's handwritten labels and Sandie's notes staring out at him. Jenny worked with Sandie in a different way, cleaning out her bed-table drawers and her bathroom. The cosmetics, she put in a box for Delphine. The medicines, she threw out, lock, stock, and barrel.

After lunch, David sought Jenny's help with a kitchen project. He wanted to clean the refrigerator and wash the neglected platters stacked on top of it. Jenny leapt at the opportunity. It was an answer to a prayer.

"May I redo the refrigerator door afterward?" she asked.

"Go ahead," he answered.

Much of the door was covered with photographs. Jenny kept all the ones of Sandie, but removed the pictures taken at the crematorium and the memorial service. In their stead, she put up recent photos of the children and of David's family, taken at Christmas. Everyone was smiling.

Then came the biggie. "May I change the little word-magnets?"

"Go ahead," he repeated.

Scattered on the surface of the door there were magnetic words spelling out sad messages. Jenny banished CRIED, WHY?, OVER, CLOUD, HOW?, GONE, and PAIN. From the box of word-magnets, she chose new words. She put PARADISE and PEACE next to pictures of Sandie, JOURNEY, VOYAGE, and SHINE next to the children and friends, and START, TOWARD, LIGHT next to David.

On Saturday evening, they went down to the lakeside to watch the fireworks celebrating the annual Festival of Geneva. Jenny clapped her hands in delight whenever a particularly spectacular display went off. Often she hugged David or squeezed him with her arm about his waist. He smiled at her glee but did not react with the same enthusiasm. He seemed remote, his mind far away. Had he and Sandie stood like this, on just such a night, watching the brilliant colors explode across the sky?

When it was over, David took Jenny's hand protectively and led her through the milling crowd in the direction of the car. Once they were out of the crush, he continued to hold her hand, but it felt suddenly awkward—a one-sided effort. She had the impression that he couldn't figure out how to diplomatically disengage himself. *What he really wants*, she thought to herself, *is to be holding Sandie's hand.* She gave him a squeeze, thanked him for the delightful fireworks, and freed her hand, using the pretext of needing to find something in her bag.

She had anticipated rough sledding, but it was increasingly clear that they were in for a roller coaster ride. Jenny had expected David's emotions to be up and down, but she was unprepared for her own instability. Insecurities she thought she had overcome were creeping back into her consciousness. Realizing there was no romance in his touch as he held her hand, she had reacted with self-doubt.

That night, as they lay in bed, she reminded herself that their mutual trust was worth gold. She could see that her love—and David's, however much it differed—would be tested again and again. But it didn't matter. For two weeks, she had tasted the reality of day-to-day existence in Geneva, learned how to operate a European washing machine, hung laundry on a clothesline for the first time in her life, and confronted the turmoil inherent in family life. When all was said and done, his question was still, "Will you come?" and her answer was still, "Yes. Yes. Yes."

The day before Jenny's return to Boston, David sent an e-mail to his brothers and their families officially announcing their plans. He had held off telling them until it was clear that Jenny had survived the visit with her commitment intact. "You sure you want to shack up with a grumpy old fart?" he asked, his finger hovering over the SEND button. The language in his e-mail was more civilized: "This will include getting married somewhere down the road," he noted as a postscript, "but we feel that is somewhat premature at the moment."

It was busy day but a calm one. Jenny moved more boxes of Sandie's clothes downstairs, then set the terrace table for lunch. David produced a platter of sliced tomatoes topped with chopped basil and fresh mozzarella cheese. He drizzled olive oil over the platter and was about to splash on some vinegar when Jenny interceded. "Could I have mine with just oil?"

"What?" he said, startled. "You don't like vinegar?"

"Only in small quantities," she answered. "It irritates my throat."

"Goddamn!" he exclaimed. "You and Sandie! She didn't like vinegar either. She always complained that my salad dressing was too sharp, and she would add more oil."

After lunch, David decided to mow the lawn. As he walked out, Jenny noticed a long tear in the back of his shorts. It was beyond repair. The surrounding fabric was worn down to bare thread. "Dearheart, you have a terminal rip in those shorts," she advised. "When you've finished mowing, we should throw them out and find you a new pair."

"Ventilation, woman, ventilation! Jeezus, you sound like Sandie! What is it with you two?" The annoyance in his tone was clearly pretend.

While David took care of the lawn, Jenny stripped lavender seeds from the pungent stalks in the garden and refreshed the hand-sewn sachets Sandie had made and used throughout the house. This was one of Sandie's annual rituals, and it pleased Jenny to continue it. When the existing sachets were redone, there was lots of lavender left over. Over the years, Sandie had made scores of placemats and table napkins. Some of her earliest efforts were now worn and frayed. Jenny took Sandie's pinking shears, cut some the frayed napkins into rounds, and brought up satin ribbon from Sandie's sewing bag. When the DuPonts arrived for Jenny's farewell dinner, she and Josette sat on the terrace, stuffing and tying sachets, some of which Josette kept and some of which Jenny packed to take back to Boston. She liked the symbolism of David's lavender, Sandie's fabric, and her handiwork, tied together and issuing a rich, long-lasting scent.

Before they went to bed, their e-mail inboxes registered congratulatory replies from David's family.

From: Nathan Perry
To: Jenny
Date: August 10, 2001
Subject: Congrats from us
Hell, Jenny, I've thought of you as family since we first met back when I visited David during his senior year. This announcement makes official what has already existed lo these many decades. In different configurations, maybe, but not in spirit. We're very happy for both of you and look forward to years of shared experiences. We love you, Jenny, for who you are, what you've done, and who you are becoming.
Best, Nate
Welcome from me, too—Margaret

Isham added a special note for Jenny in his remarks to David: "Be strong, Jenny—You'll need to be." At the time, she thought that was a joke.

On the morning of her flight back to Boston, Jenny's mug of tea was waiting for her when she came downstairs. David did this every morning, but it still surprised and delighted her. While David put her bags in the car, she stuck a funny cartoon about marriage in with his coffee filters for him to find the next morning.

Their farewell at the airport was sweet and painless, and the flight was routine. The minute she reached home, she dashed up to the loft to check her e-mail. David had forwarded more congratulatory notes, but the e-mail that pleased her most was his own:

De: David
A: Jenny
Envoyé: 14 août, 2001
Objet: Your return
I already miss being nagged.
Kisses, David

Flower Blossoms

How can flower blossoms stand to stay so long unopened,

Just sitting, hanging, standing at the end of stems,

There upon themselves closed in,

Petals overlapping petals as unsplashed drops of water or tears,

Promising, as little girls do, future poise, grace and charm,

Hinting hourly at brighter colors 'til

Further inner tinting would seem to harm?

And yet ... why do flower blossoms make me wait so long?

Do flowers have no sense of urgency, no impatience?

Then why do I? Must we both not die?

Can't they somehow see or feel themselves develop, grow?

How then can I? Somehow they too must know.

Do they have no inner image of what they will become or

May if all goes well? How then do they cope?

Does a flower see itself as I do or see me as I don't?

Why do flower blossoms give me hope?

Chapter 9

From: JWLongworth
To: DavidP
Date: August 14, 2001
Subject: Re: Your return

Arrived Boston safe and sound. Very tired, so I'll sign off. I promise a longer note tomorrow. I'll try to include some nagging.

Love you, J.

De: David
A: Jenny
Envoyé: 15 août, 2001
Objet: Cartoon

Thanks for the cartoon, but I prefer filtering coffee through bleached paper. The ink adds nothing to the taste. Yesterday I planted the herbs we bought. What am I supposed to do today?

Kisses, David

From: JWLongworth
To: DavidP
Date: August 15, 2001
Subject: Re: Cartoon

Thanks to jet lag, I'm up early (it's 3:45 a.m.), so there is still time to offer useful suggestions about your day: 1) You need to buy some khaki shorts and a new pair of jeans; 2) The remaining lavender needs to be shucked; 3) You could measure the mattress on our bed and order a much firmer one. That should get you through today. If you run short of projects, I can advance you tomorrow's list. I could even map out the whole week if that would help. Happy to do it. Love you beyond reason and common sense. J.

De: David
A: Jenny
Envoyé: 15 août, 2001
Objet: Re: Re: Cartoon
Jeeeeeeezus. Only the last remark concerns reality. Think I'll take a nap. *Bises.*

From: J W Longworth
To: DavidP
Date: August 16, 2001
Subject: Roses
Four large roses bloomed on Sandie's Abbaye de Cluny in my absence! She must be pleased with the way things are going. I know I am.
Love, J.

De: David
A: Jenny
Envoyé: 17 août, 2001
Objet: Announcements and such
Morning, Ducks. Hope somebody prepared your tea.
I will be going to Paris next weekend with Delphine. I spoke with Giselle on the phone and told her about us. She was *very* happy. I will talk to Madame Lamont when I see her with Delphine next week.
Kisses, David

From: J W Longworth
To: DavidP
Date: August 17, 2001
Subject: Friday
I made my own tea this morning pretty much on automatic. You have rarely been in this house, so I don't

yet associate you with tea in my own kitchen. That's something I have to look forward to.

I'm so pleased we have Giselle's blessing!

Love, J.

As David contacted his closest friends, Jenny began to alert her own circle about the changes ahead. Rachel Aronson closed their phone conversation with an accolade for David and offered Jenny a traditional blessing. "I bow to anyone who can surface from tragedy into a new love," she said. "May you grow old together in fortune and honor."

A fellow volunteer from the Charles River Cleanup Project rejoiced at the cosmic wonder of it:

From: Winifred
To: Jenny
Date: August 18, 2001
Subject: Your message

Got your message. Welcome back! I had a good cry as I heard your news. I am so happy for you! I have been constantly amazed at what this stage of life has brought. I never thought so many new doors could be opened. I am finding that in my own life, but you must be the poster child! Go, be happy, and make that lovely man happy. You watched your friend Sandie die and have had glimpses of your own mortality. You must have a visceral sense of the shortness of the time that is left. Know that we love you and wish you only joy. Do keep in touch!

Much love from Winnie and the boathouse gang.

Her friends and neighbors were happy for her, but except for the few who knew of her ancient passion for David, most were flabbergasted that Jenny would give up her job, leave her friends and family, and walk away from her house, her garden, her language, and her culture to go off to Geneva and marry a man they'd barely heard of. Ross knew the early history through Ramon, but most of Jenny's circle had come on board in the last two decades. If David's name came up, it was in a casual reference to "an old college friend" who was in town with his wife and children, or in a brief mention of the fact that Jenny was off to Europe for a short vacation with a Franco-American couple she knew. Jenny never hinted at the strength of her ongoing attachment to the man. David was married, and that made him off limits. No one realized how important he was to her. Small wonder that so many people were shocked by the news.

Bibi, for whom the marriage plans were old news, called to catch up and chimed in with cautionary advice. "Watch out for the children," she warned. "They may seem sweet as can be, but they can sabotage you in the wink of an eye."

Jenny had told Bibi of the incidents that upset Delphine and had described Marc's volatile behavior, but she couldn't imagine that either child would knowingly, willingly sabotage her. Delphine had gone out of her way to reassure Jenny that her stress and emotion were the result of grief at her mother's absence, not anger at Jenny's presence. Marc was difficult to communicate with, but he had been reasonably welcoming and respectful. Both children seemed relieved that her coming meant their father would not spend the winter alone.

"Yeah, but you're approaching this rationally," Bibi countered. "I have friends whose marriages were busted up by stepchildren. Kids their age are still operating on feral instinct. The advantages of your presence are theoretical. The disadvantages are physical. You're going to dismantle their nest, their safe house. You're going to systematically remove the aura of their chief protector. When you hang your bathrobe where Sandie's used to be, you're vanquishing her totems, the household gods and goddesses, and replacing them with your own. That's more than painful to kids. It's threatening. So don't be surprised if they start laying booby traps."

Jenny dismissed Bibi's warning. She had more immediate concerns—getting the car inspected, making extra keys, and a host of tedious but necessary chores. She also had to address her cat's transition to the neighbor who had often looked after her during

Jenny's absences. Since the neighbor frequently offered tuna treats, Jenny suspected Nemesis would be quite content with her new quarters.

An e-mail from Graham Wells returned her attention to the question of a wedding date. As their oldest mutual friend, Graham wanted to organize his calendar so he could attend their nuptials. Jenny wrote back explaining the parameters.

From: JWLongworth
To: Graham
Date: August 23, 2001
Subject: Re: Wedding date

The children need transition time. We're trying to balance that with Swiss Immigration. I have copies of all the documents I need, but the notary stamps have to be current within six months. If we're not married by February 28, I'll have to start all over again on the paperwork, so I'd like to do it by January rather than wait till the last minute. Might be fun to do a New Year's Eve event! Best to Barbara.

Love, J.

From: JWLongworth
To: DavidP
Date: August 23, 2001
Subject: Thursday

Hi, Cutie. I got a note back from Graham saying the last weekend in December would be good for him. If the kids could be comfortable with that, it might work out well. I was joking at first, but I actually like the idea of December 31. New Year's is a downer because I always think of Ramon—should auld acquaintance be forgot. If it became our wedding anniversary, it would no longer be sad since Ramon is bound up in this amazing saga of ours.

Love, *moi*

De: David
A: Jenny
Envoyé: 14 août, 2001
Objet: Friday
    I'm okay with New Year's Eve. We'll see. I'm off to Paris with Delphine to pay a visit to Madame Lamont. I want to tell her about us in person.
    Love, David

Jenny drove up to Maine to deliver assorted keys and pay a quick visit to her sister, Caroline, who was in Camden for the summer. Caroline had recently helped clear out the last of the boxes their mother had stored at the family cottage. In the process, she came across a small package of items from Jenny's childhood. Along with baby pictures, there was a porridge spoon and a miniature silver pitcher with JWL engraved on it. Jenny looked at the pitcher in astonishment. She told Caroline about Sandie's creamers perched on the kitchen windowsill in Morion and how David's attempt to close Sandie's collection had been thwarted by a car break-in in Paris.

"This pitcher is clearly meant to go with me to Geneva," she said. "Sandie and I will share it."

De: David
A: Jenny
Envoyé: 27 août, 2001
Objet: Re: Sunday
    Paris was good. Saw Madame Lamont. It'll be hard for her, but she understands that life goes on. Delphine enjoyed the weekend and is looking forward more and more to moving. We both felt it was easier to be in Paris than in Geneva, though I am conscious of being more at ease coming home than I was even a few months ago.
    Kisses, David

From: JWLongworth
To: DavidP
Date: August 29, 2001
Subject: Wednesday

Can't sleep. I am halfway between two worlds at the moment, which is unsettling. Had a good day yesterday, got lots of business taken care of.

I found a set of photographs from several years back when you and the children were visiting. I also came across a packet from your Florida trip. My favorite shot has Sandie, Dellie, and me squeezed together in the back of the swamp buggy at Corkscrew Swamp. It brought back wonderful memories.

Love you, J.

De: David
A: Jenny
Envoyé: 2 septembre, 2001
Objet: Gladiolas

Mornin', Luv. Forgot to tell you yesterday or the day before (this is called a list ex post facto, which I'm good at, being a historian) ... forgot to tell you that:

1) The gladiolas are blooming red and orange along with the yellow rutabagas, which the French ate during WWII while the Huns were scarfing up the potatoes;

2) I don't want to go back to school, but will, if only to meet the new kids and stir up a bit of administrative trouble;

3) I've got a pile of congratulatory letters waiting for you;

4) I seriously miss being nagged.

Kisses, David

From: JWLongworth
To: DavidP
Date: September 2, 2001
Subject: Re: Gladiolas

1) Rutabagas! Amazing. I think Fannie Farmer has recipes for rutabagas;

2) The school won't know what hit it. They don't realize yet that in addition to your stirring-up-trouble skills, you've now greatly improved your list-making capabilities;

3) We should plan to get married more often. I've heard from people I've been out of touch with for years. It's lovely;

4) Mea culpa. Perhaps I could nag you about upgrading your computer system so it can support two PCs and two printers.

Love ya. J.

This banter helped balance an emotionally charged communication David received from his young niece, Nate and Margaret's daughter LeeLee, evidencing her conflict over the marriage plans.

From: LeeLee
To: Uncle David
Date: 3 September
Subject: Worry

Congratulations, Uncle David. Jenny seems nice, but to be real honest, it feels like I'm losing more of the aunt I already lost. Love you anyway. LeeLee

De: David
A: LeeLee
Envoyé: 4 septembre, 2001
Objet: Re: Worry

Dearest LeeLee, We can't lose Sandie, though sometimes I think life would be simpler if we could forget those we loved once they've gone. What makes us remember the hurtful aspects of our past so strongly and painfully? I don't have the answers, but the question fascinates me.

You will always have Sandie and your love for her in yourself. As Bogart says to Bergman at the end of Casablanca, "We'll always have Paris." So will I. Often such evocations will make us cry, as I am doing now. It is as it must be.

Jenny has been a part of me even longer than Sandie has. Sandie often asked me why I didn't marry Jenny in the first place. It was a question I asked myself as I was making the decision to invite Jenny to come live with me in Geneva. And strangely enough, it was Jenny who provided me with the key to understanding when she gave me some books and cassettes by Joseph Campbell, who recommended that people "follow their bliss."

I followed mine when I moved to Paris in 1968, although I was not intellectually aware that I was doing so. All I knew was that Paris was where I desperately wanted to be. I had other girlfriends in Paris while Sandie and I were getting to know one another. I will never know, because it never happened, but I might have been able to marry and live happily with a different Paris girlfriend. What I do know is that the woman I married then had to come from Paris. As long as I was with Sandie, I was with Paris. I think that is why I now feel more at ease in Paris than I do in Geneva. Everything in Paris reminds me of Sandie, so she is gloriously present. In Geneva I still suffer from her absence.

Now that I am older, my bliss has transformed itself, or I have transformed it by living. What I want now is to sit next to someone I love, who knows me very well, sip a glass of wine, and be nagged at. This is where Sandie and I were before she died. Few, if any, people know me as well as Jenny. She can nag me with awareness. It's the glue of long-lasting marriages and relationships. I love it. I continue to follow my bliss. And that, my dearest niece, is my understanding of why I want to marry Jenny.

With love, Uncle David

David forwarded a copy to Jenny. It was not a total surprise to read David's comment that the woman he married in his youth "had to come from Paris," but she had never heard him articulate it so clearly before.

From: JWLongworth
To: DavidP
Date: September 6, 2001
Subject: Nagging

Thanks for forwarding LeeLee's e-mail and your response. That was really lovely.

You're the only man in my life who fully appreciates my ability to nag with awareness. In truth, however, I rarely nag. I fuss. Nagging is when you go after someone over and over, in a tone of mild to moderate annoyance, prodding him to do something he should have done a long time ago.

Fussing is when you worry out loud about someone you love because he doesn't behave sensibly and doesn't take care of himself. Imagine, for example, a spouse who walks around in shorts with holes in them or who has toenails long enough to trip over—someone who has cigarettes for breakfast instead of fruit or bran flakes. These are behavioral issues that require careful monitoring and frequent intervention. In short, they require fussing. Just want to set the semantic record straight.

Love, J.

De: David
A: Jenny
Envoyé: 8 septembre, 2001
Objet: Re: Nagging

Bullshit. I say it's nagging.

From: Jenny
To: David
Date: September 9, 2001
Subject: Sunday

I had the most amazing morning. I had an appointment with the owners of the house in Brookline where Seth and I used to live. I removed some stained glass windows from the house before we sold it but never found a way to use them. I wanted to see if the current owners wanted them. The wife, Natalie, was interested in the history of the house, so I started telling whatever stories I could remember.

One thing led to another, and this woman and I
hit it off as if we had known each other for decades.
She asked me why I was giving up the windows. I told
her about you and Sandie and Geneva. And then the
"coincidences" unfolded. Natalie's daughter's name is
Sandie. Natalie lost a very dear friend to cancer two
years ago. Natalie is now married to a man (second
marriage) she knew when they were young, and for
years and years they were "best friends."

Finally I showed her the windows, holding my
favorite one up against the light. It was a single stalk of
deep purple iris. "Iris is my favorite flower in all the world,"
she marveled. "Why haven't we ever met before? Now
that you're going to Geneva, I'll never get to know you."

Without hesitation, I invited her to come visit us. It
was an amazing encounter. This woman had a dinner
party planned. She was supposed to be getting the
house ready and the food prepared. The husband was in
and out. A neighbor came by. She and I simply couldn't
stop talking. As I was leaving, we gave each other a big
hug. There is good karma here. So I pass along her
blessings, plus several hugs from me because I am
really missing you right this minute.

Love, J.

De: David
A: Jenny
Envoyé: 10 septembre, 2001
Objet: Re: Sunday
Me, too. David

Electronic chatter. Lighthearted banter. They went to bed
assuming the next day would be like any other. They were wrong.

From: JWLongworth
To: DavidP
Date: September 11, 2001
Subject: Chaos
It's pretty grim on this side of the Atlantic right
now. Go turn on your television. The United States has

been hit with what appears to be a sophisticated and well-coordinated terrorist attack, focused primarily on New York and Washington, DC. The news reports are incomplete and speculative, but apparently airplanes, hijacked and full of passengers, have been slammed into the Pentagon and the twin towers of the World Trade Center. The towers have collapsed. A five-story section of the Pentagon has been destroyed. Washington is shutting down. New York is at a standstill.

I am stunned. I feel a need to go and seek the serenity of my garden. My visceral connection is to the people in the hijacked planes. It could have been me, thinking I was winging my way to Geneva, only to discover that a religious fanatic had decided to use my plane as a doomsday weapon. It reminds me that I should tell you at every opportunity how much I love you. Life is uncertain, but my love is not. Really want the comfort of your arms right now. J.

De: David
A: Jenny
Envoyé: 11 septembre, 2001
Objet: Re: Chaos

Oh, Jewel. This is awful, unimaginable. How I feel for the victims' loved ones. How I wish you were here. Stay safe. All my love. David

Jenny did indeed seek the serenity of her garden, pulling weeds, edging paths, deadheading spent flowers. Every few hours, she went back into the house and turned on the TV, watching the same terrible images over and over again until she felt the need to return to the garden and the sanity of nature's world, where there is neither good nor evil, only change. That evening, with the awareness of mortality heavily upon her, she composed a letter for David to read only in the event of her death. At the end she wrote, "You were my bliss, and there are not words to thank you enough for the happiness you gave me, even from afar. Love forever, Jenny."

She put it into an envelope, wrote DO NOT OPEN UNTIL MY DEATH outside, and placed it in her legal documents folder. She felt better.

From: JWLongworth
To: DavidP
Date: September 11, 2001
Subject: Chaos II
    I now understand how my parents felt when they heard the first newscasts about Pearl Harbor. I think it's going to take all day for the enormity of this to sink in, but come tomorrow, there will be a fusion of national anger terrible to behold. I don't think hate and vengeance solve anything. I think they just perpetuate cycles of violence. But I have no counsel for anyone. There is just numbness. I understand—and feel myself—some of the deep anger that is sweeping the country, but I hope wise heads will prevail, and that we will not become terrorists ourselves in our search for justice. Please hug the children and pray for Peace.
    Love, Jenny

De: David
A: Jenny
Envoyé: 12 septembre, 2001
Objet: Coping
    I find myself watching TV and searching the Internet the way I watched TV during the Kennedy assassination and searched my e-mails after Sandie's death, looking either for the bad joke or something that would calm me down. I find neither.
    Love, David

From: JWLongworth
To: DavidP
Date: September 13, 2001
Subject: Re: Coping
    I know what you mean. I keep coming back to death without warning—death with insufficient time to say

good-bye. So my way of coping was to write you a good-bye letter, to keep on file against such an eventuality.

It's still tense here, in odd ways. Normally there is an airplane approaching Logan on a flight path over the Blue Hills about every three minutes. But now, the sky is empty and silent. At the post office, there is a handwritten note on the door saying, "No Express Mail accepted until further notice." The news coverage is still nonstop, with survivor stories, victim stories, heroism stories, body counts, and the progress of assorted investigations. Everyone is braced for more incidents. I'm not personally frightened, but there is an eerie feeling in the air.

I still have a few things to attend to here, but psychologically, I'm already over there with you. If I didn't have a board meeting coming up, I would change my ticket and leave Boston earlier.

Love, J.

De: David
A: Jenny
Envoyé: 14 septembre, 2001
Objet: Re: Thursday

Still strange here, too. A lot of talk with colleagues, students writing feelings, many people affected, some directly, others almost—really close calls. Wish you were already here.

Love, David

Despite the emotional aftermath of the attacks, an e-mail from Josette caused Jenny to shift her focus back to family concerns. She got out her French-English dictionary and translated.

De: Josette
A: Jenny
Envoyé: 18 septembre, 2001
Objet: Things are difficult

Things are very difficult at the moment with Marc. You are going to arrive in a somewhat tormented period. Marc has problems in his relationship with his girlfriend, and he isn't in good shape. It is so sad to see this young man so unhappy, so uncomfortable in his skin. I think Marc has the impression that he is the only one who suffers at the death of his mother. He still so often uses this excuse to justify his inadequate behavior. For him, it is as if his father and sister no longer suffer. It is therefore very, very hard.

Your arrival will comfort David, of that I am sure. He needs help to face the problem that Marc poses for him. But be prepared that it will not be easy at all times. And if I may say something concerning your marriage—do not push too much, too early. Talk with Delphine—she is really open—and try to talk with Marc also. He has to learn that he has his place but that he does not have all the place, and that the people around him love him, but that they have their lives that have to be lived!

Big kiss, and see you soon! Josette

In the weeks following the 9/11 attacks, air travel was gradually restored. When Jenny got to Logan Airport on September 24, the once-bustling area beyond passport control and electronic screening was eerily quiet. All the concessions were closed, and her footsteps echoed in the corridor as she proceeded to her gate. The waiting area was almost empty, as was her plane.

She landed in Geneva on September 25, exactly one year after Sandie's death. David collected her, and while she unpacked, he went out and bought a bouquet of colorful field flowers in memory of Sandie. Later in the day, Josette dropped off a dozen roses.

Jenny had learned from Bibi the Jewish tradition of lighting a yahrzeit candle—a small votive that burns for twenty-four hours— on the anniversary of a loved-one's death. Not knowing where to find such things in Geneva, she had brought some with her as a simple, time-honored way of acknowledging Sandie. David had parent-teacher conferences that evening. Jenny was alone at sundown when she lit her candle and placed it on the mantel alongside Sandie's rose. It wasn't part of her belief system that Sandie could actually hear her, but she spoke to her as freely as she did to flowers and passing butterflies, thanking Sandie for her trust and promising to do her best to take care of the family

David arrived home at eight o'clock, followed shortly by Delphine. Jenny gave them each a candle, which they lit and set on the windowsill amid Sandie's creamers. When Marc came by to say hello, David invited him to join in the candle-lighting. Marc seemed glad to have a ritual to perform but was annoyed that he hadn't thought of one himself.

L'Académie Internationale was in session so Jenny was on her own for her first few days. Delphine was busy with last-minute preparations for her college debut. Marc was still living with Valerie. He had not followed through on his San Francisco plans.

David offered to prepare a farewell dinner for Delphine. She invited her friend Marie-Claire and Marie-Claire's mother, Cybèle, to join them. Marc agreed to come but said Valerie had other commitments. During the meal, the little silver pitcher Jenny had brought from Maine led to a discussion of family heirlooms, which in turn prompted Delphine to ask about her mother's wedding ring. It was news to Marc and Delphine that David had believed it was burned with Sandie until Jenny found it.

"Well, where is it now?" Delphine asked anxiously. Her tone made Jenny wonder if Delphine feared that Sandie's wedding ring would end up on Jenny's finger. David assured his daughter that he had put it away in a safe place, to be passed on to her at some future date. Delphine was mollified, but Jenny was left uneasy by the exchange.

After dinner, Delphine, Marie-Claire, and Cybèle went up to Delphine's room to look at some of the clothes Delphine had brought back from Thailand. As Jenny cleared the table, Marc told David that he had followed an Eastern tradition and launched a paper prayer boat onto Lake Leman to honor Sandie. Jenny came in at the tail end of the story. David urged Marc to tell it again, so she could hear the whole tale.

"Go tell Delphine and the others at the same time," David suggested. Marc went up to Delphine's room. Jenny followed. It was a mistake. Marc walked a few feet in, then stopped, effectively blocking her entrance. As she stood in the doorway, he kept his back to her, speaking in rapid French in a voice so low that she could barely hear him. He never looked at her. Neither did anyone else. No one invited her in. She felt extremely awkward and excused herself quickly when Marc finished speaking.

Over breakfast, Jenny asked David about Marc's boat story, saying truthfully that she hadn't been able to follow the French. She made no reference to her exclusion of the night before. She felt heartened that Marc had undertaken the exercise and was glad the boat had danced out into the lake with its candle flickering, giving him a sense of peace.

"I remember that Marc was really angry with himself for not speaking at Sandie's memorial service," Jenny offered.

"Marc has yet to forgive himself for going off to Eastern Europe while Sandie was dying," David replied.

Delphine's business college did not offer student housing, so David arranged for her to rent Sandie's old apartment on the Rue Capron. Classes didn't start until the middle of October, but Delphine wanted a little time to settle in. David borrowed a van for the drive from Geneva, and Delphine and Jenny packed it with linens, cookware, clothes, and Delphine's collection of CDs. When they arrived, they unloaded everything, then had dinner with David's oldest Parisian friends, Isaac and Camille Bloch.

Delphine had met the Blochs before, but until that night, she didn't realize that it was Isaac who had long ago taken the fabulous photograph of David and Jenny that they turned into poster-size prints. Set in a Paris park on a gray, misty day, the photo caught them with heads together and faces bathed in happiness. It had hung in their respective domiciles throughout the decades that followed. Sandie had wisely tolerated the photo's presence, and whenever she and David had a disagreement about something, Sandie would jokingly point to the photograph and announce, "Well, if you do not like the way I do things, you should have married Jenny!"

The next morning was spent unpacking Delphine's boxes, hanging pictures, and trying to figure out the directions for items with "some assembly required." The instructions were in French, so Jenny wasn't much help. They wiped shelves, rearranged furniture, scrubbed surfaces, and laid down the area rug Delphine had brought from Geneva—not exactly a romantic weekend in Paris as portrayed in the travel brochures.

When they finished, Delphine came with David and Jenny to the garage where the van was parked to see them off. It was obvious that David adored his daughter, but he simply bussed her on the cheeks as the French do, then climbed into the driver's seat. Jenny gave Delphine a hug and told her they would miss her. Delphine smiled and said, "Take care of the men." Jenny opened the car door, started to get in, and then went back to hug Delphine again. "You are the light of your father's life," she told her. David observed her emotion but made no comment. It wasn't clear whether he was amused or touched—or maybe both.

The drive back was long. They didn't bother with dinner when they got home. It was all they could do to climb the stairs and get into bed.

Monday dawned a beautiful day. It was October 1, the anniversary of Olga's luncheon. David left for work at 7:30 but came home for lunch, which was a lovely surprise. That evening, he prepared a simple supper and set it in the oven to bake while they took their wine out to the terrace. Jenny considered asking for champagne in honor of the day, but changed her mind. It was a day to mark and observe but not one to celebrate.

David's experience had been very different from Jenny's. A lot of it was a blur for him. He didn't remember the empty chair. He didn't even remember sending her home separately, so Jenny recounted her impressions of the day: David's despairing comment in the car; the terrace in the sun and the hand-picked grapes; the girls and the abandoned chair; his abrupt departure; her demand that he come for a walk; their cathartic stroll. And then, in the evening, her nausea, sipping tea and taking antacids, getting sick in the sink—his response that, "It reminds me of Sandie." His taking charge of her—their clinging to each other through the night.

As Jenny recalled the details, she found herself reliving the pain of being afraid for him rather than the joy of discovering his love. They were both affected by the rush of memories. Between the two of them, they went through nearly a whole box of tissues.

Then the mood shifted, turning on a simple question Jenny posed. "When you answered LeeLee's letter, you spoke of the process you went through while you considered inviting me to live here. When did the idea first occur to you?"

"Probably exactly a year ago today," he replied. Jenny was astonished. She presumed the thought had formed after Christmas in Chattanooga, or during the dark month of January—or even as late as their visit to Paris in April. She shook her head, saying how incredible fate and chance were—how seemingly insignificant incidents could change the course of one's life. If Olga hadn't invited them for lunch ... If she hadn't asked David about coming to the States for Christmas, thus provoking the response that frightened her so ... If she hadn't gotten sick ...

"If any of these things had been different," Jenny observed, "I doubt very much that I would be sitting here right now."

"Oh," he said, contemplating his wineglass with a gentle smile, "I think you would."

Jenny was quietly elated that David had decided so early on that their lives should go forward together. It was not knowledge she could easily share, however, lest people misconstrue it as a slight to Sandie. The truth was just the opposite. The fact that David started thinking of Jenny's coming before he had even spread Sandie's ashes was confirmation that he could not go forward unless there was some hope of filling a corner of the great, gaping hole Sandie's death had created in his world.

September, 2001

The Blackness of the Sky

The blackness of the sky against
The darker trees has not lightened
Nor added color to my understanding of the night.
Winking flashes from porch lights still sparkle
In the chilly autumn air, moving me to marvel
As a youngster does before a twinkling tree
Outside a cold and snowy Christmas Eve.
Maple leaves still redden from the tips in fall
But never as fully as I'd wish to see at all.
Starlings still swarm and veer as a flock.
So why should one years' absence
Dim your images in me of memories of before
Or stop me from expecting you to knock
One darkened evening late at our front door
Or, come to think of it,
Prevent me from loving you
- even in absentia - anymore?

Chapter 10

Marikit always came to clean on Tuesday mornings. She was a tiny, bustling grandmother, originally from the Philippines. Her warmth and cheerfulness made Jenny feel at home, as did her cleaning style, which reminded Jenny of housekeepers from her past. Marikit cleaned around things. One of Jenny's challenges was making sure, before Marikit arrived, that all the surfaces were cleared and accessible. When she told David she needed to clean the house because Marikit was coming, he laughed. She started to explain, and he held up his hand, cutting her short.

"I know, I know," he said, shaking his head. "Sandie used to do the same thing."

While Marikit tackled the rest of the house, Jenny polished the silver. David had a collection of mint julep cups, an inheritance from his Virginia grandmother, plus dozens of ornamental Victorian serving implements. The silver was nearly black with tarnish. David later teased Jenny for being compulsive, saying that tarnished silver didn't bother him one bit, but Jenny knew to a moral certainty that it would have bothered Sandie.

Next on her list was Sandie's shell collection. On one of their Christmas trips, the Perry family stopped to visit Jenny in Florida on their way to Chattanooga. Her parents were still alive at the time, and they invited the Perrys to their apartment for cocktails so they could all watch the sun set over the Gulf of Mexico. Jenny's father was charmed by Sandie. He loved her French accent and was delighted by the French custom of kissing on each cheek. As the Perrys were about to take their leave, he disappeared for a moment, then reemerged with an enormous glass jar, filled to the brim with shells gathered on his morning beach walks. He urged Sandie to take some back to Geneva as a memento of her visit. Sandie's eyes lit up like a Christmas tree. Instead of reaching into the jar, she took it in her hands and hugged it to her. She thought Mr. Longworth intended for her to take the entire collection.

"These are beautiful!" she exclaimed. "I want to decorate my bathroom with shells, and these will be so wonderful!"

Given Sandie's excitement, Jenny's father was delighted to hand over the whole lot. Jenny and her siblings had never shown such enthusiasm. When Sandie got back to Geneva, she placed the collection in a large clear bowl next to her tub.

In the year since Sandie's death, the shells had gathered dust. Jenny washed them carefully and set them on towels to dry while she took the bowl down to the kitchen and cleaned it. As she put the shells back in the bowl, she couldn't help but marvel. There she was in Geneva, taking care of shells that her father had gathered, one by one, on a beach on the far side of the ocean. Jenny had refused these shells when her father offered some to her. Now they greeted her each morning, thanks to Sandie.

Marc and Valerie came by for dinner that evening. David had been oblivious to it, but Marc immediately noticed the shining silver. He seemed surprised and pleased. As the days passed, Jenny made a concerted effort to restore order *à la Sandie* to every corner of the house. David was amused by her conversion from American community activist to Swiss hausfrau, but he was unabashedly pleased when he walked into the kitchen and saw his copper cooking pots transformed from a dirty brown to a gleaming luster. The house that had long been haunted by Sandie's absence slowly came back to life. Even Sandie became more present as the rooms became vital and vibrant again.

Jenny's cleaning campaign met with no resistance. Moving or replacing things was a different issue, however. As she had learned in her encounter with the seagull feathers, the house was a shrine. It was fine to clean it, but no one wanted anything moved. For a time, she tiptoed around the issue. And then she saw a pathway. *All I need to do is consult the goddess of the shrine and enlist her support*, she told herself.

Sandie had loved that house. She and David had watched it being built and had worked with the architect to add special features. Sandie delighted in choosing furniture and decorating, but she had only five years between the day she moved in and the day David brought home the urn filled with her ashes. There were projects never begun, much less finished. Had Sandie lived, the house would have continued to evolve.

So began a running conversation, albeit heavily one-sided.

"If you had carte blanche to change something, Sandie, what would it be?"

Jenny understood that she was generating her own answers, influenced by her own wishes. But because Sandie was so present in her mind, the ideas were consistent with what she knew of Sandie's taste, interests, and personality.

The first item was easy. Delphine had taken the area rug from the TV room for her Paris apartment. Sandie would obviously have gotten a new one to replace it. There was a silk Chinese rug beneath the glass coffee table in the living room. To Jenny's eye, the rug was too small. Although the house had tile floors with heating coils beneath them, Jenny was a New Englander, accustomed to thick rugs covering most of the floor. She wanted a rug that would underlie not just the coffee table but also the entire seating group of sofa, loveseat, and armchair.

The solution seemed obvious: move the small Chinese rug to the TV room and get a new, larger carpet for the living room. "What do you think, Sandie?" She detected no opposition.

That evening, she aired her proposal with David. He agreed they needed an additional rug, but he hesitated. "The summer sun is really strong in the TV room," he cautioned. "It might fade the Chinese rug."

"Well, to be honest, Love, the Chinese rug is badly stained. If, as I suspect, they're cat stains, they'll be impossible to get out. A little fading might actually disguise them."

David looked at Jenny over his glasses. "You're right about the cat," he allowed. "Carotte used to pee on the rug to punish us if we went on a long trip. When we had company, Sandie put magazines on the glass coffee table to hide the rug stains below."

Encouraged by David's response, Jenny moved ahead. Sandie had used large houseplants as a low-budget solution to awkward spaces and empty corners. There were a dozen such plants—straggly, overgrown, and root-bound. With David's consent, Jenny repotted everything and did some radical pruning. The spiders didn't appreciate her efforts, but the plants did, quickly generating lush new growth. "You women always have to tidy everything!" David grumbled, but Jenny could tell he was pleased with the results.

Moreover, his offhand comment provided a critical insight. Every available surface was cluttered with souvenirs, knickknacks, collectibles, and objets d'art made by the children. Jenny assumed this was Sandie's taste, yet if David's remark was accurate, Sandie was always trying to tidy everything.

Raised by a single mother in economically depressed postwar Paris, Sandie was like Americans who had grown up during the Great Depression. She never threw anything away. Damaged tablecloths were recycled into napkins and placemats. Old bath towels were stitched into dishcloths. But Sandie was also passionate about order. The answer leapt out. The surfaces were cluttered because Sandie didn't have enough storage capacity. The large houseplants were filler for spaces Sandie had not yet furnished with cabinetry.

By the front door, there was a small marble-topped vanity standing on spindly legs. Crowded onto its top were the telephone, the mail basket, a bowl full of keys and coins, message pads, a mug full of pens, and the usual detritus that collects when people unload their pockets coming into the house. The entry wall needed a much longer table with lots of drawers and cupboards underneath. Sandie had presumably put the vanity there against the day when the budget would allow her to buy something more appropriate. But then came the tricky part. The vanity had sentimental value because it came from Sandie's family. Jenny needed to shift it to a place that gave it due respect.

The TV room, half a level down, was long, narrow, and crowded. It contained, among other things, a large oak cabinet, with squares of stained glass set into the doors. Like the vanity, the cabinet had come from Sandie's family. Sandie used it to house sewing materials and table linens.

Wouldn't it make sense to store table linens in the dining area? The oak cabinet could move to the dining room, where there was lots of space, to be replaced by Sandie's vanity, which was more suitable in scale. In the TV room, the vanity's marble surface would be free of clutter, so it could be better appreciated. David claimed that the arrangement of furniture made no difference to him, but Jenny knew it mattered deeply to him how Sandie had felt.

That evening, Jenny presented her proposed transplants. "I agree that we need a larger reception table," David said, "and I don't mind the vanity going to the TV room, but I'm not sure we should move that heavy oak piece to the dining room."

"It would certainly be easier to have the table linens close at hand," Jenny lobbied.

David considered this. "Well, Sandie did say it was a nuisance to have to run up and down for napkins," he allowed.

That turned the trick. When the weekend came, they hauled the linen cabinet up to the kitchen, and the vanity went down to its new home. David was cautiously positive, and Jenny was delighted. The process exposed some cobwebs, so she went to get the stepladder that normally inhabited a narrow space between the refrigerator and the wall. It wasn't there.

"Marc might have borrowed it," David speculated. "No matter. There's a second one tucked into the back of Sandie's bedroom closet." Though it now housed Jenny's clothes, the closet, in David's mind, was still Sandie's. Jenny sometimes slipped and referred to Boston as home, so she felt no discomfort. And David was right. In the back of "Sandie's" closet, on the right-hand side, there was a small folding stepladder.

That afternoon, they went furniture shopping and found an oriental-style sideboard that could serve as the entry table. They also spotted a Chinese step-chest they liked. The chest of drawers in their bedroom was old and slightly lopsided, with deep, heavy drawers. "Does it have any sentimental value?" Jenny asked.

"No," said David, "it was left by the previous tenant in our old apartment. When we moved to Morion, we brought it with us. It has no meaning." Neither of them had any inkling how wrong David's assessment would prove to be.

They ordered a step-chest stained to match the existing bedside tables. They bought the sideboard and took it home. After putting it in place, they stepped back to admire their handiwork. "It's a good choice," David agreed.

David spent Sunday morning cooking, then dedicated the remainder of the afternoon to cleaning his upstairs office. Jenny worked downstairs, consigning old magazines to the recycling bin. An hour later, she went to get a fresh cup of tea and found David sitting at the dining room table, staring out the window at the rain. Without looking at her, he said quietly, "It's hard throwing away school memos with Sandie's signature on them." He put on the Bach cello suites and resumed his seat. Jenny knew there were times when a mourner needed to be present with his grief. This was one of them, but she found it hard to do nothing.

When Marikit arrived for her Tuesday rounds, Jenny was busy filling vases with garden flowers. Marikit saw the shining copper pots in the kitchen and broke into a big smile. "I am so glad you have come, Madame Jenny!" she said. "It has been so hard to keep the house as Madame Sandie would have wished!"

Jenny reassured Marikit that it was not her fault. "You can only do so much in four hours per week. It's taken me half an hour just to cut and arrange these flowers," she pointed out.

"They are beautiful, Madame," said Marikit in her musical Filipino accent. "They are from the garden, yes? Madame Sandie was always bringing in flowers from the garden."

"I'm pleased to know that," Jenny replied. "When Dellie comes home, I want her to feel comfortable—to feel that the house is being maintained to her mother's standards."

"Of course Delphine will be comfortable, Madame! Delphine has told me that you were one of Madame Sandie's best friends!"

Jenny was glad Delphine thought so. In truth, Sandie had far closer friends in Geneva and Paris, but their trust in one another was solid. While they didn't have proximity and the easy sharing of confidences that comes with it, their bond was unique. They both loved the same man.

After Marikit left, Jenny began sorting through Sandie's coats. David planned to donate most of them to the local equivalent of Goodwill since they were too small for Delphine. There were two fashionable jackets Jenny reserved to offer to Sandie's friends, as well as a red wool maxi-coat. The latter had a stain on it, so she set it aside to go to the cleaners. She also came across Sandie's gardening jacket—the one she had used nearly a year before during her Thanksgiving visit. She decided to ask David if she might keep it for herself. She noted that it was missing a button. It seemed an opportune moment to check Sandie's sewing supplies for spares.

There were two sewing boxes on a shelf in Sandie's office. On inspection, one had spools of thread, bobbins, packets of needles and pins, and a small pair of scissors. The second contained pinking shears, zippers, safety pins, and a measuring tape. There was not a stray button to be found. *That's odd*, Jenny thought. *Surely Sandie would have kept a supply of buttons.* She considered the area around Sandie's sewing machine. There was nothing except the machine itself and a few related tools.

But Sandie must have had buttons. Perhaps upstairs with her clothes? Jenny rechecked the abundance of little tins and boxes in the dresser. No buttons. She finally went down to Sandie's office and sat in her desk chair. "Okay, Sandie, where are the buttons?" she demanded. "I know they're somewhere here. You never threw anything out. With a family of four, times twenty-some-odd years, there must have been scores of buttons, hundreds of buttons, thousands of ..."

And there was the answer. Jenny had been looking for a small container because that's what she had in Boston, but Sandie must have collected thousands of buttons over time. She needed something big yet accessible.

Jenny sat sectioning the space, her eyes moving like disciplined searcher's through a field, quadrant by quadrant. On the top shelf of a bookcase, there were half a dozen tall canisters—decorative "presentation" casings for expensive bottles of brandy or liqueur. Jenny knew Sandie stored knitting needles in them because she had once borrowed some to create markers for Delphine's parking practice. Were they all filled with knitting needles? And then she noticed that one container was lying flat, its lid along the side rather than on top. She drew it down carefully. Inside, there were enough buttons to open a notions shop. She brought down the gardening jacket, found a good match, and stitched on a new button.

Satisfied with her domestic progress, Jenny played in the garden for the rest of the day, attacking the ubiquitous bishop's weed. In the newly cleared areas, she turned and aerated the earth. When David came home, he surveyed her work, then bent down and picked a small object out of the dirt. It was a piece of broken ceramic with a fluted design on it.

"This is what Sandie used to create the mosaic top around the indoor pond. The yard was full of pottery shards when we first planted the garden, and she collected them." He considered it for a moment. "She wanted to do the siding someday as well." And then another moment. "I'll put it in the toolshed."

David read Jenny's silence. They both knew the shard would never be used. Finally he shrugged, pocketing the piece. "I still save things for Sandie," he said.

Delphine decided to make a quick trip home before her classes started so she could pick up more clothes and a few other items she wanted for Paris. David collected her at the train station on Saturday, and they arrived at the house just in time for lunch. He had already mentioned the furniture changes to Delphine during their frequent phone conversations, but Jenny could see that Delphine was making her own assessment. Delphine scanned the living and dining rooms, then asked what had happened to the little metal trolley table that formerly occupied the corner of the dining room where the oak linen cupboard now stood.

"It's in the TV room, housing the program guide and the remote controls," Jenny said. Delphine made no comment. Something was wrong, but Jenny wasn't sure what. Everything she had done was cleared with David and seemed in tune with ideas or wishes Sandie had once expressed. But maybe it had nothing to do with the changes. Maybe it was just impossible for Delphine to walk into the house after being away and not expect her mother to greet her at the door. Perhaps the flowers and the other touches of warmth were backfiring, reminding Delphine of Sandie and thereby magnifying the pain of her absence. She was still grieving, and would be for a long time.

Jenny steeled herself for the evening ahead. They had been invited to Michel and Josette's for a potluck supper so she could meet David's school colleagues. Much of the evening would be in French, but even in English, large gatherings were not within Jenny's comfort zone. Sandie delighted in social occasions. She always had stories and jokes to share. There would be unavoidable comparisons.

Jenny dressed for the evening in a long cotton skirt, a sleeveless turtleneck, and her best antique gold jewelry. It was very American but as her mother would have said, "tasteful." She came downstairs to the kitchen where David was putting away odds and ends. He looked at her and seemed genuinely startled. Then, after a long silence, he advised that Jenny should bring a sweater or she would be cold.

He was wearing his favorite blue jeans with the torn knee. Did he plan to go like that? Was she seriously overdressed? Or worse, had Sandie perhaps worn a similar outfit once? No, she reasoned, Sandie loved strong colors. Jenny's were always subdued, so it seemed unlikely. About five minutes before departure, David went up and changed into a sweater and slacks. Maybe it hadn't occurred to him, until he saw her, that he should "spruce up" for the evening. It might have been that simple, but she was reluctant to ask. Then Delphine walked in. "Wow, you look really nice!" she said, helping Jenny feel a little more secure about her choice.

On the way over, Jenny reminded David of her shyness and asked him to stick close. The party was informal, everyone was kind, and only once did Jenny come close to panic. Fortunately, David was within range, so she just made a beeline for his side. Despite their previous conversations, David was genuinely surprised that she would prefer to stand outside in the cold with him while he smoked rather than sit in a cozy living room without him but surrounded by his colleagues.

Jenny sorted through Sandie's collection of table linens, towels, and bed sheets, reserving those she knew David wanted to keep. She put the others out so Delphine and Marc could go through them and take anything they wanted for their respective apartments. When David saw the mounds of linen, he was taken aback.

"Do you really want to give all that away?" he asked.

"It's not that I want to give it all away," she replied. "I just want the children to indicate what they want. Then I'll know what I have to work with and whether we need any new items. You have to realize that I have absolutely no idea which sheets go with which bed. If it were up to me, I would color-code the towels and sheets by room. It's a system that really makes sense—for example, green towels for the downstairs bathroom …"

As Jenny delivered the last sentence, David interrupted, speaking at the same time, saying, "Yeah, Sandie always thought it would be easier—for example, green towels for the downstairs bathroom ..." The final phrase was uttered in perfect chorus. They looked at each other, mouths open in astonishment, and then laughed. "Great minds ..." he said.

Taking advantage of l'Académie Internationale's October break, they drove Delphine back to Paris and installed themselves in a small hotel near her apartment. The next four days were spent in parent mode. David enjoyed doing things for and with his children. The big project was installing kitchen cabinets. Jenny was impressed by how totally focused David was as he drilled adjustment holes and secured the backing. Sometimes she helped, steadying the ladder or handing him tools as needed. Other times Delphine took over the assistant role, giving Jenny time to quietly contemplate the apartment that had been Sandie's home from the day she was born until after the birth of her own first child.

Taped to the mirror over the mantel was a photograph of Sandie and David, happy and smiling, standing in front of their newly occupied house in Morion. Sandie was carrying a large bouquet of red and yellow tulips, and wearing the long red coat Jenny had recently sent to the cleaners. Delphine had chosen a red and yellow color scheme for her couch, bedcover, and other accents. Was there a connection, Jenny wondered?

On the day the semester was due to start, Delphine arrived at school to find that she couldn't begin classes until her health insurance status was certified. She came back to the apartment and burst into tears before she even got her coat off. "The world is full of bureaucratic assholes, especially in France," David opined, trying to calm her. "It's probably some minor glitch. It's just a matter of perseverance."

This was perhaps true, but it wasn't what Delphine wanted to hear. She retreated to her room. Jenny went in and gave her a hug. "I'm so sorry your mother isn't here right now. I'd really like to help, but I don't know how."

"It's okay," she sniffled. "That's just life." Then she straightened up and shrugged. "If Mom were here, she'd be yelling at the school on the phone right now."

This stepmother business was not something Jenny knew how to do. Her sense of ineptitude was heightened because there were mother-daughter pictures throughout the apartment, including a beautiful one taken when Delphine was maybe four or five. In the photo, Sandie was holding Delphine on her lap and glowing with maternal love while Delphine happily sucked her thumb. Jenny stood looking at that picture for a long time, but it offered her no counsel.

Ultimately Delphine settled down, and Jenny did too. David called the school and clarified the health insurance issues. The Swiss renewal schedule was different from the French one, and they were victims of the time gap. David managed to sort everything out, and Delphine bounced back quickly. By evening she was bright and cheerful again.

David and Jenny left for Geneva the next morning. Jenny was glad to get back. The house was beginning to feel like home. Among the e-mails awaiting her was a note from Bibi, full of questions about her new life.

De: JWLongworth
A: Bibi
Envoyé: 15 octobre, 2001
Objet: Tall order

Answering your eight million questions in one sitting is a tall order. You have one of those "call anywhere for ten cents and talk for an hour free" services, don't you? Our phone is still operating on an international rate that would bankrupt the Swiss treasury if you and I got to talking. I've only been here three weeks, but I feel as if I've already experienced three years' worth of emotions, incidents, and activities. Can you call me in the morning before you go to work? J.

Bibi's call came through late afternoon Geneva time. Jenny was eager for conversation, but she yielded the floor to Bibi so she could update Jenny on her grandchildren's latest accomplishments. "And now, Miss Heidi," said Bibi in conclusion, "how are you, and how is Prince Charming?"

"Prince Charming is pretty amazing, Bibi—at least to me. He has layers of complexity that I didn't realize existed. For years, I saw him primarily in vacation mode, when he was full of fun and focused on having a good time. Here, I'm exposed to his work life and his serious interests. He loves teaching and is devoted to his students. He's developed a marvelous curriculum exploring the world's religions as a means of understanding the evolution and core philosophy of different cultures. His erudition is truly impressive, yet he's extremely modest about it. He reads voraciously, he has a strong creative bent, and he loves art, music, and poetry."

"That makes for a nice curriculum vitae, but what's your home life like?"

"David's been very sweet. He's trying hard to make me feel comfortable. I've been on my own for so long, it's a real treat to be pampered. I'm not used to someone else cooking dinner or replacing the lightbulbs or taking the car in for an oil change. Of course, there's a down side. I'm also not used to having to consult with someone when I want to toss old newspapers or move furniture around. In a way, David faces the same challenge. He and Sandie had all their routines worked out. Now he has to renegotiate everything. I'm here with the best intentions, and for the most part he's been really sweet about it, but I know I'm a source of disruption.

"Even so, it's such a joy to have my love for him out in the open. I have to pinch myself when I wake up in the morning. I can't believe that he's really lying there next to me."

"So happily ever after actually exists?"

"Well, I wouldn't say this is happily ever after. I'm not exactly riding the crest of a shining wave with a shit-eating (pardon my French) grin on my face. *Au contraire.* Since my arrival, romance has taken a back seat to learning when to put out the barrels for trash and compost pickup and how to pay bills the Swiss way."

"Someone should send you the *Good Housekeeping* seal of approval!"

"It's not all worthy of approval, unfortunately. I've learned that even when David says I can do what I want with the houseplants, that does not include throwing out his favorite cactus, despite its being dead and looking like a wilted slice of old potato that has gone gangrenous and ought to have been composted months ago. I've also been advised in steely tones not to patronize him, which means don't tease or strike a light tone when he is truly upset about something."

Bibi's tone became slightly more serious. "What does he get upset about?"

"Most of it's silly stuff. He has a temper, but once you understand what triggers it, it borders on funny. He's not methodical. He's not good at reading instruction manuals, and he doesn't have a lot of patience when he can't intuitively make something work. He has a love-hate relationship with machines and electronic equipment. I rarely encountered it in the past. When we lived together as students, recalcitrant personal computers didn't exist, and we were too poor to have the "g-d effing appliances" David finds so hard to operate. Fortunately, his eruptions are almost never directed at another human being. He likes to argue, but primarily as a game, not as a statement of genuine disagreement."

"And the not-silly stuff?"

"He's still hurting badly. The healing is very slow. He doesn't like to complain, so he holds it in. When he gets upset about something that makes no sense, my guess is that it's because he's let the pain build up. He puts on a brave face, and he jokes a lot, but it's a cover. Teaching is an outlet. Poetry is an outlet. Wine is an outlet—one that he uses more than he should. Cigarettes too. His addiction to cigarettes is absolute. He smokes outside whenever possible and uses the stovetop exhaust fan when he lights up indoors, but it's still a negative.

"I remember Sandie forbidding David to smoke in her car. They argued about it on several occasions. Once when I was visiting, she unloaded a series of laments during breakfast. Then, with a half-smile, she shrugged and said, 'But that is marriage, life as two, yes?—*la vie à deux, n'est ce pas?*' Anyway, smoking is one area where we've made progress. He won't light up with me in the car."

They discussed David for several more minutes, and then Bibi asked about the children.

"Dellie is enjoying Paris," Jenny replied. "She has been generally accepting of my presence, both there and here in Geneva, but it's hard for her to hear footsteps coming down the stairs, expect to see her mother, and then be brought back to reality when it's me. At least she turns to me for practical things—remembering messages, filing forms—since her father is something of an absentminded professor.

"Marc also has tolerated my introduction into the household, as far as I can tell, although he's not very verbal these days. Even though they're both out of the house now, Marc and Dellie are nervous about my changing things—erasing their mother's presence in a sense—so I have to be extremely careful. Being a stepmother is one of the most difficult challenges I face. When the kids have problems, I feel really inadequate, because I don't have a clear sense of how—or whether—to intervene. My best contribution is to serve as a sounding board for David."

"When's the wedding going to be?"

"That one's still up in the air—various logistical problems and some bureaucracy thrown in."

"Okay, listen, you haven't covered half my questions yet, but I gotta go to work. It's almost eight thirty a.m. on my side of the world. This timing works for you, yes? I'll call again in a couple of days. Give my best to David."

"Will do. Thanks for the call, and have a good one."

Sunday saw the arrival of Freja Dehmel, a fiftyish woman from Hamburg whose soft features and wispy golden hair reminded Jenny of German actress Maria Schell. Freja had first met David only a few months before, at the seminar he attended in Berlin during July. When he learned she was coming to Geneva in late October for a week-long conference, he invited her to stay with them. Jenny liked her instantly, even before Freja gave her a compliment that earned Jenny's undying gratitude.

"I didn't understand that you are American," Freja said. "I thought you are French because of the way you dress and wear your hair." Jenny soon found herself wishing Freja lived in Geneva rather than Hamburg. Freja was open and direct. She had never known Sandie, and Jenny was able to speak candidly about issues she couldn't raise with Sandie's friends.

"It isn't easy," Jenny confessed, "hearing every person I meet described in advance as someone who adored Sandie." Jenny had to explain the English expression "not an easy act to follow," but Freja understood immediately the dilemma she faced. Freja told Jenny about her life, and Jenny responded in kind. Jenny walked her through the house, giving illustration to stories about Sandie's seashells, Sandie's buttons, and the photo of David and Jenny taken in Paris so many years ago.

As easily as if they had been lifelong friends, they moved through the topics that naturally insinuated themselves into conversations between women who have passed the half-century mark. They talked about fate, circles, and how one's choices influence the path of one's life. They talked about death and grieving, using up a lot of tissue in the process.

"I admire the way you honor Sandie," Freja said, "and your sensitivity about Marc and Delphine's feelings. It touches me as a mother, imagining what I would want for my children if I were gone. Your situation seems like a little miracle after a tragedy. You have such balance with your own needs and the needs of David and the children. I'm sure that Sandie is watching over all of you." Freja overestimated Jenny's "balance" by quite a bit, but Jenny was grateful for her words and sorry to see her leave for Hamburg.

"Do you not become sad, Madame, being here by yourself in the day?" Marikit asked during one of her weekly visits. Marikit generally tackled her cleaning agenda with immediacy and diligence, but she was curious about Jenny and had begun to pose politely probative questions as she set out her various supplies.

It was true that most of Jenny's days were spent with only the cats for company, but she reassured Marikit that she had plenty to do, and that David often came home early. He gave proof to her response by coming back from school that day for a quick lunch, and toward the end of the day, Bibi called again, fully occupying Jenny on the phone.

"What's happening on your side of the Atlantic?" Jenny asked.

"I have trouble thinking of myself as being on any side of the Atlantic, given that the water beneath my houseboat belongs to the Pacific Ocean. That aside, life on my end is good at a personal level. Work's slow, but that allows me to spend a little more time with the grandkids. Anyway, back to my checklist of questions. What are you doing about your French? Do your neighbors speak English?"

"I'm hoping to join a French class after the holidays," Jenny answered. "I assumed I would quickly embark on French lessons, but there's been a lot to do in terms of settling in. A few of the neighbors speak English, but everybody works during the week. I'd make friends more quickly, I think, if there were some retirees in the immediate neighborhood. I've been reminded of how different being part of a couple is from being single. All our socializing, and all our neighbors' socializing thus far, is in couples. I miss the one-on-one conversations with other women."

"So what do you do during the day?"

"When David is at school, I focus on getting my bearings and being a homemaker. And odd as it sounds, I have conversations with Sandie. Not as some sentient spirit—you know I don't believe that—but I summon up everything I know about her, then process my thoughts against the presence I have conjured up. I suppose it's like playing chess against yourself, having to switch psyches with each turn, except that Sandie and I are not in competition. I just want to understand her. It makes it easier for me to organize on the domestic front. David has been incredibly accommodating—more so than I expected. It helps that most of my ideas are things Sandie had already signed off on."

"Like what?" Bibi queried.

"I asked about adding a built-in bookcase in the living room. 'You know, Sandie always said we should do that,' David mused, and *voilà*, I got an okay for the bookcase. Then I asked if we could replace the guest bed in the study with a fold-out couch. 'Sandie wanted to do that too,' he conceded.

"My approach to domestic order is almost identical to Sandie's, despite our very different personalities. I discovered, for example, that my suggestion of color-coding the towels (blue for the bathroom with blue tile, green for the bathroom with green tile) was precisely what Sandie had once proposed. The similarities have made it easier for David to trust my judgment. Even the garden is now open to my incursions. All this in four weeks, so I don't regret postponing the French lessons."

"It's impressive that you're so settled in," Bibi observed. "And to fret that you haven't started French lessons yet! I would still be trying to figure out how to get my Valium prescription filled at *la pharmacie*. I wish I were half as organized as you, but I do think that when you get down to color-coding the towels, you are ready for something more serious—like French class!"

"Well, I still have miles to go. I haven't made any inroads in the clean living department. David still smokes too much, drinks too much, and god forbid he should go see a doctor for a checkup. But other than that, we're making progress. There are difficult moments, but there are also moments when I'm so happy I'm afraid to express it, lest the gods become jealous and rain down mischief upon us. I'll keep you posted."

"Take good care," Bibi said as she rang off. "Talk to you again soon."

Although David was tied up during the week, he made time on the weekends to help Jenny with projects and purchases. One Saturday morning, David took her to Sandie's favorite department stores, where they searched for reading lamps, a new living room rug, a convertible sofa, and green towels. Jenny found only a few of the items she wanted, but it was a useful introduction to the downtown stores. In Boston, she knew where to go for anything she wanted. In Geneva, she had no idea.

They came home for a light lunch, and then the mild sunny weather lured them into the garden. Jenny got out the pruning shears and went to work, while David sat on the patio and smoked. When he lit a second cigarette, she realized that his head was bowed. He was in trouble. David had always been one of the most optimistic and cheerful people she knew, filled with energy and enthusiasm. It was heartrending to see him so low. She went over and proffered a kiss, to which there was only a shake of his head and a muted grunt in response. Then, with a sigh, he got up, picked up a pair of clippers, and began chopping away at the ivy vines on the side of the house.

Jenny kept an eye on David but gave him lots of space. By evening, he seemed in good spirits again, and they had some horseplay over the cooking pots. During dinner they teased and laughed, and the meal was a lighthearted affair until Marc burst in the front door, filled with rage and angry at the world after a fight with Valerie. He brought back the linens he had taken from the house the previous week for their apartment. He threw them into the trash bin in the laundry room, shouting that he didn't need the effing things anymore and they could effing well do whatever they effing wanted with them. He then demanded to know where his old blue-striped sheets were. Jenny directed him to the roll-out storage boxes under Delphine's bed, and breathed a prayer of thanks that she had postponed the decision to give all the worn sheets to Goodwill.

David calmly invited Marc to join them, but Marc preferred to stomp about and bang things around in his old room. Valerie telephoned. David somehow got Marc to accept the call. They were on the line for a long time, and then Marc stormed out almost as loudly as he had stormed in, slamming the front door as he departed.

"I have to tell you, David, that one of the things I fear most is the thought of Marc moving back in. I don't have the parental experience or skills to deal with him. I'm afraid of the stress he would visit upon this house and the tension that would mount if we were all under the same roof. We have a rocky enough road without that outside pressure," she said. "We're still feeling our way. I know, for example, that you had a really rough afternoon. But I don't know why or how to help."

"Yes, I had a rough afternoon," he acknowledged. "Everything we did this morning—the furniture store, the rug dealer's—all reminded me of doing those same things with Sandie. You react to things the same way she did. You have the same standards—the same priorities. It overwhelms me sometimes. But it's not your fault. There's nothing to be done about it."

"It's so hard for me to see you like this—and Marc and Dellie—and not know how to make things better."

"Ducks, you've got to accept the fact that life is never perfect. Sometimes I think you don't understand that. You really think it can be perfect. It isn't, and it can't be."

This was not what Jenny wanted to hear. "I'm not looking for perfection," she said, "but I really love you, and I'm prepared to do anything to make you happy. I've got to keep trying even if what I try doesn't—maybe even can't—work."

In the midst of this emotional exchange, Marc called back to apologize. David took the cordless phone and retreated to the terrace. He sat outside for a while afterward, then came in and turned on the late news. He made no comment about the call. Jenny watched the news with him for a few minutes but could make no sense of the French, so she went up to bed. When David finally joined her, he gave her a quick peck on the cheek, turned away, and pulled the covers around him. "One day at a time," she told herself. "One day at a time."

The following day, after their traditional Sunday market run, David started cooking—one of his chief means of relaxing. As he cut up meat and vegetables to make a *boeuf bourguignon*, he opened up about his phone conversation with Marc, who reportedly felt chagrinned about his hostile behavior.

"When Marc walked into the house, he had a moment of conflict seeing us happily chatting at the table," David explained. "He was jarred by your presence and by a gut level recognition of what it meant—that his mother was gone for good. He doesn't want me to be lonely, but the idea of me with another woman seems disloyal to his mother. Marc doesn't want Sandie replaced, and that's what it felt like for him, seeing me relaxed, laughing, and obviously happy with you."

"I understand that it was a difficult moment for Marc," Jenny commented, "coming on top of a fight with Valerie. I expect the loss, however temporary, of Valerie's good will and affection added to Marc's distress. Still, I wish the kids were as confident as you are that Sandie would approve of us—that what I'm doing is what Sandie would have wished for you."

"The ways we deal with grief are not always the healthiest," David sighed. "I haven't done you any favors tearing you away from Boston and dropping you into all this gloom while we're still thrashing about and trying to find our way. I'm not much of a prize, I'm afraid."

"We're a long way from the finish line, David. My bet's on you to walk away with the blue ribbon at the end."

"Hmpff," he replied, trying unsuccessfully to sound gruff.

Jenny watched as David seared the chunks of beef for the bourguignon. She wished Marc and Delphine could recognize that David's rush to bring her into his daily life was a tribute to Sandie, not a slight. David had told his niece that Jenny represented the same kind of relationship he had with Sandie at the time she died: familiar, comfortable, domestic—two old friends who love each other, look after each other, and know each other very well. Warmth more than fire. At least, for him. But if it was true that "slow and steady wins the race," the blue ribbon Jenny envisioned was well within the realm of possibility. "Mmmm. Smells good," Jenny said as the aromas from the stove filled the kitchen.

The Chinese step-chest they had ordered was delivered in the late afternoon, despite it being a Sunday. They hauled the old chest of drawers down to the carport to await a Goodwill pick-up and lugged the new one upstairs in sections. Jenny was delighted to have the drawer space she needed, and David was again patient and accommodating in helping to set everything up, despite his fatigue from the weekend's turmoil.

Jenny was alone the next day when the doorbell rang midmorning. She answered to find a man soliciting furniture repair and recaning work. Once she realized what he wanted, she said no but took his card for future reference. She inferred from the name on the card that he was a member of one of the Roma families—known to Americans as Gypsies—who lived in neighboring France. As he was leaving, he spotted the battered chest in the carport and asked about it. Jenny's French was running out, but she got across the explanation that they wanted to give it to a charity. He asked if he could have it. The Gypsies did not have an easy life in Europe. Giving it to him seemed as charitable an act as giving it to Goodwill, so she said fine, take it. He came back for it an hour later with a small van. Jenny felt good that it would be repaired and restored for someone else's benefit.

The rest of the day was spent on domestic chores. Her final task was ironing a mound of table linens—a direct result of her insistence on using Sandie's cloth mats and napkins. Jenny's placemats in Boston were rattan. Her napkins were of the wrinkle-resistant smooth-and-fold variety. When she and Seth were married, they both worked full time and devoted additional hours to volunteer projects. The housework got done, but it was hardly a priority—or a pleasure. It intrigued Jenny that she was now deriving such satisfaction from being a homemaker and taking care of someone.

As David got undressed that night, Jenny noticed that his shirt collar was badly frayed. "We really need to get you some new ones," she commented.

"No, we don't, Ms. Busybody. My shirt is just fine," was his response.

"It may be just fine for garden work," she countered, "but not for school."

"Goddamn!" he howled. "Sandie said exactly the same thing!" And then he grinned. "But she didn't get anywhere, and you won't either." This was said with that special tilt of the head he displayed when he was being happily and childishly obstinate.

"Ah," Jenny countered, "but the odds have changed. Now it's Sandie and me together. Two against one. You have no idea what you're up against."

An Anxious Age

An anxious age is done;
The opposite is now here, yet none
Of us has read of never
An age which - without you - ever
Shut the love out learned through
The spells of men, and women too,
Unless on there you write
Our names and softly color them white
For dark so easily opens into light.

Chapter 11

Europeans celebrate *Toussaint*—All Saint's Day—the way Americans do Memorial Day. Delphine had a long weekend and planned to come home for the holiday. David decided that a ritual, however simple, might help with the grieving process and suggested that the family hold a brief ceremony to honor Sandie.

Delphine and Jenny helped David prepare things for the ceremony. Marc arrived at noon. They ate lunch, then assembled on the terrace. It was so mild that they were able to hold the "service" outdoors. Delphine read a French poem, Marc read one in English, and David drew from texts in both English and French. At the end, he looked at Jenny and asked if she wanted to speak. She shook her head. She had not planned to and could not have anyway because she had started to choke up. She was not alone.

David went in search of a box of tissues and brought it out to the terrace. After they all steadied themselves, David asked each of them to choose an area of the garden to sprinkle some of Sandie's remaining ashes. He also gave them shells brought back from the seashore where Sandie's ashes had been cast into the sea.

There was a gentle moment with Marc. Jenny's tears had touched him, and he gave her a hug. "I don't weep for Sandie," she told him. "Sandie's okay. It's the three of you I cry for. It hurts to see you in such pain." Perhaps it was good for Marc to witness the opposing sides of the contradiction she represented. Jenny understood very well the confusion the children felt, because she often felt it herself.

After the youngsters left, David and Jenny did some heavy garden work, giving them a welcome release from the day's tension. When a cold front moved in with the setting sun, they called it quits. David laid and lit a fire, and they ended the day sharing some quiet intimacy in the living room, watching the flames dance in the fireplace.

As they moved into November, Jenny continued the process of revitalizing the house. Sandie's office was to become her office, so she immersed herself in Sandie's organizational systems to understand what she should keep and what she could change. She and David shopped for a convertible couch to replace the office bed, ordered an ergonomic chair for the office, and purchased a large Berber rug for the living room. Jenny then suggested they look at some armoires. "Armoires? Why?" David asked.

"Because you desperately need a second closet," she told him. "There is no room to hang your shirts. Even Sandie couldn't have fit anything else into your cupboard."

"I can always find a place," he argued.

They sparred good-naturedly and finally reached a compromise. Some of his older shirts no longer fit him. They would offer those to Marc, then give the remainder to Goodwill. That might eliminate the need for increased storage capacity.

The following day, Jenny went through David's closet and put a pile of shirts in Marc's old room for him to try on. She kept one for herself—a formal dress shirt. She liked using men's shirts in lieu of nightgowns, and this one, with smocking, pleats and ruffles, could even pass for feminine wear.

That evening, Delphine called, tearful and upset. She didn't like the business institute and regretted choosing it. She felt trapped— obliged to continue because the fees had already been paid for the semester. David urged that she give the school—and herself—a little more time. Remembering discussions with Sandie regarding the education trust, Jenny reassured Delphine that she and Sandie had both felt education was less about studying and more about learning to think. Making a mistake was not a waste of money, nor was changing direction a waste of time. The waste occurred only if no lessons were learned.

"You have your mother's good sense and your father's passion, so I have every confidence in your ability to seek out whatever wisdom can be derived from this experience," she told her. Jenny was pleased that she had been able to do something supportive for Delphine. That night she celebrated by donning the ruffled dress shirt she had rescued and wearing it to bed.

"Do you like it?" she asked David.

He considered the shirt, smiled an odd smile, and said, "Oh, yes."

"So do I," Jenny echoed. "It's actually quite pretty."

"Sandie liked it too." He paused. "That's the shirt I got married in."

Jenny froze for a second, then recovered her breath. "I had no idea," she said. "Does it bother you," she asked, watching his face carefully, "that I'm using it this way?"

"Not at all. I'm happy that it pleases you. It seems fitting."

She was tempted to ask what he meant by fitting but decided to let it be.

The furniture store had promised a morning delivery of the new living room rug, so Jenny busied herself going through Sandie's bookshelves while she waited. In one folder, there were several years' worth of school yearbook photographs. The last one of Sandie was not flattering—not surprising given her illness—but there was a lovely portrait taken two years earlier in which Sandie looked serene, elegant, and very beautiful.

Jenny found a frame and placed the portrait on the new entry table beside the front door. There, David would be able to see it each morning when he left for school and each evening as he emptied his pockets of keys. After the carpet arrived, Jenny pulled back the furniture from the center of the room, rolled out the rug, then negotiated everything back on top of it. The rug warmed the room and brought everything together. "Do you like it, Sandie?" she asked, addressing the portrait.

When David walked in, he approved of the rug and also liked Jenny's choice and placement of Sandie's portrait. Shortly afterward, Marc appeared to pick up some clothes he had left drying the day before. He walked three feet into the house and stopped dead. He stared at the rug, then turned and went down to the basement to gather up his laundry plus the old shirts Jenny had set aside. When he came back up, David asked Marc directly what he thought of the carpet. Marc hesitated and then said, "It's very thick, isn't it?"

"Yes!" Jenny replied with enthusiasm. "And great with bare feet," she added, slipping off her shoes and wiggling her toes in the deep wool pile. Marc shrugged, but there was a hint of a smile, so Jenny assumed it was okay. That weekend, David helped Jenny frame photos she had brought from Boston, and they hung them in the bedroom. For the first time, she felt the room was hers as much as Sandie's. Her favorite addition was a set of six photographs, taken long ago in Paris, showing David and Jenny as the young lovers they were then, smiling radiantly at one another. Among the series was a smaller version of the poster-sized blow-up David kept in his atelier—the one Sandie had sometimes teased him about.

Marc and Valerie came for Sunday lunch. Marc had again decided he wanted to go to San Francisco and needed to send in an application to San Francisco State College. "Would you like some help with the forms?" David offered. Marc's response was ambivalent and testy. He was agitated, but the cause was unclear. While father and son sat at the computer, Valerie came up to the kitchen. She wanted to talk about Marc.

The primary Swiss languages are German, French, and Italian, but Valerie had studied English in school and had enough fluency that she could communicate effectively. She was thinking seriously of breaking up with Marc, she confided. She cited his capricious conduct, his changing moods, his anger, and his sensitivities. Until recently, she reported, he had often passed the evenings drinking and doing drugs with his friends. She threatened to throw him out of her apartment, but finally he made a promise to change. She clearly cared about him, but she had little confidence he would hold to his promise. She spoke of Marc's confusion about the house. "Marc has a good heart; he isn't angry at you, but he has, in his head, images of his mother in the house," she explained. "He wants time to stop, and the house to remain unchanged. In this way, his mother remains alive."

Jenny understood Marc's wish to keep the image of Sandie and her house unchanged, but she took an opposite view. Marc wanted to honor Sandie by freezing her house—and in a manner, her family. Jenny wanted to honor Sandie by helping the house—and the family—go on living. Life is change. And life is what David had chosen. Sandie would never have tolerated a dead house. But how to communicate this vision to Marc and Delphine?

Downstairs, Marc, still stressed, finished with the computer. David, who had retreated some time back, was sitting in the living room, staring at the fire, chain-smoking his Gauloises. When Marc and Valerie left, Jenny gave David a kiss and a hug.

"Something's wrong," she said. "What is it?"

"Same old problem," was his reply. "I'm afraid for Marc. He's obviously unhappy—lacking in confidence, without direction, without discipline, and without any positive vision of the future. He has no idea what to do about it. Neither do I." He sighed.

As the new week began, Delphine called. After further conversations with her father, she decided to finish the first semester at the business institute in good standing, then transfer into a liberal arts college. None of the French universities permitted a transfer midyear. The American University of Paris, however, was a private college that operated with American academic flexibility. If Delphine took her second semester at AUP, she could end the year with full credit and transfer into the Sorbonne the following fall. It seemed a sensible step.

While Delphine was completely bilingual, she didn't trust her written English and wanted her father to proofread her application essay. In her draft, she cited her mother's Parisian heritage and her own original interest in going to college in Boston. Attending AUP in Paris would be a way of combining both. She also wrote of how much she missed her mother and how important it was to her to have her father and brother nearby as sources of support. Jenny wanted Delphine to see her as a source of support as well. She knew it was foolish to expect a mention in Delphine's application—there was no slight in the omission—yet Jenny felt left out.

David sensed she was subdued, and he was lighthearted and teasing at supper. There was some leftover paté wrapped in foil, which he started to put on the table. Jenny got out a small plate. "What do you want a plate for?" he asked.

"The paté is nicer on a plate than on an old, rumpled piece of tinfoil," she answered.

"She wants a plate!" he exclaimed to Carotte. "My wife wants the paté on a plate!"

The wedding had yet to be scheduled, but when David referred to her as his wife, Jenny was oddly reassured.

"That's another thing for the list," he said, smiling.

"What list?" she asked.

"The list of traits you share with Sandie. Like insisting on a plate."

"What are the others?" Jenny queried.

"Oh, almost everything," he said. "You like playing with the photographs on the refrigerator door. You don't like a lot of vinegar in your salad dressing. You nag me about cleaning out the toolshed. You salvage broken flowers and put them in Sandie's little creamers. You save wrapping paper. You want me to get rid of the blue jeans with the torn knee. You keep the copper pots polished. I don't know. Almost everything."

Just days before Thanksgiving, Jenny came down with the flu. Her sore throat turned to laryngitis, and her chest tightened into a knot. They canceled Thanksgiving dinner, but Delphine already had her train ticket and came for the weekend regardless. Jenny encouraged everyone to safeguard their own health by respecting her self-imposed quarantine, so she saw Delphine only twice, when she poked her head in to say hello, and later, good-bye. When Jenny finally felt well enough to rejoin the world of the living, she wanted to hear about Delphine's visit.

"How did Delphine like the entry table and the new rug?" she asked.

There was no way David could duck the question. "Delphine was upset by it," he said wearily. The story gradually came to light. Marc had been telephoning Delphine on a regular basis, angrily reporting each and every change Jenny made. Marc was furious about the rug, and both Marc and Delphine were extremely distressed about the removal of the old bedroom chest of drawers.

Jenny remembered asking David whether the chest of drawers had any sentimental value. "No," he had assured her. "Sandie had no attachment to it at all." What David didn't realize was that the children had memories of going to that dresser to borrow their mother's socks and wool scarves when they couldn't find their own.

"I'm sorry that the children felt hurt," Jenny ventured, "but why on earth didn't they say something? You told them about the Chinese chest. It would have been perfectly easy to store the old dresser if they had expressed a desire to have it, but neither one of them said a word," she noted, annoyance creeping into her tone.

"Delphine said that she felt silly trying to express herself," David explained, "because she recognized that her response was purely emotional."

Marc's reaction was harsher, David admitted. "Marc said you showed his mother's furniture no respect because you 'gave it to some gypsy.'"

David's take was that Marc also understood, although not as well as Delphine, that his feelings were not rational, but they were strong nonetheless. "You have to let go," he had told the children. "You have to let Sandie be where Sandie is. You have to let Jenny be who Jenny is."

David could see from the look on her face that Jenny was crestfallen. He tried to reassure her that no one really blamed her. "The process is internal," he counseled, "and there is nothing you can do except be sensitive to how people feel."

Jenny recognized that illness and fatigue played a role in her distress, but that didn't make it any easier to handle. When David went out, she turned to her journal, trying to exorcise the demons by writing out her feelings. *Bibi was right*, she steamed as she booted up her computer. *Watch out for the children*, Bibi had warned. *They can sabotage you in the wink of an eye.*

Jenny opened the journal and let fly. There it was safe to be angry.

11/28/01—Am I wrong to expect them to behave like adults? Do they really think I would be careless with anything Sandie valued? Why would they not say a word about wanting the dresser when we spoke openly about giving it to Goodwill?

Marc took linens and dishes and glassware to Valerie's apartment. Why is it okay for him to shift things but not me?

Dellie took cookware and kitchen items to Paris and has revamped Sandie's old Rue Capron apartment. Her efforts to refresh the apartment are a tribute to her mother, not a criticism. Why can't she see that the same holds true with my efforts regarding the house—that changing things to suit your own needs can be accomplished in ways that are totally respectful of what (and who) was there before?

I've tried at every turn to blend Sandie's taste with mine, and mine with hers—to do things she would approve of. I'm feeling seriously raw over this. Worst of all, if the children are unhappy with me or what I'm doing, that wears on David.

I'm really wallowing in it, aren't I? Okay, enough. Ask yourself this one, Jenny. If they're not really grown-ups yet, then their behavior is forgivable. But what about you? Are you a grown-up? And if you are, what is the loving thing to do?

Jenny turned off the computer and considered her options. After a moment's thought, she went into Delphine's room and pulled out the large binder labeled "Maman"—Delphine's compendium of condolence letters and presentations made at Sandie's memorial service. Jenny started through the pages, and within minutes her sympathy for the children was revived. The power of the words and images transported her back to the week of Sandie's funeral. Poems, drawings, lyrics, e-mails, prayers, letters, tributes—it was devastating.

Several of Jenny's own e-mails to David were included, along with the farewell letter she sent Sandie and the "Conversations with Sandie" excerpts she had mailed to the children. Near the front of the collection, handwritten on school notebook paper, was Delphine's contribution. When Delphine spoke at the ceremony, her words were punctuated by sobs, and Jenny understood only the closing lines. With the written version in front of her, she could translate the French far more easily:

When I was little, you used to come tuck me in at night and together we would sing a children's song. A few months ago, we sang it again. *C'était bon*. It was good.

In the mornings, when we left for school, just the two of us, sometimes we would talk and sometimes not. It was our routine. *C'était bon*. It was good.

On Saturdays, when we went shopping, we used to laugh, and argue, and eat lunch, and try things on, and buy things (sometimes). *C'était bon*. It was good.

In the evenings after dinner, we curled up on the couch to chat. I told you about my boyfriends, my worries, my successes, my joys. *C'était bon.* It was good.

When I was late getting dressed, I would rush into your room, pressed for time, upset. I would empty your dresser, and then it was your turn to be upset. I never went out naked. *C'était bon.* It was good.

I am going to have to learn to do all these things all alone. I'm afraid I won't be strong enough. I miss you.

Jenny's tears had joined Delphine's at the ceremony. They came again reading her anguished words. The line about "your dresser" cut like a knife. Jenny read further outpourings of pain and love, but a third of the way through the album, she had to stop.

De: J W Longworth
A: Ross
Envoyé: 28 novembre, 2001
Objet: Pain

Ross, I need some serious honesty. Has the pain ever stopped? Do you still weep for Ramon? I've got my friend Rachel to coach my understanding of grief when it's still new and raw. But you're the only one I'm close enough to whom I can ask about the long haul. Is David ever going to get over losing Sandie?

If my questions hurt, I'm sorry, and if you don't want to talk about this, I will understand.

Much love, Jenny

She was about to turn off the machine when she realized there was a response coming back from Ross.

From: Ross
To: Jewel
Date: November 28, 2001
Subject: Re: Pain

Has the pain ever stopped? It depends how you define pain. I haven't cried in a long time. I haven't even felt like crying in a long time. I live in the present, not the past. When something reminds me of Ramon, it usually makes me smile. What hurts—what's hard still—is when something happens that I wish he had lived to see. But then, there are things I'm glad he missed, like when the Twin Towers went down. We would probably still have been in New York.

When I joined you in Paris, David and I had a couple of chances to talk about Ramon and Sandie and coping with loss. He made a comment that I thought was very powerful, alluding to the famous Frost poem, the one that ends, "and miles to go before I sleep."

"I'm sad that I can't take all the paths in the woods simultaneously," he said. "None of them is perfect, but each offers its own riches, and I hope to profit from the walk."

Sandie's loss has forced David to take up a different life. That different life has led him to you. Sandie's death didn't dictate what his future would be. It only dictated what it wouldn't be. The path he expected to follow was suddenly cut off. He could have just sat down and gone nowhere. He could have taken a path that spiraled into darkness and despair. But instead he chose life. He took the energy inherent in loss and used it to propel himself in a new and positive direction. Every road offers the possibility of beauty and joy, and David is actively searching for that on the road he's walking with you. His vision may be blurred by tears, but he's walking with his eyes wide open.

"Getting over" Sandie's death is the wrong phrase. "Going forward" is what you really want to happen. As far as I can see, David's doing a great job of it. I just wish Ramon were alive to see it. He loved his Ware Street friends. He'd be really glad for both of you. As am I. Ross

Jenny heaped mental blessings on Ross. Despite the anguish of the day, she was back on the up end of the seesaw by the time David got home and optimistic enough about the future to revisit the issue of a wedding date.

"Unless you think it's a lost cause, we should get in touch with the consulate about whatever hoops we have to jump through. My tourist visa is running out, and the notarized documents have an expiration date. If worse comes to worst, I could always go back to the States for a while but ..."

He cut her off. "Woman, if you go back to the States, who the hell is going to make sure I clip my toenails?" He frowned and tried to look very stern but failed. Jenny's face broke into a smile. David's romantic verbiage was unorthodox, but Jenny knew how to translate it. "I don't think it's a lost cause," he continued, his voice softening. "I'll call the consulate and set up an appointment."

Over the next few days, Jenny resumed the domestic organizing that had been stalled by her bout with the flu. In preparation for her new computer setup, she needed to shift a large bookcase in Sandie's office. She removed the contents and worked the bookcase to its new site. She spotted a pile of sheet music and other choral material and made a mental note that David should consider donating it to the school. She also found some lighthearted poems David had written for Sandie to celebrate birthdays and anniversaries. Then she got blindsided. There was an old worn teddy bear, presumably Marc's or Delphine's, sitting on one of the shelves. As she cleaned, she set it on the floor. It fell forward with a small plop, prompting the little music box inside to release the tinkling notes of "Rock-a-bye Baby." It played a line and a half, then stopped. Silence. She stared at it. Sandie had loved her children so much—and they missed her so much. Jenny had to leave the room and occupy herself elsewhere for an hour before she could come back and finish with the bookcase.

She thought about telling David what had happened, but put it off. *If a music box tune in a teddy bear can do that to me, what must David's every waking hour be like?* she wondered. She forced herself to refocus by composing a response to recent inquiries about their wedding date, doing her best to sound optimistic and chipper:

De: JW Longworth
A: Family & friends
Envoyé: 5 décembre, 2001
Objet: Status

We don't have a wedding date yet. The course of true love never runs smooth. The latest problem is that the Swiss require US certification of our documents. This means a trip to the US consulate in Geneva. The consulate, however, has been closed since the 9/11 attacks, except for a few unpredictable sessions when they conduct essential business for people who can't make the three-hour trek to the US embassy in Berne.

Since David's weekday availability is so limited by his teaching schedule, a sympathetic staffer finally gave us an appointment. We went haring over to the consulate during David's lunch hour only to find that they had moved to a more "secure" building on the other side of the lake. They neglected to mention this when we made our appointment. David called again to reschedule. They are now officially operating from ten to one, Mondays, Wednesdays, and Fridays, but they aren't giving appointments, and the hours are subject to change. No, they won't be open during the winter holidays. No, they aren't sure what the schedule will be in January. As David would say, it's a hoot! If it weren't for the health insurance and residency permit issues, it would be a whole lot easier just to live in sin.

Stay tuned!
Best, Jenny

David's Christmas vacation began the third week of December. They took advantage of the open weekdays to go to the consulate. They had to pass two checkpoints where rifle-toting guards examined their papers and searched Jenny's pocketbook before they were allowed to enter the office and fill out forms for their affidavits.

Delphine came home for what would be the family's first Christmas in Geneva without Sandie. Jenny had put a rose in a bud vase on Delphine's bedside table to welcome her, but Delphine made no comment about it. That, combined with the fact that Marc had blown off a second application to San Francisco State, led Jenny to brace for some rough sledding.

Surprisingly, the holiday activities were launched without incident. Marc came over and helped David put outdoor lights on the shrubbery in front of the house, and then the two of them went off to buy a tree. Delphine took charge of setting up a nativity scene using carved and painted wooden figures dating from Sandie's childhood.

Given the turmoil of the previous months, it was reassuring to see them having fun together. David and Marc strung the tree lights. Delphine joined in, placing the ornaments. There were lots of references to Maman liking it this way or Maman doing it that way, but the memories seemed to be happy ones. Jenny had her own ways of liking and doing, but she stayed discreetly on the edges and occupied herself making rum-spiked eggnog.

David invited the DuPonts to join the family for dinner Christmas Eve, along with Mehrak and Manuela Pashoutan. Jenny set the table with Sandie's silver and her good cutlery. Delphine added some decorative touches that were favorites of Sandie's, placing candles in groupings, then taking a small bottle of sparkling star shapes and sprinkling them over the tablecloth.

Michel and Josette arrived at 7:30, followed shortly by the Pashoutans, then Marc and Valerie. The assembled company ate and drank their way through the next three hours. The menu included, but was not limited to, oysters, smoked salmon with *cornichons*, *paté de foie gras*, goose with chestnut stuffing, Swiss chard baked with chopped onions and cream, Christmas salad made from the traditional white chicory, an assortment of cheeses, and finally a sweet-and-sour lemon pie based on a recipe from David's mother. There was champagne to start, a light white wine for the fish, a sweeter white for the *foie gras*, and two different reds for the goose and the salad. It was a splendid meal.

On Christmas Day, David was up early, despite not getting to bed until three. Jenny rose shortly after he did, to find he had already cleaned most of the kitchen. The children had hung the family's holiday stockings on the mantel, including Sandie's. Jenny's assigned receptacle was a medium-length sports sock.

Sandie's stocking was empty. While David was occupied, Jenny withdrew a rose from the bouquet Josette had brought them the evening before, wrapped the stem, and carefully deposited it in Sandie's stocking. As she turned away, she spotted, peeking from the top of Delphine's stocking, the decorative little box that she knew contained Sandie's wedding ring. She and David had agreed that, when they married, they would give Delphine her mother's ring and Marc his grandfather's gold pocket watch—their wedding presents to them.

David had said nothing about giving Delphine the ring at Christmas. Was this also a surprise for Jenny? Had the children finally given their consent? She had a moment's elation, then a moment's doubt. The doubt stayed with her.

Marc and Valerie weren't due until noon. Delphine was still asleep. David focused on the luncheon menu, making a rich stock from the goose carcass and starting a pumpkin soup simmering on the stove. Despite his love of cooking, he was edgy. After absorbing three generous servings of eggnog, he disappeared to take a midmorning nap.

Delphine emerged around 11:30. Marc and Valerie arrived an hour later. It was decided to eat first, then open presents afterward. After the last crumbs of dessert were consumed, they settled in the living room.

The pace was slow enough that everyone could see what everyone else received. Jenny had ordered her favorite snapshot of Sandie and herself, reproduced in three different sizes. The smallest one fit perfectly in the key chain frame she tucked into David's stocking. The midsized copy was for herself—for her/Sandie's office. The large print, suitable for a stand-up frame, was her "big" present to David.

The gifts were a success. Marc served as the family photographer and chronicled the whole performance. The stockings were last. David withdrew Sandie's rose from her stocking, and Jenny immediately put it in water. There was also a rose in her own stocking. It was the first time David had ever given her one. And then it hit her. That rose had been intended for Sandie's stocking. Realizing Jenny had inadvertently preempted him, David stuck it in Jenny's stocking instead.

Marc and Delphine were both cautioned to unpack their stockings carefully. Marc found his grandfather's pocket watch and was intrigued. David supplied some of its history and helped him decipher the inscription.

When she saw her mother's ring, Delphine burst into tears. She tried to put it on, but the ring was too small for her. "You can always have it refitted," Jenny suggested.

"No, I'd rather put it on a chain and wear it around my neck," she replied.

From across the room, David called to Delphine, "It was Jenny who found it." He had already told her that months before. Jenny wondered at the reminder. She waited hopefully for a "surprise" gift of the children's blessing and a date for the wedding, but it didn't come.

The young people went out in search of entertainment. David and Jenny stayed home with a simple supper. Except for her unspoken (and she hoped unnoticed) disappointment about the lack of resolution regarding the wedding, it had been a good Christmas. The day was free of tension, and the enjoyment seemed real.

The following day, David retrieved a frame one of his students had given him and inserted the picture of Sandie and Jenny. When Delphine popped her head in the door, David showed her the photo and asked if she recognized the setting. It had been taken at Corkscrew Swamp several years before when the Perrys and Jenny were in Florida. "Nice," Delphine said and immediately changed the subject to her afternoon plans.

After Delphine went out, David checked his e-mail, then lay down on the couch in the living room. He warned Jenny off. "I'm down at the moment. I'll come back up eventually." They had been trading runny noses and sore throats throughout the holidays, so at first Jenny thought it was just the illness and the cold medication. Eventually, she realized that he was down emotionally as well.

After an hour, he stirred himself, lit a fire in the fireplace, and resettled himself next to the end-table lamp with the newspaper. Jenny went in quietly, plopping down on the rug in front of the fire, and laid her head against his knee. She might as well have been in some other part of the house. It wasn't until Minuit arrived on the scene that David absentmindedly reached out his hand and patted ... the cat. *His mind is on some other planet,* Jenny concluded as she quietly withdrew.

Thanks to a good night's sleep, David was cheerful in the morning. Jenny's laryngitis had reappeared, and he teased her about sounding like a frog. He went shopping with Delphine to get some items she needed for Paris. When they came back, Jenny set up the ironing board in the dining room, thinking to keep David company while he cooked, but he retreated to the living room and started to read the newspaper. His mood was difficult to decipher.

Marc and Valerie joined them for Delphine's farewell dinner. Jenny was acutely conscious that this constituted the last opportunity for David to talk to the children, together and in person, about committing to a wedding date. She excused herself immediately after dessert and retreated to the bedroom. She had hoped to get a report afterward, but David didn't come to bed until she was sound asleep.

David had trouble getting into his e-mail in the morning. From the next room, she heard him muttering, "Goddamn piece of shit!"

"Do you need help?" she offered.

"I'm in a bad mood, Jenny." He minced no words. "I don't want any help, and you'd best stay clear."

David was preoccupied when they took Delphine to the station, distant when they went shopping for office supplies, and testy during lunch. There was little improvement by evening, but when the phone rang after dinner, David managed to sound cheerful as he exchanged greetings with the caller in English. "It's Bibi," he told Jenny after a minute.

"Thanks," Jenny said. "I'll take it downstairs."

David wished Bibi a Happy New Year and hung up when he heard Jenny pick up on her office phone.

"Hey, Bibi, how were the holidays!"

"Hanukkah is getting to be as commercial as Christmas, and we had eight days of it to get through," she complained. "It was over on the seventeenth, and I'm still recovering! How was Christmas in the Alpine snow?"

"Geneva had thick clouds and icy winds instead of snow, but we survived. Actually it wasn't bad. The kids seemed to enjoy their father and each other, and David prepared a fabulous Christmas dinner."

"So all goes well?"

Jenny debated about how to phrase her answer. Bibi's radar instantly picked up her hesitation.

"Or is there trouble in paradise?" Bibi amended.

"I don't know that I'd use the word *trouble*," Jenny responded, "but neither would I use the word *paradise*. If this were a Hollywood script, we would have had an emotional scene overflowing with love and reconciliation. The kids would have given us their enthusiastic support for a Christmas Day wedding wrapped up in shiny paper with a big red bow, and the ceremony would have proceeded, performed by an angel in disguise, sent by Sandie."

"I take it this was not the case?"

"This was definitely not the case. The kids are still resistant to the wedding and unsettled by the changes in their lives. David still grieves for Sandie, and he feels the children's pain as well as his own. I accept that this is all going to take a long time, but I get a little discouraged sometimes."

"Jenny, I know you may not want to hear this, but if David is still so conflicted, maybe you should back off and give him more time to get over Sandie's death. I know you want to help him, and I understand that you have to get married in order to stay in Geneva, but it sounds to me as if the family isn't ready. You're the one who kept worrying about whether this was happening too fast. Maybe you were right. Does it make sense to push the marriage thing under the circumstances? I mean, it's not as if you're pregnant and there's a loaded shotgun somewhere."

"For sure I'm not pregnant, but as to the shotgun, I still get nervous that David might end up loading one if he sinks to the bottom, and there's no one on hand to pull him back up again. He needs me here, Bibi. He's not strong on sweet nothings, but the need is very clear."

"I know you're a stiff-upper-lipper, but are you getting enough back to make all this baby-sitting worthwhile?"

"Bibi, that's not fair. David is hardly behaving like a baby. If anything, he's the one who's trying to tough it out, not me. It seems to me that vowing allegiance 'in sickness and in health' includes standing by someone you love when they're felled by emotional pain, not just physical illness. If David were fighting cancer, you wouldn't suggest that I skip out just because he was drugged and barely responsive."

"Okay, okay. I hear you, but somewhere there's a limit. What I'm really trying to say is that if this doesn't work out in the long run, no one is going to blame you if you chuck an unsatisfying relationship and go home."

"David is bowed, Bibi, but he's not broken. The man I've known for thirty-some-odd years is still there. I see glimpses, and the rest is just beneath the surface. This is going to work. It may take time, but it's going to work."

"From your lips to God's ears. Meanwhile, Happy New Year. Talk to you in a week or so?"

"A week or so is good. Happy New Year to you too."

Sunday brought their weekly market run, which perked up David's spirits. He actually got excited when he spotted black-eyed peas. He bought a kilo so he could make hoppin' John, a traditional southern dish, for New Year's Day. Afterward, they stopped at the florist's, and he picked out a fresh rose for Sandie. He gave it to Jenny to hold. Then he picked out a second rose. "And this one is for you," he said. He tilted his head down so he was looking into her eyes over, rather than through, his glasses. The look was long and deep. There were no further words attached to it, but Jenny suddenly found herself blushing.

When they got home, Jenny set Sandie's rose in its usual site on the mantel and put hers in her office. She, too, had received a picture frame as a Christmas gift. She took the midsize print she had ordered for herself, featuring Jenny and Sandie in Florida, and slid it into the frame. It was a perfect fit. She set it on her desk next to the rose. "I'm not the one who needs a sign, Sandie," she told the photograph. "Besides, I don't really believe in them. But it would be nice if you'd send one to David and the kids, to reassure them that you're okay with how things are going."

New Year's Eve was spent quietly at home, just the two of them. They drank champagne with dinner to toast the New Year. Jenny started yawning at nine o'clock. "Do you want to stay up until midnight?" she asked David.

"Sandie used to stay up, but it doesn't mean anything to me," he replied.

"Even if I loved New Year's Eve, which I don't, I'd have trouble staying awake that long," Jenny confessed.

"*Gone with the Wind* is on the movie channel," David told her. "That'll get you close to midnight. It's dubbed in French, but you know the story so you won't have trouble following it."

"I'm not really a fan of dubbed movies. If you're going to watch, I'll go get into bed with my book."

David watched the film for an hour, but turned it off at, "*Franchement, Scarlette …*"

Jenny had fallen asleep, but she stirred as David got into bed. She moved to give him a good-night kiss, and they made love for the first time in weeks. Jenny smiled with relief as much as pleasure. The hiatus had unsettled her.

Shared Time

For Jenny - Happy New Year, with love

We've walked on separate paths, scarred
By storms whose churning, raging turbulence
Ravaged inner sculpted lands
And comfortable but fragile spaces.

Now shared time erodes the older pain.
Reshapes streams and rebuilds hills.
Newly opened trails will no doubt give us
Ample joy to fill the empty places.

D.P - 1 January, 2002

Chapter 12

New Year's Day was devoted to designing a card for their New Year's greeting. Rather than a Christmas card, the French custom was to send a note in January with best wishes for the coming year. The Perry tradition was a family photograph with a message in both French and English. David selected a photo taken Christmas Eve, with David, Marc, Delphine and Jenny standing side by side next to the tree. Just above and behind them, clearly visible in the photograph, was the oil portrait of Sandie that David painted and gave to her on her fiftieth birthday. Christmas past, Christmas present, Christmas future. Everyone was smiling—including Sandie.

As Jenny worked on the design, David handed her a brief poem. "Happy New Year, Ducks," he said, planting a kiss on the top of her head. The poem had a melancholy edge, but it contained words of hope and healing. "Shared time erodes the older pain," he had written, and, "Newly opened trails will no doubt give us ample joy."

The New Year was starting on a positive note. Buoyed by David's words, Jenny started on her Christmas thank-yous. The most important ones were to Delphine and Marc. In Delphine's, Jenny acknowledged her gift and her help during the holiday. At the end she wrote:

> I know it hasn't been easy to adjust to a new presence in the house, and to the changes my coming has brought about. I also know, because David has been candid about it, that there have been times when we did something that, despite our best intentions, caused pain

or anxiety for you. Regardless of these difficult incidents, you have consistently been respectful and considerate. It's natural to feel confusion and anger when a surviving parent chooses a second spouse—and to vent some of that anger in the direction of the newcomer. But I have never felt any personal resentment from you, and I am grateful beyond words. Thank you again for everything, and may the New Year bring you many blessings.

Love, Jenny

She then composed a similar note to Marc. Confronting their discomfort seemed to Jenny to offer the best chance of diminishing it.

Delphine came back to Geneva for her birthday in early January. Her gift was the promise of a necklace of her choice to carry her mother's ring. David prepared a family dinner, and Jenny followed Sandie's tradition of baking Delphine a rich American devil's food cake. The conversation at table was wide ranging, but the subject of a wedding date was not broached. The expiration date on Jenny's notarized documents was getting closer and closer, and her concern was increasing at a parallel rate.

Jenny woke up the next morning with a cough and a raspy throat. She went down to the kitchen and started emptying the dishwasher while David fixed her a mug of tea. She broke a glass in the process. Despite her diminished vocal power, the spontaneous, "Shit!" that escaped was clearly audible.

David reacted instantly to her distress, moving in to soothe and calm. Jenny rarely swore, so he knew something was definitely wrong. "Happens all the time," he said. Jenny insisted that she was just worn down from the holiday hubbub. David gave her a warm hug, and they stood for a moment in a gentle embrace. As she leaned against him, it occurred to Jenny that the incident highlighted the contrast in their personalities. Had David been the one who broke the glass, he would have sworn a blue streak, bellowed his rage, and not allowed her anywhere near the kitchen—or him—while he cleaned up, solo, cursing under his breath.

Later, true to form, Jenny heard profanity issuing forth from the basement. Carotte had apparently missed the cat box. When Jenny trotted down the stairs to help, David ordered her to stand clear. He didn't permit hugs when he was upset.

Delphine was due to leave the next day for Paris. As far as Jenny knew, David had not yet gotten Marc and Delphine to agree on a date for the civil ceremony that would legalize her presence. *Why is he waiting?* she fretted. Were there pressures she was unaware of? Were there others besides the children lobbying for a delay? Before Jenny moved to Geneva, Michel had offered words of caution concerning Marc and Delphine.

> *De: Michel DuPont*
> *A: Jenny*
> *Envoyé: 7 septembre, 2001*
> *Objet: Conseil*
> *Chère* Jenny—The fact that you and David enjoy each other and have decided to live together neither shocks the children nor perturbs them. *Au contraire.* But I sense that they need time to accept that this cohabitation should regularize itself by a marriage, which they see no reason for at present. I think that a certain patience is necessary for David and for you, even if certain administrative difficulties are associated, because your happiness will suffer if your family life is established on a decision incomprehensible to them.
> *Amicalement,* Michel

At the time, Jenny agreed with Michel and appreciated his counsel. But several months had passed. The "administrative difficulties" were mounting, and so were the social ones. She had not told her siblings of Marc and Delphine's resistance to a marriage. She didn't want her family's first impression of them to be colored by a negative note. She wanted to believe that David was moving things along as quickly as possible, but by Sunday morning, Delphine's last day in Geneva, Jenny's anxiety got the better of her. Over breakfast, she cautiously reminded David that this was the last chance he would have to talk to Delphine in person about their getting married.

"Don't push me, Jenny," he snapped. She immediately backed off and apologized.

"Shit, Jewel, I'm sorry," he rejoined. "I know this is frustrating for you. It is for me too. I've been turning this over and over in my mind and getting nowhere. I'm caught between a rock and a hard place. I was hoping to talk to the children together last night, but that got torpedoed when Marc canceled on dinner. Now I'll have to do it another way."

Delphine had an early-afternoon train. David drove her to the station alone, so they would have a chance to talk. When he came home, he was preoccupied and mute. Jenny sat silently with him in the kitchen while he smoked a cigarette and stared out the window. Finally, he looked at her. "I couldn't talk to Delphine. The setting just wasn't right."

"It's okay," Jenny said simply. It wasn't okay, but pushing the issue was obviously counterproductive. "We'll figure something out," she added. What that would be, she wasn't sure, but she wanted to show solidarity. Suddenly David was on the move, heading down the stairs.

"This whole thing is too goddamn complicated," David announced to the air as he descended. Jenny heard the computer click on. He started typing. He was at it for two hours straight. When he was done, he asked her to look at what he had written. It was the draft of a letter to Marc and Delphine.

De: David
A: Marc; Delphine
cc: Jenny
Envoyé: 6 janvier, 2002
Objet: My Promise
    Dearest both of you,
    I am going to take back my promise concerning Jenny and me. I wanted to discuss it with you this past

weekend, but I couldn't find a time when we could be together.

For me, marriage is a practical relationship and has little to do with feelings; it's a social, legal arrangement. Jenny is in Switzerland on a tourist visa. She can only stay here legally if she is married to me. Her American insurance policy will only pay for emergencies abroad. She cannot get Swiss health insurance because she has no legal status here. Only when we are married will she be eligible. For someone with her cancer history, this protection is very important.

Similar problems exist at the bank. I am counting on Jenny to take over management of our finances. To do this, I need to modify the title of my accounts, but the bank doesn't want to deal with a "foreign signatory." They want to wait until Jenny and I are married, and Jenny has a residency permit. All this sounds terribly material, but that's what the legal side of marriage is all about.

You say that you are not yet ready to have a second Madame Perry. That's fine if you have a great deal of time before you, as I hope you do. But do Jenny and I? She worries that my smoking and drinking and aversion to seeing doctors will cut short our time together. I worry that her massive radiotherapy of six years ago may do the same. The one thing we both know is that life is uncertain. Given our age and circumstances, waiting a few years is not a reasonable option.

Jenny is *not* Sandie. She does not pretend to be. We have no right to expect her to be anyone other than herself. Nor do we have any future in wanting Sandie to be with us except in our minds and hearts.

For all these reasons and more, I have decided that Jenny and I will get married this month. I have chosen 25 January because I want to associate this event closely with Sandie's birthday. I am certain Sandie would want this for us all. It will be my birthday present to her.

I would like you to serve as our witnesses, but I will not hold it against you if you decide not to. I love you very much and hope you can understand this letter and what is behind it. Even if you do not understand fully today, I know you will understand later in your lives.

Love, Dad

Jenny read it carefully. The first time through was to absorb the gist. On the second reading, she tried to look at it from Marc and Delphine's point of view. In doing so, there was an issue that concerned her. In saying he was going to renege, David was denying the children an eleventh-hour chance to give their okay. "This may not be necessary," Jenny suggested. "It's always possible that if you ask them now, they'll agree to a date."

"I've already asked them," he said.

This was new information. "And they said no?" she queried.

"They said no," he confirmed

"How long ago was this?" she asked. "If it was early on, they might, by now, have gotten used to having me around."

"Two weeks ago," he said.

Two weeks ago meant Christmas. David had been carrying this burden around for two weeks without telling her. When she had casually mentioned what a nice Christmas gift the children's blessing would be, David tried to arrange it and was thwarted by their opposition. Small wonder he didn't want to talk about what was going on.

Jenny tried recalculating the logistics of her legal status. She wanted to get David off the hook and give the children more time, but the practical pressures were enormous. She didn't want to risk being in Switzerland as an illegal alien lest it foreclose the possibility of a future residency permit.

"It would help to have a sense of how much time they need," she commented, trying to get a handle on the parameters. "In August, a delay seemed reasonable. Neither of them knew what it would be like to have me around the house. But at this point, we've settled into a pattern. The way things are now is pretty much the way things are going to be. Do you know what they're looking for? What they're waiting for?"

"I think they just want to hold onto the status quo as long as possible. It's not you they object to, only the circumstances. You've been a real trooper, Jenny. You've been patient and kind and caring.

Their feelings aren't rational, but they're understandable. Believe me, they're understandable." He sighed.

Perhaps this is like packing up Sandie's clothes, Jenny considered, *or cleaning out her medicine cabinet. Perhaps my role, painful though it might be, is to move things forward even though no one wants to move. Maybe I am best, not as the person who is patient, kind, and caring but as the person who pushes, confronts, and forces essential change.*

Jenny gave her signoff regarding the letter. David planned to e-mail it that evening so the children would receive it simultaneously. Before he did so, however, Delphine called, upset by a snafu at school. David tried to calm her down, but the academic problem was serving as a release valve for other tensions, and Delphine was not easily pacified. "Not a good time to send the letter," he concluded.

The following evening, David called Delphine and was pleased to learn that her school problem had been resolved. Her distress had dissipated, and she was back to normal. Jenny wondered if David would therefore send the "marriage" e-mail, but she didn't ask. *He will tell me when he tells me,* she said to herself.

When he returned from school the next day, David went straight to his computer. After twenty minutes, he announced that he had amended the letter to the children. He suggested that Jenny review the final version while he started supper. There was only one change. After the opening paragraph, he had inserted a new one:

> First of all, I'm happy being with Jenny, living together, growing old together, sharing what's left of this life with someone who knew and respects your mother as much as I loved her, someone who respects you, enjoys your company, wishes only your well-being, someone I've known and loved in another way for almost forty years.

Jenny read the amended version twice. As she returned to the kitchen, she considered David's reference to their loving each other "in another way" during her marriage to Seth and his marriage to Sandie. It was a love that remained steadfast though time and distance, undiminished despite the demands of other commitments. It didn't fit the traditional definition of romance, but it was a testament to love's resilience, however varied its expression.

She wrapped her arms around David, and they held each other as the pan of sliced potatoes on the stove began to sizzle. "I love you so much," she told him. These sweet moments had the power to wipe out all the previous anxiety.

David started the marriage process in earnest, stopping by the *Mairie*—town hall—to find out what dates were available for the required civil ceremony. He discovered that their US documents had to be translated into French by an official Swiss translator. The translation alone might take three weeks, and the *Mairie* could not proceed without it. There was no way they could schedule a wedding in late January. Late February was more likely. David was disappointed, yet he had no choice but to accept the *Mairie's* dictates.

"This doesn't preclude a January 25 wedding," Jenny said. "We can still hold a private spiritual ceremony on the twenty-fifth. It just means that the private event and the legal contract signing will be on separate dates."

The legal ceremony required witnesses. That was the role they hoped the children would fulfill. Jenny suggested that David send his e-mail right away. "The longer the children have to adjust, the greater the chance they will say yes," she reasoned.

David sent the e-mail, then called Marc to tell him it was coming. He next called Delphine. The conversation ended swiftly. Afterward, he sat at his desk for several minutes, silently rereading the letter.

The evening was chaotic. A colleague called about a seminar. Germaine St. Jean called from Nîmes, lonely and grieving, needing someone to talk to. Michel called. In between were two calls about school politics. But there was nothing from either Marc or Delphine in response to David's missive. He was moody and remote by the end of the evening.

In the morning, David checked his e-mail. There was still no word from the children. As he got ready for school, he asked Jenny to prepare a packet of documents for the Swiss translator. "I'll swing by and pick it up after my last class," he promised.

That afternoon, David was on his way out the door with the packet of documents in hand when Delphine called. They spoke for a few minutes, then he called up to Jenny that he was off to the *Mairie*. He was in a good mood when he came home.

Jenny asked about Delphine's phone call. "She sounded okay," he reported. "She didn't say anything about the wedding, and I didn't ask, but she confirmed that she'll come home on the twenty-fifth and stay for the dinner party on the twenty-sixth that we always hold with the DuPonts, in honor of the multiple January birthdays."

"Do we need to hear from Marc, or may I tell my side of the aisle that we've doing a private ceremony on the twenty-fifth, even though we don't have a *Mairie* date yet?"

David let out a sigh. "Marc will likely take his time, if he responds at all. Go ahead and tell whomever you want."

Jenny hoped to add some details to her announcement. "Do you have any thoughts about the private ceremony?" she asked.

"Well, we'll do the wedding here at the house and have a special dinner at home with just Marc and Delphine. I'm thinking of making Julia Child's *fondue de poulet à la crème*, in honor of the first French dish I cooked for you back in our Cambridge days."

Jenny wasn't picking up anything substantive about the wedding ceremony. She was looking for more than chicken poached in cream. "Our private ceremony is the really important one," she said, "more so than the *Mairie* event. I'd like vows of our own making."

"Fine," he answered. The nonculinary details didn't seem to be of interest.

Michel and Josette stopped by for coffee and chat. After discussing school politics, David mentioned that Delphine was coming in from Paris for the joint birthday celebration on the twenty-sixth.

"Ah, but we have forgotten to tell you! There is now a problem with the twenty-sixth," Josette said apologetically.

Michel suggested the twenty-fifth instead. "Delphine is coming home that afternoon, yes?"

"Yes," David confirmed.

"So, we shall all be together on 25 January!"

"Fine," said David.

Jenny was dumbstruck. "But that changes everything!" she told him as soon as the DuPonts had gone. "Why didn't you tell them we've chosen the twenty-fifth as our wedding date?"

"The twenty-fifth is the only night they're free when Delphine can join us. We can do the wedding ceremony before we go to the birthday dinner."

"Dearheart, if we commit to a birthday dinner with the DuPonts on the twenty-fifth, the children's presence at our private ceremony is moot. Even if she wants to participate, there won't be enough time to collect Dellie from train station at six-thirty, bring her back to the house, do a wedding ceremony, and then meet the DuPonts at a restaurant at eight—or even eight-thirty. The only way we can fit the wedding into that scenario is if we do it during the day, before Dellie arrives."

"We can't do it during the day. I have school until three-thirty."

That left them between the time he got home until he left at 6:00 to pick up Delphine. Jenny could feel herself going tense. How invested was she in this date? Was it just a momentary confusion that made David agree to the twenty-fifth for the joint dinner? Did he think they could exchange vows on their way out the door? Or was there some subconscious resistance to proceeding without the children's blessing?

Jenny took a deep breath. "Okay, let's rethink for a minute. I've already told people that the wedding will be on the twenty-fifth. I'd like to stick with that if possible. It's right next to Sandie's birthday, as you wanted. The children don't have to be present for our private exchange of vows. If they were enthusiastic about it, that would be a different matter, but they're not. The ceremony we really want them to attend is the one at the *Mairie*, in February, where we have to have witnesses, and where your friends will be present. If our spiritual wedding is just me and thee, we won't need more than half an hour. We can do it as soon as you get home and then collect Dellie and go to the birthday dinner."

She could see David working this through his mind. She zeroed in on the logistical problems.

"Unless Dellie cancels her Friday classes, the earliest train she can take is the three o'clock, which arrives at six-thirty p.m. What if the train is late? What if there's a traffic jam? You might not even get back to the house until seven-thirty or eight. She would barely have time to change for dinner, much less watch us get married. This is not a setting for the kind of thoughtful exchange of vows I have in mind."

He was still processing. Jenny shifted to reason.

"There's no need to push the children about January 25. Focusing them on the civil ceremony in February gives them several weeks of reprieve. To be honest, I think it will be better this way. Our private vows may involve some serious emotion. I'm guessing the *Mairie* event will be impersonal and legalistic. It will be a lot easier for the children to watch if all we're doing is raising our right hand and signing on the dotted line." Jenny paused to see if David was still with her. He was.

"So, we stay on the schedule, yes?" she asked.

"Yes."

"I love you, David Perry."

"Hmpff," he replied.

The next week saw David inundated with meetings at school, but he managed an appointment at the *Mairie*. They handed in their translated documents and filled out a double set of forms. "Once the forms are approved, you will receive an official notice in the mail," said the young woman who processed the material. "Then," she explained, "you must wait for ten days—a mandatory period of reflection. If you still wish to proceed, the documents are valid for two months after the period of reflection, and you can perform the ceremony at any time within those two months."

"Can we reserve a date now?"

No, they could only reserve after the notice and the ten days of reflection, but she was able to tell them which dates were open. They needed a weekend so Delphine could come back from Paris. The *Mairie* only did weekend ceremonies once a month during the winter. The Swiss were disinclined to hold weddings during ski season. The first weekend option was Saturday, February 23. The validation dates on their documents expired on March 1. Barring disaster, they would make it under the legal wire with five days to spare.

With that out of the way, their evening conversations touched on the political problems at l'Académie Internationale. The faculty was squaring off against the administration over a series of new policies. David was a key figure in the drama, though he didn't consider himself as such.

"I'm the one who calls the meetings," he explained, "but I'm a negotiator, not a leader," he argued. "It's easy for me to facilitate because personally I have no ambition. I'm not bucking for a promotion. I don't have my eye on a future administrative post. I am already living the life I want to live. I am following my bliss." Then he locked his eyes on Jenny's. "You have no idea—no idea—of the impact of your introducing me to the works of Joseph Campbell. I will be forever grateful to you for that. It has allowed me to truly live my life."

While David struggled with school problems, Jenny consolidated three different Perry address books plus her own into a computerized master list for the New Year's card mailing. The first book had been recently updated, making it easy to work with. The second book was Sandie's 2000 appointment calendar, with a section in the back for addresses and phone numbers. The summer was progressively filled with references to medical appointments. In August, Sandie's handwriting began to deteriorate. Jenny could almost feel her energy draining away. Could Sandie see it when she looked at the pages?

The third address book was the oldest, with lots of cross-outs and changes. There were several listings for hairdressers, nail salons, and health spas. David once remarked that part of what drew him to Paris was its incredibly elegant women. Sandie clearly made a point of maintaining and maximizing her physical attractiveness. Her bathroom overflowed with cosmetics, lotions, skincare products, and perfumes. Her tub rack had bath capsules, scented soaps, scrubbing sponges, and probably six or seven different shampoos and conditioners.

Jenny shook her head at the contrast. Her own bathroom array, not counting toothbrush and dental tools, contained all of eight items: one comb, one bottle of lotion, one small perfume jar (a gift), one tin of baby powder, one bottle of shampoo, one deodorant stick, one blemish stick, and some eye makeup to compensate for nearly invisible eyelashes. The cosmetic industry would perish if it depended on women like her. She cut her own hair, accepted the gray that was creeping into it, filed her own nails, and had never set foot in a spa.

This last address book was a history of David and Sandie's marriage. There were references to restaurants, hotels and vineyards, railway and airline ticket offices, and vacation rentals. There were lists of pediatricians, school personnel, old friends from their Paris and San Francisco days, and newer ones from their life in Geneva. The addresses and phone numbers represented thirty years' worth of experiences and memories. The gap between what David and Sandie had shared in the past and what he and Jenny might share in the future was huge. It was a depressing exercise.

Over dinner that night, Jenny asked if David had chosen a restaurant for the twenty-fifth.

"The Lipp," he replied. "Sandie always wanted oysters on her birthday, so we always went to the Lipp."

As they finished their meal, Jenny remarked that the bride's family traditionally pays for the wedding dinner. "I think that should include the Lipp," she concluded.

David hesitated. "I don't want the marriage to overshadow the celebration of the birthdays," he said. "That's why I don't even want to tell Michel and Josette until that night."

"Dearheart, if we were celebrating an anniversary, it might be qualitatively the same as celebrating a birthday, but this is the wedding itself—a once-in-a-lifetime event. If you want it downplayed, you'd better alert the DuPonts in advance so they don't make a big deal out of it. On top of that, we don't know how the children feel yet. Or do we?"

"No, I haven't asked them, and they haven't offered. I'm letting them feel their way."

"If they're still uncomfortable, we should give them room to maneuver and protect their pride. For example, toasts should be multi-issue, like, 'Here's to three birthdays and a wedding!' That way they can raise a glass to Sandie's birthday and the other birthdays as well, even if they're not thrilled about the wedding. This is why we need to warn Michel and Josette. We also need to tell the children that the spiritual wedding will be just the two of us. There's nothing for them to officially witness on the twenty-fifth."

Marc came by late the next afternoon, laundry in hand. David was direct and open with him about his findings at the *Mairie*. "The legally recognized wedding won't happen until late February," he told him, "but Jenny and I are still going to make a private commitment to each other on January 25."

"Why not wait until the *Mairie* date?" Marc asked.

"I want to give this as a gift to Sandie, and I want it as close to her birthday as possible without taking the day itself. Sandie's blessing is important to both of us. Jenny and I will mark January 25 as our anniversary in whatever years we have to come."

Whatever was in his mind, Marc accepted David's answer without argument. Jenny suspected he was relieved that his presence on the twenty-fifth was neither requested nor required. Marc stayed to finish his laundry run and then headed back to Valerie's apartment. Michel and Josette arrived not long afterward in response to David's request that they stop by for a drink. David told them about the plans for the twenty-fifth and his wish to have the evening celebrate all the January birthdays, with no emphasis on the marriage. They understood what he was trying to do and agreed to help by example.

As the evening progressed, David invited the DuPonts to stay for supper. He and Michel went into the kitchen to have a cigarette and start the meal. Josette and Jenny stayed in the living room where Josette asked, with genuine curiosity, what Jenny did with her days. "You are so often alone, *n'est-ce pas?* I am not able to imagine how you fill the hours."

Jenny couldn't handle the answer in French, so she switched to English. Speaking slowly, she told Josette how much remained to be organized and cleaned out. She cited, as an example, her efforts with the address books and also described her emotional reaction to them. Jenny told other stories as well, including her tale about the teddy bear and how devastating it was to hear the first few notes of that soft lullaby. It was a relief to talk about it, even with the limitations of the language difference.

On January 24, Sandie's birthday, Jenny discovered in the course of a casual breakfast discussion that David had said nothing to his siblings about their getting married the next day. "Too many things to do," he explained. "I'll get around to it one of these days." Jenny didn't view it as a slight. David had never been bound by convention. But after he left for school, she decided to correct the breach of etiquette with a lighthearted e-mail to her about-to-be in-laws:

De: J W Longworth
A: Perry family
cc: DavidP
Envoyé: 24 janvier, 2002
Objet: Blue Jeans?
I have a sneaking suspicion that your big brother hasn't mentioned it yet, so I'm going to preempt. The news—better late than never—is that we're getting married tomorrow and having a multi-celebration dinner with Marc, Dellie, and the DuPonts. David considers the menu to be the most important item on the agenda, hence his absentmindedness about the lesser events of the day. This will be our spiritual wedding, with vows and a ring. In February, when it suits the town hall's

301

schedule, we'll take care of the legal nuptials—the official registration.

David chose January 25 because he wants to offer our marriage as a present to Sandie. With the Perry-DuPont tradition of celebrating the January birthdays together, it seemed ideal to plop our wedding right in the middle of it.

The question of the moment is whether I can get David to upgrade to slightly worn corduroys, or whether his side of the wedding is going to happen in blue jeans with torn knees. I promise to send an uncensored report.

Love to all of you, Jenny

The eloquence of David's reaction was fueled by several glasses of wine in celebration of Sandie's birthday.

De: David
A: Perry family
cc: Jenny
Envoyé: 24 janvier, 2002
Objet: Recent Rumors

I learned this afternoon that certain rumors have been circulating concerning my civil status and imminent changes. The question is, should you believe a busybody bluestocking from Boston or not?

The question is pertinent. To what, you ask? To the relative merits of blue jeans with holes in them or corduroys with a worn seat. Sixteen months ago this same Boston bluestocking got on my ass about wearing blue jeans (she says it's a goddamn lie!) to my wife's cremation. Sandie herself would have been scandalized, but I didn't give a shit then and don't now so who gives a damn about what one wears to one's own wedding that according to some is going to take place tomorrow?

Is it the case? Should we inform the society editor of the *Boston Globe* and the *Chattanooga Times Free Press*? Jenny is threatening to turn off the computer because she thinks I'm crazy and weird. But she wants to get married anyway. So why not? I guess we'll just do it.

Love, David

The women of the Perry family accompanied their congratulatory responses with requests for detailed descriptions of the ceremony, the flowers, and the dress. The men took a slightly different tone.

From: Isham
To: Jenny
Date: January 24, 2002
Subject: Re: Recent Rumors
    I feel for you, Jenny. Good luck

Nate's reply was addressed to David and cc'd to Jenny.

From: Nathan Perry
To: David
cc: Jenny
Date: January 24, 2002
Subject: Re: Recent Rumors
    Congratulations, Big Brother, for finding another person who will put up with you! Nate

During dinner, David got a call from a faraway friend who remembered it was Sandie's birthday and wanted to offer comfort on what she sensed would be a difficult day. After the initial exchange, David said, "It's been one year and four months." Jenny couldn't hear the other end of the conversation, but the caller must have asked how long it had been since Sandie died. David needed no time to calculate the time span. He could probably have given the days and hours as well. Then he reached for his wineglass and brought the caller up to date. They were only halfway through sending out New Year's cards, and there were still friends unaware of recent events.

"I'm giving Sandie a very special present: I'm getting married tomorrow to Jennifer Longworth, an old friend from Boston—someone Sandie knew and respected. She often asked me why I hadn't married Jenny in the first place. A silly, rhetorical question, but she was French. So now I'm doing it."

The morning of the wedding, everything seemed normal, and indeed was, until they finished breakfast. When he had emptied his second cup of coffee, David handed Jenny a sheet of paper, rolled up and tied with a red ribbon. He went downstairs to gather his papers for school while she removed the ribbon and flattened out the paper.

For Me the Time Has Passed—
For Jennifer on Our Wedding Day

For me the time has passed
When love lay soft and light,
When shadows bittersweet
But shaded ardors of my past,
Lit brightly save by youthful memories,
Callow passions unrequited -
Mere irritants, I now perceive with age
And loss, to love which lasted
Thirty summers and a month.
And ours... which covers thirty-seven ?
Is it, being interrupted, simply different,
Or played out about these pools of grief,
Which filter through the cracks of life,
Souring our heaven,
Will it with time provide forgetfulness
And thus for both us relief ?
I cannot say today no light's gladdened
Our stroll together of late,
Scattering momentarily my memories,
Soothing my hurt, lightening my gait.
Rather it does so as shade shifts in a summer storm
Among trees tightly grown,
Ignoring briefly, as we walk below,
Both us and certain spots of earth,
Returning with a sudden gust of thought
To throw sad shadows of my own
On what should be by all gods' rules
Our wedding's mirth.

For one terrible moment, on first reading, Jenny thought David had decided to call off the wedding and was using the poem as explanation and apology. He called up the stairs that he was heading off to school. Jenny raced down and hugged him. She searched his face for clues. Nothing. "What you wrote is beautiful," she offered. "And very sad."

He gave no direct response, substituting instead a quick kiss and a, "See ya later."

Did he want to go forward with the wedding? And if not, was her love strong enough to withdraw gracefully? Had she pushed him into this? Walking around the house, doing the morning chores, she tried to sort out her feelings—and his. She moved from task to task, clutching a packet of tissues to deal with the tears and runny nose that accompanied them. Whenever she felt strong enough, she read the poem again.

She finally decided, since he did say, "on our wedding day," that they were going ahead with it. *Be a grown-up, Jenny,* she chided herself. *This is real life, not Disney. You can handle it.*

She set up the dining room table for the wedding. She laid out a white linen cloth. Over that, she spread antique lace passed down from David's grandmother. She put Sandie's birthday roses on the table, removing one to refresh Sandie's vase on the mantel. Then she retrieved the silver box that contained the last of Sandie's ashes and carefully placed it beside the roses. Sandie was to be their witness.

To Jenny's surprise, David walked in the door at noon. He had forgotten to take his lunch. He came into the kitchen to claim it. He saw the table with the lace, flowers, and silver box, but he made no comment. They talked instead about an elusive leak in the basement and how best to deal with it, as if they'd been married for decades and this day was like all others. He ate his lunch sitting at the kitchen counter. She joined him with a yogurt. Then he headed back to school.

Jenny read the poem once more after David left, then rolled it up, replaced its ribbon, and set it on the table next to Sandie's flowers. She reminded herself that her insecurities frequently moved her to blow things out of proportion. If David wanted to call things off, surely he would have done so at noon when he saw the dining room readied. It began to dawn on her how much courage it had taken for David to give her the poem. On the eve of their wedding, depressed and melancholy, his memories focused on the celebration of Sandie's past birthdays, he had chosen to convey his mood through the poem rather than pretend it didn't exist. To be so candid, he had to have enormous confidence in the strength of her love.

His last class ended at 3:30. Jenny expected him by 4:00. At 3:45, she changed into a lavender-hued outfit with a small neck scarf tied in the French fashion so she would be ready as soon as he got home. At 4:15, there was no David. He had mentioned picking up some milk on the way home. Was it crowded at the supermarket? It turned to 4:20, 4:30. She was getting butterflies in her stomach. Finally, at 4:40 the car pulled in. He had groceries and two lovely orchids—one with slender purple striations as a birthday gift for Josette and one that was pure white for Jenny. She gave him a kiss and the option of changing into his torn blue jeans and grungy espadrilles for the ceremony.

"Oh no," he insisted with a grin, "I'm wearing these corduroys so I can tell people how you coerced me on our wedding day. The backside is a bit worn, but there are no holes in the knees."

"You have to leave at six to get Dellie," she cautioned. "We don't have much time."

"What," he said, "are you planning a high mass? This ain't gonna take more than a few minutes."

"Well," she replied, "you can be as short as you wish, but I have things I want to say."

He got out a bottle of Veuve Cliquot and two champagne flutes, while Jenny retrieved the engraved gold ring from her jewelry box. She thought they would sit opposite each other, but David took the chair at the head of the table as he poured the champagne. They raised their glasses.

"To us," he said. Then before she could add anything, he picked up the ring and asked, "Jennifer Longworth, do you want to marry me?" If she had been in a teasing mood, she would have commented on the careful phraseology. But she was not in a teasing mood. Her heart was in her throat.

"Oh, yes," was the best she could muster.

He put the ring on her finger, then stated, in a highly unorthodox vow, that the ring could come off as easily as it went on. "If the day ever comes when you want to be quit of me, I will honor your wish to leave."

"Considering how long we've been working on this relationship," Jenny retorted, "I wouldn't say it went on all that easily, and I certainly have no intention of ever taking it off."

David managed a wry smile. He raised his glass again and pushed back his chair as if to conclude the ceremony.

"Wait!" Jenny cried out. "This isn't the end! There are things I want to say!" She reached for the scrolled poem and held it up. "For starters, I want to talk about this. I must have read it a dozen times today, and I was in tears for most of them. I am awed by the amount of courage it took for you to write such a piece and give it to me on our wedding day."

"Courage? I don't think it took any courage," he said, frowning.

"Well, if it didn't, then it constitutes an extraordinary compliment, because it means you were prepared to trust me with a very painful truth. You didn't tell me anything I haven't already observed. But to put it into words, so there can be no pretending that I don't know the score—that's courage."

"Accept the compliment then. I do trust you with it." He took her hands in his and didn't let go.

"Well, I'm glad, because for me, that's part and parcel of the vow 'for better or for worse.' I am deeply in love with you and always will be, but I have no expectations you will ever be in love with me in the same way. That's about as significant a 'worse' as I can imagine—and I accept it. It doesn't alter how I feel or the fact that I want always to be with you."

David stopped her. "You're wrong," he said. "I'm not sure what you mean by being in love, but as I use the term, I am indeed in love with you."

Jenny backed down. She certainly wasn't going to try to talk him out of such a perception!

"Maybe what I'm trying to say is that you don't really have romantic feelings, whereas I do."

"Romantic feelings? What does that mean to you?" he queried, genuinely puzzled.

"It means my heart leaps when you enter the room. When you come home, I want to be there for you. I want to hear what you have to say and decide if you're down and in need of distraction—or just in need of help carrying in the groceries."

David insisted that he did have romantic feelings for Jenny. "But it's not like a Hollywood movie, with unbridled passion eclipsing all else," he added. "There's always a high in the early stage of a relationship, but biologically, it settles down. I initially felt that high with Sandie, and then my feelings shifted into friendship and appreciation. The marriage worked because when the biological high diminished, a more mature love and commitment replaced it. I expect that's true of all successful marriages over the long run. It's the mature love that has the deeper meaning. And it's the mature love that's harder to lose."

He quietly described the first few months after Sandie's death, sitting at the kitchen table, with a view of the front door—sitting for hours, waiting for the sound of Sandie's footsteps, waiting for the sound of her key turning in the lock.

Then he looked at Jenny and shook his head. "Do you realize how incredibly much it means to me to know that you're home waiting for me when I walk in the door? I start thinking about it the minute I get into the car at school. It's why I asked you to come, why I want you to stay. Because you and I have that same maturity—that bedrock kind of love—that makes life worthwhile."

IF YOU NEEDED ME

What a heart-melting, soul-lifting thing for him to say. Yet he had never before mentioned it—never said a single word to tell Jenny how he felt about coming home to her. Often he walked in at the end of the day, distracted or tired, offering a quick peck, then occupying himself with the paper or his e-mail. Why was he so shy about verbalizing affection? Did he not understand how much she needed his words of reassurance?

"When you went back to Boston at the end of the summer," he continued, "I didn't like it. I was agitated and uncomfortable and unhappy about your absence the whole time you were away. I'm not likely to say it a lot, but I do love you, Jenny. I can't believe, after all these years, that you have any doubts about that."

"I am so glad we chose to do this with just the two of us, David. This conversation would never have happened in front of Marc and Dellie."

Finally they unglued their hands. "Well," he said, swallowing some champagne, "we've offered up the sacrifice of water. Now I shall offer the sacrifice of fire." He got up, flipped on the stove fan, and lit a cigarette. They raised their glasses in the direction of the silver box, put the leftover champagne in the refrigerator, and rinsed the glasses. They were husband and wife.

David went to pick up Delphine while Jenny put away the lace and the table linens, replacing them with her favorite among Sandie's tablecloths—a yellow and blue Provençal print with classic olive and laurel decor. When Delphine arrived, she offered congratulations. The words sounded sincere. Delphine had a way of making the best of any situation. After she changed her clothes, the three of them drove to the restaurant. They were the first to arrive, then the DuPonts, followed by Marc and Valerie. Marc was pleasant and smiling, though Jenny could see from his eyes—glazed, red, and slightly unfocused—that his good mood was drug enhanced. It was not the first time she had seen him that way. Sadly, it would not be the last.

After half an hour of struggling with the French that flew around her, Jenny gave up and let her mind wander. Her eyes strayed to

Delphine. She was growing into a beautiful woman. Jenny knew there were bumps ahead, but she didn't worry about Delphine. Even when she was upset by something, Delphine usually retained her ability to analyze what was happening and address the problem objectively. Marc, however, left Jenny increasingly uneasy. Though he was two years older than Delphine, he didn't have her maturity. On top of whatever drugs he had used before dinner, he was drinking wine as if it were water. He had problems, and he wasn't going to solve them with pills and alcohol. Without apology, she was glad he wasn't living under their roof. Under present circumstances, there was little she could do to help him fight his demons. She could only hope, as David did, that he would survive this phase of his life and come out the other end a calmer, happier person.

It was nearly midnight by the time the meal was finished. Given the late hour, the five-course menu, and the volume of wine consumed, Jenny had no expectations that their marriage would be officially consummated when they finally got home. She was delighted to be proven wrong. They managed a slightly geriatric romp that left Jenny giggling and coughing at the same time and David going into a sneezing fit.

The morning mail brought a letter from the Swiss government asking them to confirm that the information on their application for a marriage license was correct. The confirmation the government sought was for data already confirmed and notarized by the US consulate, translated by an officially approved Swiss translator, and reviewed in their presence by the staff at the *Mairie*. Jenny understood that bureaucracy had its place, but this was unbelievable. She felt as if they were in the middle of a farce.

Their first full day of "spiritual" marriage was a good one. David had relaxed dramatically since the day before, and they sparred like an old married couple, teasing and fussing. After lunch, he put on a Vivaldi recording, settled down on the couch, and within a short period was asleep and snoring. Jenny e-mailed friends with a carefully edited report on the ceremony and a lengthy description of the birthday dinner. Responses arrived in short order.

From: Rachel Aronson
To: Jenny
Date: January 26, 2002
Subject: Happy Future

I am drinking a toast to the two of you and sending very best wishes. Jenny, you have handled this complicated situation with such diplomacy and love. I know Sandie is wishing both of you happiness. And I know how much David must appreciate that you can give him space to grieve and remember and yet be close enough so he can always find you. For me, one of the most difficult things, now that over a year has passed since Josh's death, is that for most people Josh is history. I must always be the one who brings him into the conversation, which I do because he is still so much a part of my life. David is fortunate because you understand that same need in him.

Much love, Rachel

De: JW Longworth
A: Rachel
Envoyé: 27 janvier, 2002
Objet: Re: Happy Future

I appreciate the compliment as well as the good wishes, but much of the credit belongs to you. More than anyone else, you helped me understand the grieving process, and that's made me a better partner for David.

We who stand on the sidelines need a lot of instruction regarding what is helpful and what is hurtful. I am lucky that David and I have a relationship built on a long history of trust. This allows David to be honest about whether he's up, down, or in between. I need this honesty because I can only understand pieces of his grief, not the whole. Sandie is an integral part of David, as Josh is an integral part of you. I could not be a good partner to David if I didn't respect his love for her.

Thanks again for all your wise insights.

Love, Jenny

After his nap, David composed a report of his own.

De: David
A: Family & friends
Envoyé: 26 janvier, 2002
Objet: It's done, but it ain't legal.

It's done, but it ain't legal. The gods know, so you might as well too, but that don't cut the mustard with Swiss bureaucracy.

As of yesterday afternoon, Jenny and I are spiritually married, whatever the hell that means. Carotte and Minuit witnessed the entire ceremony. I'm sure Sandie was present as well because she had her roses on the table. Never was one to ignore roses. If Jenny and I ever decide to get unhitched, we're gonna need us a high-powered lawyer.

Now all we have to do is deal with Switzerland. Got a letter from the local city hall, telling us they needed more information. They don't believe the US consulate, which seems understandable these days. Nevertheless, it adds to the red tape for us.

To celebrate the spiritual wedding, we all went to Chez Lipp for oysters, seafood, and wine, which was excellent. Good food, good company. We're off to a good start.

Love to you all, David

Despite what he said in his e-mail, David quietly acknowledged that the dinner at the Lipp, while splendid, barely qualified as a wedding celebration because everyone avoided mentioning the nuptials. He suggested a small, relaxed luncheon at the house—ten people at most. He would include the DuPonts because they were the equivalent of family, but otherwise it would be a predominantly English-speaking guest list—their neighbors, Mehrak and Manuela; Olga and her husband Jacques; and Edie and Jeremy Duval. Edie had recently retired from teaching and had spent the fall traveling. She and Jeremy had only just returned to Geneva. Jenny had not seen them since Sandie's funeral, but she remembered Edie's strong New York accent and her tale of winning over her mother-in-law in a discussion about chicken soup.

"Edie and Sandie were very close," David told her. "Given their respective New York and Paris backgrounds, they recognized each other as big-city girls—understood each other. Despite their different cultures, they tended to see things the same way."

They spent the morning of the luncheon in preparation. David was clearly in good spirits. When the guests arrived, David alerted them to Jenny's difficulty with smoke and designated the patio as the official smokers' lounge. Despite it being February, the sun was shining, there was no wind, and in the sheltered backyard, the temperature was in the high fifties. Everyone immediately moved outdoors to have a cigarette, with the exception of Edie, who thoughtfully kept Jenny company inside.

Edie had been to the house often when Sandie was alive. She commented favorably on the changes she noticed but clearly appreciated that Sandie's albums, photographs, and knickknacks were still prominently displayed. She excused herself for a moment to use the guest lavatory. She emerged wide-eyed and asked, in a slightly tremulous voice, what scent Jenny had used to freshen the room.

"I'm not sure," Jenny admitted. "Sandie had a huge collection of perfumes. Dellie took some, but there are still a lot. I don't want to wear them because perfume seems like such a personal thing, but I use them for the house. Whenever a sachet needs refreshing, I put some of Sandie's perfume into it. I could probably figure out which bottle I used."

"No, that answers my question," said Edie. "I was washing my hands, and I got a whiff of scent that made me feel like Sandie was standing right beside me."

Jenny felt a bit uncertain. "Do you think it's okay to use her perfume that way?"

"Whatever you do," Edie answered, "I know you do it with good thoughts. Listen, I've got to tell you that when David invited us, I wasn't sure I could handle coming to the house. I was afraid Sandie would have been blotted out. It's a relief that she's still so present— that so much of her remains here. You've obviously taken care of her things with respect. Including her husband!" she joked, lightening the mood.

"Thanks, Edie. I know how hard this all must be for Sandie's friends."

"Hey," Edie replied, her tone very matter-of-fact. "Don't worry. Sandie would be relieved to see David in such loving hands."

Lunch was very relaxed. David offered a toast. "To Jenny, who is doing her best to clean up my act, my pots and pans, my garden, and my language. I like being nagged at by someone who knows me inside out. Keeps me ornery."

After the meal, everyone but Jenny took advantage of the mild weather and went out for a postprandial smoke. Olga returned after just one cigarette, to offer a hand clearing the table.

"No, truly," Jenny said, "don't worry about the dishes. But now that we're alone, I have something to tell you. I've wanted to say it for a long time, but there's never been a good opportunity before. I want you to know that my marriage with David is due in large measure to you. It all started with the luncheon you gave after Sandie died."

Jenny told Olga about the luncheon's aftermath—her fear for David, her decision to confront him, their shared tears, their long walk—explaining how powerful that day was (without touching on that night) and how it influenced their future. Jenny also offered her gratitude for the support Olga and others had given David during that first winter.

"He couldn't have made it through without the love and encouragement of his friends and colleagues. You were his safety net, and for that, a million thank-yous are too few."

Olga considered Jenny for a moment. "It is you who were the safety net," she said firmly, in her deep Eastern European accent. "We are all convinced that it is you who got him through—especially for those darkest days immediately after Sandie died, but also now and over time. The luncheon was important, yes," she continued, "but not because of us. Because of you." She studied Jenny's face, her reaction. "Do you remember the decorations of the table?"

"Yes," Jenny replied. "I can still picture it. The table was lovely. You had set little clusters of grapes beside each plate, and there were nuts and colorful berries scattered all over the tablecloth."

"And do you know what is the symbolism of these nuts and berries?" Olga asked.

Jenny was puzzled. "Symbolism? No."

"It was the first time," Olga said, "that we decorated with the fruits and nuts, with the harvest of a long summer. These were not the flowers of spring. This was the life that comes after a long growing time. It was obvious to everyone," she went on, "that David absorbed all your attention. You didn't worry about convention or what anyone else thought. You were emotionally there next to David every minute. We could see it. And somehow he knew it, that you would be with him."

Her next words sent a shiver up Jenny's spine. "And Sandie knew it too."

Olga and Sandie had been very close. Sandie often confided in her. Many times through the years, Sandie had discussed Jenny with Olga, keeping a close and analytical watch on her relationship with David. Olga confirmed what Jenny had always presumed. Sandie was well aware that she loved David.

"At first," Olga said, "Sandie was very threatened by you, by the idea of you, because she always felt she had caught the train between stations. But once you became real, and not just an idea, she was able to see that while the love was very strong, it was also pure. And so she processed you in her mind and finally accepted that your love was important to David and was not harmful to her. You were different from all other women because here was not a new relationship beginning but an old relationship that had never ended and was still going on and always would."

Sandie and Olga had engaged in long talks about Jenny's proposal to set up an education trust for the children. A careful evaluation took place, but Sandie found no negatives, no obligation, and only long-range value in the arrangement for the children. It was another affirmation of her belief that Jenny's motives were benign.

Olga was part of the rotation of caregivers during Sandie's final stay in the hospital. In one of their conversations, Sandie said she was sorry they had canceled Jenny's August visit to Geneva. "It would have helped David to talk to Jenny," Sandie said.

"That makes me really regret not coming," Jenny interjected. "I'm not sure it would have helped David. His denial was still strong at that point. But I regret missing the chance to talk with Sandie, to hear her thoughts and wishes about David firsthand. Most of the time I think she would be glad I'm here, but I still have moments of uncertainty. Had I come, we might have talked, woman to woman, about the future. It would have meant a lot to have her blessing. I thought then that we had more time. Now I'll never know for sure what she wanted for him."

"Oh, Jenny," Olga said, shaking her head. "Do you not understand?" She fixed her eyes on Jenny's, leaning close and placing her hand on Jenny's arm.

"Sandie knew she was dying. Her thoughts were all for her family. For Marc and Delphine, she believed they would be okay. With David, it was different. 'I do not think that David will be able to cope on his own,' she told me. 'But,' she went on, 'I do not worry for him, because I know that Jenny will come, and she will take care of him.' Now do you understand? Now do you see? Sandie knew what we who watch you with David have all come to know—that when he needed you, you would come to him. You would cross the sea. You would bring him hope. You would keep him safe."

"This is the answer to a prayer, Olga," Jenny whispered as she gave her a hug. "It will really help David and the children to know this. Thank you. Thank you a million times."

"It is you who are the answer to a prayer," she replied. "Sandie's prayer, and certainly David's. And others too—the prayers of all of us who care about David. Be happy, Jenny."

"What are you girls talkin' about?" David called as the smokers came back indoors.

"We're talking about you, of course," Jenny replied.

"Watch out, Olga," he warned. "Jenny's a goddamn busybody."

Open Book Editions
A Berrett-Koehler Partner

Open Book Editions is a joint venture between Berrett-Koehler Publishers and Author Solutions, the market leader in self-publishing. There are many more aspiring authors who share Berrett-Koehler's mission than we can sustainably publish. To serve these authors, Open Book Editions offers a comprehensive self-publishing opportunity.

A Shared Mission

Open Book Editions welcomes authors who share the Berrett-Koehler mission—Creating a World That Works for All. We believe that to truly create a better world, action is needed at all levels—individual, organizational, and societal. At the individual level, our publications help people align their lives with their values and with their aspirations for a better world. At the organizational level, we promote progressive leadership and management practices, socially responsible approaches to business, and humane and effective organizations. At the societal level, we publish content that advances social and economic justice, shared prosperity, sustainability, and new solutions to national and global issues.

Open Book Editions represents a new way to further the BK mission and expand our community. We look forward to helping more authors challenge conventional thinking, introduce new ideas, and foster positive change.

For more information, see the Open Book Editions website:
http://www.iuniverse.com/Packages/OpenBookEditions.aspx

Join the BK Community! See exclusive author videos, join discussion groups, find out about upcoming events, read author blogs, and much more! http://bkcommunity.com/